Texas Angel

CAROL FINCH

ZEBRA BOOKS

KENSINGTON PUBLISHING CORP.

ZEBRA BOOKS

are published by

Kensington Publishing Corp.
475 Park Avenue South
New York, NY 10016

First printing: September 1987

Printed in the United States of America

WAR OF WILLS

"You will do what I tell you, when I tell you, like it or not," Wade said in that low, imposing voice of his. But as fate would have it, Shianne carried the inborn trait of the proud Cheyenne warriors who chose to fight to the death to protect their pride and rights. Wade was challenging her self-respect and her independent nature. She was too outraged not to defy him.

"Hear me and hear me well, you despicable son of a . . ."

With the quickness of a rattlesnake Wade coiled himself around his hissing prey. His lips came crushing down upon hers before she resorted to profanity. Shianne fought the restraining arms that kept her against his rigid body and struggled against the traitorous sensations that followed in the wake of his overpowering kiss.

He might have won this round, but the real battle had just begun . . .

To my husband Ed for his love and support.
And to my children
Christie, Jill and Kurt . . . Love you . . .

Chapter 1

San Antonio, Texas

When Jedediah Winston had finished treating his last patient of the day, he sighed tiredly. Bending his gaze to his attractive young nurse, he mustered a smile. "I am deeply indebted to you, Shianne. I fear I would have collapsed many times the past few years if you had not been here to offer a helping hand."

Shianne Kimball retrieved the satchel of medical supplies the doctor had bestowed on her and then tossed him a weary smile. "I can only hope my father, wherever he is, has been receiving the same treatment . . . if he is suffering."

"Still no word about Blake?" Jedediah questioned in concern.

Shianne gave her head a negative shake and fought back the tears that threatened to mist her eyes. For the most part, Shianne had managed to conceal her apprehension about her father, but there were times when the mention of Blake's name brought a lump to her throat.

In a gesture of consolation, Jedediah laid his hand on her shoulder. "I'm sorry, honey. I know it must be difficult for you to sit and wait for word about your father. That damned war was hell on all of us . . . those who served and those who stood in wait."

His rueful gaze strayed back to the battered soldier who had come within a hairbreadth of losing his life and his mental capacities while fighting with the Texas Brigade. Only now, years later, had the soldier begun to recuperate from his devastating injuries and harrowing experiences. His wounds were a constant aggravation, ones that still plagued him long after the South surrendered to the North.

"I do admire your spirit, Shianne. You have held your father's ranch together and spared the time to come to my assistance." A quiet chuckle bubbled from his lips as he ushered the shapely young woman toward the office door. "You have been burning the candle at both ends and searing the middle these past years. For one so young, you have handled your responsibilities amazingly well."

"Is twenty-one young?" Shianne asked with a skeptical frown. She felt every bit of eighty. "I thought I had already reached my declining years."

Jedediah directed her attention to the mop of gray hair that covered his head. "No, my dear, you are far from viewing the downward slope of aging. *This* is what you can anticipate in the winter of life." Then he gestured toward the glorious mane of ebony hair that lay in a braid on Shianne's shoulder. "You have yet to enjoy snow on your head or miles of wrinkles on your face."

Shianne looked up at the kindly doctor and graced him with an affectionate smile. Doc Winston had become the father who she was so desperately missing. She adored this old man. Her hand moved gently across his tired features. "These lines are merely a ledger of all the lives you have touched and saved with your skillful hands. And your white hair counts the number of good deeds you have performed for the citizens of San Antonio."

"Now don't go filling me with praise, girl," Doc Winston chided with a gruff snort. "You will have me believing myself to be some sort of saint."

"You *are,* Doc," she insisted before striding into the street.

"I am not," he denied. "And don't you show your face around here tomorrow. You deserve a rest."

Shianne grinned at his harsh command and waved good-by. Doc Winston *was* a saint by everyone's standards, and she wished she could be more like him. Although Shianne had pursued the compassionate ways of the doctor she was still quick to temper. Shamefully, she admitted that her temper could fire as rapidly as the Colt .45 revolver that hung on her hip.

A contemplative frown knitted Shianne's brow as she urged her black stallion into a trot. Life had been peaceful before that cussed war. Blake Kimball sold hides to the leather manufacturers in the East and supplied beef and horses to army outposts in the West. But when sixty thousand Texans marched off to fight the Civil War, and twenty-seven thousand more were assigned to defend the state, Blake felt obligated to offer some sort of assistance.

Blake and several other ranchers near San Antonio were contacted by a rebel scout from Louisiana. The Texans were encouraged to gather their cattle and horses to sell to the Confederate cavalry and starving armies. Shianne had been away at Miss Brown's Young Ladies' Seminary in Houston when Wade Burdett approached her father. If she had been home she most certainly would have protested Blake taking an active part in the war. The man had fought in the war with Mexico, for Heaven sake! One war should have

9

been enough.

At first Blake had come and gone, his longest absence five months. Then, he had dropped out of sight, and Shianne had no communication from her father. She had been greatly relieved when the war came to an end, thinking her father would reappear. But too soon she realized it was to be the beginning of a new brand of frustration. Her life was filled with apprehension and loss of direction. For two years the veterans of the country's most brutal war filtered back to their homes. Eagerly she watched the procession of those who had traveled east to take arms against the Union army. The healthy soldiers had come first, and later, the bone-weary stragglers—the wounded, limping, and broken infantries who had been devastated by battle. But Shianne's father was not among those who hobbled back to Texas to pick up the pieces of their broken lives. Blake had mysteriously dropped out of sight.

Each passing day left Shianne with the apprehension that her father would never return and that she would never know what had become of him. Although Ramona and Carlos Santos had cared for her as if she were their own daughter, Shianne yearned to know her father's whereabouts or if he was still alive. This lack of direction exasperated her. She feared making any major decision until she knew what had happened to Blake.

"It is all that Wade Burdett's fault," Shianne hissed resentfully. "If not for him, Papa would be where he belonged!"

Although Shianne had never had the displeasure of meeting the man who had persuaded Blake to aid the cause of the South, she detested Wade Burdett, sight unseen. Her father had allowed that smooth-talking Confederate scout to convince him to drive longhorns

10

across the dangerous routes that were heavily infested with Union troops. Shianne had heard of other cattle drovers being imprisoned for aiding and supplying the rebel forces, and she suspected her father had been captured or worse. . . . Only now, two years after Lee surrendered, was the Union army granting pardon to Southern prisoners.

If Blake had been rotting away in some hideous prison, Shianne spitefully wished Wade Burdett was suffering along with him. Blake had made enough sacrifices during the Mexican War to compensate sitting this one out, Shianne mused bitterly.

Wasn't it enough that she had lost her mother to cholera? Must she lose her father because some daring rebel had insisted that Blake drive cattle into harm's way?

Shianne jerked up her head, jolted from her silent reverie by the braying of a mule in the distance. Keen, dark eyes focused on the creek bank. Her heart skipped a beat when she focused on the scene that lay before her. For a moment, Shianne simply sat in the saddle, her jaw gaping wide enough for a prairie chicken to nest. There, staked out beside the braying mule, lay a man. There was not a stitch of clothing on his long, lean body. He was tied spread-eagle beside the stream. Judging by the summer's blistering heat, Shianne speculated that every inch of the man's torso was burned to a crisp.

Once she recovered her ruffled composure, indecision etched her brow. The last thing she wanted was to ride up on a man who was as naked as the day he was born. It would surely embarrass the both of them, and the next to the last thing she wanted was to become involved with some vagabond or desperado whose stroke of misfortune had found him strapped to the ground to be sunburned and snakebit.

11

Since the end of the war there were hoards of homeless Southerners swarming Texas. Some came to make a fresh start. Others were ruthless outlaws who preyed on struggling ranchers and homesteaders. These days one could never tell what kind of man one would meet, and that was precisely why Shianne refused to set foot outside the hacienda without her pistol. It was difficult to speculate on what sort of man she had stumbled on. Without his clothes, Shianne could make no predictions. The man was simply naked and undoubtedly looked no different than others of the male species.

Whoever this stranger was, he had obviously crossed paths with raiding Comanches, desperados or Haden Reems's band of roving bravoes. Any of the three groups were capable of pulling such a prank. It was also apparent that this man had not been easily subdued, she noticed. Most unfortunate travelers were merely frightened within an inch of their lives and urged to ride out of Texas, or stripped of their valuable possessions and left afoot. Obviously this man refused to submit without a fight. He had probably angered his assailants, provoking them into employing drastic measures to make their point.

Heaving a perplexed sigh, Shianne looked past the long braid of raven hair that cascaded over her shoulder and stared at the saddle bag behind her. Doc Winston would not have hesitated in galloping up and tending the stranger. No doubt, he would chastise her for ignoring the Hippocratic oath of caring for the sick and wounded, no matter what the circumstances.

Resigning herself to the fact that she could not detour around the victim who was in dire need of medical attention, Shianne urged her steed toward the creek. If she did not offer assistance her conscience would hound her. But as the distance between them

12

dwindled, the more reluctant she became to approach a man who was baking in the sun without meager covering.

Shianne willed her eyes not to stray past the stranger's blistered face, for fear of embarrassing herself. As near as she could guess, the man was in his early thirties. An abundance of crisp, wavy hair capped his head, glowing blue-black in the sunlight. Thick, dark brows protected his eyes from harsh weather, and pronounced bone ridges stretched across his forehead. He had been blessed with an aquiline nose, high cheekbones and a strong chin. Although his eyes were closed, she could see the long black lashes that caressed his cheeks. Full, sensuous lips, parched though they were, turned up in a natural smile. That was a pity, Shianne thought to herself. At present, the stranger had very little to smile about. It seemed to Shianne that the good Lord had collected the most becoming features He had created and molded them into this man's face. There was no other way to put it, Shianne admitted. Even if the man were a scoundrel, he was the handsomest rapscallion she had ever laid eyes on.

Her inquisitive eyes dipped to the broad expanse of his chest to note the thick matting of hair. Shianne willfully concentrated on the bulging muscles of his arms that were strapped to stakes. Several scars traced his ribs and shoulders, assuring her that the man may have been a stranger to this part of Texas, but he was no stranger to the art of self-defense. He had seen his share of fighting and, judging by the size and length of his brawny body, he would be an ominous opponent.

Although Shianne's intentions were honorable, feminine curiosity got the best of her. The path of her betraying brown eyes slid below his waist, and she blushed up to her eyebrows. Gasping at her first view of a completely naked man, Shianne fought for hard-won

13

composure. With her heart slamming against her ribs Shianne hopped to the ground and retrieved the blanket that was tied behind the saddle. When she wheeled around, a pair of vivid green eyes were boring into her, making mincemeat of her already crumbling composure. The intensity of his gaze nearly knocked her out of her boots. He was leering at her as if *she* were the one wearing not a stitch! Shianne was being stripped naked, picked apart, piece by piece, and glued back together in the span of fifteen seconds.

When beet red splashed her cheeks, the man chortled and cast a skeptical glance at the quilt that was clenched in her fists. "The last thing I need at the moment is a wool blanket, lady" came his low, raspy voice. To Shianne's surprise, his tone crackled with amusement. His gaze lifted to peer squint-eyed at the blinding sun. "In case you failed to notice, it's as hot as hell out here."

A deeper shade of red flushed her cheeks. Dammit, the blanket wasn't for him. It was for *her* and they both knew it, Shianne thought flusteredly. The stranger had to know she was apprehensive about approaching a naked man. Even in her dealings with the sick and ailing, Doc Winston had taken particular care to ensure that his patients were properly covered when there was a lady present.

Without uttering a word, Shianne tilted her chin high in the air to prevent her betraying gaze from wandering. Determinedly, she strode forward to drop the quilt over the private parts of the stranger's anatomy. When she pivoted to fetch her medical bag, she heard soft, mocking laughter behind her, and her back went rigid with irritation.

This stranger was obviously an outlaw, Shianne surmised. What other breed of man could retain his warped sense of humor when he found himself in such

14

an uncomfortable situation? This hooligan behaved as if the incident that left him scorching in the sun was a mere inconvenience instead of calamity. Even in dire straits he dared to taunt her for coming to his rescue.

It was at that critical moment that Shianne seriously contemplated stepping into the stirrup and galloping away. This desperado deserved to bake in the sun until someone else happened by to offer emergency aid.

"If your only reason for stopping was to protect yourself from embarrassment, take your quilt with you when you go," the man called after her. "I prefer to fry alive than to smother beneath this itchy wool quilt."

The man had incredible nerve, Shianne thought huffily. How dare he mock her while she was portraying the good Samaritan. Silently fuming, Shianne yanked the satchel from the saddle. Well, this arrogant dolt would not receive a smidgen of compassion, she vowed spitefully. She would hurriedly tend his burns and be on her way!

Shianne resolved to ask no questions or strike up a conversation that might throw them together in the future. Compressing her lips, she said not one word as she went about her chore. With noticeably shaky hands, Shianne fished into the bag for a cloth and squatted beside the stream. With the rag saturated, she returned to her patient's side to drip the soothing liquid over his reddened skin. Shianne could have sworn she heard the water sizzle as it made contact with his overheated flesh.

A sigh escaped Wade Burdett's lips when the cold water brought temporary relief. His assailants had tormented him by tying him on the creek bank . . . close enough to stare at the water without being able to drink it or bathe in it.

"Would you kindly either kiss me or apply that cloth to my lips," he requested, his voice lightly threaded with sarcasm. "Although I am sorely sunburned, I am apt to die of thirst first."

Rattled by her obvious blunder of putting the cart before the horse, Shianne dragged her hat from her head and dipped up a drink. The stranger gulped down the water like a camel that had been stranded on a desert for weeks on end. His thirst quenched, he slumped back on the ground and heaved a heavy sigh.

"Aren't you the least bit curious to know how I came to be in such a predicament?" Wade questioned as Shianne applied the soothing poultice to his blistered body.

Although the stranger's devil-may-care charm had piqued her curiosity, Shianne held firm to her vow to remain uninvolved. Deftly, she worked the lotion over the man's shoulders and chest. He was like a lion in repose, his powerful body rippling with muscles. Unwillingly, Shianne admired the potential strength that was strapped to the ground, and before she completed her ministrations, she knew the stranger by touch, even when she would have preferred not to make his acquaintance at all!

"God, that feels good," Wade breathed as her gentle hands glided up and down his chest. He sucked in his breath when Shianne concentrated the salve on his upper thighs. This massage was becoming more arousing by the minute, and Wade was beginning to realize the importance of having particular parts of his anatomy covered!

While Wade was being tended, his gaze wandered at will. He was intrigued by his mute nurse. Since the first moment he had opened his eyes to see this beauty staring down at him, he swore he was living a dream. There, perched on her prancing black stallion, was a vision of exquisite loveliness. His guardian angel was garbed in boots, tight-fitting breeches and a revealing shirt. Although the young woman's generous assets had drawn his immediate attention, Wade had been fascinated by her flawless face and dark eyes that twinkled with a brilliance that held him spellbound. Perfectly arched brows set above fathomless pools of ebony, and those sultry eyes were rimmed with thick lashes. Her creamy olive skin reminded him of the intriguing complexion of an Indian princess. Her finely etched mouth looked so soft and inviting that Wade would have yielded to the temptation of kissing her if he could have freed his hands.

Her strikingly lovely features had drawn his eyes like a magnet and held him entranced. When this goddess moved toward him with perfect poise and grace Wade swore he had fallen in love . . . at least temporarily. He had seen his fair share of Southern beauties, but this dark-eyed, curvaceous nymph was in a class all by herself. Her sylphlike grace excited him. Her tender touch aroused him. He could not help but wonder what it would be like to feel her caresses. Lord, if this mere massage had a stimulating effect on his male body, he could well imagine what she could do to him if she touched him with other intentions.

Suddenly, Shianne jerked back as if she had been scorched by this stranger's flaming flesh. It had just occurred to her that she was actually *enjoying* this task, and *far* more than she should. Heavens above! What had come over her? She was not in the habit of fantasizing about a man, but that was exactly what she had been doing. Shianne sorely resented her attraction to this good-for-nothing outlaw.

One heavy brow arched, and Wade broke into a rakish smile. The woman's dark, expressive eyes mirrored her uneasiness. He could tell this encounter was having a disturbing effect on her as well. His unrelenting gaze worked its way past the becoming

17

blush on her cheeks to linger on the taut peaks of her breasts that were pressed against the thin gauze blouse.

Again Shianne was struck by the odd need to cover herself from those unnerving green eyes. The man had an uncanny knack of looking right through her, as if he were plucking the thoughts from her mind and, at the same time, speculating on how she would look in the altogether. Instinctively, she withdrew and busied herself by gathering her medical supplies.

"What is your name, princess?" Wade questioned, his voice husky with unmistakable desire.

The throaty inquiry brought Shianne to her senses and to her feet. She was not about to offer one shred of information to this rudderless drifter. Although he was virtually harmless lying there, staked securely to the ground, Shianne had the premonition she had met a man she couldn't handle. He had rattled her composure with his words and suggestive glances. She had no intention of encouraging the man. She would not have this rogue pounding on her door to renew their acquaintance. Lord, she had seen quite enough of him already!

When Shianne pirouetted around to replace the satchel on Delgado's saddle, Wade let out his breath in a rush. "Dammit, woman, don't you have a tongue? You saved my life. At least tell me your name!"

She never broke stride. Wade watched helplessly as she ambled to her steed. The gentle sway of her hips hypnotized him, provoking his breath to come in uneven spurts. Sweet mercy! The sun must have fried his brain, he thought bleakly. This gorgeous creature had made not the slightest attempt to be provocative. Indeed, she had remained cool and unapproachable. Yet, his thoughts had detoured onto a most arousing path. It was only that she was irresistibly alluring, Wade concluded. Mother Nature had been overly generous with this Texas temptress. A man was instinctively drawn to her simply because it was impossible not to be.

His thoughts halted abruptly when Shianne spun around, displaying the dagger that was clasped in her hand. Wade wilted when he detected that mischievous sparkle in her eyes. Being a gambling man, Wade was prepared to wager the lady was toying with the idea of cutting him into bite-sized pieces instead of cutting him loose.

His body tensed nervously when she sashayed back to him, wearing that ornery smile. Wade grimaced when her shadow fell over him, but to his relief Shianne leaned out to lay the sharp-edged blade under the leather strap that bound his left leg. With the lithe grace of a cat she severed the strap, offering him an ounce of freedom. Then to his further amazement, Shianne stepped back and drew her revolver.

Now she was going to blow him to smithereens, he predicted, gazing down the barrel of her pistol. Why the hell had she bothered to apply salve to his sunburned body and free his left leg if her ultimate purpose was to put him out of his misery . . . permanently? His tangled lashes drifted up to stare her straight in the eye. Remaining as stiff as a corpse, Wade watched as Shianne lowered the barrel of her revolver to blow away the leather strap that restrained his left arm.

When the smoke cleared Shianne replaced the pistol in her holster. Without a word she sprang into the saddle as her steed stretched out into a gallop, leaving a cloud of dust billowing behind her.

Wade was dumbfounded. For a long moment he lay there staring after her. He had encountered a most unusual woman who rode with the expertise of the Indians and who handled a pistol as well as any man. This fetching beauty was not only a vision of loveliness, but she had obviously been blessed with many rare talents.

He was intrigued. If this bewitching sprite lived near San Antonio, he vowed to seek her out to satisfy the compelling craving she had instilled in him. She would not slip away from him that easily, he promised himself. As soon as he saw to his business, he would begin a relentless search for this mysterious nymph.

Since Shianne had freed his left hand, Wade twisted around to untie his right hand and then his right leg. Slowly, he gathered his feet beneath him and rose to full stature. When he had worked the kinks from his back and tied the makeshift robe made from the quilt around him, he snatched up the trailing reins to his mule.

His arrival at the K Bar Ranch headquarters would have to wait a few more days, he decided. Not that he was anticipating the confrontation to begin with. Wade was in no hurry to make Shianne Kimball's acquaintance. He had the sneaking suspicion that Blake had attempted to set him up with his spinster daughter. That was probably why Blake requested Wade make the trip to Texas instead of coming himself.

If the wench was as short and stout as her father, it was little wonder why she hadn't married, but Wade was not about to be roped into a wedding to solidify the partnership between himself and Blake Kimball. If Shianne was part of the bargain, Wade fully intended to make other arrangements. His future plans did not include taking a wife, not when the world was full of beautiful, available women who could appease a man's needs without tying him to a hitching post.

Determined in that thought, Wade aimed himself in the direction from which he had come. His first order of business was to return to his campsite and fetch some clothing. When he had recovered from his burns, he would ride into San Antonio to purchase another rifle and some supplies. *Then* he would approach Miss Shianne Kimball.

A concerned frown furrowed his brow. The men who had confiscated his weapons and valuables had also absconded with the letter Blake had sent with him. Damn, now he would have no proof that he was obeying Blake's wishes when he confronted Shianne with his intentions.

An ironic smile pursed Wade's parched lips. It probably wouldn't matter, he told himself. The plump, hook-nosed spinster would believe anything if she thought it would land her a man in the house. Hell, he wouldn't be surprised if he had to fight off the eager wench with a stick! By damned, he wasn't playing up to some homely excuse for a woman just because she was Blake Kimball's daughter! Yes, he and Blake had become close friends and confidants these past four years, but Wade was not about to sacrifice his freedom for the sake of his friend, not by a long shot!

The vision of a well-rounded spinster with dark, beady eyes and stringy hair faded from his thoughts. Wade smiled to himself, recalling the sweet fragrance that had hovered about him while his mute angel massaged his seared flesh. He could still feel her tapered fingers gliding over his skin, see that dazzling glint of spirit that blossomed on her face when she approached him with her dagger. Now *that* was his kind of woman. Wade felt warm and tingly inside, just imagining what it would be like to take that curvaceous beauty to his bed, to touch what his eyes beheld.

Absently, Wade swung from the mule's back and strode inside the cave to fetch his clothes. He was going to find that dark angel and satisfy this hunger she

21

aroused in him . . . just as soon as he fulfilled his obligation to Blake Kimball's love-starved daughter.

Shianne forced a smile when she entered the hacienda. After the unnerving incident that afternoon, she was anxious to hear Ramona Santos's idle chatter. It would distract her from thoughts of the bold stranger who disturbed her more than she cared to admit. Shianne was not disappointed. The moment she strolled through the mosaic tiled foyer, Ramona began her nonstop prattle in Spanish, forcing Shianne to concentrate if she hoped to translate. Within five minutes Shianne had received a detailed account of the day's happenings at the K Bar Ranch.

The buxom maid rattled on for another ten minutes, chiding Shianne for making the trip to San Antonio without a proper escort. Shianne had endured the lecture each day she rode in to assist Doc Winston, but it didn't stop her from venturing into town.

"*¡Dios Mio!*" Ramona exclaimed. "This country is thick with bad *hombres*. I have not raised you from a babe in arms, only to have you molested by desperados and Comanches!"

"You worry too much," Shianne said with a reckless shrug. She tossed her hat aside and accepted the cool drink Ramona offered her. "Haden Reems's hired henchmen have strict orders not to harass me, and I have no quarrel with the Comanches. I can come and go as I please without fearing trouble."

Ramona sniffed distastefully. "If you continue to refuse Señor Reems's marriage offer, you will no longer be granted amnesty," she warned. "And no one can trust Comanches. They may ignore you today and scalp you tomorrow! And what about this mysterious band of outlaws that is terrorizing the countryside?"

22

Ramona wagged a stubby finger in Shianne's unconcerned face. "Mark my words, *chica.* You will find yourself stewing in your own juice if you continue to come and go without a chaperone. If Señor Kimball were here, he would see to it that you took better care of yourself. You have become like a tumbleweed since he left." She threw up her hands in exasperation. "I swear, your *padre* will not recognize you when he returns!"

The mention of her long lost father sent Shianne's spirits plunging to rock bottom. "What does it matter?" she murmured as she trudged up the steps to her room. "I'm beginning to think Papa is never coming back at all."

Ramona's shoulders slumped. Ruefully, she watched Shianne ascend the stairs and disappear down the hall. The cruel war had forced Shianne to become a woman of obligation and responsibility long before her time. Without Blake to tend to the ranch, Shianne was forced to stand in his stead, ramrodding a ranch of fifty thousand acres with only a handful of vaqueros to help her. Although Ramona's husband, Carlos, had offered instruction and guidance, Shianne had been handed a tremendous responsibility. There had been little time for the young girl to pursue her whims. Shianne had been doing a man's job for more than four years.

What Shianne needed was a strong, dependable man to lift this yoke of responsibility from her shoulders, Ramona decided. But definitely not Haden Reems! *Fijese!* They would never be compatible. Shianne had grown too independent to tolerate a tyrant like Haden Reems. *Si,* the man possessed vast wealth, and he played the perfect gentleman in Shianne's presence; but they would clash like a mongoose and a cobra if they were to become man and wife. Ramona did not trust the man who was smitten with Shianne's rare beauty. She had heard rumors, shocking ones that bore no proof, but ones that left her with doubts about Haden's integrity. No one in San Antonio dared to confront Haden with accusations or suspicions. They feared him and the repercussions of speaking out against him.

The very thought of Shianne wedding Haden made Ramona shiver uncontrollably. *Caramba,* such a marriage would create catastrophe. But then, Shianne would never consent to taking Haden for her husband, Ramona reassured herself. Indeed, it seemed the señorita was determined not to marry at all, at least not until she knew what had happened to her father. Shianne shied away from such decisions and continually put Haden off when he insisted that she set a wedding date.

Ramona heaved a doleful sigh, wondering if Shianne would ever find her perfect match. No man in the county suited her. Shianne found fault with everything in breeches. Although she was one of the most sought-after heiresses in Bexar County, Shianne remained polite but distant in her association with men. Why? Ramona could only speculate. It seemed Shianne had conjured up the picture of the perfect man, and no male met her description. Not that it mattered, Ramona grumbled. Haden discouraged any man from courting the woman he had designated as his fiancée.

"Such high expectations," Ramona muttered as she clambered up the steps to prepare the señorita's bath. There was no man on God's green earth who could fill the boots of the handsome prince who galloped through Shianne's dreams. If he had existed, he probably perished in the disastrous war that took Blake Kimball from his daughter. *Si,* Shianne was searching for a man who was everything her father was and more, and Haden was doing his damnedest to prevent prospective beaux from finding their way to Shianne's doorstep.

"Such a pity," Ramona mused aloud. Shianne needed someone to fill the emptiness in her life. She had lost her mother before she could speak the woman's name. Now she had lost her father before another man came along to take Blake's place in Shianne's eyes.

Ramona glanced heavenward. What they needed was a miracle—a bold, handsome man who could withstand Haden's threats and command Shianne's respect. But he could not be an ordinary man, Ramona tacked on to her prayer. If he were, he would not last a day in this lawless state that was overrun by desperados and Comanches!

Chapter 2

A strange restlessness settled over Shianne, provoking her to pace the confines of her room. Try as she
may, she could not eradicate the ruggedly handsome
stranger from her mind. Not when his well-sculptured
physique had been branded on her brain, she thought
in annoyance. It had been her intention to ride off in a
cloud of dust, never granting the man another thought,
but his husky voice kept echoing in her ears, and his
rakish smile kept materializing from the shadows.

Shianne had busied herself with her father's ledgers
until she was certain her eyes would slam shut, but the
moment she closeted herself in her room a pair of
dazzling green eyes, flecked with gold, came out of
nowhere to haunt her.

Giving way to impulsiveness, Shianne wandered
onto the balcony. The sound of a screech owl caught
her attention. With sharp discerning eyes she scanned
the darkness. Sparing only one backward glance,
Shianne threw her leg over the railing and climbed
down the vine-covered trellis. She ran barefoot toward
the corral to fetch Delgado. Her quiet whistle brought
the steed to her side. Delgado nuzzled against his
mistress and made no complaint when she grasped his

mane and swung onto his back for their midnight ride.

Another beckoning call from the screech owl sent a tingle of anticipation trickling down Shianne's spine. Pressing her knees to the black stallion's flanks, she raced against the wind, anxious to reach her destination.

As the clouds paraded across the star-studded sky, swallowing and then releasing the moon, Shianne thundered away from the dim lights of the hacienda. It had been two months since she had heard the cry of the owl. If Ramona would have known who had sent that eerie call, she would have keeled over in a lifeless heap.

A beaming smile blossomed on Shianne's features when the tall aristocratic savage emerged from the shadows to stand in the moonlight. When Shianne had brought Delgado to a halt, Maman-ti strode forward to pull the trim beauty into his arms.

After a greeting hug that very nearly squeezed her in two, Shianne stepped back to peer into the Owl Prophet's broad, angular face. She greatly admired Maman-ti whose name translated as Sky Walker, He-Who-Touches-the-Sky. More often he was called Do-ha-te, the medicine man, or the Owl Prophet of the Kiowas and Comanches. Although Quanah, Satanta, Lone Wolf and Wild Horse were well known names to the U.S. Army, the Owl Prophet was elusive to many white men. He lurked in the shadows behind the great chiefs of the Kiowas and Comanches, but his power among the embattled tribes was omnipotent.

Other whites who had the rare opportunity of laying eyes on this lean yet muscular shaman may have deemed him a dark, sinister figure, but Shianne idolized him. While Maman-ti struck terror in the hearts of her neighbors and the homesteaders of the Texas frontier, Shianne had no fear of him. The Owl Prophet was known for his bravery in battle and his

27

kindness to his people, and his people alone. Since the day the Texas Rangers charged into Indian Territory to murder an entire band of Comanches, including women and children, Maman-ti had declared war on Texans. He swore all of Texas would pay for the massacre at Rush Creek.

Long before the war, Comanches and Kiowas had raided Texas, pushing the frontier more than one hundred miles south. The area surrounding San Antonio was a favorite sight for Maman-ti, not only because of the many horses he could steal, but because of this rare beauty who had been named Shianne.

When Maman-ti had approached Shianne five years ago, she had very nearly jumped out of her skin. She had heard horror stories related by those who had survived encounters with the renegade Indians. But the Owl Prophet smiled kindly at her, assuring her that he had no intention of harming her. Maman-ti told her that he had been blessed with the gift of prophecy and that one of his dreams had led him to her. The Owl Prophet knew that her grandmother was the daughter of a powerful Cheyenne chief, an ally of the Comanches and Kiowas. After Maman-ti had bravely rescued many women and children who were about to be massacred by the cavalry, he became a blood brother to Black Kettle, the great Cheyenne chief. His association with the tribe provoked a strange dream, compelling him to seek out the young girl who was one-quarter Cheyenne, the cousin of Chief Black Kettle.

When Maman-ti first explained about his premonitions and dreams, Shianne was skeptical, but her cynicism lasted all of one night. Maman-ti took her with him to the council he conducted with the war chiefs, a meeting held before each battle against the hated white men.

In astonishment, Shianne listened to the Owl

Prophet mimic the sound of the feathered oracle. From out of the blackness, an eerie semblance of an owl appeared to perch on Maman-ti's wrist. The great medicine man then proceeded to prophesy the outcome of the upcoming battle. He foretold of the revenge raid in Texas. Maman-ti assured the warring chiefs that no Indians would be killed and that two of their enemies would perish. He also claimed that the greatest heroes of the battle would be striding gray horses.

After Shianne was returned to the hacienda without bodily harm, she later learned of the raid in north Texas. Shianne half collapsed when the incident was reported to her exactly as the Owl Prophet had predicted. It was not to be the last council meeting Shianne attended. Each time she heard Maman-ti's eerie predictions they came true, much to her amazement. The shaman made no ill-founded boasts, and the Indians hailed him as one of the greatest leaders of the times.

"Your beauty makes your forefathers proud," Maman-ti murmured. His dark eyes flooded over the shapely maid who had earned his admiration and affection. "Each time a dream beckons me to you, I swear you grow more lovely."

Shianne blushed self-consciously as Maman-ti's keen eyes swept over the thin white gown she had neglected to change in her haste to answer his call. "You are generous with your compliments, Maman-ti," she chortled. "There are far more attractive women than I. Your two wives for instance. I have heard it said that the great medicine man of the Comanches and Kiowas has surrounded himself with women who surpass all others in beauty."

Maman-ti laughed softly. His perceptive eyes made another thorough inspection of Shianne's bewitching figure. "If not for the will of the Great Spirit who commands that we remain no more than friends, I would sweep you into my arms and take you to my village near Medicine Creek. If you were mine, there would be no room for other women in my tepee."

"Surely you did not come here to shower me with empty praise," Shianne mocked lightly. "We both know I am where I belong and that you are content with your devoted wives and children."

Maman-ti brushed a callused hand over her creamy cheek. "But had we met in another time . . ." His hand dropped away and then folded around her elbow. "In truth I have come to replenish our supply of horses and cattle. My warriors and I have just returned from the Sun Dance ceremony with the Cheyennes, Apache and Navaho," the shaman muttered under his breath. "We had taken many ponies to trade with the Navaho, but they came into our camp to partake of our feasts and then *stole* the horses we planned to sell to them. The Navaho are foolish with their horses. They ride them into the ground, and when their steeds perish they butcher their mounts and seek out others. The Navaho even dare to steal from the red man who would call him friend."

Maman-ti sighed with frustration. He hadn't intended to spoil his meeting with Shianne by rehashing the unfortunate incident on the banks of the Washita. "Come, Little One. I have something to show you."

Frowning curiously, Shianne allowed herself to be propelled along with Maman-ti's long, swift strides. They walked for almost a quarter of a mile with Delgado trailing along behind them. Maman-ti paused beside the gurgling spring that bubbled from a mound of boulders in the side of the hill.

"What is so . . ."

Maman-ti laid a tanned finger to her lips to shush her. "Listen. . . ."

Shianne heard strange, muffled noises flowing with the rippling water. Wide eyes lifted to Maman-ti's amused smile.

"The water speaks. Perhaps that is why the Great Spirit led me to you, Little One. This is the sacred ground of our ancestors. I will hold council here and follow the prophecies of other oracles, as well as the owl."

Another council of the chiefs meant more raids, she thought dismally. "Must there be more war against the Texans?" she blurted out.

Maman-ti smiled tolerantly. He had come to expect such remarks from this feisty beauty. Shianne was not like his obedient wives who did not dare to question his decisions. "The Comanches and Kiowas will raid to acquire horses and cattle from the white man until the moon no longer climbs into the night sky. We have suffered injustices because of the white man. He murders our women and children, drives the buffalo into its grave and offers treaties that are no more than convenient lies." Maman-ti's voice grew more bitter by the second. "Our brothers are being pushed from their homelands and ordered into Indian Territory as if we were no more than herds of elk or buffalo. It is in the wind, Little One. The white man wishes the Indian to be no more . . . forever."

Reluctantly, Shianne bit her tongue and did not argue the point. As far as she could tell, both the Indian and the white man were at fault. The whites boldly claimed Indian land for their homesteads. The Indians retaliated by burning and raiding cabins that stood upon their territory. The whites cried to the cavalry for protection, and the army obliterated entire bands of Indians. It had become a vicious circle, and Shianne wondered where it would end. Even her own family was at fault. The K Bar Ranch set upon the vast hunting grounds of the Kiowa and Comanche. Only because of her link with the great Cheyenne chief and her friendship with Maman-ti was she granted amnesty. Other whites were not so fortunate. On numerous occasions, ranches were relieved of their cattle and horses. Maman-ti and the tribal chiefs felt it was fair compensation for the atrocities the Indians had endured and for the white man's intrusion into regions where he did not rightfully belong.

When Maman-ti set her atop the black stallion, he was tempted to tell her about the dream that compelled him to seek her out, but he bit his lip and kept his thoughts to himself. Another time, he mused as he peered into Shianne's bedazzling features.

"When will I see you again?" she murmured.

"I will send for you more often than I have in the past." The Owl Prophet half turned, staring pensively at the river that glowed like silver in the moonlight. "Here lies the Speaking Springs, the spiritual ground of our ancestors. We will come here often to listen to the voices of the spirits, and I will call for you."

Reluctantly, Shianne urged Delgado into a trot. She felt trapped between two different civilizations, unable to devote her loyalty to either side of this volatile conflict. She knew the Owl Prophet's presence meant trouble for the ranchers and homesteaders, and yet, she could not betray the medicine man's confidence.

Shianne truly admired the bronze-skinned warrior who possessed the features of a Greek god. He was the only man who looked upon her with something other than lust in his eyes. Although the Owl Prophet had made it known that he desired her, he was content to call her friend. Most of her other male acquaintances seemed more interested in a woman's body, not the mind and personality that was attached to it. Most men were like the bold stranger she had met the previous

32

afternoon, Shianne reminded herself cynically.

Although Shianne was determined to detest the arrogant desperado who had been stripped of everything but his monumental pride, she found his image coming uninvited to her thoughts the split second she left Maman-ti. *Stop this nonsense!* Shianne scolded herself. She had a ranch to run, and there was no time to dawdle over a stranger who appeared one day and vanished the next.

Besides, any relationship which began under such unusual circumstances could only lead to trouble, Shianne assured herself. There was enough trouble brewing in Texas after the war between the states without piling catastrophe upon disaster. The Texas Rangers had been disbanded and replaced by the state police. Shianne frowned disconcertedly at the thought. The police were no more than a swarm of carpetbag badge toters who delighted in suppressing Texans who had fought on the opposite side of the war. They were n'er-do-wells who had flooded the state on the coattails of the Northern Republicans who had assumed command of the government after the defeat of the South.

To make matters worse than they already were, the Indians were stealing the white man blind in spiteful retaliation. The general economy was at an all time low. Although cattle outnumbered humans ten to one, the markets of the South offered no relief and money was scarce.

Just what was she to do about gathering the herds that had wandered here and yonder during the war? Lord, one roundup to brand K Bar cattle would require more men than she could afford to pay without assuming staggering debts.

Dammit, where was her father? Why were all these critical decisions dumped in her lap? Although Carlos

33

Santos managed the ranch, Shianne was forced to make the final decisions. Should she take the easy way out and accept Haden's long-standing marriage proposal? He was eager to assume command of the K Bar and make her his wife.

Shianne sighed heavily. She wanted something more from marriage than a convenient solution to her problems or the joining of one vast ranch with another. Haden had behaved like the perfect gentleman in her presence, but she had also heard the quiet rumors. She could not completely put her trust in a man who hired himself an army to discourage grass pirates from gathering unbranded cattle and claiming them as their own.

Was it too much to ask for a woman to want a strong, enduring love instead of security? Could she ever come to love Haden Reems? Shianne scoffed at the absurdity. The man had no sincere love to offer. He was a cold, calculating rancher whose greed to possess half of Texas had become his obsession. Shianne was only a conquest to him. Haden craved to surround himself with objects that caught his eye. Although she did not consider herself a raving beauty, one glance in the mirror assured her that she was far from homely. Haden had made it obvious that he liked what he saw and that he would not be adverse to seeing more.

Haden liked to collect pretty things. His hacienda was a monument of elaborate decor and expensive, imported furnishings. Shianne laughed bitterly, wondering if Haden would think to prop her in the corner beside the mammoth grandfather clock he had shipped to Texas all the way from Italy.

The fact that he ruled his one hundred thousand acre ranch like a tyrannical king agitated Shianne. Haden had declared war on the homeless as well as the desperados. He was of the opinion that every mustang and maverick in Texas should have *his* brand on its hip, and he sent out his army of bravoes to discourage others from crossing his land or setting up housekeeping.

Shianne's respect for the cattle baron had dwindled when he chose to sit out the war. Haden was in his mid-thirties and able-bodied, but he chose to remain on his ranch while Blake rode off to do his duty. Indeed, Haden had been so apathetic that he drove his herd through Mexico to sell to buyers from the European market. His only loyalty was to himself, and Shianne could never tolerate such a selfish man as a husband.

Haden had become persistent the past two years, but Shianne kept putting him off. Although she would not give him the answer he demanded, he discouraged other men from actively courting her. In truth, Shianne did not mind his interference in her love life. She had too many responsibilities without becoming involved with a man. One thing was for certain; she would not be prodded into a marriage she could not abide. She would become a spinster before she sacrificed her independence and her identity.

Her eyes took on a dreamy glow as she trotted across the prairie. Shianne longed for a man who was the master of his own soul—someone like Maman-ti who was bold, daring and brimming with wild nobility. She also wanted a man who possessed her father's perseverance and delightful sense of humor, and someone with Doc Winston's generous heart and tender ways. Unfortunately, it seemed impossible to bottle up all those good qualities and pour them into one man, a man who could touch her wild, restless heart.

A bubble of laughter gushed from Shianne's lips. Impulsively, she gouged Delgado in the ribs, sending him into his swiftest gait. Her expectations of the perfect man were no more than a child's whimsical dream, she told herself. She longed for a creature that did not exist, and yet, she refused to settle for anything less.

Shianne leaned against Delgado's neck, urging him to sprout wings and fly. "I will grow old yearning for what I cannot find," she mused aloud, her gaze focused on the distant lights of the hacienda.

Wade Burdett stood at the mouth of the cavern, listening to the sound of hooves pounding the ground. His breath caught in his throat when he spied the enchanting vision who sailed through the darkness like the dancing shadow of a dream. There, silhouetted against the silvery moonlight, clinging to the back of a devil stallion was the woman he had seen the previous afternoon. Her sheer gown sparkled with moonbeams. A mane of midnight hair trailed wildly behind her as she spirited across the prairie. Over the pounding of hooves Wade could detect faint laughter, a hauntingly compelling sound that sent ripples of excitement flooding down his backbone.

As the echoes of laughter and the call of a distant owl melted into silence, Wade sighed forlornly. Who was this mysterious woman who roamed the sprawling range of Texas? Had she ridden by his campsite to torment him again, to ensure that her memory still lingered in his mind?

Try as he may, Wade could not forget that bewitching face and enticing body. Even after a day he could still feel her hands sweeping across his burned flesh and smell the feminine scent that had invaded his nostrils. By damned, he was going to find that dark nymph and ease the hunger she had instilled in him. Once he satisfied his curiosity and his lust, those

36

glimmering brown eyes would no longer torment him. Perhaps if he could find sweet release in this mysterious angel's arms, he could endure his forced association with the witch of K Bar Ranch.

Another image leaped to mind, causing Wade to swear under his breath. Shianne Kimball. An intriguing name, Wade thought to himself. But he could well imagine the face and body attached to Blake's unmarried daughter. She was probably no more than five feet tall and as round as a barrel. Her skin was most likely as dry and rough as rawhide, and her eagerness for a lover would probably send even the most desperate of men scampering away in search of alternative affection.

"Thanks a helluva lot, Blake," Wade muttered at the darkness. If this was Blake's idea of a practical joke, Wade wasn't laughing. He would have much preferred to travel to Springfield, Illinois and allow Blake to deliver his own messages to Texas. Surely, Blake knew he could not corral Wade into an unwanted marriage with some wild-eyed witch. Wade was a dedicated bachelor, and he was not about to tie himself to the likes of Witch Kimball, not for all the mavericks in Texas!

Dammit, Wade had agreed to this proposition and partnership because he wanted to make a new beginning after the war, but after riding and contemplating for a hundred miles, it occurred to him that Blake might have set a trap for him. Grappling with the possibility of what awaited at journey's end, Wade began dragging his feet. He had drunk and whored his way through Louisiana to Texas. For more than three months he had been followed by the lurking image of a woman who could give a man nightmares. Wade had only to conjure up Blake Kimball's craggy, weather-beaten features and stout body. Suddenly he was visualizing the same features and torso on a woman. Lord, what a sight Shianne must be!

Cringing at the hideous image, Wade muttered under his breath. The next few months were going to be pure hell, he warned himself. For God's sake, the past four years had been no picnic either. How could his association with Shianne Kimball be worse than being gouged by longhorns during cattle drives and dodging Union bullets in battle? He had survived the war, he reminded himself. He could dodge the arms of a homely, love-starved witch who would leap at the chance of having a man take charge of her responsibilities.

For some reason Wade didn't feel better after having this little talk with himself. He kept wondering if the wench would plant herself in his bed one night and then scream the house down the following morning, swearing she had been seduced and demanding a shotgun wedding by nightfall.

"What the hell are you grinning about?" Wade snorted sourly.

Jacob brayed in response to Wade's harsh tone and then went back to grazing on the plush grass beneath his hooves.

"I'm not certain which one of us is the jackass," Wade grumbled as he attempted to hobble the lanky mule for the night. "At the moment I would gladly exchange places with you. When we were swarmed by outlaws no one thought to stake *you* out without a stitch of clothes, and you don't have to fret over being mauled by a witch who hungers to snare a man, any way she can get him."

Jacob curled his upper lip, laid back his long ears, and bellowed. Roughly, Wade yanked on the lead rope, forcing the contrary mule to follow or risk having his neck pinched in two.

"If you have nothing pleasant to say, don't say anything at all," Wade demanded. "My prize steed has been stolen and I am left with you. If those outlaws had known what a sparkling conversationalist you are, maybe you would have been led away instead of Galahad."

Muttering over the loss of his experienced steed and growling about the upcoming encounter with the woman who probably had as many arms as an octopus, Wade stalked back to the cave. Damn, why did he feel like a lamb being taken to slaughter? Confound it, this was all Blake Kimball's fault. That conniving rancher had set Wade up, and it was too late to turn back. The plans had already been put into motion.

Although Wade was a man who had learned to take adversity and setbacks in stride, he was having difficulty overlooking the problems he faced with Blake's daughter. He had not become *completely* poisoned with bitterness when the Union army burned the plantation home and then confiscated the land that had been in his family for generations. Gritting his teeth, Wade had accepted his loss and sought out other avenues to reestablish his fortune. He needed Blake and his generous proposition as much as Blake needed Wade to ensure that they turned a profit. What Wade *didn't* need was a clinging vine to strangle him while he was devoting his time and effort to business.

No, he wasn't going to like Shianne Kimball, not one iota. Not that he was a prize catch, but he was probably the only available fish in Shianne's evacuated sea. That plump little witch was going to cause him trouble. He could feel it in his bones!

After completing several important tasks in San Antonio, Wade purchased a new holster and strapped the Colt .45 on his hip. He emerged from the stone and adobe store to survey the bustling of activity. His perceptive gaze circled the town square to see his stolen horse tied in front of the cantina.

With his mouth set in grim determination, Wade strode across the street as boldly as a lion stalking a jungle. Without hesitation Wade marched to his steed and swung into the saddle. One of the vaqueros he had met two days earlier was leaning against the supporting post of the cantina. When Wade dared to recover his horse, Gustavo Ruiz spun on his heels to alert his friends.

Wade waited for the horse thieves to swarm from the tavern and then blew away the wooden steps where they stood. When Gustavo Ruiz whipped out his pistol, Wade sent it sailing from his hand with a well-aimed bullet.

Four pair of bewildered eyes lifted to the muscular cowboy who sat in the saddle. A slow smile curved one corner of Wade's mouth upward as he assessed the desperados' reaction to his daring affront. "Thank you kindly for taking such good care of Galahad." His astute gaze caught the movement of one desperado inching his hand toward his revolver. "I wouldn't if I were you, *amigo*. I lost my taste for killing during the war, but I can easily be provoked to it again." Wade's eyes drilled into the man's taut features. "When a man loses his land and has little left except his horse, he has a tendency to cling fiercely to it." His gaze drifted to the outlaw's dusty boots and then returned to survey the tense lines around the man's mouth. "If you were to die trying to reclaim the horse you *stole* from me, shall I tell the undertaker that you wish to be buried with your boots on?"

Juan Mendez broke into a wide grin. He could not help but respect the daring stranger who counted his odds four to one and did not bat an eye at defying disadvantage. Juan was still sporting the bruise on his jaw after the confrontation. He was well aware this *hombre* had the strength of three men. Self-confidence exuded from Wade Burdett. He looked to be a man who had tested his abilities to the very limit and lived to tell about it if he were inclined to do so. But Burdett seemed to be a private man who had no need to boast. Juan had the feeling Burdett didn't exactly set out to find trouble, but when and if it found him, he was not the kind of man who walked away from it.

The *gringo* was very calm and controlled . . . almost to the point of deadly ease. Juan had dealt with many men during the years he worked for Haden Reems. Men like this stranger were the dangerous kind. Wade was slow to anger, but when provoked to killing fury, he had already weighed every possibility, and he reacted with calculated accuracy. If Juan were to reach for his pistol, he had the uneasy feeling he would be dropped in his tracks, and before Juan fell into a lifeless heap, the rest of his friends would be joining him on what was left of the wooden step.

Considering the alternative, Juan decided to sacrifice the blood-bay stallion and spare his own life, not to mention the use of his valuable gun hand. *"No hay de que, gringo.* I brushed the bay down last night and fed him well."* Juan's grin broadened when Wade eased his finger from the trigger of his pistol. He gestured his head toward the garments that stretched across Wade's broad chest and muscular thighs. "I approve of your new set of clothes, *hombre.* They become you far more than the dusty breeches and vest you wore the first time we chanced to meet."

For a long moment the two men continued to grin at each other, sizing each other for reference, in case of future confrontations. Satisfied that he would not be shot in the back when he presented it as a target, Wade reined Galahad toward the mule he had ridden into San Antonio.

When Pedro Tecovas reached for his pistol, Juan grabbed his arm. "Let him go, *amigo*. He is more than the two of us put together. I like him."

"But Señor Reems may not like it if the *hombre* accuses us of horse theft and sends the sheriff to ask questions," Pedro insisted. "As of yet, no one has dared to link our names with the outlaw band that roams the county." His narrowed gaze drilled into Wade's broad back. "This *gringo* could be the one who dares to name names. We did not strike fear in him the way we did the others."

Juan's dark eyes followed Wade as he walked the blood-bay stallion around the town square. "I do not think that is the stranger's way. If it were, he would have hidden behind the sheriff and begged protection instead of retrieving his stolen horse by himself." Juan gave his head a slow shake. "This *hombre* is the kind who fights his own battles. And I, for one, think we are fortunate that he is satisfied to forget about what we did to him and merely fetch the bay."

If the truth be known, Juan was beginning to care less and less about what Haden Reems did or didn't like. After the brutal incident the previous spring, Juan was losing his taste for Haden's brand of cruelty. There was a world of difference between strong-arming and unprovoked violence. Although Haden paid Juan well to overlook his conscience it still hounded him occasionally.

As Wade rode past the tavern, an attractive señorita appeared on the balcony. His thick lashes swept up to appraise her voluptuous figure and her come-hither smile. Wade pulled his steed to a halt, silently deliberating the invitation. But that hauntingly lovely face that had taken up permanent residence in his mind squeezed its way to center stage.

Hell, what was the use of tumbling another wench into bed when he craved the elusive goddess who had spirited in and out of his life? What he wanted couldn't be bought, and he was frustrated that he had seen nothing of the mysterious nymph during his visit to San Antonio. Dammit, Wade was prepared to swear the girl existed. She wasn't a figment of his imagination. She had rescued him from the creek bank, and she had sailed through the moonlight on her coal-black stallion. He *had* seen her!

Cordially, Wade tipped his hat to the lady (if one could call her that) and nudged Galahad toward the edge of town. Indecision clung to Wade's brow as his gaze swung from the path that led to his campsite to the trail that would take him to the headquarters of the K Bar. He had confronted the desperados and walked away unscathed. Perhaps this was the time to face Witch Kimball. He may as well get this over with, Wade lectured himself. He could not procrastinate forever. A wry smile pursed his lips as he aimed Galahad toward the K Bar. By the time he escaped Shianne Kimball's clutches, he would probably be beating down that señorita's door to touch something warm and feminine.

Suddenly soured by his unenthusiastic anticipation of meeting Witch Kimball, Wade muttered under his breath. If Shianne offered him room and board he would most certainly decline. Wade would much prefer to camp by the cave than attempt to sleep with that overeager female prowling the hall. No amount of money could persuade him to play up to that homely wench with sagging jowls and hips as wide as an axe handle. Wade shivered repulsively at the thought. Each time Shianne Kimball's image popped to mind, the woman grew uglier and wider.

My God, he had conjured up a monster, Wade realized with a bitter laugh. Just because she was Blake's daughter and still unwed at twenty-one, didn't mean she was all *that* bad, for God's sake! He could tolerate plain-faced women as well as the next man. After all, he didn't consider himself a handsome, refined gentleman with his dark skin and rugged features, and he had never been one to display stiff, polite manners that might lump him in the class with the chivalrous gentlemen of the South. Wade had been carved from a different scrap of wood. True, he was a mite rough around the edges, but he saw no harm in that.

"Oh, what the hell," Wade snorted, encouraging himself to stop moping. The only way he was going to know for certain what kind of creature Shianne Kimball was, was to march up to her door and take a look at her. If she were as dreadful as he imagined he could always . . . He could always what? Wade was stuck, just like a longhorn bogged down in quicksand. Blake Kimball was his partner and, as in that unpleasant institution known as marriage, it was for better or worse.

Haden Reems glanced up when he heard the faint rap on his study door. His deep-set eyes focused on the portal, and he bade entry in that rough, brisk voice of his.

Although Juan Mendez had urged him to forget about the daring stranger who escaped his torment to prowl the streets of San Antonio, Pedro Tecovas feared repercussions. Pedro had found the letter stashed in Wade's shirt while he was rummaging through the garments. He was certain Haden would be

44

most interested to read its contents. Ignoring Juan's warning, Pedro hastened to Haden's study the moment they returned to the ranch.

"Señor, I found something I think you should see," Pedro declared, walking forward to lay the letter on Haden's desk. "It was stashed on the man we staked out this week."

Haden unfolded the letter and hurriedly scanned its contents. "Damn," he burst out. Angrily, he wadded the paper in his fist and hurled it toward the hearth. "So Blake *is* alive. And not only that, but he has taken himself a partner to help him manage the K Bar." Haden vaulted to his feet and snatched up his hat as he breezed into the entryway. "I'll not have any man dallying with Shianne. She is mine. It's time I paid her a visit and reminded her of that fact!"

Like a bat out of hell, Haden tore off down the path that led to Shianne's hacienda. He had hoped Blake had perished during the war, offering no resistance when Haden finally persuaded Shianne to be his bride.

There had always been a strain between Blake and Haden. Blake never approved of Haden's tactics of acquiring land or his techniques in business dealings, and Blake was the type of man who dared to make his opinions known. Although Blake appeared to be preoccupied with his new investment, he had sent Wade Burdett to ramrod the K Bar. Surely, Wade would not be as difficult to deal with as Blake, Haden thought confidently. He was eager to meet his competition and issue his warning. If this Wade Burdett valued his hide, he would take a wide berth around Haden and keep his distance from Shianne. Haden may never gain sole control of the vast acres of the K Bar Ranch, but he was not about to lose the raven-haired beauty whose vision could keep him pacing the floor in unfulfilled desire.

There were other ways to acquire the land, Haden reminded himself. He had already resorted to skull-duggery to obtain land holdings that interested him. He could always find ways to maneuver around Blake. Haden was obsessed with becoming the most powerful cattle baron in Texas, and one day that dream would collide with reality, he reassured himself. The minor inconvenience of a stranger managing the K Bar was not going to deter him from his goals. His men had already dissuaded scores of homesteaders from purchasing the land he wanted, and they had thwarted the branding of several thousand head of cattle that roamed the region. No one would stand in his way. Haden would see to that.

By the time Haden and his army rounded up the stray mavericks, he would own the largest herd in Texas, and when he returned from driving the beeves to market, he would triple his wealth. That thought brought a smile to his thin lips. Very soon Shianne would rule his cattle kingdom by his side and ease the obsessive craving he held for her. She could not reject his proposal forever. He would not allow it!

From the time Shianne had blossomed into womanhood, Haden knew he had to have that high-spirited minx. She challenged him, aroused him. Although he could have bought any wench who met his whim, Haden hungered for the olive-skinned beauty with the wide, spellbinding eyes. He would have to master her feisty temperament, but she would mellow when she realized she could not battle Haden Reems and win. He had been patient with her, but within the next few months Haden vowed to take her as his bride, whether she wanted to marry him or not.

Satisfied that Wade Burdett's intrusion might hamper his plans but never destroy them, Haden galloped across the open range to restake his claim on

San Antonio's most stunning beauty. If Burdett knew what was good for him, he would not oppose the marriage. A fiendish smile swallowed Haden's bony features. If Burdett tried to interfere he might find himself in the same uncompromising situation as that defiant traveler he had disposed of the previous spring. Haden had made short work of the man who had dared to trespass on the Lazy R Ranch. The man would never make that mistake again, nor did he live to talk about it. Yes, if Burdett proved to be the stubborn sort, he would also meet his demise.

Chapter 3

Wade fished into the saddle bag that was strapped on his mule and grasped a bottle of courage. After downing a drink of whiskey, he recorked the bottle and returned it to its resting place. Drawing himself up, he made the long walk to the vine-covered veranda that surrounded the hacienda. The Spanish styled home of sun-dried brick had been well kept during Blake's absence, he observed. No doubt, Shianne had little else to occupy her, Wade thought with a smirk.

After rapping on the intricately carved door, Wade allowed his gaze to sketch the two-story structure. It was so unlike the plantation house the Union army had burned to the ground, he mused. Huge arched windows boasted a view of the sprawling ranch set in a valley that was ablaze with wild flowers. Wide terraces encircled the hacienda, allowing its inhabitants to enjoy the natural beauty of the surroundings without enduring the heat of the hot summer sun. Beyond the courtyard was a wooded spring that supplied water for the grand home and the servant's quarters and bunkhouse that were located in back of the hacienda.

It seemed Blake Kimball lacked for nothing, Wade speculated as he impatiently shifted from one foot to the other. Except a charming daughter who could attract the kind of man Blake wanted for a son-in-law, Wade tacked on.

When the door swung open to reveal the plump maid, Wade forced a sick smile. Lord, Miss Kimball had hired a servant to match her looks, and Wade was willing to bet his right arm that there were no mirrors dangling from the walls in this house. Blake's ugly daughter probably didn't want to frighten herself when she happened to glance at her own reflection.

"I have come to see Shianne Kimball," Wade announced with all the bravado he could muster. Damn, he should have consumed the entire bottle of brandy to help him endure this encounter!

"Un momento, por favor," Ramona replied.

Her critical gaze slid up and down the stranger's muscular physique, and she smiled to herself. Now here was a man who could transform Shianne's indifference into immediate interest, she predicted. *Caramba!* If Ramona were twenty years younger she would be drooling over this darkly handsome *hombre*.

As Ramona waddled away to announce the visitor, Wade slumped against the door casing. *Lord, make time fly,* he prayed. He would storm the hacienda, rattle off his reasons for being there and get the hell back to the cave as fast as Galahad could gallop!

"Señorita?" Ramona poked her head inside the study where Shianne was laboring over the ledgers. "There is someone here to see you."

"Who?" Shianne questioned without glancing up.

"I did not think to ask his name. I was too busy marveling at his fine stature," she guiltily admitted. "Shall I show him in?"

Shianne absently nodded approval and concentrated on computing the month's expenses. When she completed the tally, she sank back in her chair to massage her aching head. Her expenses were mounting all too quickly, and she sorely needed to gather a herd to put on the trail north. Damnation, where was Blake? She needed him, and she did not have the slightest idea how to begin searching for information about him. Not that she would have the time, she thought dismally. It would take the rest of the summer to round up the wide-spread herd, cut out the marketable calves and brand them for the drive north in the fall.

The sound of boots and spurs clanking against the tiled foyer drew her from her troubled musings. Shianne lifted her eyes and gasped in disbelief when the man she had spent two days trying to forget barged into her study. Bug-eyed, she peered into those disturbing pools of emerald. Without thinking, Shianne surveyed the stranger from the top of his black felt hat to the tips of his boots. The man was as awesomely attractive in clothes as he was when he was lying na . . . *Banish the thought!* Shianne chastised herself. She did not want to remember how this man's muscles rippled when he moved, how his hair-roughened flesh felt beneath her inquiring fingertips, how his lips parted in a roguish smile.

If Shianne was shocked beyond words, Wade was struck dumb. For a moment he could only gape at her. This mysterious angel was Shianne Kimball, the woman he had bitterly referred to as a hag with stringy hair and a hooked nose. Lord, he retracted every spiteful, derogatory thought!

Blake had not put a curse on him after all. Wade would not only be eager to share living quarters with this provocative nymph, but he would have no qualms about sharing her *bed.* The thought caused a rakish grin to tug at the corner of his mouth. Mmmm, he could just imagine how tantalizing she would be in his arms.

Wade's arousing fantasy shattered when Shianne's stunned expression transformed into a glacial glare, one cold enough to turn the arid climate into a barren arctic. "What are you doing here?" Shianne snapped.

There should have been icicles dripping from her voice, Wade mused. But they could not extinguish the slow burning fire that had kindled inside him. From under the brim of his hat, his probing gaze worked its way over her high thrusting breasts and swanlike neck. Wade took his own sweet time about appraising Shianne's attractive assets, not overlooking even the smallest detail.

She had it all, the delicate bone structure, the creamy olive coloring, the flawless skin and the sculptured features of a goddess. Wade could only speculate as to how she would look in the altogether, but he seriously doubted if he would be disappointed.

When Wade finally got around to refocusing his attention on her face, his confident smile sagged on his lips. Shianne looked as unfriendly as an Indian war party, but Wade was not to be intimidated. He had every right to be here, and gawking was not a crime, certainly not in lawless Texas.

Noticing that Shianne's dark eyes had begun to roam over him, Wade chuckled softly. "Am I overdressed?" One eyebrow climbed to a mocking angle. "I realize you are not accustomed to seeing me in clothes." His smile grew wider, displaying flashing white teeth. "If you prefer I can peel off a few layers. . . ."

His taunt struck like a well-aimed arrow. Shianne's agitation was compounded by the fact that this haughty rogue knew where her mind had wandered. She could have kicked herself for being so obvious!

Shianne put out her chin, attempting to remain cool

51

and aloof. "Did you come here to display your distorted sense of humor again or do you actually have a practical purpose for interrupting me?" Her voice carried an unpleasant edge. If Wade had not been a confident man he would have tucked his tail between his legs and crawled away before she slashed his male pride to shreds. "I am very busy at the moment. If you have come to chat, you are wasting my time and yours. I had nothing to say to you when we first met, nor do I now."

The lady *did* have a tongue, Wade realized. It had been frequently filed and permanently sharpened. His brow wore a condescending frown while he raked her up and down. "Are you always so rude and abrupt with your guests?" he taunted. "Tsk, tsk. You will never win friends with such a sour disposition."

Wade tossed his hat on a nearby table. He strutted forward, filling up the room and making Shianne more uncomfortable by the second. This stranger had a way about him—a calm reserve nothing seemed to shake. Shianne had resolved to have no association with the man she had met under most embarrassing circumstances. Since he refused to be routed with rudeness, she found it necessary to resort to more extreme measures. Her tapered fingers folded around the pistol she always carried on her hip. As Wade approached like a charging infantry, Shianne lifted the revolver above the desk, freezing the grinning cowboy in his tracks.

"There are some men in this world who are either too ignorant to ignore a warning or too mule-headed to take a woman at her word," Shianne gritted out, her black eyes snapping. "Into which category do you fall?" Without awaiting his reply she rushed on. "Agreed, it is difficult to overcome stupidity. A man who possesses the intelligence of a fence post is to be pitied, but there

52

is a cure for stubbornness." Shianne emphasized her point by cocking the trigger of her pistol. "The treatment may often be drastic, yet effective." The faintest hint of a smile rippled across her heart-shaped lips, but it was more a display of taunt than pleasantness. "As I have found in dealing with jackasses, it often takes a pounding between their ears to get my point across." One finely etched brow elevated as her gaze drifted over his masculine torso. "The last time I turned my pistol on you it was to split the strap that bound your hand. This time my mark will be the vital parts of your anatomy. Have you a particular preference as to which one?"

Wade took one retreating step, but there was delightful amusement glistening in his eyes. Ah, how he adored a feisty woman, one who didn't cower or whimper. It was obvious Blake had raised a she-cat. No wonder this dark-eyed enchantress wasn't married. She was hardly the shy, retiring type who would fawn over a man and bolster his male pride with her glowing accolades. Indeed, Shianne Kimball had Wade counting his saving graces and contemplating his faults—the most obvious of which was approaching a tigress without a chair and a whip. While it was true that the lady had the body and face of an angel, there was fire and brimstone in the region of her heart.

Wade let out the breath he had been holding and shrugged nonchalantly. Doing an about-face, he sashayed toward the door. "Very well, Miss Kimball, if you choose to be so mean and nasty, I will keep my information about your father to myself. Your icy attitude leaves me to wonder why Blake bothered to relay a message to you through me."

"My father?" Shianne chirped. Tossing the pistol aside, Shianne bounded from her chair to block the stranger's exit. "My father is alive? You have spoken with him?"

Wide, expressive eyes lifted to meet Wade's sly smile. Taking advantage of the opportunity, Wade reached around the shapely blockade to close the door. Leisurely, he lifted the lustrous braid from her shoulder, marveling at the silky strands that caressed his fingertips.

Shianne endured the stranger's closeness, even though it was having a strange effect on her blood pressure. All five senses seemed to come to attention, each vividly aware of the raw, masculine strength that towered over her. Willfully suppressing her nervousness, Shianne dragged the long braid from his callused hand and replaced it on her shoulder.

"Well? What did my father say?" she demanded impatiently.

"What he *didn't* say was that I would risk life and limb to convey the message to his lovely daughter." His astute gaze flooded over her curves and swells, speculating on the measurements of her enticing figure. "I have nothing to say until you apologize for talking so nastily and holding me at gun point. I came to relieve your fears about your father and you, Miss Kimball, have behaved abominably."

"I'm sorry," Shianne said hurriedly, her tone hardly apologetic. She was much too eager to know of Blake's whereabouts to delay with long-winded regrets.

Wade gave his raven head a disappointed shake. What he wanted in the way of an apology needed no words. He had bargaining power, and he damned well intended to use it. "That isn't good enough, princess. But I think a kiss would heal my bruised pride."

Shianne stared at him as if he had sprouted another head, one equipped with devil's horns. Her glittering glare said it all. She would not be cowed into a clinch by this wily fox!

Seeing the adamant "no" stamped on her exquisite features, Wade detoured around her. His body brushed against hers, determined to enjoy a smidgen of physical contact. "Then I guess this is good-by, honey. I would say it has been a pleasure to meet you, but I promised my dear mother I would never lie."

Shianne gnashed her teeth until she very nearly ground them smooth. That ornery sidewinder! He was delighting in taunting her. Oh, what the hell, she thought to herself. What could one little kiss hurt? If it would loosen the man's lips and encourage him to relate the incidents that kept Blake from returning home, it was worth it.

Before Wade's outstretched hand clamped onto the door knob, Shianne reached up on tiptoe to plant a hasty peck on his bronzed cheek. "Now tell me about my father," she pleaded. "I have been very concerned about him."

Disappointment clung to his craggy features. "I said a *kiss,* not a peck on the cheek," he clarified. "My mule displays more affection than that. Your technique leads a man to believe you know nothing about kissing." One dark brow slid to a teasing angle. "Lack of practice, Miss Kimball?"

Shianne clenched her fists at her sides, trying to control her temper. She itched to smear that arrogant smirk all over his handsome face. Grumbling at this stranger's infuriating tactics, Shianne moved closer. By damned, she would give this cocky cowboy a lesson in kissing that he would not soon forget! And what she did lack in practice Shianne vowed to compensate with inventive originality. She wasn't going to stamp his lips with a kiss; she was going to leave him sizzling in frustrated desire. That was exactly what this rascal deserved!

Her supple body molded itself to his hard contours.

55

Boldly, her hands slid up his muscled chest to curl her fingertips in the crisp, wavy hair that clung to the nape of his neck. Her lips parted in a seductive smile.

"Is this more to your liking?" she whispered as she drew his head toward hers. Her moist breath caressed his mouth long before the actual kiss began, leaving Wade hungering to devour her.

What had begun as a spiteful retaliation to reduce this mass of brawn and muscle to quivering mush, backfired in Shianne's face. His touch altered her breath. The feel of his male body blending familiarly into hers sent a cavalry of goose bumps galloping across her skin. The brutish scent of the man who enveloped her in his arms caused her heart to tear loose and slam against her ribcage.

Shianne was not being kissed in return; she was being ravished! In less than an instant she became painfully aware that this stranger had probably *forgotten* more about kissing than she had learned in her twenty-one years of existence. She was being held in experienced arms—not too tightly to squeeze the breath out of her—not too loosely to let her collapse when the bones in her legs turned to rubber. This charismatic stranger had perfected kissing-in-the-clinch into a masterful art to be envied by every Cassanova between the Mississippi and the Pecos!

Sweet mercy. Shianne had blundered in over her head. She was swamped and buffeted by unfamiliar sensations that affected every nerve and muscle in her naive body. Each place his virile body touched sizzled like wildfire consuming dry kindling. Faintly forceful, his sensuous mouth rolled over hers. It was hard and warm and intoxicating. His questing tongue tugged her lips apart to trace the trembling curve of her mouth before investigating the sweet moistness within.

Shianne thought it impossible to deepen such an

56

intimate kiss. But oh, how naive she was, she realized. This bold stranger knew how to tenderly assault a woman and crumble her defenses. Wild sensations riveted through her. Shianne was left to wonder if she had somehow managed to wrap her hand around a lightning bolt. Her entire body was being seared by electricity, paralyzing her, causing her to melt all over him. His practiced expertise was ripping holes in every barrier she sought to construct between them, making her respond when she hadn't really wanted to.

Then, as abruptly as lightning struck, sizzled and evaporated, Wade released her. Shianne wilted against the wall, her dark eyes smoldering by what she could only assume to be desire—a sensation with which she had even less experience. Was this man some sort of mystical wizard? How could a mere stranger evoke such turmoil within her? How could he spin her nerves into tangled twine with his first kiss? From whence had these feelings come and what could have possibly set them off? Shianne wasn't even certain she liked the man who had very nearly kissed her senseless!

While Shianne was contemplating her unusual reaction, Wade was attempting to draw a normal breath. He had done far more than kiss a woman in the past—a helluva lot more—but in his vast experience with the female of the species, he had yet to have the props knocked out from under him by a first kiss. This ebony-haired sorceress had done just that, even with her innocent ways. Wade hated to think what a dynamic effect this minx would have on a man when she had gained more experience. She could become the kind of temptress who could and would drive a man mad with desire.

Wade tugged at the collar of his shirt to release the steam that was pocketed inside his clothes. When his heart finally slowed its frantic pace and began to beat at a methodic gait, he expelled a breath. "Lady, I would gladly endure another verbal lynching if that is your usual form of apology," he declared, his voice ragged with the side effects of passion.

Shianne blushed up to the roots of her hair. She wasn't certain how to counter his comment without making matters worse than they already were, so she said nothing at all. She merely wobbled back to her desk and plopped down before she fell down. Lord-a-mercy. Was that what kissing was really about? Shianne wasn't certain she wanted to undergo such an experience ever again. It left her feeling vulnerable, as if her own body sought to betray her.

Wade navigated his way to the vacant chair and parked himself in it, still grinning at the stunned expression on Shianne's face. "Your father is alive and well and living in Springfield, Illinois," he announced.

Shianne corraled her runaway thoughts, attempting to concentrate on the stranger's words. "Illinois?" she questioned bewilderedly. "Why didn't he come home?"

"I will get to that in a minute," Wade assured her as he eased back in his seat to pour out the events of the past few years. "The trail drives to Louisiana led to more trouble than we had anticipated. The war had reached a critical stage. Blake and I found ourselves ambushed by Yankee snipers, and our herd was confiscated to feed Union soldiers. Your father and I both sustained serious injuries, and we sought a safe place to recover from our wounds." Wade hesitated, wondering if this was the proper moment to explain about the dramatic change in Blake's life. No, he decided. Shianne had enough to cope with. This was not the time to drop a grenade in her lap. Later he would explain why Blake had not come himself.

"After Lee surrendered, the South was under military occupation. Not that it mattered," Wade grunted resentfully. "Blake and I could barely stand, much less walk away from the smoldering ruins of the South. When things had simmered down, we decided to make plans for the future, to attempt to return to a normal life after we picked up the pieces of a disastrous war."

Wade squirmed to a more comfortable position under Shianne's intent gaze. "We heard it rumored that a man named Joseph McCoy was interested in negotiating trade with Texas. The state is drowning in cattle that were left to multiply to more than six million during the war. Since the price of beeves sold in the South cannot turn a profit, McCoy is urging Texans to drive their cattle north. Beef is worth only five dollars a head in Louisiana, but it sells for twenty-five dollars or more in the North. At this very moment, Blake and Joseph McCoy are making arrangements to build stock pens near the railroad sights. They are also trying to encourage other investors to join in the crusade to reestablish trade between the North and South. Abilene, Kansas has been selected as the end of the cattle trail. There, buyers from Chicago can congregate to purchase Texas beef."

"Abilene, Kansas?" Shianne repeated skeptically. She had never heard of such a place. "I thought the only profitable market was in Sedalia, Missouri. That is where many of the ranchers are planning to take their cattle this fall."

Wade nodded slightly. "It *has* been the only outlet for cattle," he agreed. "But McCoy wants to move the herds straight north, bypassing the belligerent Missouri farmers who fear the spread of tick fever from Texas cattle. Cattle drovers have already met with resistance in the form of armed vigilantes who refuse crossing, not to mention the roving bands of outlaws who steal entire herds and murder range hands."

Shianne was not convinced. "You seem to forget that Indian Territory lies between Texas and Kansas, Mister . . ." Her voice trailed off, realizing she had yet to learn the stranger's name.

"Wade Burdett," he supplied with an easy smile.

"Burdett!" Shianne could not believe her ears. She had hated this man for years because he had taken her father from her, and here he sat in her study . . . after he had subtly maneuvered her into giving him a kiss that rattled her composure. No wonder her father had been unable to refuse any request this man made, she thought bitterly. Burdett was some sort of magician who could bend one's will until it coincided with his own.

Judging by her reaction and the angry frown that was plastered on her face, Wade surmised that he was as welcome as a swarm of hornets. No doubt, this firebrand held him personally responsible for stripping her father from her arms. But dammit, a war had been going on, and a man had to do what he thought was right. The government was attempting to dictate policy, refusing to allow states to write laws that corresponded to their individual needs. Blake felt obliged to do his part to preserve the South, but Shianne held Wade in contempt for contacting Blake to drive cattle to the starving Confederate army. No doubt, she would resent him even more when she learned the whole of it, Wade mused. No, this definitely wasn't the day to tell Shianne everything, he decided. She would be on the warpath for sure!

Wade frowned disconcertedly, watching the mutinous thoughts flash through Shianne's dark eyes. "Yes, I'm the despicable bastard who reminded Blake of his obligations, but let me assure you, it took little talking to convince him." He arched a quizzical brow. "Now, would you like to throw something at me to satisfy your bitterness or shall I continue my explanation?"

How could Wade Burdett read her thoughts so accurately? Surely they were not printed on her face. Was she so transparent or did Wade also possess the gift of mind reading? The man was a bundle of surprises. He defied every rule she had ever observed when encountering a man.

Smoothing her ruffled feathers, Shianne begrudgingly sank back in her chair and waited for Wade to continue. "Do go on," she purred with a sarcastic smile. "I'm sure I will like you even less by the time you finish relating the chronicles of the past few years."

Such a temper, Wade thought to himself. Shianne was quick to anger and incredibly defensive. If she had endured the battles of war it would have rounded off her sharp edges, but Wade liked her youthful spunk. It proved she possessed a passion for living and an even greater passion that had yet to be tapped by a man's touch. That particular passion intrigued him most. When they had sorted out the details of the past and placed the K Bar Ranch in working order, Wade intended to devote his spare time and energy to the seduction of Shianne Kimball. Like the wild mustangs of Texas, she could be tamed if a man had the perseverance to approach her with a gentle hand.

"Your father and McCoy are well aware of the hazard of crossing Indian Territory and confronting other outlaw bands who will prey on the herds, and we know it will be necessary to pay Indian tax for the right to traverse Indian land," Wade commented. "But by following the trail north there will be fewer large rivers to ford and more open range to graze the vast herd we intend to take to Abilene."

"How many head of longhorns are we discussing

here?" Shianne demanded to know. She was becoming more suspicious by the second. Had Wade talked her father into an investment that would drain the K Bar Ranch? What exactly did Wade Burdett want? Did his long-range plans include riding on Blake Kimball's coattails to build the fortune he probably lost during the war? Was he using Blake as a spring board, launching himself into the cattle business with Blake as his backing?

"I plan to take a herd of three thousand to Abilene," he told her matter-of-factly.

"Three thousand!" Shianne echoed incredulously.

She mentally tabulated the expense of feeding, equipping, and paying the many ranch hands required to herd that many beeves on a three-month trail drive. The estimate was staggering. It would cost the ranch nearly everything she had managed to save during the lean years of the war. Wade must have thought her father to be a multi-millionaire. Either that or Blake was suffering from delusions of grandeur! Did her father imagine she had managed to turn the same amount of profit they had enjoyed before the war? My Lord, Blake had not only lost the war, but he had obviously lost his mind!

"I don't know if my father has taken you into his confidence on the financial matters of our ranch, but I have just completed a tally of profit versus expenses, Mr. Burdett . . ."

"Wade," he inserted with an intimate smile that Shianne purposely ignored.

"Wade," she amended and then rushed on, "We cannot afford to herd such great numbers of cattle, even if there is a pot of gold waiting at the trail's end. The initial investment would force me to sell several hundred acres of the ranch!"

Wade squirmed in his seat. Shianne had taken

62

offense to everything he had said thus far. What was upcoming would undoubtedly annoy her, he predicted. "Your father has foreseen the problem and has sold me five hundred acres. That money will be used to defer part of the expenses."

Dumbstruck, Shianne gaped at him. Blake had sold part of the ranch to this . . . Shianne sought the exact word to describe the calm, self-assured man who was willing to gamble on any venture that might bring him a profit. Unfortunately, no single word seemed to fit Wade Burdett.

Taking advantage of her silence, Wade hurried on, "The land deeded to me by Blake lies north and east of the hacienda at the source of the springs. I have already set up camp on my property."

Wade Burdett had bought the land where Maman-ti intended to hold council. Damn, Wade couldn't have selected a worse place to pitch his tent. Rumors had been flying for months. Several of the vaqueros swore the cavern was haunted, and Maman-ti was certain Indian spirits lived inside the hill. That area was already subject to suspicion. What Shianne did not need was Wade Burdett prowling about.

"I'm sure you would prefer another plot of land to that one, Mr. . . . Wade," she corrected herself. "The ranch is large. If my father has indeed sold you land, it will not be too much trouble for you to relocate."

Probing green eyes assessed Shianne's carefully guarded expression. That piece of land was extremely valuable. Had Shianne somehow managed to learn why? If she hadn't, why was she so anxious to have him transplanted elsewhere? "Do you have some complaint against the area I selected?" he questioned point-blank.

Yes! Wade Burdett might find himself in the middle of a Comanche war dance, roasting over their ceremonial campfire, but Shianne couldn't tell him that. If the other ranchers got wind of the fact that the Owl Prophet and his council of war chiefs were camping on the K Bar Ranch, the Indian wars would break out in her own back yard. Dammit, first it was the Civil War and now this. Would there ever be a convenient catastrophe? Didn't she have enough to fret about without being caught in the middle of an Indian uprising and a trail drive that might cripple the ranch?

My, but the lady looked apprehensive. Wade had become adept at reading people's faces. He deciphered the downward slant of Shianne's brows to mean she was wrestling with inner turmoil.

"Why don't you want me to have that particular plot of land?" he put the question to her again, hesitant to drop the subject until she supplied him with an acceptable answer.

"It is only because it was an intriguing spot when I was a child," she hedged. "There have also been reports that the cavern is haunted by ghosts, and I never thought Papa would consider giving that area up . . . especially to a stranger."

Wade didn't buy that excuse. No, there was another reason why Shianne was apprehensive about surrendering that piece of ground. Did she know what he knew? Damn, if she did, chances were others might discover the truth of the caverns. Allowing that Shianne might have accidentally stumbled onto the secrets of the cave, Wade decided to table the subject until he was certain how much Shianne knew. Letting the matter die a quiet death, Wade turned the topic of conversation to the other reasons he had been sent to the K Bar Ranch. He may as well get part of this over with, he mused. After Shianne threw her temper tantrum, they could continue on from there.

"Since Blake decided to journey to Springfield and then to Abilene to oversee the construction of the railroad sight, he sent me here to serve in his capacity. The letter of explanation was stolen, along with my clothes and valuables, but it is Blake's wish that I become your guardian. My other duties will include gathering and branding longhorns for the drive north."

Just as Wade anticipated, Shianne split apart at the seams. As the words soaked in, color gushed into her cheeks.

"What?" She came straight out of her chair, and Wade calmly waited for the feisty beauty to hit the ceiling which she most certainly did! When she came down, black sparks were spewing from her eyes. "Do you think for one minute I am going to allow a total stranger to waltz into my hacienda and announce that he has been granted power of attorney? Do you think I will allow you to make decisions for me and my father without protesting? You had better think again, Wade Burdett," she fumed as she stormed around the side of the desk to breathe fire on him.

"I am the one who held this ranch together for the past few years. I have made all the decisions during the crises . . . and, believe me, there have been scores of them!" Shianne tapped herself on the chest to emphasize her point. "I run the K Bar. Does my father think I am still the same little girl he left to keep the home fires burning while you dragged him away to fight a lost cause and sacrifice our cattle to a defeated army?" Wade's eyes crossed when Shianne shook a slim finger in his face. "Well, I am not some simpering twit who will happily relinquish my responsibilities to the man who stole my father from me in the first place!" Shianne was gathering steam, and it felt ever so good to vent her wrath on the man who had caused her such heartache and inconvenience. "You will not give one order to my vaqueros. You have no proof of purchase and no handwritten affidavit stating that I am to step down and bow to the temporary king of K Bar Ranch. . . ."

Nonchalantly, Wade drew the bill of sale from his pocket and laid it in Shianne's hand. "Signed, sealed and delivered, Princess Kimball." An ornery smile stretched across his lips, making his eyes sparkle like priceless emeralds. "You need not call me *Your Highness*. I prefer we refer to each other on a first name basis and bypass formality."

Shianne glared at the bill of sale and then glowered at the mocking grin that displayed Wade's gleaming white teeth. "There is only one thing about your trek across Texas to assume your throne that baffles me, *Your Majesty*," she gritted out with a poisonous smile.

"Only one?" Wade purred, his tone bordering on sarcasm. "Then by all means, ask and I will set the matter straight."

Shianne's eyes were as hard as ebony. "Did you, perchance, walk on water to get here, *Sire?*" She spat out the word as if it left a bitter taste in her mouth.

Undaunted by her attempt to shave him down to size, Wade countered her murderous glare with his dazzling smile. "No, actually I came by horseback," he informed her flippantly. "The position of boss and guardian are mine at Blake's insistence. The only way for you to be reinstated as resident queen is to marry your newly appointed king . . . a possibility I think Blake considered when he requested that *I* come to Texas while *he* traveled to Abilene."

Shianne strangled on her breath and her face whitewashed. Marry this rattlesnake? Her father must have suffered shell shock. "I'd rather be whipped," she spumed. "You stole my father from me, kept him with you when I needed him. I resented your interference in my life then and even more now!"

Wade pushed himself out of the chair. He loomed

over the fiery minx who was glaring daggers at him.
"I'm really not all that bad," he assured her haughtily.
"Once you get to know me, you might even like me.
Why, I can name any number of women who would
eagerly accept my marriage proposal . . . not that I am
offering you one," he tacked on. "I may not be
dashingly handsome, but my looks are at least
tolerable . . . or so I have been told."

He knew damned well he was strikingly attractive,
Shianne thought furiously. Wade Burdett had an
interesting face and a virile physique that would create
a riot if he were to prance, stark naked, through San
Antonio. But a handsome man was the worst kind,
Shianne reminded herself. Wade was confident, arrogant and not beneath using his seductive charm to have
his way with women. Shianne had already decided that
if she were to marry, she would make her nest with a
prairie rooster not a peacock! A man's outward
appearance was not half as important as the qualities
within. She insisted upon traits she could admire—
dependability, honesty, sincerity—*not* thin-skinned
beauty.

"If there is a passel of women eager to wear your
wedding band then I suggest you round them up and
migrate your harem to Utah where you can wed them,
one and all," she smirked caustically. "I am not the
slightest bit interested in any proposition my father
thought to conjure up without consulting me. I am my
own woman, and I will not be dictated to, not by my
father and certainly not by you!" Her voice had grown
higher and wilder by the second, and she was all but
screeching in Wade's face.

My, but Shianne was glorious when she was in a fit
of temper, Wade thought to himself. It was as he
predicted. This tigress lived with a passion, hated with
a passion and she could probably love. . . . His

contemplations came to an abrupt halt when Shianne gave him a forceful shove, sending him sprawling in his chair.

Shianne loomed over him, refusing to be browbeaten by a total stranger. "You can take your proposal and your plans and stuff them in your saddle bags, Wade Burdett! Find some other willing rancher to offer you his headquarters for a roundup. And get . . . off . . . my . . . land. You will not have the plot my father offered you in a moment of madness. You will not have one acre of the K Bar Ranch! I will protest the bill of sale until my father returns to assure me that he was of sound mind when he scrawled his name on your wrinkled document!"

Now Wade was a man who had learned the meaning of patience and tolerance, but he did have his breaking point. This feisty female could try the patience of a saint, Wade reckoned. So it was hardly inconceivable that she had located his high threshold of temper and snapped his patience.

With pantherlike grace Wade unfolded himself from his chair to trap Shianne between his hard, unyielding length and the desk. Although he was still smiling, as was his custom, there was a venomous twist to his bottom lip and a dangerous glitter in his eyes. Shianne could feel the coarse tendons of his thighs mashing into her hips, feel the heat of his breath as he bent his head to demand her undivided attention.

"We can go about this in two ways, woman. You can step down from your lofty pedestal or I can *drag* you off of it. But either way, I am taking charge of the K Bar."

Too furious with him to be afraid of him, Shianne raked him up and down with scornful mockery. "Did you bring along your crown and robe, Your Grace?" she queried sarcastically. "You must forgive me for neglecting to dust your throne before you arrived. Had I known you were coming I would have prepared a great feast and gathered a dozen virgins to sacrifice to you."

His fingers clamped around her shoulders. Wade was sorely tempted to shake this she-cat until her teeth rattled. He had done battle with the most formidable opponents, but never had he confronted a woman who tested his patience and his self-control.

"You can hurl sarcastic rejoinders if you wish, vixen, but I am assuming control of the K Bar. You will do what I tell you, when I tell you, like it or not," Wade said in that low, imposing voice of his—the very same tone that warned Juan Mendez to back off or face the deadly consequences.

As fate would have it, Shianne carried the inborn trait of the proud Cheyenne warriors who chose to fight to the death to protect their pride and their rights. Wade was challenging her self-respect and her independent nature. She was too outraged *not* to defy him. Dammit, this was a matter of principle. If she did not make her stand, here and now, this bold breed of man would walk all over her. Shianne didn't relish the idea of having Wade Burdett's footprints on her back.

"Hear me and hear me well, you despicable son of a . . ."

With the quickness of a rattlesnake Wade coiled himself around his hissing prey. His lips came crushing down upon hers before she resorted to profanity. Shianne fought the restraining arms that kept her mashed to his rigid body, struggled against the traitorous sensations that followed in the wake of his overpowering kiss. She cursed herself for feeling anything except repulsion. But, being a strong-willed woman, she overcame her feminine emotions. Shianne refused to respond to a kiss that was meant to prove male supremacy.

When Shianne went rigid in his arms, Wade swore he had planted a kiss on a stone statue. Frustrated, he grumbled under his breath. He had accomplished nothing by allowing his temper to snap or by manhandling this stubborn minx. If anything, he had intensified her mistrust and hatred. Shianne was proud of her accomplishments, and she had every right to be. From what he had seen, the K Bar retained its dignity while many of its men were away fighting the war. Other ranches had been ill-managed and left to deteriorate, but not this one. Although this petite little spitfire was not big enough to fill her father's boots, she had compensated with sheer will and grim determination. As much as he hated to admit it, he could understand why she fiercely resented being ordered about by an outsider.

But blast it, that changed nothing. Wade still had his purpose as well as a score of loose ends to retie before putting a herd on the trail in the fall. He and Blake had made a bargain, and Wade wasn't bowing out just because this five-foot-one-inch bundle of fire and undaunted spirit appeared as an immovable obstruction.

They squared off, each firm in his belief. For a long silent moment they glared at each other through an invisible wall of tension. Wade wasn't sure how to proceed from here, and Shianne was contemplating scratching out Wade's eyes for attempting to force her into submission. They had reached an impasse. Neither of them intended to yield, and yet they were uncertain how to emerge from the situation without coming to blows.

Ironic though it was, Wade found himself wishing Shianne Kimball *were* a homely witch who was starved for a man's attention. She would have been a damned sight more agreeable about dumping responsibility in his lap and a helluva lot more affectionate than this proud, obstinate chit.

Even though he shouldn't have given a whit, Wade did care about Shianne's feelings. He didn't want to walk out, having her detest him because he had invaded her personal domain, and for that reason he refused to relay the last part of the message from Blake. This was no time to add fuel to a blazing fire. Shianne already regarded him as the most contemptible creature ever to slither through the sagebrush. Dammit, he wanted her respect, but judging by the agitated frown that was stamped on her face, he didn't have a snowball's chance in hell of acquiring it. Her expression was worth a thousand words, and there was not one complimentary word among them. Wade had set foot on the wrong side of Shianne Kimball, and they would be crossways of each other until she could look upon him with something more than blatant hatred.

Although Wade had contemplated all the considerations, he still had no idea how to gracefully bow out of this situation without retreating. Shianne was waiting for him to speak, and, no matter what he said, she was going to come at him with claws bared. Hell, he could have said he was madly in love with her and still she would scratch him to shreds. The lady was primed for a fight, and Wade was not about to let her pound him flat and mail him back to Louisiana. If he backed down from this firebrand now, she would have him so henpecked that he would moult semiannually. By damned, *that* was not going to happen!

Chapter 4

Haden Reems steamed and stewed while he galloped from his ranch to Shianne's hacienda. When he saw the blood-bay stallion tethered outside, he could guess who sought an audience with his fiancée. Wade Burdett, Blake's new partner. Damn that man for interfering in Haden's carefully laid plans.

When Ramona opened the door, Haden burst inside and propelled himself toward the study. Finding Shianne in Wade's clutches, Haden exploded in outrage.

"Get your filthy hands off my fiancée!" he bellowed.

Wade ignored the harsh command and swiveled his head around to survey the fuming rancher who threatened to reduce himself to a pile of smoldering ashes. His critical gaze swept from the crown of Haden's brown felt hat, across his puffed chest and spindly legs, to stare at his silver-toed boots. Slowly, his eyes retraced their course, unimpressed with the severe expression on Haden's narrow mouth and the tautness in the muscles of his protruding chin.

A wry smile touched Wade's lips, thinking the man would never have to fear his hat falling down over his eyes with that set of large ears holding it up. The

72

agitated rancher reminded Wade of a goat with his thin goatee and his beady, deep-set eyes. The pronounced knuckles on his hands could have been described as hooves, and his rounded shoulders suggested he was more aptly suited to walk on all fours. The heavy-footed rancher had sounded like a stampeding herd as he clomped through the tiled entryway. A man would never have to wonder who was approaching his blind side, Wade thought with a smirk. It was most fortunate this clumsy excuse for a man had not been born an Indian. He couldn't sneak up on a covey of deaf quail.

After thoroughly surveying Haden Reems, Wade bent his gaze to Shianne who was still glaring fire-tipped arrows at him. "Pardon me for saying so, but I would have thought you could have made a better selection."

Let the vermin think Haden was her husband-to-be, she thought spitefully. If it would keep Wade Burdett from chaining her in his powerful arms it would serve a useful purpose. When Wade's grip eased, Shianne threw herself away and hastily rearranged her bolero.

"What brings you to the K Bar, Haden?" she questioned more calmly than she felt.

"Him!" Haden thrust a bony finger toward the nonchalant cowboy who had yet to apologize for squeezing the stuffing out of Shianne. "I know what he is doing here, and I came to ensure that this man does not expect you to be part of the bargain he made with your father."

His rough voice bounded about the room. It was not until he heard his own echo that he realized he had blundered.

Wade eased a hip on the corner of the desk and crossed his arms over his chest. Amusement flickered in his eyes as he watched Haden suffer with his affliction of hoof-in-mouth disease. "Now how would you know about my partnership with Blake Kimball unless you had read the letter I was carrying with me when I was robbed and left to toast naked in the sun?"

Flustered, Haden struggled to gather his thoughts. "News travels as fast as a cyclone in this part of Texas, Mr. Burdett, and nothing moves here without my knowing about it. I have always made it a point to keep abreast of matters that concern me." His gray eyes swung to the shapely young woman who had collected her composure and had propped herself against the other front corner of the desk. "Shianne belongs to me, and I will fight any man who thinks to steal what is mine."

"If I followed that logic, you and I would be squared off at this very moment," Wade remarked with a faint smile. "It was your men who stole my horse and valuables yesterday." With that infuriating air of nonchalance Wade braced his hands on the top of the desk and crossed one boot atop the other. His eyes shifted to Shianne, regarding her with a possessive glance that had Haden gnashing his teeth. "And as for the lovely lady, I didn't notice your brand on her. You do stamp your initial on all your possessions to signify its proper owner, don't you, Mr. Reems?"

Haden was taken aback that Burdett knew him. It left him to wonder if the partial owner of the K Bar Ranch knew him by reputation in San Antonio or if Blake had besmirched his name.

Shianne scolded herself for silently applauding Wade's ability to put Haden on the firing line. Haden was not accustomed to finding himself at a disadvantage. But then, Haden usually traveled with an escort of heavily armed bravoes whose gun hands were ready and eager to speak for him.

"Your arrival at the K Bar changes nothing," Haden barked, detouring around Wade's previous question.

"Everyone knows Shianne and I will one day be married. It is undisputed fact!"

It came again—that goading smile that Haden had already begun to despise. Wade pushed away from the desk to saunter around to the chair behind it. He sat down as if he belonged there. Negligently, he propped a boot heel against the partially opened top drawer.

"I seriously doubt that *rumor* sent you thundering to the hacienda, but if that should be the case, let me restate my position on this ranch. Blake has given me full power of attorney in his absence. I have the right to manage business as I see fit, and I make all decisions concerning his one and only daughter." A grin as wide as Texas spread across Wade's dark features. "In short, Mr. Reems, the only way for you to get to the lady is through me. I decide where she goes and with whom. If you come barging into my study, snapping orders and voicing harsh demands, I might consider you far too uncivilized to court this gently bred young lady. I have heard that Texas is proud of its unblemished roses. We can't have them mingling with the sagebrush, now can we, Mr. Reems?" A taunting smile clung to Wade's lips. "Blake has strongly insisted that I am to watch over San Antonio's rarest rose as if she were my own cherished sister."

Wade's eyes shifted sideways for a split-second, noting that Shianne's knuckles were turning white. He could guess that the stranglehold she had clamped on the edge of the desk would have been on his neck if they were not entertaining a visitor. When Wade focused his attention on Haden he silently chuckled. Reems looked like a loaded cannon waiting to explode.

Haden's jaw clenched. His gray eyes burned like hot silver. "Any man who dares to mock me, lives just long enough to regret it, Burdett. You are no different. I have my own ways of dealing with those who persist in

75

defying me."

The threat hung heavily in the air, but Wade had been forewarned of Haden's unscrupulous tactics. Blake had offered a detailed account of how Reems had bought his land holdings with blood. Wade knew his opponent long before he laid eyes on him, and he had his own personal reasons for disliking Reems.

If one matter had been understood, it was that Haden Reems would never claim Shianne as his bride. Blake had avoided writing to Shianne because of Haden's interest in her. He knew his absence would deter Shianne from making any major decisions about her future until she knew if and when her father would return. Obviously, Blake had read his daughter right. She kept her life hanging in limbo, refusing to make any drastic changes until she received word from her father.

Wade shared Blake's adamant insistence that Haden be held at bay. The thought of this unsavory scoundrel touching this exquisite young woman very nearly nauseated him.

"We have both been forewarned," Wade remarked. His emerald eyes locked with smoldering silver. "Don't slam the door on your way out, Haden, and do employ the courtesy of knocking the next time an ill wind blows you onto our doorstep."

The sarcasm in Wade's voice stoked the fires of Haden's volatile temper. Displeasure was written all over Haden's face. Calling upon every ounce of self-control he possessed, he forced a tight smile and bowed stiffly before Shianne. "Before I go, I would like to invite the lady to the fiesta that will be held in two weeks."

Shianne waited tensely, certain Wade would object and a battle would ensue. To her amazement, Wade shrugged carelessly. "I'm sure she would be delighted to accept your invitation. She has been working overly hard, and all young women deserve to enjoy festivities occasionally. What time will you come calling for us?" he inquired.

"Us?" Haden lifted a thin brow.

"Surely you do not expect me to send her off without a chaperone?" Wade retorted in mock surprise. "How else can I ensure that your intentions are honorable and your manners impeccable?"

If Haden could have located a nail to chew on he would have bit it in two. Burdett was taunting him and deriving wicked pleasure from it. "My carriage will arrive at six o'clock," he managed to say without sneering.

"We will be ready. It should prove to be an interesting evening," Wade enthused.

Haden couldn't wait to return to his ranch. The moment he located Juan he would order him to plan Burdett's demise. The quicker the better, Haden thought bitterly. The man had already become an aggravating thorn in his side.

As Haden spun on his heels to make his melodramatic exit, Wade's quiet voice reined him to a halt. "Oh, by the way, *amigo,* I took the precaution of leaving a letter with Blake's lawyer in San Antonio. It is to be opened in the event of my untimely death. The first part of the statement declares that my stolen horse was in the possession of one of your vaqueros. The second half of the letter supplies evidence as to why you should be considered the prime suspect since I have been named guardian of your fiancée. You provided the motive, and I have provided the court with a strong case . . . should it become necessary." Wade uncurled his long body and came to his feet. His eyes were on Shianne as he moved to brace himself beside her. "I would have arrived earlier this afternoon, my dear

Shianne, but I had to scribble out several copies of the letter to stash with several of your father's friends. But you mustn't fear. If anything should happen to me, another guardian will be appointed, and he will be directed by the courts to see that there will be no impending marriage between you and my malicious murderer."

Shianne smiled despite herself. Wade was giving Haden fits. Wade Burdett had blown into Texas like a whirlwind, leaving no life untouched by his presence. What Blake had attempted to do in a decade, Wade had accomplished in the course of the afternoon. He had Haden bulldogged.

Haden glowered at his nemesis and stalked out the door, muttering epithets with every step he took. Burdett may have won the first skirmish, but the battle was far from over, Haden vowed. Once he got over being furious and had time to think clearly, he would formulate his counterattack. The arrogant Wade Burdett hadn't seen or heard the last from him! Perhaps he couldn't kill Burdett without putting his life in jeopardy, but he could make life unbearable. Every man had his breaking point, even the cool, calm veteran of the Civil War. Haden promised to throw obstacles in Burdett's face until the man was prepared to admit he couldn't win. Damn, Haden would have much preferred to deal with Blake. He detested the strong, controlled vitality that exuded from Wade Burdett. He was too sure of himself, too calculating to be disregarded as an unworthy opponent. Blast it, what a shame Burdett had dodged a Yankee bullet with his name on it. Haden could have been spared a great deal of trouble!

When Haden's footsteps died into silence, Wade

picked up his discarded hat and aimed himself toward the door. Shianne stared at his departing back in disbelief. Wade Burdett had taken on the dragon of Bexar County, and now he was walking out in the middle of their unfinished argument.

"You still have not told me how you propose to finance this monstrous cattle drive," she called after him. "Have you, perchance, decided to take a room in the brothel and sell your body to the many women who would pounce at the chance of sharing your charming company?" Her voice crackled with mockery. "I have heard that women are not the only breed of whores who sell their bodies for profit."

This gorgeous she-cat never let up, Wade mused as he turned to face her goading smile. "Maybe it is *your* body I considered placing on the market for profit, princess," he said glibly. "You could use the practice. I know. I was the recipient of your novice kiss, but there are men hereabout who are so starved for affection they will not bat an eye at taking whatever they can get."

Oh, how she itched to slap that aggravating grin off his face. Didn't the man ever quit smiling? He probably even grinned in his sleep! That mocking expression was beginning to creep beneath her skin, and Shianne wasn't certain how long she could tolerate it before she succumbed to the urge to implant her hand on his bronzed cheek.

"Mr. Burdett, how can you possess so many annoying qualities and tolerate yourself? It amazes me that you bear such a remarkable resemblance to a man I used to hate," she sniped, employing his technique of smiling while she hurled a biting rejoinder.

"Could it be something I've said?" Wade questioned with sticky sweet sarcasm. "It surely couldn't be the way I look in the altogether. I have the distinct feeling I am the first man your innocent eyes have touched and that you found no complaint with what you saw."

Wade won the battle of wits, and Shianne found herself to be a sore loser. Impulsively, she grasped the wooden figurine of a longhorn steer that set regally on her desk—or at least it had until it became her weapon of retaliation. She had every intention of poking a sizable hole in Wade's inflated arrogance, but to her chagrin, Wade's hand snaked out to catch the flying bovine before its horns collided with his head.

As if nothing had happened, Wade strolled over to replace the statue. "We really must do something about these tantrums of yours, sweetheart," he drawled. "You will have the K Bar in shambles. If you are going to fling insults, you should be able to take them as well as you dole them out."

"Another of your mother's proverbs, I suppose." Shianne mocked, clamping a bridle on her temper.

Wade nodded affirmatively. He positioned himself in front of the firebrand who looked incredibly appealing in her blue bolero and matching merino skirt. "She also taught me to extend my gratitude when someone comes to my rescue. I was in dire need of assistance when you applied your healing salve and cut me loose. A simple thank you does not aptly convey my sincere appreciation." His tone grew softer and huskier by the second.

Shianne knew what he intended. He focused on her lips as if they were the first pair he had ever seen at such close range. She wanted to fight him. She truly did, but Wade held her captive with those intriguing green eyes that were flecked with gold dust. Being curious by nature, Shianne felt compelled to reacquaint herself with the unique tingles Wade could send tumbling down her spine. The seed of curiosity he had planted with his embrace had sprouted into a strange, illogical need.

This was to be an experiment of sorts, Shianne assured herself. She would retest her reaction to this bold cowboy who had suddenly walked in and taken over her life at her father's insistence. After the way Wade had adeptly handled Haden Reems, a smidgen of respect dawned in her eyes. She could not help but admire Wade's forethought and manipulation of the powerful rancher. They would inevitably clash, but Shianne had the sneaking suspicion that Haden Reems had just met his match . . . and so had she.

When Wade slid his arm around her waist to draw her to him, there was no forcefulness in his touch. He was determined to dispel any apprehension Shianne might have had after their last bruising kiss. His lips hovered over hers like a honey bee courting nectar. He was tender yet persistent in sampling the sweetness within.

"You are like a banked campfire, Shianne. . . ." It was the first time he had voiced her name. The velvety softness with which he whispered it sent a wave of goose pimples rippling across her skin. "You may not be prepared to admit it just yet, but there is something magic between us, something that kindles a flame. I knew it the moment I saw that mischievous glint in your eyes." As if to make his point, his sensuous lips skimmed her cheek and feathered over each eyelid. "When we touch, we set off sparks. . . ." His raven head tilted forward as he bent her into his hard, masculine contours, acquainting her with the vast differences between a man and a woman. "Feed the fire, Shianne . . . let's see how hot it can burn. . . ."

Shianne was shocked to learn the results of her experiment. When his mouth took possession of hers, the thought processes in her brain broke down. Her pulse pattered like the rain. She couldn't analyze; she could only feel the delicious tremors surging through her bloodstream, the unfurling of need that spread through her limbs.

He kissed her with deliberate thoroughness, as if he could not get enough of her, and the hindering garments that separated his flesh from hers stood like tormenting obstacles between them. Her naive body was speaking in a language all its own, inching closer to the sinewed columns that were so unlike her soft flesh. Her arms wound around his neck, feeling the corded tendons flex and relax beneath her innocent touch.

His hands were never still for a moment. While he settled down to the serious business of kissing her insane, his exploring caresses mapped the graceful curve of her hips and then settled on her waist. Shianne gasped at his arousing fondling, startled by the shock waves that sailed down her backbone like nimble fingers flying over a keyboard, making sweet music echo in her soul.

Shianne hadn't meant to, but she was kissing him back, using the arousing techniques she had learned from her skillful instructor. Her tongue darted inside his mouth to trace the inner softness of his lips, making Wade groan in unholy torment.

Yes, he had intended to be gentle with this inexperienced nymph. He had also planned to introduce her to the rudimentary elements of desire, but the introduction into the pleasures a man and woman could find in each other had skipped past mild arousal and leaped right into hungry passion!

Lord, if Shianne could read his mind she would be walking through the walls to elude him. Wade wasn't going to be satisfied until he held her naked body against his, until he had made her his total possession.

He could imagine how she looked, the way her silky skin would feel beneath his inquiring caresses . . .

Fighting the difficult battle of self-conquest, Wade set Shianne away from him and heaved a shuddering breath. God, *she* was supposed to melt into a pool of liquid passion, not him! If he didn't put some distance between them and quickly, Wade wasn't certain he could trust himself. He found himself wanting things from Shianne that could truly frighten one so inexperienced in the ways of love. One look in her bewitchingly innocent face had Wade mentally kicking himself. Yes, there was a white-hot fire blazing between them, and it was about to engulf him.

For a long, breathless moment, Shianne merely gaped at him. She was wrestling with the chaotic sensations Wade had instilled in her. He left her wanting something she couldn't quite comprehend, something his kisses and caresses couldn't satisfy. The need had begun to blossom into craving. He had given her a foretaste of pleasure, and she found herself wanting more . . . but more of what? Shianne wasn't certain. Wade Burdett had come along to leave her questioning needs she never realized existed, ones that left demons of curiosity dancing in her head.

"I think I had better leave," Wade murmured. His tone was husky with the side effects of a kiss that had burned hot enough to melt him in his boots.

Shianne watched him scoop up his hat and move toward the door. Her eyes ran the full length of his broad back and tapered hips, seeing right through his well-fitting trousers and cream-colored chambray shirt. An impish grin caught the corner of her lips which Wade had left tingling after his devastating kiss.

"I have one last question, my dear guardian." She waited until Wade half turned to meet her teasing smile. "Just in case neither of us can make a killing in the brothel, which bank are we going to rob to acquire the money to afford this preposterous cattle drive?"

One heavy brow arched and he chuckled to himself. If he set Shianne up in a house of ill-repute, her line of eager clients would stretch from the east border of Texas to the sprawling Pecos, but the thought of sharing this adorable minx was distasteful. He would sooner rob a bank.

"Are you offering your gun hand, Shianne?" he inquired, his mind on anything but her slim fingers, lovely though they were.

"I can think of no other hasty way to collect the amount of money it will take to put three thousand head of longhorns on the trail."

Wade set his black felt hat on his head and pulled it low on his forehead. Veiled green eyes twinkled at her from the shadows of the broad-brimmed hat. "Let me worry about obtaining the money, my dear ward. You inform the ranch hands that we will begin our roundup at first light Thursday."

Shianne could not help but stew about the money. It had to come from somewhere. How was Wade going to get it? Then another apprehensive thought shot across her mind. "Wade, about the plot of ground you bought . . ."

His eyes narrowed on her. Did she know or didn't she? Damn, he couldn't say for certain. "I thought you said you had only one last question," he reminded her. Wade's thoughts were carefully guarded by his lackadaisical smile.

Shianne chewed on her bottom lip, contemplating how she could coax Wade to another section of the ranch without drawing his suspicion. Nothing reasonable came to mind so she decided to ponder it before presenting another argument. Besides, the Owl Prophet would probably not return for a few days.

By the time he did, Shianne would find a way to relocate Wade.

"You're right," she admitted with a careless shrug. "I have already posed my last question."

Wade studied the ebony-haired beauty for another few seconds. "Tomorrow night we will venture into San Antonio. I have heard the city boasts of its Casino Club, a social and cultural organization for aristocrats. I hope you will do me the honor of sharing a meal and a play with me."

Without waiting for Shianne to accept or decline, he touched the brim of his hat and strode out the door. He debated about reopening the subject of the cave. Instead, he had impulsively invited this lovely firebrand to share his company. Why? Wade couldn't say for certain. Disturbed that he had no answer to that question, Wade told himself that it would merely be an attempt to pry information from Shianne about the cave. She might drop hints that would help him determine if she knew what lay at the bottom of those cold, damp chambers.

If and when he felt he could trust Shianne, he might take her into his confidence, but now the bond between them was strained. If the information got out it could prove disastrous. As adept as Haden Reems was in keeping surveillance on every activity in the county, he would be snooping around the cave, Wade reminded himself. No, the less said about his campsite, the better. He faced enough trouble without being forced to defend the cave.

Wade left the hacienda feeling relieved that Shianne had begun to accept his interference in her life. Her irritation with him had fallen several degrees, hovering around a tolerable dislike. She had mellowed after the initial shock wore off, but she would rise to new levels of fury if he had confessed the other reason Blake was

85

delaying his return. Wade was far from her good graces, but at least he had taken a step in the right direction.

Their last kiss had set them both to thinking, and Wade was deliberating it far more than he should. As he rode back to camp, he kept picturing that flicker of desire in Shianne's dark, expressive eyes. The scent of her lingered on his clothes, and the taste of her clung to his lips.

"Damn, woman," he muttered to the alluring vision that sailed just ahead of him. "You have an unnerving way of making me forget why I came here." There were umpteen duties to attend, and all he could think of was satisfying his unfulfilled desires for that feisty, high-spirited sprite who had a startling effect on his blood pressure.

The moment Wade disappeared out the door, Ramona waddled into the study, beaming like a cat that had dined on a canary. "I approve of the *hombre* Señor Blake has sent to watch over you," she gushed with excitement.

Shianne flashed the bubbling housekeeper a disgruntled frown. "I am not at all sure the *hombre* can put the K Bar back on its feet. He has some very drastic ideas."

Ramona's dark eyes glistened with mischievousness. "Perhaps not, *chica,* but I think he has set you back on your heels."

A condescending glare pelleted over the housekeeper's wrinkled features. "And I think you have been spying on me," said Shianne.

"*Si,*" Ramona confessed with an unrepentant grin. "I saw the way the stranger kissed you, and I did not see you putting up a fuss."

Shianne was in no mood to be taunted about her baffling reaction to Wade Burdett. She had yet to understand why she responded to the raven-haired devil in reckless abandon. It was not at all like her to allow a man such privileges.

Refusing to answer the questions that flocked to the tip of Ramona's tongue, Shianne strode outside to inform the curious congregation of vaqueros that they would soon be taking orders from the temporary king of K Bar Ranch.

The remainder of the evening and the following day was a blur in Shianne's mind. Her thoughts were full of the green-eyed stranger. Each time she remembered the feel of his hands and lips, a knot of longing began to uncoil deep within her.

Shianne didn't appreciate what she was feeling. It was new and a little frightening. Wade Burdett disturbed her with his soul-shaking kisses and familiar caresses. He annoyed her with his crooked smile, one that assured her he knew what she was thinking and feeling. She should have been relieved that he had come to lift the yoke of responsibility from her shoulders, but his devastating presence made her as skittish as an untamed mustang. One thing was for certain, Shianne would be forced to deal with Wade Burdett. He had pranced into her life and turned it upside down. Now it was up to her to ensure that he didn't walk all over her just because her father had given this self-confident *hombre* free run of the K Bar Ranch.

Chapter 5

Shianne stared at her reflection in the mirror. Painstakingly, she smoothed a renegade strand of hair back into the immaculate coiffure of curls that lay atop her head. For the life of her she didn't know why she was fussing over her appearance. What did she care what Wade Burdett thought of her? Gnawing on her bottom lip, Shianne reassessed her image. She should peel off this scooped-necked velvet gown and step into a high-collared dress that did not so greatly complement her figure. And so she would, she mused, a deliciously wicked smile bordering her lips. Shianne wiggled free of her gown to don the prim and proper attire that would assure Wade it was not her want to encourage him.

Ramona poked her head around the partially opened door, and Shianne watched in amusement as the housekeeper's beaming smile slid off her lips. It was obvious Ramona expected Shianne to be bound up in the fancy trappings of an available young lady in hungry pursuit of a man.

Shianne pirouetted in front of the housekeeper. "Do I look presentable?"

If the sweet, innocent expression on Shianne's face

was any indication of her angelic nature, she should have sprouted wings and a halo, but Ramona wasn't fooled for a minute. She knew a devil had perched on Shianne's shoulders.

"Si, if you were on your way to a church social," Ramona sniffed in disapproval. "The señor is downstairs. I'm sure he will be as disappointed by your selection of clothing as I am."

"You seem to forget that Señor Burdett is my guardian, not my date for the evening," she reminded Ramona as she breezed out the door.

"He is still a man and a very handsome one at that," Ramona grumbled. "Your attire is a purposeful insult, and you know it as well as I do."

Shianne shrugged away the housekeeper's criticism of her apparel. Her wandering thoughts evaporated when she approached the head of the staircase. Below her, draped casually on the balustrade, stood Wade. He was garbed in a fitted linen shirt and sleek black breeches. His expensive clothes strained across his muscular form, subtly reminding Shianne that there was nothing but finely tuned muscle beneath those tailored garments.

Blast it, could she ever glance in that man's direction without remembering how he looked the first day they met? Shianne detested being so aware of Wade Burdett as a man. She wanted to perceive him as nothing more than an interference in her life, an annoying thorn that required extraction.

One dark brow lifted as Wade's astute gaze flicked down the tiny buttons that lined the front of her blue muslin blouse. With dedicated deliberation Wade sketched the trim indention of her waist and the soft folds of her matching skirt. Amusement flickered in his eyes when he retraced his path to survey Shianne's exquisite face.

"Are you afraid of me perchance?" he chuckled softly. "Heaven forbid that I view even an inch of bare flesh."

Shianne's dainty nose elevated as she gracefully swept down the steps. "Did you come to escort me to dinner or ridicule my clothes?"

Wade laughed low in his throat, his eyes dancing with deviltry. "You might be surprised at my purpose," he murmured as he laid his hand on Shianne's rigid back.

"I doubt it," she parried, purposely outrunning his touch. "Men like you are easy to predict. You will purchase my meal and pay for my ticket to the theater. In return you will expect an appreciative goodnight kiss. You consider it my dutiful obligation since you spent money on me," she prophesied.

Wade reached a long arm around the saucy bundle to open the front door. "What a dreadful cynic you are, my lovely ward."

His velvety voice came from so close beside her that Shianne winced uncomfortably. Wade had already stared holes through her clothes. The last thing she needed was for this rake to breathe down her neck.

Shianne stepped outside and then spun to face his wry smile. "Please kiss me and get this over with," she impatiently blurted out. "I would prefer to do it now instead of dreading it all evening."

What a firebrand she was, Wade thought to himself. Shianne stood before him, defiant as hell, preparing herself for an embrace that she had no intention of enjoying. She reminded him of a sick patient puckered up to accept her dose of castor oil.

Wade sighed heavily as he studied the begrudging expression that was glued on her perfect features. Shianne knew sparks flew when they kissed, and yet she detested the attraction. He was not about to give her the satisfaction of ravishing her. That was what she wanted—another reason to loathe him.

"You have your heart set on disliking me, don't you?"

"Why shouldn't I?" Shianne shot back. "A man is only as good as his worst fault. Your most annoying peccadillo is your domineering arrogance. I detest overbearing men."

His hand lifted to trace the delicate line of her jaw, feeling the creamy flesh beneath his unhurried exploration. Shianne compressed her lips and willed herself to endure his touch without feeling anything, not even a twinge of arousal. Wade had caught her off guard that day in the study, but now she was prepared for him, and nothing short of a cyclone was going to knock her off course.

Wade frowned at the stubborn defiance in her eyes. "You really need to overcome your defensiveness, Shae." The nickname he had given her rolled off his tongue like a tender caress, demolishing the barriers she was attempting to erect between them. "That chip on your shoulder is the size of a tree trunk." A wry smile rippled at the corner of his mouth. "As your guardian it is my responsibility to offer you various advice and instruction, my dear." He moved closer, his eyes focused on the grim set of her mouth. "I think it's time I taught you the proper techniques of kissing. Open your lips to me, princess," Wade commanded. His voice whispered over her face, breathing fire into her already flushed cheeks.

Shianne opened her mouth alright, only to fling a sarcastic rejoinder, not to obey his command, but Wade was an opportunist. He wasted no time in teaching her another thing or two about kissing. Soft sensuous lips fitted themselves to hers, his mouth moving languidly over hers. She could feel his hard male strength brushing ever so slightly against her as his tongue traced her inner lips. The masculine fragrance of his cologne invaded her nostrils, making her even more aware of Wade than she wanted to be.

Blast it, while she had purposely defied him, thinking to annoy him from the onset of their evening together, Wade had foiled her plans with a kiss that was so soft and tender she could find no complaint. Shianne was shocked to realize that she was anticipating the feel of his powerful arms closing in on her, but Wade made no move to deepen the embrace. She didn't *want* to want for more than his moist lips, but she did. God help her, she did!

Ever so slowly Wade withdrew, but only far enough to hold her entranced in the depths of his emerald eyes. "Now you can enjoy the remainder of the evening, knowing the worst is over," he murmured with a quiet smile. "But to be perfectly honest with you, princess, I had intended to be on my best behavior tonight. I had planned to escort you back to your doorstep, expecting nothing in payment except the pleasure of your company. My sole purpose for inviting you out was to ensure that we became better acquainted. . . . After all, we will be working as associates of sorts. . . ."

While Wade brushed past her to amble toward the carriage, Shianne silently fumed. Had she forced herself to pay the price when she could have breezed through the night without offering the slightest compensation? Damn, she was too clever for her own good!

Exasperated, Shianne flounced down the stone walkway, begrudgingly accepting Wade's assistance into the buggy. For some reason Shianne felt the need to pick a fight with the man who had barged into her life. "Don't you think you are being a bit extravagant with your money?" she questioned as she settled her flowing skirt about her. "We will need every spare penny for this insane roundup you are planning."

"I thought I asked you not to worry your pretty little head over money," he chuckled. Lifting the reins, Wade urged the horse into a walk.

"One cannot manage a sprawling ranch without giving serious thought to profit and expense," she defended tersely. "My head has been filled with figures these past few years."

"My head is preoccupied with only one figure," Wade remarked.

Shianne didn't have to ask him to explain himself. The look in his eyes said it all. He was speculating as to what lay beneath the score of buttons that stretched from the waistband of her skirt to her throat.

"I am built like every other woman you have known," Shianne said flippantly.

She was determined not to become rattled by their subject of conversation. Wade Burdett would not have her blushing, she promised herself. He was baiting her and she knew it. Wade delighted in ruffling her feathers. It was an amusing pastime for him, but Shianne refused to accommodate him.

Extending both arms, Shianne turned them in front of him. "You see? I come equipped with two hands, each boasting five fingers." She lifted a slippered foot for his inspection. "And like all other creatures of the species I possess two legs, a right one and left one. If there is some sordid fascination in that, I cannot imagine what it might be."

Wade snickered at the pert pixie. "Don't pretend to be naive, Shianne, though you are in many respects. One look in your mirror assures you that you are assembled far better than most women. Your parts are magnificently well-proportioned and perfectly as-sembled. You need not be ashamed of nature's generous gift by hiding it beneath an old woman's garb."

"I suppose you would have preferred I wear nothing at all," she sniffed caustically.

"To dinner and the theater?" Wade wore an expression of mock horror. "Certainly not. It would be most indecent. But when we make love, I expect you to wear no more than a willing smile."

Shianne gasped at the blunt remark. Although she had vowed not to be shocked by anything Wade Burdett said or did, her composure cracked. "You are deluding yourself to think that will ever happen. You may have wedged your way into my life, but you will never set foot in my bedroom!" she spewed.

Wade tilted his head back and laughed out loud. It only took a moment to realize he had been teasing her to get a rise out of her. Shianne chastised herself for exploding at him.

"Ah, Shianne, you are so quick to temper. I do delight in watching your temperature roll up and down like a yo-yo." Wade flung her another smile. "I do hate to disappoint you, but the figure to which I referred before you burst into your lengthy speech was the total sum required to put this trail drive en route. As you have so plainly pointed out, women are all the same . . . although some are more attractive than others." His gaze lingered on her face, which was enhanced by moonlight. "I doubt that you were fishing for a compliment since you are so suspicious of men and their ultimate intentions. I am offering one only because I have been taught to give credit where credit is due."

Shianne gulped when he leaned close, as if to relate some confidential remark. It baffled her that she was so affected by this man's nearness.

"You are a breathtakingly lovely woman, Shae." The

94

faintest hint of mischief flared in his eyes as he reached over to undo the top three buttons on her blouse. "And if you ever decide to use your feminine charms on a man, you will be dangerous."

The feel of his knuckles brushing against her throat sent an unwanted tingle darting down her spine. Although Shianne had been affected by his light touch of intimacy, Wade did not appear to be. That frustrated Shianne. She did not appreciate meeting a man she wasn't sure how to handle.

Shianne studied his carefully controlled expression, wishing she possessed such amazing willpower. Wade was forever smiling and nothing seemed to surprise him. He took life in stride, no matter what difficulties confronted him, and he was incredibly sure of himself in the presence of a woman, more so than any man she had ever met.

"Does nothing disturb you?" she questioned.

He shrugged evasively. "I have pondered my share of worrisome thoughts," he admitted.

"Such as . . ." Shianne prodded.

"Such as why you strongly disapprove of the acreage I purchased from Blake." Wade awaited her response with seeming nonchalance.

It was Shianne's turn to shrug noncommittally. "I cannot imagine why you would fret over that. It should be the least of your concerns. One plot of land is as good as another."

"Not so," Wade argued. "Some acreages are brimming with their own special treasures—a dependable water source, for instance, or perhaps a lush stand of grass to feed a sizable herd. Other plots make a perfect landscape for a man to build his home."

Shianne relieved Wade of the reins, turning the steed to the west. "Can you find complaint with this section of land?" She drew the horse to a halt and gestured toward the scenic beauty that stretched out before them. The creek meandered through the property like a silver rope threading its way across the open prairie. "Why not make your camp here? It is closer to San Antonio. The grass land is every bit as plush as it is near the cave."

"Why does it matter so much where I pitch my tent?" he questioned. "You and your father own thousands of acres. I don't think sentimentality or haunted caves are the real reasons you want me to relocate."

His face was only inches from hers, his eyes probing into hers. Shianne suddenly forgot what they were discussing. "I think we had better go," she said shakily.

As Wade leaned closer, Shianne scooted as far away as the carriage seat would allow. Wade approached like a poised predator, slowly cutting off every means of escape. "I intended to behave like a perfect gentleman tonight," he rasped, mesmerized by the tempting curve of her lips, "but your insistence on an initial kiss planted a seed. It has begun to sprout. Now it is sorely in need of watering. . . ."

There was nothing forceful in his advances, but they were no less devastating to Shianne. Her lips parted to accept his kiss, one that subtly knocked her sideways and left her carefully hidden emotions seeping toward the surface. His tongue thrust into her mouth, exploring the dark recesses, gradually stripping every ounce of breath.

Shianne's eyes flew open when she felt his nimble fingers on the buttons of her blouse. Her hand grasped his, discouraging him from continuing. Still staring into her wide eyes, Wade slid his hand inside the gaping blouse with her fingertips still clinging to his wrist.

"You feel as soft as satin, Shianne," he whispered before his mouth slanted over hers.

When his caress delved beneath her chemise to

wander over the swell of her breast Shianne gasped for breath. Unexplainable sensations were erupting deep inside her, making her entire body tremble. Brazenly, he continued his intimate explorations. He savored the softness of her, tested the firmness of her sweet contours.

Touching Shianne was pleasure in itself. Wade wondered where he would find the will to stop. The way he was feeling at the moment he could have continued all night without hesitation. He wanted to trace his hands and lips over every inch of her shapely body, to lift her to the same heady plateau of desire that he had scaled when he first dared to touch her.

These were not the feelings she had expected to endure when Wade boldly touched her in places that were unfamiliar with a man's caress, and she was not reacting the way she had anticipated. Instead of pushing him away and spouting her indignation she was breathlessly waiting to feel the other sensations that would grip her naive body.

His moist lips abandoned hers to glide across the exposed flesh of her breast. Instinctively, Shianne threaded her fingers through his raven hair, but she was not yanking him away. She was holding his head against her, allowing him to press enticing kisses wherever it met his whim.

What devil possessed her? She was enjoying his intimate touch, delighting in these giddy sensations that smothered logic. A soft sigh died beneath his savoring kiss when his hand strayed to the other throbbing peak. He was so close and yet her innocent body was not satisfied.

Wade had delivered himself several stern lectures before approaching the hacienda that evening. He had vowed not to give Shianne another reason to despise him, but he had not counted upon this mind-boggling attraction. Yes, while he knew this spitfire could trigger a man's primal instincts, he had intended to resist the temptation and remain on his best behavior. Yet, this ride in the moonlight was more than a healthy man could endure. He was left aching for things from this shapely goddess that he had no right to take. Knowing that did not discourage him from wanting them, Wade painfully realized.

Hell, he didn't care if he got past this delicious appetizer to feast on the main course of dinner! No staged play could be as emotionally stirring as the scene in which he was presently involved. He could not seem to satisfy this insane craving for this curvaceous nymph.

As if his hands possessed a will of their own, they delved farther beneath the muslin blouse to map the full swells of her breasts. But touching was not enough. He wanted to see her exquisite skin glowing in the moonlight. As he withdrew, his gaze fell, lingering on the rosy peaks and the contrasting flatness of her stomach.

God, she was gorgeous, he mused with an appreciative sigh. When Wade finally noticed the conflicting emotions that were chasing each other across her moonlit features, he felt the need to speak. He yearned to erase her humiliation before it took root and set fuse to her volatile temper.

Reverently, his fingertips whispered over the dusky bud and ascended to tilt her face to his tender smile. "You are truly exquisite, Shae. You have nothing to be ashamed of. I took unfair advantage of your innocence, but I cannot say that I regret it. You are alluring, even when you are not trying to be, and, although my intentions were honorable, my attraction for you and my need to know you by touch, are much too strong."

Still she was staring at him with that heart-wrenching expression that made him want to contort his body so he could be the donor and recipient of a swift kick. Wade reached down to rebutton her blouse, his gaze clinging to hers. "I wish I could say this will not be the end of it." His voice cracked with barely contained desire. "But I cannot. There is some mystical fascination between us, princess. You are trying very hard to deny it, and I have tried to ignore it." With his task complete, Wade braced his arms on either side of her shoulders, his face only a hairbreadth away from hers. "The magnetism grows stronger with each passing moment. It may not be what either of us intended, but the time will come when neither of us will be able to control the need to begin where we left off. . . ."

As Wade pushed away to take the reins, Shianne collapsed against the side of the buggy. It was as if she had just emerged from a trance. Her heart was still racing around her chest and her knees were weak. Her eyes drifted to his handsome face and she swallowed with a gulp.

Attempting to rewind her unraveled composure, Shianne pushed into an upright position on the seat and stared straight ahead. She had allowed Wade to assume the blame for what had transpired between them, but in her heart she knew it was not all his doing. She could have stopped him, *should* have stopped him, but she hadn't. She had encouraged him to satisfy the craving, to teach her of passion's pleasures.

Shianne squeezed her eyes shut, trying to forget those delicious sensations that his kisses and caresses aroused. Even during the ride into town she concentrated on erasing the mental picture, but it was imprinted on her mind like a compelling chapter waiting to be completed . . . another time . . . another place.

Much to her relief Wade began to rattle on about his journey from Louisiana, relating several amusing anecdotes from his experiences in Nagodoches and Austin. When they arrived at the Casino Hall and Club, Wade reached up to lift Shianne down beside him. Shianne had only thought she had recovered from her experiences in the moonlight until she felt his long, lean fingers folding about her ribs.

Her lashes fluttered up to meet the rakish smile that brimmed his lips, and Shianne could not suppress the burst of color that flushed her cheeks. He knew full well what she was thinking and that rattled her.

"It's curious, isn't it . . . this chemistry between a man and a woman," he murmured as he wrapped his hand around her elbow. "The ingredients are always there, but occasionally, between two people, elements that usually remain dormant begin to react." Wade sighed forlornly. "In my case it creates a craving." He paused to open the door to the Casino Hall, his breath murmuring against her cheek. "You are most fortunate there is a chef hereabout. Otherwise, I might be overly tempted to make a meal of you."

Confound it, why couldn't he allow the incident to die a graceful death, Shianne thought in exasperation. She was having enough difficulty analyzing her reckless response to this rake. Why did he insist upon adding fire to an already simmering stew.

Shianne directed his attention to the dining hall that was brimming with patrons. "I think perhaps we should find you something to chew on and quickly, my dear guardian, lest I am forced to find someone to *protect* me from my guardian. . . ."

Her voice trailed off when they rounded the corner

to see Haden Reems sitting at a nearby table with the local banker. Shianne was immediately uncomfortable, but Wade showed no signs of uneasiness. Indeed, he seemed to delight in the encounter.

Haden paused in midsentence when he spied the striking couple. His jaw tensed at the sight of Wade Burdett's ornery smile. His frustration was further compounded by Wade's possessive attitude toward Shianne. The moment Wade met Haden's gaze he drew Shianne even closer than necessary. It was as if her guardian was silently expressing his dominance in the situation. Haden hated the fact that Wade stood directly between him and what he desired.

When Wade had seated Shianne at the table he dropped into the chair beside her so he could stare across the room at Haden. Although all outward signs pointed to the fact that Wade was calm and collected, Shianne knew she was no longer in Wade's thoughts. Only his eyes gave him away. His expression clouded with an emotion she could not comprehend. There was friction between these two men, and Shianne had the feeling it had nothing to do with their first confrontation. But what? Shianne was at a loss. Wade and Haden had not known each other before the three of them clashed in the study.

The appearance of the waitress forced Shianne to set her contemplations aside. During their meal Wade behaved like the perfect gentleman, but the ease with which he conversed with her earlier became strained. He was polite but much less attentive. When Haden and his companion left, Wade turned his full attention on Shianne.

"Is your meal satisfactory?" he questioned.

Shianne touched her napkin to the corner of her mouth and nodded affirmatively. "And yours?"

Wade eased back into his chair to swirl his wine

around the rim of his glass. "Excellent," he admitted. He stared at her through a veil of thick, sooty lashes. "But there is only one thing missing. Otherwise, the meal would be perfect."

A curious frown puckered her brow. The Casino was noted for its fine cuisine. She could not imagine what could be lacking.

"And just what would that be?" Shianne asked innocently.

Wade lifted his drink, assessing his stunning companion from over the rim of his glass. "Dessert." The resonance of his voice was as effective as his caress. "But I don't think the Casino serves what will satisfy my sweet tooth."

Shianne fumbled with her fork. Averting her eyes, she glanced about the dining hall, seeing several women ogling Wade with obvious interest. "It appears that you have your pick of the pastry in the Casino, my lusty guardian. If you decide to satisfy your appetite, I will see myself back to the hacienda."

Wade made visual contact with every pair of female eyes that were giving him the once-over. "And leave you unchaperoned? I would be neglecting my duties," he chuckled softly. Wade set his glass aside and unfolded himself from his chair. "Besides, when a man finds himself tormented by a particular craving, there is usually only one item on the menu that will satiate him. Why settle for a biscuit when one's mouth is watering for a luscious, cream-filled tart?"

He knew that was the wrong thing to say even before he finished his sentence. Shianne jerked away and glared at his fading smile.

"You may call me many things, most of which I probably am," she hissed, striving to keep from screaming her irritation in his face, "but I am not your *tart,* nor any other man's. And why I didn't chop off your hands earlier this evening is beyond me, for now I sorely regret what happened. I am thankful our tête-a-tête went no further. If it had I would not have been able to face myself."

As Shianne sailed toward the door, Wade hurried his step to close the distance between them. With Shianne clamped in one hand, Wade fished into his pocket to retrieve the cash to pay for their meal. Shianne's mouth dropped open when she spied the roll of bills Wade flashed before her.

Where had he obtained that kind of money? Hadn't he said he had come to Texas to make a new beginning? Didn't that imply that his old life had left him seeking new ways of earning a livelihood?

"You are much too sensitive," Wade grumbled as he propelled her toward the huge ballroom. "When I referred to you as a tart, I did not mean to insult you. Far from it. Quit throwing obstacles between us. We have enough problems facing us without tripping over your stumbling blocks."

"Where did you get that money?" Shianne demanded to know. Wade was not about to sidetrack her by drawing her back into their previous argument. At the moment she didn't care what lurid name he called her, so long as he answered her direct question.

"I'm impressed," Wade commented as he paused to survey the large room where an elaborate stage and balcony had been constructed. "This theater must have a seating capacity of at least four hundred. I didn't realize San Antonio was the social and cultural center of Texas. We will have to make it a point to come here often."

"Dammit, I asked you a question," Shianne muttered as he led her to their seats on the third row. "And do not think to evade the issue by complimenting our city's cultural activities."

Wade squirmed to fold his long legs into the confining niche and then spared his annoyed companion a glance. "I came here to enjoy the theater not to be interrogated by an inquisitive little imp who is beginning to develop the disturbing habit of meddling in my affairs." That infuriating smile returned, making Shianne itch to scratch it off his craggy features. "But if you insist on being an integral part of my *affairs,* we had better search out a secluded little nest, away from this packed house. For if you demand to know *everything* about me, I will see to it that you *do* know every intimate detail."

That sounded like a challenge, but Shianne had begun to realize that Wade's bark was no more than a playful taunt aimed to poke fun at her naivete. If Wade thought he could put her off with his seductive innuendos he thought wrong.

"Perhaps what I chance to lose in my quest for the answers you have skillfully evaded would be well worth the cost." She returned his saucy smile, refusing to be baited again. "Then I would know what *I* know as well as what *you* know. I would say it would give me a great advantage in dealing with you."

Wade chortled huskily. "Ah, I do enjoy fencing words with you, Shae. Your sharp wit keeps me on my toes. I think our association is going to be very educational . . . for both of us."

"Are you ashamed of your ill-gotten gains?" she persisted.

When the curtain went up the applause drowned out Wade's voice. Shianne frowned disappointedly when the performance began, bringing quick death to their conversation. Wade Burdett had piqued her curiosity in more ways than one. Shianne had the uneasy feeling her inquisitiveness was going to lead her into trouble. She had never been one to dismiss a notion once it had taken root in her mind. No, she wanted to know what made a man like Wade Burdett tick. She wanted to know what motivated him and how he acquired the funds to accomplish the task he had come to Texas to perform.

Shianne suffered through the performance, delightful though it was. She squirmed in her seat, impatient to unleash the questions that stampeded to the tip of her tongue. Wade, on the other hand, was satisfied to sit back and watch the actors' performance of a lighthearted comedy. When the curtain dropped after the final act, Wade gathered to his feet to usher Shianne back outside.

The moment they were in the carriage, Shianne released the questions that were buzzing through her mind for over two hours. "Where did you get that wad of money? Who is financing you, Wade? Did my father pay you to escort me about town when you were not rounding up mavericks? Did you make some sort of deal with him that you have not bothered to explain?"

Damn, the woman was like a leap frog bounding from one ill-founded conclusion to another. "No one. No, he didn't, and no," he answered just as rapidly as he had been assaulted by her questions.

When they reached the edge of town, ensuring their privacy, Wade brought the buggy to a halt. "Somewhere along the way you are going to have to begin trusting me," Wade told her matter-of-factly.

"Why? Just because my father does?" Shianne put out a stubborn chin. "Well, I am not my father, and I will not be wooed into offering blind faith to a man who refuses to explain himself."

"You have been just as elusive." Wade tossed her an accusing grin. "I am still on the edge of my seat, wondering what fascination you hold for the cave where I have set up camp. You seem all too eager to have me evacuate the sight. Is there something there worth protecting?" he questioned, knowing full well there was.

"How should I know what is in that cave?" Shianne shot back. "I have never bothered to explore it since I was a child, and even then I was much too afraid of the dark to walk more than ten feet into the mouth of the cavern. Now it is rumored there are phantoms lurking there. Is that the kind of company you prefer to keep?"

Wade broke into a rakish leer. "I think you know whose company I would prefer," he growled seductively.

Her remarks put his mind at ease. At least Shianne had no notion as to why he was compelled to stay at the cave. Whatever her reasons for wanting him resituated didn't have anything to do with what lay at the bottom of the cavern. Although Wade was curious to know what other reason she might have had for being partial to the sight, he was far more intrigued by the way the moonbeams caressed her lively features.

As his body moved deliberately toward hers, Shianne retreated to her favorite corner. That roguish flicker in his eyes brought out her cowardly instinct, one that had seen little action the past few years. "You promised . . ." she squeaked, holding him at bay with a dainty but determined hand.

"I did, didn't I," Wade murmured absently. He studied her as if she were a rare beautiful bird he had captured. His gaze focused on the intriguing curve of her upper lip which appeared as moist and inviting as dew setting on a flower blossom. "I also warned you that I would be tempted to begin where I left off. . . ."

Shianne squealed when his hard lean body pressed her into the carriage seat. She could feel his arousal, a state she had never been forced to deal with . . . until now. She was being forced to deal with it and Shianne was shocked at the sudden change in his male body.

His soft laughter echoed about her. "Ah, my naive little nymph, you are so very innocent of men. I find it refreshing but very exasperating." Reluctantly, Wade pushed away to allow Shianne room to breathe. "Have you no idea how painful it is for a man when he denies himself to save a lady's reputation?"

"Painful?" Wide, innocent eyes searched his strained features.

Wade shook his head in disbelief as he reclaimed the discarded reins. When he had encouraged the steed to a trot, he chortled again. "It seems Blake has left me with a far greater task than I had anticipated. Haven't you the faintest idea what transpires when a man and woman make love?"

Shianne fought the flush of color that invaded her face. "I don't think I want to know," she mumbled uneasily. "Can we please change the subject?"

"We could," Wade acknowledged, "but pushing it aside will not solve anything. One day you are going to have to face facts. Talking about it will make the moment much easier to accept."

"What makes you such an authority on the subject?" Shianne sniffed caustically. "I would have thought you to be more interested in *when* it all comes about rather than how and why."

Wade burst out laughing. This feisty little chit was a constant source of amusement. Although he had always been one to break into a smile at the drop of a hat, he had not laughed so often in years. Shianne was like a potion of mirth. One dose had him chuckling. Two heaping portions left him giggling like a carefree child.

"Experience is the best teacher, little princess," he assured her, his voice still bubbling with amusement. "I do not mean to boast, but I have not spent these past

107

years in celibacy." Wade slid her another teasing grin. "I am a man with the normal amount of cravings and needs. That in itself is reason for you to put stock in what I can tell you about those of the male persuasion."

"Well, I wish I were one," Shianne burst out. "I detest being considered the weaker sex. I cannot help it that the good Lord thought to place my frustrated soul inside a woman's body. I have been forced to think like a man and behave like a man while my father was away. Then here you come, stripping me of my responsibilities and attempting to lecture me on those facets of my education that Papa overlooked." Shianne folded her arms beneath her breasts and raised a stubborn chin. "I think I will become a spinster so I won't be forced to fret over the complications that disrupt other women's lives."

"My dear Shianne, you should never resent your femininity. I happen to find it fascinating," Wade inserted with an approving glance. "You will never escape life without being forced to consider your feminine needs. You are much too attractive for men to disregard in their quest for affection—the physical kind that you are so afraid of."

"I am not afraid," Shianne denied, her protest a mite too loud to be convincing. "There is very little in the lawless state of Texas that reduces me to trembles."

In an effort to prove his point, Wade slid his arm around her. His hand made bold contact with the undercurve of her breast and Shianne nearly jumped out of her seat. She had yet to learn to control herself when Wade dared to put his hands on places they didn't belong, places that were not accustomed to a man's attentions.

"I seem to detect a tremor of sorts," he mocked. "Since I am not holding you at gunpoint, threatening your life, I can only conclude that the intimacy of my touch has an unsettling effect on you." His straying hands folded about her breast, provoking sparks to dance down her spine. "Now what was it you were saying about not being afraid of men?"

Shianne removed his hand and scooted farther away. "Very well," she begrudgingly admitted. "I *am* wary of what I do not understand, but you have no right to amuse yourself at my expense. My attraction to a man has to be more than the satisfaction of physical needs. I am not like you, Wade. I view love as part of a lasting commitment. You see it as a passing fancy, one you will not allow to *pass* you by. If it means nothing more than a moment of appeasing animal lusts, it has no value to me."

"What makes you think an intimate affair with me would have no worth?" His emerald gaze held her captive. "You might gain valuable insight about yourself, things that have gone undetected in your attempt to remain cool and aloof with men."

Dark eyes flashed. "And if I should surrender to you? What then, Wade? Will you declare your undying devotion or will I become just another of your conquests?"

A lopsided smile touched his lips. "There need not be chains for a man and woman to enjoy each other, princess. It is better that way. People change like the seasons and so do their needs. What a man thinks he wants today may not be what he needs tomorrow. Binding commitments only cause resentment."

"Not if two people truly care about each other," Shianne argued. "I happen to think you have a distorted outlook on life."

Wade snorted disdainfully. "War has a way of changing a man's outlook. I found myself living for the moment because I never knew if I would be around the next week, much less the next day."

Shianne would have preferred to debate the issue, but she couldn't, not when Wade had firsthand experience in living through hell. He accused her of being cynical of men and their intentions, but he was cynical of women and of love. She and Wade would never agree on the issue because they each held firm to their contrasting convictions.

When the steed paused in front of the hacienda on its own accord, Wade scooped Shianne off her perch and put her to her feet. Shianne hurried to the house, anxious to put a safe distance between her and this bold breed of man who had her questioning herself and contemplating his opposing values of morality.

"Shianne?" Wade grasped her arm before she could seek shelter within the adobe walls. "You are like a naive little girl lost in an idealistic dream, waiting for a mythical knight to come along and whisk you away to the enchanted land of Camelot, but there are no knights on white chargers and life is uncertain. In these troubled times we must take what we can when opportunity presents itself. The fall of the South provided a valuable lesson, and we should all profit from it." He moved closer, his rock-hard strength pressing her back against the wall.

"I meant what I said. There is unfinished business between us, something very potent and difficult to ignore. The day is coming when I will find no more excuses *not* to enjoy what I know would be pleasurable for both of us." His somber gaze drilled right through her, piercing her soul. "And when that time comes, princess, it will be up to *you* to stop what our natural instincts have set in motion. I will have exhausted my reasons as to why I shouldn't make love to you. . . ."

For an agonizing moment, Shianne stood there watching him stare at her with those incredible green eyes. She couldn't breathe. She couldn't look away, even if her life depended on it. His head came steadily toward hers, his mouth taking firm possession. His kiss spoke of pent up passion, a hunger he had no desire to control.

Muttering in frustration, Wade set her from him. When he wheeled away to disappear into the shadows, Shianne dragged in a ragged breath. Disturbed by his prediction, Shianne wobbled into the hacienda. Destiny had thrown them together, and she wondered if any woman, no matter how strong-willed and independent she was, could refuse a man like Wade Burdett. But she had to, Shianne lectured herself. If she allowed herself to care for him, to surrender to this irrational attraction, he would swallow her alive! Then, when he walked out of her life, she would be left to pick up the pieces of her heart.

No, Shianne thought resolutely. She had resisted the advances of a dozen other men. She would find a way to resist Wade's dark charm. He was only a man and he held no mystical powers over her. Perhaps she was clinging to whimsical dreams, but she was holding out for a love that could endure the test of time, not a fascination that would last a month at the most.

Clinging to that determined thought Shianne ascended the stairs. She may be forced to have Wade Burdett underfoot for the next few months, but he would be her guardian, not her temporary lover. If he wanted a woman in his bed he could search elsewhere for that kind of lusty satisfaction. It was not so difficult to say *no,* Shianne reassured herself, and she would mentally practice denying him. If and when the moment came she would be prepared to reject his advances firmly, unequivocably, knowing in her heart that passion was empty without the reinforcement of love.

111

Chapter 6

Heaving a perplexed sigh, Shianne settled herself in a warm, relaxing bath. She prayed the tepid water would ease her frustrations and help her sleep. A contented moan tripped from her lips as she laid her head against the rim of the tub. For a full minute Shianne was free of the looming image that had been following in her shadow for the past few days, but a moment of peace was all she was allowed before Wade's captivating features began to form in her mind's eye. She could see his dark hair absorbing the sunlight. She could see those, sometimes infuriating but always intriguing, crinkles that fanned from the corners of his eyes when he smiled. His full lips were curved upward, parting slightly, invitingly, and those fascinating green eyes that were flecked with gold danced within the perimeters of his long, thick lashes. His high cheekbones and firm jaw were deeply bronzed. His skin was much coarser than hers. It felt like tanned leather beneath her exploring fingertips.

And the rest of him . . . Shianne sighed heavily. He was built like a mythical god. His body was a mass of finely tuned muscles—like a lion in repose. Wade could be gentle when it met his mood, but when he was provoked to anger, he was like a mountain of steel—hard, unyielding, unconquerable.

Damn, why was she punishing herself like this, Shianne wondered. She had resolved not to allow that charismatic cowboy to invade her thoughts. She had employed distraction and preoccupation, but the treatment had proved ineffective. Wade's memory came uninvited each time she let down her guard.

Shianne had watched Wade come and go the past few days while he rounded up the *cimarrones* and *mestenas,* the wild breed of cattle that roamed the country. After working long, tedious hours Wade drove the longhorns into the pens that he and the vaqueros had constructed, hoping to gentle them before driving them north.

Each time Wade cast a glance in Shianne's direction, she was reminded of that night when he had issued his warning. She was tormented by what had transpired between them and by the longings she foolishly thought time would erase.

Since then nothing had changed, Shianne thought dismally. He had but to look at her and sparks sizzled across her skin. There seemed no remedy for this maddening attraction. Shianne cursed herself for remembering the musky scent of him, the tantalizing sensations that engulfed her when he had kissed and caressed her. There was a storm brewing between them, a dark cloud of unfulfilled desire that billowed higher with each passing day.

Wade had made it a point to join her for midday meals, planting himself at the opposite end of the table. She could feel his eyes on her, eyes that seemed to look through her, touching her just as surely as if he had reached out his hand in a bold caress.

Each time she turned around, Wade was in her way, staring at her with that charismatic smile of his. She swore he had mapped out every nook and cranny in the hacienda and strategically positioned himself so that he could corner her. Shianne would find him hovering over her, his masculine body brushing seductively against hers. He would whisper some intimate remark and swagger away, leaving her to regather her composure and scattered thoughts. He was touching her physically and emotionally, refusing to let her forget the magnetic attraction between them.

His subtle but unnerving tactics were driving Shianne mad with frustration. Oh, why wouldn't he go away and turn his attention on some other woman, one who could be content with passion for passion's sake?

Even now, while she was alone in her room, she could feel the heat of his gaze, feel the stirrings of desire for a man whose philosophy of life and love were in direct contrast with hers. Why was she preoccupied with this need to touch him in a different way than she had that first day when she applied salve to his burns? Would he respond if she touched him as a woman caresses a man? Shianne groaned miserably and closed her eyes to squeeze back the titillating thoughts.

"What have you done to me?" Shianne murmured to the image that floated above her. Wade compelled her to discover what lay beyond her experience—a world of sensations that she had just begun to realize existed. "There was a time when I never considered such things about a man. I was happier then . . . not knowing, not wondering how it would be between us. . . ."

Shianne mulled over her frustrating reaction to Wade for the hundredth time. She *had* to cling to her convictions. She and Wade were not right for each other, no matter how strong the physical attraction.

This was all her father's fault, Shianne mused resentfully. Why had he thrown her to this lion of a man? What did Blake see in Wade? Had Wade saved her father's life in battle? Did Blake feel a strong obligation to return the favor by making Wade his partner? And why had Blake sold Wade a portion of their ranch? Did Blake really expect her to contemplate matrimony to this bold, arrogant stranger? Or was that Wade's way of throwing her off guard? After all, he did take wicked delight in provoking her. He would make some blunt remark; she would lose her temper. He would taunt her with that lopsided grin of his, and she would forget why she was so furious with him.

Deliberating her father's motives, Shianne took up the sponge and inhaled the aroma of jasmine. It was time to rid her senses of the lingering scent of Wade Burdett. She had lived with that enticing male fragrance much too long. Tonight she would cleanse away the demon with coal-black hair and a devilish smile. . . .

The distant lights of the hacienda drew Wade's gaze like a moth lured into a compelling flame. He had conversed with the voices in the cave. He had carried on a one-sided discussion with his horse and mule. In frustration he had mentally listed the myriad of reasons why he should stay put, but nothing eased his hunger after Shianne whetted his appetite. He knew he should pursue her at a snail's pace, but following his own sensible advice was damned near impossible.

Wade had employed every tactic known to man in an effort to cool his lust for that shapely goddess. He had worked until he was ready to drop in his tracks. He had occupied himself with dozens of other thoughts, but Shianne's vision was still tampering with his mind. A long swim in the creek proved to be temporary relief for what ailed him. Feeding his hunger for food did not satiate the gnawing craving, and talking to the phantom of the cave, not to mention two dumb animals, had been a miserable substitute for what he really wanted—Shianne.

The name seemed to fit her, he mused as he paced the campsite. It sounded soft and yet mysterious as it rolled off his tongue. He had never thought to ask Blake how she had come by that unusual name, but it was a unique mixture of the wild, lawless breed of Indians and the compelling intrigue of femininity.

The haunting memories of the times he had spent with Shianne, battles and all, settled around Wade like an avalanche. After staring at the beckoning lights for an hour, Wade threw caution to the wind. He was never going to be the same until he satisfied his craving for that minx. Haden Reems would probably have him stripped and staked out again if he knew, but Wade didn't care. He had worked himself into a frustrated frenzy, and Shianne was both the cause and cure of his torment.

Once he had appeased this maddening need, he would be assured that Shianne was merely a woman, like all the others who had come and gone from his arms in moments of passion. She was old enough to become a woman, Wade rationalized. Someone had to be the first to introduce her to passion. Why not her guardian, the man who had been given control of her present and future? Perhaps if they were to become lovers Shianne would grow fond of him. It would ease the blow he had yet to deliver about the ultimate reason Blake had not returned to Texas.

Satisfied with that thought, Wade swung onto Galahad's back and then muttered at his lack of willpower. His eyes fell to the folded blanket Shianne had left with him when she found him staked to the creek bank. Perhaps he would merely return the quilt, he told himself. It would provide the perfect excuse for riding to the hacienda.

It was just that, an excuse, Wade scowled as he snatched up the wool blanket and tucked it under his arm. There was no sense kidding himself. He was journeying to the hacienda for one reason—to make love to Shianne, to see for himself if her passion for loving was as fierce as her passion for living.

Wade slowed his pace when an apprehensive thought flashed through his mind. What if she adamantly refused him? What if she tried to back him down with her pistol as she had a habit of doing? Well, he would cross that bridge when he came to it, he told himself courageously.

Tethering Galahad a good distance away from the back of the hacienda, Wade moved silently through the gardens toward the vine-covered lattice that led to the second floor. With ease he swung his legs over the railing to stroll past the dark rooms. When he reached the bed chamber that glowed with gold lantern light, his legs froze under him, refusing to move.

There, stretched out in a porcelain tub, was a mermaid. Midnight hair cascaded down her back and bare arms protruded to tantalize him. When one shapely leg lifted, Wade swallowed every ounce of air that hovered over Texas. God, what he had seen thus far was exquisite. His eager eyes drank in the magnificent sight of her, and excitement spiraled through his bloodstream.

Once his legs began to function, they took him ever closer . . . until he was engulfed in the velvet drapes that hung beside the open terrace doors. From his inconspicuous lookout post, Wade gawked like a schoolboy taking his first peek at a woman. He ached to touch what his gaze beheld, to caress every inch of satiny skin that shimmered with water droplets.

His curiosity should have been satisfied, Wade

preached to himself. He had spent a week contemplating how this angel would look without her
robes. She was what dreams were made of, just as he
expected. He willed his legs to move in the direction
from which he had come, but they betrayed him. They
held their ground, allowing his hawkish gaze and lusty
thoughts to run rampant.

This was all wrong! His wilting conscience screamed
before it was completely strangled by potent male
desire. He shouldn't be peeping at Blake's daughter.
Hell, he shouldn't be here in the first place. Shianne
already considered him as low as a snake. What would
she think of him when she learned he had been spying
on her? She wasn't some common trollop whose
profession it was to satisfy a man's lust. This was
Shianne Kimball, for God's sake! She was his ward.
How was he to protect her when he was his own worst
enemy?

When he overheard Shianne's hushed voice echoing
in the silence, he knew there was no turning back. Her
whispered words encouraged him, and Wade was
quick to presume she was referring to him. It seemed
Shianne was as baffled by this budding need as he was.
Shianne might vehemently protest if he took her in his
arms to further her lessons in love, but her vocal
contemplations assured him that he had stirred
something in her.

Shianne heard the rustling of the drapery behind her
and assumed the evening breeze had caused the
muffled sounds. A bemused frown knitted her brow
when she did not feel a sudden breath of wind racing
over her skin. She twisted around and gasped in
surprise when she realized it was not a Texas gale that
had blown into her bedroom. It was Wade Burdett,
alias Peeping Tom, the same man who had crowded
her into corners and crumbled her defenses, bit by

118

excruciating bit!

"What are you doing here at this hour? We do have a front door," she chirped, her voice failing her when she needed it most. "If you had one shred of decency you would have at least made your presence known instead of clinging to the shadows, watching me while I was unaware."

Frantically, Shianne groped for the towel to cover herself. Blushing up to her hairline she watched Wade approach her in soft methodic strides. His bold affront shocked her. If she could have located her swallowed tongue, she would have ranted and raved at him again for invading her privacy, but she couldn't and she didn't. She just sat there, stunned that even Wade Burdett would come prancing right up to her when she was not wearing a stitch!

"I wanted to return your blanket," he said absently, his exploring gaze devouring every inch of her bare skin. "If I would have announced my arrival, I would have missed the lovely scenery."

Shianne had never found herself in such a threatening situation. Seeing Wade naked wrought emotional turmoil but having him see *her* in the same state of undress was even worse. She knew he was making comparisons when she could not, and she had no practice in watching a man sketch her naked flesh with his all-consuming gaze.

After what seemed forever, Shianne recovered her ability to speak. By damned, she would not allow this daring rogue to embarrass her again, she promised herself. She could pretend to be as casual and nonchalant as he was . . . or at least she would die trying. He must have heard her words. There was no sense pretending she hadn't said them.

With more bravura than she felt, Shianne sat upright, clinging to her meager covering. One finely arched brow lifted, returning his probing stare. "I suppose we are even now," she managed to say without her voice cracking completely. "There are very few secrets left between us."

Wade folded himself to a crouch and braced his elbows on the edge of the tub, making no attempt to disguise the fact that he liked what he saw. He had half-expected Shianne to scream at the top of her lungs when he approached her, but then, he remembered her stubborn streak. She was far too proud to be intimidated by any man.

Leisurely, he tunneled his fingers through the waterfall of raven hair that streamed down her back. "You were wondering what it would be like between us?" His hand moved to cup her chin, tilting her flawless face to his. He was quick to detect the hint of fear in her eyes. She was not as afraid of him as she was of the unknown. A seductive smile passed his lips. "It would be like walking into a forest fire, I think," he rasped as he moved deliberately closer. "I didn't really come here to return the quilt, princess. To be perfectly honest, I have run out of reasons to keep my distance from you. My curiosity is killing me. I came here for this. . . ."

His mouth slanted across hers and Shianne felt like a swimmer going down for the first time. He smelled of the whole outdoors and tasted of brandy. Her heart pounded like hailstones against her ribs, strangling her breath. Shianne felt herself sinking a second time, drowning in the depths of delicious pleasure. As his wandering hands explored the unclaimed territory of her body, Shianne's resistance fell down around her ankles, and she sank into the sensual darkness for the third and final time. She was drowning in his masterful kiss, and she didn't care if she was rescued. She had spent days practicing saying "no," but the word would not form on her lips when he touched her so tenderly. Wade Burdett was making her will his own and causing her brain to cease functioning.

His practiced hands glided down her arm and then receded to survey the slope of her bare shoulder. His lean fingers dived beneath the damp towel to encircle the peak of her breast. As his caresses roved over her stomach, Shianne moaned softly. His touch set her afire, making her want things she never craved from a man. His gentle explorations left her limp and pliant, but beneath her yielding flesh, sensations were wreaking havoc.

Wade marveled at the exquisite texture of her skin, the titillating curves that lured him to bold intimacy. The palm of his hand swam over the silky flesh of her hip, his thumb sketching the softness of her inner thigh, but these arousing investigations were not enough. He wanted her pressed intimately to him, glorying in the feel of her naive body. He wanted to be as close as two people could get, to teach her to satisfy him as he intended to satisfy her.

Wade withdrew, his smile evaporating. The expression that was etched on his craggy features caused Shianne to catch her breath. Livid hunger burned in his eyes, hypnotizing her. As he lifted her from her bath, Shianne curled her arms about him, aching and breathless to learn where these maddening sensations would lead.

When he set her to her feet, Shianne worked the buttons of his shirt to expose the hair-covered expanse of his chest. Brazenly, she stroked his muscled flesh, wanting to stir the same excitement that claimed her when he caressed her.

Wade waited, allowing her to undress him. When each article of clothing lay on the floor, he slipped his arms around her trim waist and drew her close. His

121

huge body trembled with barely contained passion. He wanted many things from Shianne's first encounter with love, things he had never offered a woman. This had nothing to do with lust, though it had initially set fire to his male curiosity. In a way, this was a new experience for him too. He had the premonition that this could never be a mere appeasement of physical needs, not with a woman like Shianne. She would demand more of him than he had offered any other woman.

Shianne hadn't the faintest notion what awaited her. She was naive and innocent. If he allowed his male instincts to assume control, she might not find pleasure in lovemaking. She had just begun to trust him, and he could not destroy that trust, not if he intended to live with his conscience. When he finally took her she would be eager for him, so eager that she would overlook the pain, he promised himself.

As he laid her onto the feather bed, he stretched out beside her. His gaze flowed unhindered over her curvaceous body. "You are exquisite, Shae," he breathed, his voice laced with genuine emotion. "You are everything I thought you would be and more. . . . It will take the entire night to love you the way you need to be loved, and I intend to love you properly . . . in all the ways you have never dared to imagine. . . ."

His kisses traced the rapid pulsations of her throat and then hovered over her collarbone. His tongue flicked at the pink bud of her breast, and then he teased it with moist lips. His caresses flowed like a lazy river coursing over silted sand, erasing what had come before, obliterating all except this rapturous moment. As his kisses trailed over her ribs, evoking a tiny moan from her throat, Shianne dug her nails into the rigid muscles of his back. She ached with the want of him and yet she hungered for more of his intimate caresses.

Need mushroomed into intense craving and fanned the flames of passion into a blazing inferno.

When his probing fingers invaded her feminine softness, Shianne closed her eyes and mind to all except the tormenting feelings that spilled over her like wine toppling from the rim of a glass. As if her hands possessed a will of their own, they moved to and fro across his back and then swirled along the scar that marred his hip. Another wave of ineffable sensations crested upon her. Instinctively, Shianne urged him to her, pleading with him to make the aching go away, to satisfy this sweet agony that consumed her.

Wade prolonged passion's torment with featherlight kisses and butterfly caresses. It was as if he had touched some unattainable star and could not force himself to sacrifice the pleasure of holding its precious light in his hands. Lovemaking had never been like this, this unhurried exploration, this generous giving of pleasure. The past boasted a simpler kind of passion, but it could not compare to the satisfaction he derived from working sweet magic on this innocent nymph.

When Shianne's brazen touch crept along his thigh to return his caresses, he felt his entire body shudder. Then she twisted to allow her kisses to follow the thick matting of hair that trailed across his belly, and Wade could no longer inhale a breath. Her moist lips worshipped his skin, sending tremors ricocheting through every nerve ending, causing raw passion to rear its head. Gentleness evaded him as her adventurous hands and lips sought out each sensitive point and brought it to life.

When Wade could endure no more of the maddening torture of having her so close and yet too far away, he pressed her to her back. Her silky hair spilled over the pillow, framing her enchanting face. Wade looked into her dark, glowing eyes, eyes that beckoned him, lured him to satisfy the hunger that had gnawed at him for days. He wanted to tell her what was coming, reassure her, but he could not find the words. They were trapped in his throat. It was as if he had been deprived of oxygen and he couldn't breathe.

As his muscled hips settled over hers, his lips consumed hers, stealing the breath that eluded him. The impact of raw masculine power frightened Shianne more than she had anticipated. Wade felt her tense when he pressed intimately against her, felt her push at him, but it was too late to back away. Wade was a man possessed by uncontrollable passion. He tried to be tender, and he knew he would tear her asunder if he didn't make an attempt to spare her pain. But God, it was asking the impossible!

Shianne's hazy cloud of pleasure parted when he entered her. Her pained cry died as his mouth swooped down on hers. Instinct told her to struggle, but she could not escape. Wade's sinewed body was a part of hers, bringing a strange, almost agonizing pleasure. Then, the moment before she swore she could no longer endure this unfamiliar sensation, an erotic feeling bubbled from within. It was like a warm, soothing spring that drowned love's first pain beneath a wave of rapture. As he moved within her, setting a cadence that drew her beneath his spell, Shianne began to respond. She arched to meet his driving thrusts, compelled by some wild, unexplainable longing. The sensations began to mount, piling one upon the other, and when she was certain she was about to die from the pleasures of his lovemaking, she was lifted onto yet a higher plateau of pleasure.

Shianne clutched at him like a kitten clinging to a swaying limb high atop a tree. The winds of passion engulfed her, flinging her into mindless abandon. She hung on to Wade as if he were the only stable force to be found in ecstasy's tempest. The dark world that swirled about her suddenly came alive with pure white light, as if she had burst through the tornadic clouds to face the sun. Then an uncontrollable shudder erupted from the very core of her being. Shianne knew what awaited at the end of passion's rainbow. It was an experience so unique, so satisfying that no words could describe it and no other sensation could compare to it.

While Shianne was discovering rainbows, Wade was skyrocketing past the distant stars. The intimate flight left him dangling in mid-universe. A tremor of rapture rocked his soul, causing him to tremble, to clutch Shianne to him and hold her tightly until the mystifying sensation ceased. It was as if every emotion he had ever experienced had converged into one. It exploded within him, leaving him a mass of shudders. Just when he thought he had regained control of his emotions, aftershocks riveted down his spine. His mind was numb, his strength drained, his nerves tingling.

When Wade finally mustered the energy to raise his head, he couldn't hold it up! My God, he thought. What spell had come over him? Passion had never been quite like this. In the past it had never been so devastating that he couldn't rise and walk away. He had never been a man to linger with the woman he had taken in his arms. Each female had served her purpose, and he was eager to trot off on his merry way, to seek out a new conquest who could offer him a smile and a moment. . . .

"Wade?" Shianne's husky voice cut through his pensive contemplations. Her warm lips caressed his temple. "I saw rainbows? Is that normal?"

Her innocent question caused him to chuckle in disbelief. Only this naive nymph would dare ask such an intimate question. "I can't say for certain," he commented, his voice cracking with amusement. *"I* was dangling from the tip of a star."

Shianne blinked and then stared at the ceiling, watching the flickering lantern light skip across the rough supporting beams. "Before that I was flying into the sun. Is it always like this? I mean . . . we are still alive, aren't we? I feel as if I'm floating in a dream, somewhere on the other side of reality."

Wade lifted his head. He was grinning again. "Why are you asking me all these questions? I can barely hold my head up, much less formulate a sane thought!"

Shianne mistook his teasing for a scolding. It was always difficult to read Wade's moods and emotions. Even when he had been in pain the previous week, he smiled. Who could know what the man was really feeling? He could mask murderous fury or utter boredom behind a smile, and no one could know for certain what he was thinking. "Well, you are the one who should know," she grumbled, worming from beneath him. "I have never made love to a man before."

"Neither have I," Wade snickered and then grunted uncomfortably when Shianne retaliated by swatting him on the head with her pillow. Playfully, he reached for her, pinning her to the mattress. "Minx! Lie still a moment. You make me dizzy when you bound around the bed."

Shianne was in an odd mood. His lovemaking left her with an exhilarating sensation that did indeed have her bouncing off the walls. Wade's energy had been drained, but hers had been regenerated. Living fire leaped in her dark eyes as she looped her arms over his shoulders and stroked his back.

"Make love to me again. I want to see the stars. . . ."

Wade did a double take. Good God, he had fallen into bed with an insatiable witch! He predicted her passion in love would far excel that of the other women he had known, but her stamina was incredible. He

126

wasn't even sure he could stand upright, much less repeat a performance that had exhausted his emotions and his strength!

The soft echo of an owl in the distance invaded the silence. Shianne tensed. What was Maman-ti doing in the county again tonight? What poor timing! Without making an excuse, Shianne wiggled away. Hastily, she threw on her gown and fled across the terrace. Wade stared after her, his jaw gaping wide enough for a covey of quail to roost.

"Shianne? Where the hell are you going?" He was met with silence. As he eased into a sitting position he heard the thunder of hooves pounding the ground. He didn't have to guess whose horse had just left the hacienda without its master. "The woman is mad," Wade declared to the walls.

Summoning his strength Wade grabbed his trousers and shirt and tugged them on. He was the one he was supposed to ride off into the darkness. Dammit, that woman defied the rules. No wonder she wasn't married. No mortal man could keep up with her. He had planned to bow gallantly before her and then fade into the shadows, but instead, *she* tore off like streak lightning when the hoot owl began croaking at the moon. . . . A muddled frown plowed his brow as he tucked his shirt tail in his breeches. He had heard the cry of an owl the previous week. Then he had seen Shianne spiriting off on her black stallion.

"Sweet mercy, she *is* a witch!" She had gone to consort with the demons of the night. "There were a few things you neglected to tell me about your daughter, Blake," he muttered grouchily.

It was a long walk back to camp, and Wade grumbled every step of the way. To his surprise Galahad was there waiting for him, but Shianne wasn't.

"Where the hell have you been?" A voice echoed from the hollowed darkness of the cavern.

Wade frowned bemusedly. "Tell you the truth, I'm not sure. I thought I was in heaven, but now I'm beginning to wonder if I have just returned from a trip in the opposite direction."

"Heaven?" A sour voice erupted from the cave. "I think the heat fried your brain when you were left to bake in the sun. We've got troubles and you're lollygagging around until all hours of the night!"

Wade dragged himself from his pensive musings and concentrated on the shadows. "What kind of troubles?" Had Shianne darted off into the night to ensure that Wade had not disturbed the secret of the cave? Was she hereabout? Investigating?

"Indian troubles," the voice grumbled. "I could hear them whooping and hollering at the other end of the cavern. They are chanting to the great spirits."

A wry smile pursed Wade's lips as he took up the torch and strode into the mouth of the cavern. The trouble to which the phantom referred might well be a blessing in disguise, Wade mused. He veered around the huge rock sculptures that reminded him of the open mouth of a shark with its spiny teeth jutting from the ceiling and the floor of the cave. His footsteps took him through a narrow tunnel to the small opening where the underground spring tumbled from the rocks.

Lying flat on his belly, Wade peered through the pigeonhole to see a congregation of bare-chested savages hovering around the bank of the stream. A shocked gasp bubbled from his chest when he spied Shianne in their midst. What the devil was she doing consorting with wild Indians?

His narrowed gaze focused on the tall, swarthy chief who had draped his arm around Shianne's waist. "Well, I'll be damned," he breathed in disbelief.

A wave of jealousy ricocheted through him. Was this the man Shianne had *truly* wanted earlier this night? Had she used Wade to satisfy her curiosity about passion? The way Shianne was staring at the muscular warrior annoyed Wade. Admiration and respect were written all over her face, and Wade growled in disgust. He had the infuriating feeling he had been used as a substitute for this . . . this wild heathen who was holding Shianne as if it were old habit.

"What's going on?" the phantom voice demanded to know.

"They're having some sort of a council," Wade whispered back. "And guess who is right smack dab in the middle of them?"

"I'm in no mood for guessing games. Who is it?"

The flickering torchlight displayed the strained smile that stretched across Wade's lips. "The lovely, but very mysterious Shianne Kimball, mistress of the K Bar Ranch. It seems the lady leads a very interesting life."

"What are we going to do? We can't have those heathens snooping around here. If they find out what is stashed in this cavern, it will take a cavalry of soldiers to run them off . . . which, may I remind you, we don't happen to have with us at the moment."

Wade wedged the torch against the rock formations where the underground spring poured over the boulders below. "If the savages think this river boasts the voices of their gods, we'll give them what they want."

Cupping his hands around his mouth, Wade began to howl like a banshee, mimicking every eerie, wailing noise he *thought* he had heard all those nights he had spent alone in the darkness. The phantom of the cave chimed in the chorus. Their low voices echoed around the underground chamber and trickled from the mouth of the spring.

Maman-ti stood on the delta of sand where the water forked to flow off in opposite directions. He flinched when a faint golden light seeped from the mouth of the spring, causing the water to glow like morning sunshine. Pricking his ears, he listened to the haunting sounds that belched from the crevice. It sounded as if a parade of phantoms were begging to be released from the bowels of the earth.

"Do you hear the voices of our ancestors?" he questioned the war chiefs of the Comanches and Kiowas. "They are answering our chants, bidding us to avenge our losses to the white man."

A quiet murmur echoed through the small band of Indians. In awe they stared at the sparkling water until the light and voices faded and the murmuring river whispered with the familiar sounds of nature. They were certain Maman-ti had led them to sacred ground where the spirits spoke into the bubbling springs.

Shianne watched and listened, her brows furrowing in a skeptical frown. She was prepared to bet her share in the K Bar Ranch that Wade had something to do with the wailing voices. The fact that Wade had taken up residence near the cave and began playing pranks on the Comanches worried her. What if he alerted the ranchers to the presence of Indian warriors on her ranch? What if Wade learned she had fled from his arms to meet with the Owl Prophet? Damn, the man might blackmail her with that information, forcing her to do his bidding. Lord, that man would cause her trouble, just as sure as the world was round.

Calm yourself, Shianne scolded the inner voices that sought to unravel her composure. Whoever or whatever was in that cavern couldn't see through solid rock. Wade didn't have the slightest notion where she had gone, and she was not about to tell him. He had his secrets and she had hers. The source of the eerie sounds might not have anything to do with Wade Burdett, Shianne reassured herself. There was no sense working herself into a nervous frenzy until she had just cause.

When the council meeting ended, Maman-ti lifted Shianne onto his steed and swung up in front of her. While the raiding party thundered off to confiscate horses and cattle from unsuspecting ranchers, Mamanti took Shianne back to the hacienda.

"I was visited by a strange dream, Little One," the Owl Prophet confessed as they rode through the darkness. "I wanted to tell you of the vision the last time I sent for you, but I hesitated. I see much difficulty, much turmoil in your future, but the dream was hazy, the images vague. You must guard your footsteps or trouble will find you."

Shianne frowned disconcertedly. Had Maman-ti envisioned disaster for her in the form of Wade Burdett? That should come as no surprise, Shianne assured herself. Since the moment she laid eyes on that devilish libertine she had been unable to rout him from her thoughts. Shianne inwardly groaned, thinking how she had allowed Wade to waltz into her life, take command and then take possession in *every* sense of the word.

"You are very quiet tonight, Little One," the Owl Prophet murmured.

Shianne eased her grasp on his waist and sighed heavily. Regret was beginning to catch up with her. She had allowed her curiosity about the bold stranger to swallow her alive. Wade had invaded her bedchamber, and she had submitted to him like a shameless trollop. Damn, that had been a foolish thing to do, she chided herself. She could well imagine the triumphant smile on Wade's lips. Why, at this very moment, he was probably carving another notch on his belt. How could he respect her when she had been such an easy conquest? How could she respect herself when she had fallen into bed with a man she barely knew?

Lord, have mercy on her soul! She could never face Wade again, she realized. He had taken what he wanted from her and she had not even put up a fight. Well, there would be no more dallying with Wade Burdett, Shianne vowed to herself. She had made a tragic mistake, and she would not repeat it. She had wondered what it was like between a man and a woman. Now she knew, but what a high price she had paid for that knowledge!

"You are trembling, Little One." Maman-ti drew his steed to a halt and eased Shianne to the ground. When he had dismounted he gathered her in his arms, offering her a strong shoulder to lean on. "Tell me what troubles you. I know there are difficulties facing you. Whatever they are, I will make your battle mine."

Shianne gazed up into the wild, angular features of the face that hovered just above hers. She could not ask Maman-ti to fight her private wars for her. She could not pit this fearless warrior against a man who equaled his strength and cunning. One man was her friend and the other, regretfully, had become her lover.

"You and your people have your own wars to fight," Shianne said after a long silence. "I have been fending for myself much too long to allow anyone to stand in my stead."

"There is a man," the Owl Prophet predicted. "Who is he, Little One? What hold does he have on you?"

Damn, she was transparent, Shianne mused. Both Wade and Maman-ti could see through her. Slowly, she retreated from his arms and presented her back. "I wish you and your war chiefs would find another meeting place," she requested, purposely avoiding the probing question. "I'm not certain it is safe for you to

132

congregate at the mouth of the springs."

"What other place is safer, more sacred than the springs where the great spirits rise to speak to their people?" he snorted. "You worry for nothing, Little One. It is the white men who deserve your pity. We will continue to take from them what they have stolen from us. It is the only way to prove to the Great White Father that the Indian will not be herded onto reservations and confined like livestock. This land belongs to the red man. It is our hunting ground, the land where our fathers have been buried." Maman-ti grasped Shianne's arm, spinning her around to face him. "You entreat me to let you be what you are, not to sweep you away to my village to make you one of our people, your grandmother's people, to make you *my* woman." His dark eyes bore into her with fierce intensity. "I have respected your wishes, Little One, and so you must also respect mine. I am compelled to the place of the speaking springs, just as I am called upon by the feathered oracle to advise my people in the ways of war."

Shianne nodded slightly, knowing she could not ask Maman-ti to deny his fierce convictions. The Indians held strong to their superstitions and beliefs. Shianne did not dare dispute the authenticity of the springs. Her only alternative was to convince Wade Burdett to pull up stakes and move elsewhere . . . before he found himself strung upside down between two cypress trees.

"Are we still friends, even if you are annoyed with me?" Shianne questioned demurely.

Maman-ti melted beneath her wan smile. His lips brushed her forehead, his hands folding about her forearms to give her a loving squeeze. "Always, Little One," he insisted softly. "Many things may change, but never my affection for you."

Shianne lingered by the lattice until Maman-ti had

133

become one of the swaying shadows. Breathing a heavy sigh, she scaled the lattice to return to her room. Her rueful gaze swung to the crumpled sheets where she and Wade had made love. Shianne cursed her weakness. It was unlike her to become a man's pawn, but when Wade touched her it had felt so good, so right. It was only an illusion, she lectured herself. There was nothing right about taking a tumble in bed with a virtual stranger, especially one like Wade Burdett. He was far more than she could control. Somehow he would punish her for giving in to him without protest. No doubt it would come in the form of taunts, sordid illusions to the night she had surrendered to a weakness of the flesh as well as the spirit.

Shianne froze in her tracks when she spied the dark stains on her bed. God, what had she done? She had given herself and her innocence to a man who wanted nothing from her but passion. She had intended to save herself for the man she loved and would one day marry. Now she would come to her husband as a tainted woman.

Suddenly, she remembered the remark Wade had made about her father scheming to link her with her new guardian. She had detected the cynicism in Wade's voice, and she knew he was not eager to wed her nor any woman. His kind never married, Shianne told herself bitterly. What Wade Burdett wanted from a woman had nothing to do with lasting ties and commitments.

Well, the next time she saw that scoundrel, she would treat him as if their tryst had meant nothing more to her than it meant to him. She would be distant and aloof, insisting that she had only succumbed to him to appease her feminine curiosity. He would never know how disappointed she was in herself, how she was hurting. Let him think she was as much a rogue as he was, she thought spitefully. That should put a dent in his male pride.

Satisfied with her plan of action, Shianne climbed into bed. Tomorrow would be a better day, she promised herself. She would be prepared to deal with Wade Burdett, and he would never know her shame. She may have lost her virginity and command of the ranch, but she would not sacrifice her pride and her heart!

Chapter 7

When dawn blared into the open window, Shianne came slowly awake. The well-meaning lectures she had delivered to herself the previous night had not bolstered her spirits. Shianne cursed herself for allowing Wade to bring out the cowardly instinct in her. She couldn't face him, not yet, not until she had adequate time to reinforce her firm resolve.

Shianne hurried through her toiletries and then jumped into her clothes, anxious to make the journey into San Antonio. The defenders of Texas had taken cover inside the walls of the Alamo, and Doc Winston was the key to *her* salvation. She could only pray that her battle against her irrational attraction to Wade Burdett would not end as disastrous as the attack on the mission some thirty years earlier. The defenders of the Alamo had stayed to fight, but she chose to retreat. Shianne smiled slyly to herself. She wasn't really turning tail and running to Doc Winston; she was only falling back to regroup.

On that positive note Shianne aimed herself toward the bedroom door. As she breezed by the mirror she paused to survey her reflection. Her hand brushed across her cheek, wondering if anyone could tell she had surged from maidenhood to womanhood. If the differences were not obvious on the outside, they certainly were on the inside, Shianne thought in dismay. She had experienced a passion she never believed possible, and yet, she knew she had turned to the wrong man.

Luckily, she had not fallen in love with that virile rogue whose touch had temporarily erased logic. If she had, she would have been in worse condition than she was now, Shianne reckoned. She considered herself fortunate to have escaped with her soul intact after consorting with that raven-haired devil.

Tossing all thoughts of Wade Burdett aside, Shianne grabbed a slice of homemade bread and strolled outside to saddle Delgado. In the distance she noticed the tall figure of a man approaching on his bay stallion. Riding behind him were the vaqueros who worked for the K Bar Ranch. Shianne gouged Delgado, sending him off in the opposite direction. Let Wade take command of the roundup while she regained control of her emotions. When she was forced to face Wade's smug smile, she would be remote and reserved, just as she had been the first day she found him lying on the creek bank. And that is exactly where she should have left him, Shianne thought resentfully. Thus far, the man had been a threat to her pride, morals, and independence.

Shianne leaned against the steed's neck, urging Delgado to cover the ground at breakneck speed. The feel of the wind whipping through her hair sent her apprehensions flying in the breeze. Thank goodness for Doc Winston. His companionship would keep her preoccupied. If wishing could make it so, Wade Burdett would never cross her mind again . . . ever!

* * *

Jedediah's broad face split into a welcoming grin when Shianne bounded into his office, eager to make herself useful. "Has someone set a fire beneath you, girl? You look different today."

Shianne's spirits sank down around her ankles. Doc could have talked all day without lighting on that sensitive subject. Forcing a smile, Shianne ambled over to the basin to cleanse her hands. "If I look and act differently it is because I have received good news," she enthused. "I have learned that my father is alive."

"That is indeed reason for that new sparkle in your eyes," Doc Winston said excitedly. "I have prayed Blake had not met with disaster. It is a relief to all of us to know he will be returning home to the K Bar Ranch."

While they tended Jedediah's first patient, Shianne related the events of the previous week and the news that her father was alive and well and making preparations for Texas cattle to reach the northern markets. Doc Winston listened to Shianne's account and then frowned curiously. "You approve of having this Wade Burdett take control of your duties?"

Shianne's shoulder lifted in a shrug, and she concentrated on wrapping the bandage on their patient's arm. "It seems no one is concerned whether I approve or disapprove. My father left instructions with Wade Burdett, and he is a very imposing man. He has already informed me that he will either walk around me or over me, but that he will complete the job he was sent here to do."

Jedediah assisted his patient from the table. "I don't suppose you put up a fuss," he chuckled.

"To no avail," Shianne muttered resentfully. "That is when Wade assured me I could stand aside or be trampled."

"From what you have said about Wade Burdett, he

138

seems to be a very determined man."

"He is that," Shianne concurred begrudgingly, "but I fear he and I will constantly clash. He is much too pushy for my tastes."

Jedediah grinned at the distasteful frown that was etched in Shianne's bewitching features. There was something curious about the man who had ridden into Shianne's life. Although she protested his interference, his name had been on her lips since the moment she set foot in the office. It set Jedediah to wondering if Shianne weren't protesting a bit too much. But he didn't press the matter. He simply listened each time Shianne reopened the subject to list all Wade Burdett's faults. To hear her talk one would think the man had hundreds of them. Shianne made Burdett out to be a tyrannical dragon who breathed fire and gobbled up humans as a between-meal appetizer, but Jedediah had the sneaking suspicion this feisty Texas beauty was trying very hard not to like the man whom Blake had designated as her guardian and interim boss of the K Bar Ranch.

By late afternoon Jedediah had a distorted picture of the man who strode into the office to fetch Shianne home. The doctor bit back a grin when the tall, muscular cowboy with the charming smile stepped into the room. Wade introduced himself and announced that he had come to escort Shianne home.

She was furious that her guardian thought she needed a chaperone to ride the miles between San Antonio and her ranch, as if she were an imbecile who could not remember her way home. But what rankled Shianne the most was that she was forced to confront the man she was trying desperately to forget. Dammit, why couldn't he leave her be? Wade was the last person on earth she wanted to see at the moment.

When Wade attempted to take her arm to escort her

onto the street, Shianne jerked away as if she had been stung, and indeed she had. His touch singed like fire, thwarting her attempt to feel nothing when she was forced to face the grinning rake.

"I will thank you kindly not to humiliate me by coming to fetch me home," she hissed as she stomped toward her steed. "I am quite capable of fending for myself. I have been doing just that for the past several years. As you can plainly see, I have survived without anyone's assistance."

"You purposely avoided me today," Wade stated as he lifted her into the saddle, despite her vocal protest. "Are you having regrets about last night?"

Shianne focused on some distant point and gritted her teeth. "Hundreds of them."

Wade ambled over to retrieve the package that was tied behind his saddle. "Perhaps this will cool your temper, princess."

Casting him a suspicious glance, Shianne opened the gift and then stared bug-eyed at its donor. "Where did you get this?" Her astonished gaze fell back to the expensive burgundy gown he had bought for her.

"I purchased it at the boutique," he said pleasantly. "Do you like it?"

"But why?" Shianne croaked. "And how?"

"Why? Because I could picture you in it, attending the fiesta. And how? With money, of course." Wade swung into his saddle, awaiting the inevitable question. It came, just as he anticipated it would.

"Did you decide to rob a bank without waiting for me to play your accomplice?" She couldn't help but ask.

Where else could he have obtained the money to buy such an expensive gift? Blast it, they needed every cent they could scrape together to organize the roundup and cattle drive. Why was he splurging money on her? They

140

meant nothing to each other, not really.

Wade leaned out to grasp Delgado's reins, urging the stallion down the street. "I thought I asked you not to worry about the money. I will find a way to purchase everything we will need without draining the K Bar's funds."

"Even if it includes resorting to illegal means?" Shianne flung at him.

Wade grinned slyly. "There is no reason for you to fret over my methods, my dear. The ultimate end should be your only concern. I doubt that I have crippled the trail drive by going on a shopping spree."

Shianne eyed him suspiciously. He was being far too secretive to be up to any good. Obviously, Wade had stooped to skullduggery to obtain funds, and then he had splurged to buy her this elegant gown for reasons she could not begin to understand. Was this to be some sort of compensation for what had transpired the previous night? Did he think he could buy her gifts to ensure her door would always be open when he was overwhelmed by a lusty fit? That would be the day the Sahara froze over! she thought huffily.

"I will not accept your lavish gift," she declared. "Kindly return it to the store."

Although Wade was still smiling, Shianne noted the twitch in his jaw. That was the only outward sign that he was annoyed with her.

"You are keeping the gown, and you will wear it to the fiesta, even if I have to come to your room and fasten you in it," he told her in no uncertain terms.

Shianne puffed up indignantly. "I will not be dictated to! If you are so fond of the dress, *you* wear it." With that, she hurled the package at him and thundered down the street, leaving a cloud of dust at her heels.

Grumbling at the woman's damnable spirit, Wade

141

hooked the strings of the package around the saddle horn and charged after Shianne. Although Delgado was swift of foot, Galahad was faster. When they passed the outskirts of town the two stallions were racing side by side. Wade extended himself to yank Shianne from the saddle. To her dismay, she was forced to clutch her arms around Wade or wind up in a broken heap on the ground.

As Delgado thundered off without his mistress, Wade reined Galahad to a halt and abruptly released his grasp on Shianne. Unprepared, she fell in an unceremonious heap, cursing a blue streak.

"It serves you right," Wade snickered, "and I wish you would quit resorting to profanity. My God, woman, you can curse as proficiently as your vaqueros."

Angrily, Shianne scraped herself off the ground and glared holes in Wade's blue gingham shirt. "Who do you suppose is responsible for increasing my vocabulary in the first place?" she sassed. "I have spent years working beside my ranch hands, learning all there is to know about cattle and cussing, and there are times when swearing fits the situation. This is one of those times! Damn you, Wade Burdett!" she yelled at him.

Unshaken by her disrespectful tirade and the mutinous glowers that would have sent a panther cowering in his den, Wade leaned out to hoist Shianne up in front of him. He stuffed the package in her lap and touched his heels to Galahad's flanks.

"You weren't cursing me last night. In fact, I rather thought you were encouraging me," he had the nerve to say.

Shianne reacted instinctively. She twisted around in the saddle to whop him up side the head with the package that was clenched in her fist. Wade burst out laughing, making her all the more furious.

"I detest you, Wade Burdett. If I had it to do all over again, I wouldn't! Any man could have appeased my curiosity. You were merely convenient."

Wade was no longer snickering. Her remark cut him to the quick. He was again set to wondering if Shianne had used *his* body and attached that half-naked savage's face to it. The thought of this curvaceous nymph surrendering to another man, especially a renegade Indian, agitated him. Damn, why was he suddenly so possessive? He had never been before. Because Shianne was different, he reminded himself. He had accepted that fact—begrudgingly—but there was no way around the truth. For God's sake, he didn't have to turn envy green when she spitefully suggested that she might succumb to other men, did he? Hell, yes he did! Shianne was not the kind of woman who took a tumble with whoever happened by. She was Blake Kimball's daughter, and Wade would be damned if she became indiscriminate, at least not while he was her guardian as well as the only man who had sampled her charms.

"I'll not have you gallivanting about, perfecting your new found talents in bed," he growled in her flushed face. "You are not a peddler who passes out free samples!"

Shianne swiveled around to glare straight ahead. "I will see whomever I please, whenever I please," she snapped brusquely. "You may have been the first, but you will hardly be the last. I'm sure there are any number of men in the county who would not be opposed to sharing my bed, even if I demanded a fee."

Damn, this little firebrand could spoil his good disposition faster than anyone he had ever met. Wade never considered himself to have a hair-trigger on his temper until now. But Shianne had indeed tampered with his patience. She could set him off faster than an exploding cannon.

"Since I am financing this cattle drive there is no need for you to put your charms up for sale," Wade muttered, his tone sour enough to curdle fresh milk.

"Oh? Are you implying that since you have already robbed a bank to gain funds for our venture that I can keep whatever I might make as a harlot?" A mischievous smile rippled across her lips, making her eyes gleam like ebony. "Perhaps I *will* keep this dress. Men like passion-red gowns, don't they? It should serve to entice one or two eager males to my boudoir. I'm sure I can put their payments for services rendered to good use, and, as you so rudely reminded me, I can use the practice."

If Wade would have had a free hand he would have strangled the ornery minx. "I sorely wish I would have delivered the news about Blake to you and kept riding," he grumbled resentfully.

"Nothing would have made me happier," Shianne retaliated, turning up her dainty nose. "Then I would not have found myself in cohoots with a thief!"

"I am not a thief!" Wade vehemently protested.

"Then where did you get the money for this dress?" she fired the question at him.

"That is none of your damned business, woman," Wade breathed down her neck.

Shianne silently smoldered for several minutes. For the life of her, she could not fathom how Wade had secured the funds for such an extravagant purchase. The economy of the South was in dire straits, and Wade had yet to make his fortune driving mavericks to Kansas.

When Shianne spied the hacienda in the distance she slumped in relief. Another quarter of a mile and she would be free of Wade's sinewy arms and masculine scent. Their closeness was playing havoc with her

144

emotions. She had picked a fight with him to protect her vulnerability, but even an argument had its limitations as a means of defense. She would have to be stricken deaf, dumb and blind if she hoped to ignore the man who held her to his muscled chest and kept her captive with his hard thighs and restraining arms.

When they reached the corral, Wade curled his hand around her waist and set her to her feet. "I feel better knowing you arrived safe and sound," he drawled, the faintest hint of sarcasm in his voice. "I heard Indians raided one of the ranches west of here last night." A slow grin slid across his lips when Shianne glanced the other way. "It would grieve me if you were to be abducted by savages. . . ." His voice trailed off momentarily before directing a pointed question. "By the way, where did you spirit off to last night, princess? I have heard the fairy tale about Cinderella dashing off before the stroke of midnight. She feared having her coach transformed into a pumpkin. What was your excuse?"

Shianne raised her gaze to peer into those unnerving green-gold eyes. Had he guessed her destination? Had he indeed been the one to taunt the Comanches by pretending to be the great spirit? How much did he know and how much was he trying to pry from her?

A deliciously mischievous smile caught the corners of her mouth. She could be as evasive as this ornery cowboy was. If he wouldn't divulge the source of his funds, she wouldn't answer his probing questions.

"To quote my dear guardian: 'It is none of your damned business.'" Flinging him a smug glance, Shianne pivoted on her heels and strutted toward the hacienda with her gift dangling from her fingertips. "And thank you for the gown," she threw over her shoulder. "I will try to put it to good use."

Wade ground his teeth and glared at her shapely

backside. It seemed they were back to pistols and hatchets again. Damnation, there were two contradicting personalities spiriting around inside that curvaceous body. One was soft and seductive like a slow burning fire. The other one was a block of ice. A man could get scorched or suffer frostbite, and the pitiful thing about it was that he never knew his fate until the moment was upon him.

Resigning himself to the fact that he had become involved in a battle of civilized warfare against the mistress of the K Bar Ranch, Wade reined Galahad toward the cave. Shianne was going to spite him at every turn, he speculated. One night of passion had not mellowed that spitfire. She was as ornery and stubborn as ever!

The nerve of that woman, suggesting she would spread herself before any man who met her whim! Damn her. If she allowed another man to touch her Wade would. . . . He expelled a harsh breath. Taming a woman like Shianne would take some doing. Challenging her only made matters worse. Blast it, Blake had allowed her to grow like a wild weed while he was away fighting a war. Why hadn't Blake seen to it that someone with a firm, capable hand had been left in charge of his feisty daughter? Lord, now she was so strong-willed and independent that she was practically unmanageable. No doubt Blake had decided that Wade was indirectly responsible for Shianne's lack of guidance and that he should be the one to right the situation.

Wade muttered under his breath as he urged Galahad to sprout wings and fly to the cave. He should marry that misfit if only to bring her under thumb. Then he would have full control over her. She would be forced to do his bidding, and if she didn't, he had every right to exert his power over her. As her guardian he could only guide her, but that woman didn't need a guide, he thought acrimoniously. She needed someone to take her over his knee and throttle her!

The thought caused a smile to mellow Wade's chiseled features. He could well imagine Shianne's fury if he dared to paddle her shapely derriere, but she had it coming after the way she behaved. Yet, a man couldn't very well marry a woman just to vent his irritation with her. Hell, he wasn't the marrying kind, Wade reminded himself. Even if he were, Shianne Kimball would make a hellacious wife. She was far too contrary, too headstrong, too set in her ways and so was he.

Ah, but the nights . . . he thought with a sigh. Theirs was a wild, reckless sort of passion. It was spontaneous and sweet and . . . *Don't think about that,* Wade lectured himself. If he allowed his mind to drift, he would find himself trotting back to the hacienda at twilight. Then that little witch would know she held some sort of power over him. No, he wasn't going to crawl back to her, begging for her affection. He would tie himself to a tree long before he gave way to his weakness for that ebony-haired enchantress who could make him feel every bit a man when she allowed herself to be a woman.

A thoughtful frown knitted Shianne's brow. Since the previous day when Wade had escorted her home, her mind had been in a quandary. It disturbed her that Wade had become so free with his money. What was his source of funds? Had he stolen and looted during the war, building himself a sizable nest egg for his new venture in Texas? How had he been able to afford to pay Blake for the acres he had purchased? Where had he found the funds to hire on a dozen extra men to help

147

with the roundup? Had the man discovered a money tree in the forest? Just where was Wade stashing this mysterious wealth?

Shianne had the uneasy feeling she knew why Wade was so determined to keep the plot of ground where the dark, unexplored cavern lay. As a child, she had been too frightened of the dark to venture past the mouth of the cave, but now she could deal with her childhood fears. Perhaps it was time for her to prowl around the cavern. Since Wade was with the men, gathering stray mavericks, she decided to seize the opportunity.

With two torches and a supply of kerosene, Shianne aimed herself toward the cave. She was determined to satisfy the demons of curiosity that spurred her to investigate Wade's hideout. When she reached the entrance in late afternoon, she watched the swarm of bats blacken the sky. With the pesky rodents off feeding, she felt reasonably safe. After lighting a torch she moved bravely forward to follow one of the three tunnels that led into the bowels of the earth. Her footsteps echoed in the musty darkness, sending an eerie tremor tripping down her spine. The darkness of the cave was like nothing she had ever experienced. Outside, on the blackest of nights, even when the stars and moon were blotted out by thick clouds, she could determine the sizes and shapes of images. But Shianne had the uneasy feeling that if she allowed her torch to die, she would be unable to see her hand in front of her face.

The deeper she journeyed into the unknown, the more apprehensive she became. Swallowing with a nervous gulp, Shianne inspected the dark chamber that dripped with long spindly mineral formations. The strange colored pillars that jutted from the floor of the cave triggered her imagination, one that was dangerously close to running away with itself.

In the distance she could hear the murmuring of an underground river. She began to wonder if the Owl Prophet had indeed heard voices of spirits frolicking in the underworld. Her mind and body froze when the sound of footsteps echoed in the silence, footsteps that did not belong to her and certainly not to Wade, she thought uneasily. He was off chasing *cimarrones*.

A doleful wail floated down to her from the shadowed ledges high above. Shianne's courage pulled up stakes and abandoned her. Her heart catapulted to her throat to strangle her, and it was all she could do to prevent collapsing in fright.

"Who's there?" Shianne questioned shakily.

She waited to hear a human voice, but she was met with another round of spine-tingling cries. Shianne took one step backward and then another. Her back brushed against something cold and hard and she screamed for all she was worth. When she managed to get herself in hand, she shined the torch behind her, finding another slick mineral deposit flooding over a jutting rock.

Pulling a tight rein on her runaway heart, Shianne swallowed down her nervousness and turned back in the direction she had come. Damn, she would have to work up enough nerve to return at a later date, she told herself. It would take several trips just to learn to tolerate the eerie experience of descending into the musty bowels of the earth. The path she had chosen had led to no mysterious treasure. Indeed, it had been no more than a lesson in self-control.

As Shianne retraced her steps she continued to hear strange noises in the distance . . . or were they directly behind her? In this black pit it was difficult to tell since her senses had not adjusted to this new form of darkness.

When she finally reached the antechamber of the

cave, she shrank away from the radiant light that sprayed into the portal between the rocks. When her eyes became accustomed to the sunlight, she inched toward the opening and then cursed her rotten luck. There, just outside the mouth of the cave, stood Wade. Damn, she had no intention of letting him know she was snooping. She had tied Delgado a good distance away as a precautionary measure, but never in her worst nightmare did she anticipate being trapped inside the cave.

Grumbling over her stroke of misfortune, Shianne rolled the torch in the dust to extinguish the flame. She plopped down on the floor to wait for Wade to disappear from sight, giving her the opportunity to escape without making her presence known. But to her dismay, Wade built his campfire and placed his freshly skinned rabbit over the flames to roast, and there she sat fuming, praying Wade would wander off to bathe or fetch fresh water . . . anything!

A wry smile pursed Wade's lips as he tossed more logs on the fire. He had returned from a successful day of corraling twenty head of unclaimed calves. He had marked one steer with the K Bar brand and the next with the Circle B brand. When he returned to camp he heard the whinny of an unidentified steed and went to investigate.

Finding Delgado tethered in the brush provoked his devilish chuckle. It wasn't too difficult to guess why Shianne was snooping around his campsite. She was determined to learn where Wade kept his funds. Consequently, her search led her into the cave.

The daring little imp, he mused as he sank down crosslegged to stoke the fire. Shianne was bound and determined to satisfy her curiosity, no matter what the consequences. Well, it was time to teach that little minx a lesson, Wade decided. Grabbing a nearby blanket, he fanned the flames and directed the smoke toward the entrance of the cave. She couldn't last long when engulfed by smoke and the tantalizing aroma of fresh meat cooking over the fire, he reckoned.

As the rabbit-flavored cloud rolled toward her, Shianne stuffed herself in the corner and covered her face with the hem of her skirt. The aroma reminded her that it was the supper hour, and her stomach responded as Wade had predicted. Even with her face covered, Shianne could almost taste the juicy meat. The fabric that clogged her nostrils absorbed the appetizing fragrance instead of blocking it out. Shianne cursed her predicament and her growling stomach. Praying Wade would find some reason to wander off, Shianne waited several minutes, strangling her need to cough.

Cautiously, she crawled toward the entrance and then jerked back when Wade peeled off his shirt and dug into his sack to fetch his eating utensils. Lord, he wasn't leaving, and she would be forced to endure the night in the eerie darkness, she thought dismally.

Wade had employed every tactic that came to mind in hopes of enticing Shianne from the cave, but the stubborn imp wouldn't budge. She seemed determined to outwait him. After an hour of encouraging smoke clouds to invade the cavern, Wade was at wits end. His arms were about to fall off from waving that confounded quilt, but Shianne still hadn't shown herself.

Finally he marched over to the portal between the rocks. "Come out of there, Shianne. I know you're in there."

Shianne swore under her breath. Begrudgingly, she climbed to her feet and raced through several excuses as to why she had trespassed on his property, but they were lame excuses, none of which Wade would believe. Tilting her chin to a proud angle, she walked through

151

the wall of smoke to face his taunting grin.

"Had I known you were interested in exploration I would have invited you to scout out the cavities of the cave sooner," he mocked dryly.

"Had I known you would return so soon to catch me, I would have arrived earlier in the day," she snapped back at him.

Shianne cursed her betraying eyes for roaming over the broad expanse of his chest and following the thick matting of hair that dived into the waistband of his breeches. Damn, why was she so magnetically attracted to this ornery rascal? His sole purpose in life was to taunt her, and he did it very well.

"Were you searching for something in particular or snooping in general, princess?" he questioned flippantly.

"What do you think?" she smirked, refusing to explain herself. If Wade thought he was so damned smart he could figure it out for himself.

Wade's green eyes slid down the chemisette that clung to her breasts and then wandered over the gentle curve of her hips. "I'm beginning to wonder if your true intention was to finish what we began the other night. . . ."

Shianne drew herself up, her eyes spitting black flames. "If you believe that, you are incredibly arrogant."

His dark brow arched, and he regarded her defiant expression for a long silent moment. "Or perhaps you were using me when it was another man you truly wanted in your arms."

His comment caught Shianne off stride. Where had he gotten such a notion? Not that she was opposed to allowing the exasperating varmint to think he had been a substitute, she mused spitefully. It suddenly occurred to her that Wade might have seen her with the Owl

152

Prophet, and she didn't know whether to fret or gloat.

For a strained moment they stared each other down, both harboring their own secrets. Wade spoke first, voicing the thought that had plagued him throughout the day.

"Are you in love with that Indian chief you ran off to meet the other night?" he questioned point-blank.

Shianne flinched, her worst fears confirmed. Hastily she recomposed herself. The feat was becoming easier with each passing day. Dealing with Wade provided plenty of practice in self-control. With her wits regathered, Shianne looked him square in the eye. "Are you hiding some sort of treasure in the cave, a stolen treasure perhaps?" She answered his question with one of her own.

The smile that usually lighted his handsome features had faded into an annoyed frown. "What does he mean to you, Shae? What ties do you have with the Comanches?"

"Where did you get the funds to hire extra men and purchase lavish dresses, Wade?" she prodded.

Damnation, she had done it again! She had stretched Wade's patience until it snapped. This woman had the uncanny knack of turning his emotions wrong side out. Impulsively, Wade clutched her arm, yanking her to him, his breath hot against her cheek.

"Answer me, damn you. Was it *his* face you saw when we made love? Was he the one you longed to pleasure that night I heard you whispering to the shadows in your room?"

He was so close, so masculine, and Shianne was all too aware of him. Wade did impossible things to her self-control. She detested her weakness for him, but his forceful touch set off a chain reaction that affected every part of her being. No, it wasn't Maman-ti she wanted, but she couldn't tell Wade that. It would destroy her pride and feed his arrogance.

A saucy smile tripped across her lips. "I never thought you to be the sensitive type, my dear guardian," she purred in sticky sarcasm. "I knew you came to my room, wanting a woman, knowing any woman would do. You came to satisfy your curiosity and your lust. Why does it disturb you that I might have eyes for another man or that I might have been searching for the same things that brought you to my bedchamber?"

Confound it, why did this firebrand upset him so, Wade asked himself. He had wandered about, taking his pleasures from scores of women. He knew nothing of jealousy . . . until now. By damned he was jealous, he realized. Shianne stirred emotions in him he had never experienced. He had dedicated himself to ensuring that her first taste of passion was pure and sweet, and in his tenderness, he had sacrificed a part of himself.

With determined effort, Wade regained control of his temper. His grasp eased on her arm, and a token smile returned to his lips. Gently, he reached beneath her chin, tipping her exquisite face to his, demanding her undivided attention.

"I never thought to ask your father how you came by your name. Is it a namesake of sorts? Do you have some tie to the Cheyenne Indians, one that makes you an ally to *all* Indians?"

Shianne thoughtfully chewed on her bottom lip, wondering whether to confess the truth to Wade. Perhaps if Wade knew of her relationship with Maman-ti he would consider relocating.

Suddenly the smell of burning meat overcame the musky scent that had fogged her senses. Shianne glanced back to see the charred rabbit above the fire. Following her gaze, Wade hurried over to snatch his supper from the flames. An apologetic smile crept to one corner of his mouth.

"I would have invited you to join me, but I doubt you would be interested in cremated rabbit."

Shianne grabbed a fork and carefully peeled away the outer layers. "I think we can salvage a few nibbles, at least enough to curb the hunger pangs."

For several minutes they worked in companionable silence. When Shianne had cut up bite-sized pieces, she offered one to Wade. He munched on the meat and then nodded approvingly.

"I've tasted far better, but this will suffice." He lifted a slice of rabbit to Shianne's lips. She was prepared to accept the morsel, but Wade's mouth rolled over hers. "Another substitute for what you truly wanted, I suppose," he whispered, his jewel-like eyes probing the fathomless pools of ebony.

"You are very persistent," Shianne giggled as she retrieved a leg of rabbit and chewed upon it. "I . . ."

Shianne found herself pressed to her back. Wade's muscular body moved intimately against hers, his hands wandering at will.

"A bashful man never gets what he wants," he assured her huskily, his voice like rich velvet. He focused on the seductive curve of her lips. "What I want is to skip the main course and nibble on dessert."

Without waiting for Shianne to accept or reject his request, his lips slanted across hers, devouring her, making her heart skip several vital beats. His lean body half covered hers. The sinewed columns of his thigh gently guided her legs apart, letting her feel the bold urgency of his desires. Shianne protested his advances for all of a half second. But her resistance tumbled down when Wade molded himself against her feminine contours.

Wade dragged his lips away and drew in a ragged

breath. He wanted to satisfy his cravings for this doe-eyed enchantress, and yet he wanted to know what mysterious spell the Indian held over her.

"Tell me about him, Shae," he beseeched as he trailed a lean finger over her kiss-swollen mouth.

The kiss worked like a truth serum. The confession flowed from her lips before she could bite back the words. "He is called the Owl Prophet by both the Comanche and Kiowa. His name is Maman-ti—He-Who-Touches-the-Sky. Maman-ti is the highly respected medicine man of all Indians, a great mentor who has been blessed with the gift of prophesy. The war chiefs come to him to council, to learn the outcome of their battles and raids before they engage in them."

When Wade cast her a skeptical glance, Shianne grinned smugly. "You can discredit his powers if you wish, but I have attended his councils and listened to him speak from a trance. Once I heard him order a party of braves to stand watch at a certain point along the Butterfield Trail in Texas. He predicted that two wagon trains of whites would pass a few hours apart. The first would be a small congregation that would be easy to overcome. He cautioned the war chiefs to allow this group to pass unscathed. The second would be a much larger party. The Owl Prophet prophesied that the Indian losses would be small, but that many of the enemy would perish. He assured the chiefs there would be much plunder and many supplies to save the hungry tribes."

The expression on Wade's craggy features still held a hint of cynicism. Shianne reached up to smooth away his frown. "Maman-ti led the raid himself. The impatient braves begged to attack the first convoy of whites that approached, but the Owl Prophet forbade an attack. Three hours later a train of ten wagons rumbled down the Butterfield Trail. The whites were captured, and forty-one mules and several loads of needed supplies were confiscated.

"When I later learned about the raid, I discovered that the first wagons were headed by General William T. Sherman. He and his escort had been sent by the government to investigate the Indian atrocities. If Sherman had been slain a full scale war would have been launched against the tribes. Perhaps you find it difficult to believe that Maman-ti has such supernatural powers, but one cannot doubt fact. That is only one of the many predictions I have heard, and *all* of them have come to pass," she informed him.

Wade remained silent for several minutes, seemingly preoccupied with combing his fingers through the glorious raven strands that spilled across the grass. "You greatly admire this savage, don't you, Shianne, even when it is your neighbors who suffer from the Owl Prophet's raids."

Shianne nodded slightly. "Maman-ti makes an ominous figure when he ventures into battle. He strips to the waist and paints his dark skin white. Blue owls are etched on his chest and back. Even his warhorse is painted and decorated with signs of the feathered oracle."

"Has your admiration turned to love?" He hated to ask but he had to know.

Her eyes strayed, seemingly distracted by the flickering flames of the fire. "The Owl Prophet is considered the master of all medicine men among the allied tribes. His bravery is unrivaled in battle and his gift of compassion is legendary among the Indians," she replied evasively.

"That is not what I asked you, princess. Is he the reason you never gave in to marrying Haden Reems? Are your feelings for the Owl Prophet the reason you have held yourself from other men these past years?"

157

Wade demanded to know.

Shianne would not be sidetracked. She intended to make an important point, long-winded though it had become. "Maman-ti is a force to be reckoned with, Wade. When I hear the call of the owl, I go to him because he expects it of me."

"Does he desire you?" Wade questioned point-blank.

"Yes," she said with a frustrated sigh. Why couldn't he listen to her explanation without inserting personal questions? What did he care anyway? Wade had taken what he wanted from her, something she had offered no other man. He was as farsighted as a mole if he couldn't see that his kisses and caresses melted her into a pool of rippling passion. "But he respects me and accepts my place among the whites. I care about him and he cares about me. I cannot betray him, and that is why you must make camp elsewhere." Her dark eyes pleaded with him. "I will do as you command if you will grant the Owl Prophet space. He believes the mouth of the springs to be sacred ground, a haven where the great spirits reside."

As if on cue, a strange, haunting voice echoed in the cave, making Shianne wince uncomfortably. She had suspected that Wade was the cause of the eerie sounds she and Maman-ti had heard, but it was growing more apparent that the cavern was inhabited by some sort of creature—flesh or spirit, she didn't know for certain.

Seemingly unalarmed, Wade glanced toward the cave where the howling noises had erupted. When the sounds died into silence, he focused his full attention on Shianne's bewitching face. "And because of your affection for this gifted shaman you want me to ignore his presence and to tell no one that I have seen him," Wade said somberly, ignoring another round of howling sounds that trickled from the cavern. "You are prepared to do anything I request to keep this secret?"

"He means a great deal to me," Shianne admitted. "The Owl Prophet's visions led him to me many years ago . . . when I was a child. He knew my grandmother was the daughter of a great Cheyenne chief. The Kiowa and Comanche are allies with the Cheyenne, and Maman-ti was my strength while my father was away. Although I am caught in the middle of the conflict between the Indians and whites, I could never betray the Owl Prophet. His friendship is priceless, even if you cannot understand how I could be drawn to a renegade savage."

Her gaze drifted toward the pitch-black tunnel that was spewing with eerie sounds and then turned questioningly to the sober-faced cowboy. "What do you suppose causes those nerve-tingling noises?"

His shoulder lifted in a careless shrug. "How do I know what ghost haunts the cavern?" he lied without batting an eye. "If the sound discourages unwelcomed visitors, I have no complaints." Wade flung her an accusing glance. "And quit changing the subject. Are you prepared to obey my demands without complaint in exchange for my silence in this matter?"

Damn, she should have known this wily rascal would attempt to blackmail her. Confessing the truth had only offered him another weapon to use against her.

A condescending frown set upon her brow. "You are a scoundrel, Wade Burdett," she muttered acrimoniously.

A roguish grin lifted the corners of his mouth. "I have been called worse, but I want the same privileges you grant the Owl Prophet," he demanded. "I want you to come when I call, and I expect no resistance when I make requests."

Shianne was entertaining several spiteful thoughts, not the least of which was siccing Maman-ti and his braves on this pesky cowboy.

"You know what I want, don't you, princess?" he murmured suggestively.

"I should have the Owl Prophet lift your scalp and make it my prize," she hissed, attempting to push him away.

Wade braced his arms on either side of her, his dark face looming only inches from hers. "But you value your precious Indian, and you know I would ensure that all San Antonio knows of his presence if he were to bring about my demise."

Shianne knew all too well. She had seen Wade wrap Haden Reems around his finger, making the arrogant rancher dance like a puppet on a string. Wade was an opportunist, a calculating machine who contemplated every situation and twisted it to his advantage. When Wade hobbled Haden, she admired his ingenuity, but now the boot was on *her* foot, and she felt the pinch.

"One day I will devise a way to make your crafty scheme recoil on top of you," she vowed determinedly. "Then you will know how it feels to be backed against the wall. I only hope it squashes your arrogance flat!"

The vengeful glitter in her eyes evoked a skirl of deep laughter. Damn, but Shianne was a spitfire. She may give out occasionally, but she never gave up. Wade didn't doubt for a minute that this feisty beauty could give what she got, but he was willing to take the risk if it meant having her in his arms, enjoying a passion that excelled any encounter from his past.

"Spite me if you wish, my dear ward, but the bargain is struck. You will be allowed to protect your cherished secret, and I will reap the rewards for my silence in this matter."

A tight smile thinned her lips, and Wade swore they would snap from the fierce pressure. "I have yet to inquire about your ancestry, my dear guardian. Were you by chance raised by a nest of vipers in the Louisiana swamps?"

"It was a gator-infested bayou," he corrected with an ornery chuckle.

"I wonder why that doesn't surprise me?" Shianne smirked sarcastically. Catching Wade off guard, she gave him a forceful shove, sending him sprawling beside the fire. Scrambling to her feet, she snatched up the charred rabbit and hurled it at him. "Here, chew on this, Gator Burdett. I do not relish being gobbled up as your next meal."

As she stomped toward her horse, his goading laughter nipped her heels. "Tonight . . . when the hacienda is quiet . . . you will join me by the creek—the place where we first met. Don't disappoint me, vixen. After all, the magnificent Owl Prophet's future—or lack of it—hangs in the balance. . . ."

Shianne wheeled around. The glower she gave Wade would have burned a normal man to a crisp, but Wade's beaming smile deflected the sparks that flew from her eyes. "You'll regret this," she hissed venomously.

"I doubt it," he chuckled and then munched on his meal. "Oh, by the way, if you decide to do more snooping, don't veer off to the left." His offhanded warning drew Shianne's dubious frown. "Take any other direction in your search for my supposed treasure, but shy away from the narrow, winding tunnel. You might get yourself in trouble. The hideous monster of the cavern just might *gobble* you up." His taunting gaze sketched her well-sculptured figure. "And I would be greatly distressed if you were to miss one of our evening rituals of passion."

"I swear I will find a way to retaliate," Shianne sneered at him. "I will not become the object of your lusty desires!"

161

Wade lounged on the ground, propped on one elbow, an ornery grin dangling off the corner of his mouth. "Odd, sweetheart. I thought I was the subject of your experimentation. You wanted the Owl Prophet and you settled for me instead." His mouth had a derisive slant to it. "Ironic, isn't it, Shae? I want you because you excite me, but in your eyes, I will never have any appeal unless my skin turns red and I take up residence in a tepee."

Damn that man! He was giving her fits! Shianne was seeing shades of furious red as she shoved bushes out of her way to reach her steed. How dare he bribe her like that! In the first place, he didn't know what the hell he was talking about and in the second . . . Shianne let her breath out in a rush. What purpose would it serve to rehash the conversation; it would only frustrate her all the more. By damned, she was *not* going to steal off into the night to meet Wade just because he demanded it. If he followed through with his vicious threat of exposing Maman-ti, she would stake him out, just as Haden did. Wade could lie there and rot for all she cared!

She should have known better than to appeal to Wade's sense of decency. He didn't have one! She had confided in him, hoping for compassion, and what had she received in return? Blackmail! Wade wanted to use her as his plaything, his convenient strumpet. Wait until her father learned the truth about his partner, she fumed. Blake would tear Wade to pieces and serve him to the bobcats that roamed the prairie. That is, if there was anything left of that sidewinder when she finished with him, she thought vindictively.

Chapter 8

The moment Wade strode into the hacienda, Shianne knew something was amiss. There was no smile hovering on his lips, no attractive crinkles fanning from the corners of his emerald eyes. His jaw was clenched, and his features looked as if they were carved from stone.

Shianne had been furious with him the previous night, and while she anticipated that he would be annoyed with her for refusing to keep their tryst, she had not expected him to be so completely bent out of shape. Lord, Wade looked like black thunder. She had never seen him quite so angry.

Wade did not voice a greeting. He merely stormed across the room, handcuffed Shianne's arm and dragged her toward the door. "You are coming with me," he barked sharply.

"What devil is hounding you this morning?" she muttered, attempting to worm her way from his bone-crushing grasp.

"A she-devil with wicked black eyes," Wade snapped back at her. "I expected you to be angry with me after the demands I made last night, but I didn't anticipate such viciousness. You seem to have forgotten that, by defying me, you are cutting Blake's throat as well as your own."

The man was a lunatic, Shianne quickly concluded. It would be useless to argue with him in his present state. Resigning herself to the fact that she could follow peaceably or be dragged in his wake, Shianne hastened her step.

As if she were light as a feather, Wade scooped Shianne off the ground and stuffed her in the saddle. Without offering an explanation, he stepped into the stirrup and reined Galahad toward the west. After they had galloped in silence for several minutes, Wade slowed his laboring steed to a trot. Within a quarter of an hour they reached the hill overlooking the location of Wade's cattle pens. He gestured a long arm toward the upended poles that had been planted in the ground to hold the cattle he had spent weeks gathering.

"It will cost me a helluva lot of time, energy and manpower to reconstruct what once was a solid pen around hundreds of longhorns," he ground out between clenched teeth. "What did you do? Race off to summon your Indian cousins to take the plunder and destroy the stockade?"

Shianne's mouth fell open as she stared at the broken timbers that were strewn about the pasture. "This was not my doing."

Wade scoffed bitterly. "Don't lie to me, Shianne. The night watchmen informed me that Indians wearing war paint swooped down to frighten the cattle. No one could stop the stampede. The longhorns were charging through the barricades, practically killing each other to escape the thundering horses and wild screams of the raiding party."

Tugging on Delgado's reins, Wade led Shianne down the hill to the congregation of men who were attempting to gather the timber and begin again. But this time, Wade intended to move the sight of the pens to *his* acreages.

After issuing orders to load the timbers in wagons and begin construction near the creek, Wade turned back to his silent companion. A threatening smile caught his lips when he focused his annoyed gaze on Shianne.

"And don't warn me away from relocating the stock pens on my land," he ordered harshly. "I control the area where the spring forks to nourish your pastures as well as your splindly-legged neighbor. The cattle will drink to their heart's content."

Shianne met his smoldering gaze with an unblinking stare. "You are asking for trouble, Wade. I told you Maman-ti believes the springs to be sacred ground. If you flaunt your herd of cattle under his nose, he might be tempted to take what his people need and your work will be in vain."

"*Our* herd," Wade corrected, a distinctly unpleasant edge on his voice. "Half of these cattle carry your brand, and every obstacle you throw in my face poses a threat to you and your father. If you sic your renegade Indian on the longhorns again there *will* be a full scale war between the Comanches and whites." His green eyes narrowed and there was no mistaking the anger in his stony features. "If the Indians and whites do battle, you will be caught in the middle, Shianne. I'll make damned certain every man in the county knows you have been harboring that hostile war chief."

Shianne clutched the reins until her knuckles turned white. Oh, how she itched to claw out those smoldering green eyes of his. She responded to his threat with one of her own. "If you put the Owl Prophet's life in jeopardy I will spite you every chance I get. The blood that flows through Maman-ti's veins is *mine*. I will not stand by and allow you to write his death warrant."

165

"But you would not bat an eye at having his arrow in *my* back," Wade scowled bitterly. "Why don't you marry the medicine man and take refuge in his village? Then both of you would be content, and I could do the job I was sent here to do!"

"He already has two wives, and I refuse to be the third," she hurled at him. "And if you believe it was Maman-ti who raided cattle on *my* land you are a bigger fool than I gave you credit for being." Flashing brown eyes raked him with scornful mockery. "The Indian is blamed for all misfortune in the area, but if you were not a foreigner to Texas, you would know that it has long been the ploy of outlaws to apply mud and war paint to their faces and bodies. More than one fallen warrior has been found to be white. There are numerous renegades who loot and steal and allow the blame to fall on the Indians. As a matter of fact, it was the white man who invented scalping, not the Indian." She told him coldly. "You are like all the other ranchers who have met with misfortune. You are quick to blame the Indian for your troubles. There are times when I am ashamed of my white heritage. I do not wish to be lumped into the same category with a narrow-minded idiot who makes loud accusations without evidence."

Shianne glanced purposefully about her. Suddenly she hopped from the saddle and stormed over to retrieve the arrow that lay in the dirt. When she had walked back to the man who sat fuming on his bay stallion, she lifted the shaft of the arrow and shook it in Wade's face. "Take a close look." She indicated the steel tip and then directed his attention to the feathers at the opposite end of the arrow. "This is neither Comanche nor Kiowa, and believe me, I have seen my share of them. This is a white man's attempt to copy a technique the Indian has spent centuries perfecting."

All the fire went out of Wade's eyes. Damn, he had

jumped to the wrong conclusion. But he was so certain Shianne had meant to defy him after the demands he had made on her last night. He should have known she would never thrust her precious medicine man into a situation that might bring him disaster.

Slowly, Wade leaned out to retrieve the arrow, thoughtfully turning it in his hand. "I'm sorry, Shae. I retract every biting remark I made." The faintest hint of a smile touched his sensuous mouth. "Am I forgiven for charging off, half-cocked?"

Shianne was not to be softened by his charismatic charm. Wade had treated her abominably, flinging accusations and threats he had no right to make. *"I'm sorry,* even when it is uttered with a smile doesn't right the injustice," she assured him tartly. "And relocating your cattle pens where the spring forks to feed the creeks is asking for trouble. As long as the longhorns remain here you will be granted amnesty, but that portion of the ranch where the cave is located will never belong to any white man. The Owl Prophet considers it the stomping ground of ancient spirits and nothing will convince him otherwise. Even if *I* were to erect pens on that spot, Maman-ti would be angry with me." Her somber gaze held him captive. "Don't defy him, Wade. He is a force to be reckoned with, a warrior who does not know the meaning of defeat."

Dammit, there she went again, praising that Indian as if he were a saint. If Shianne felt even a smidgen of the respect for *him* that she felt for Maman-ti, theirs would not be such a stormy relationship, Wade predicted. Blast it, why was it suddenly so important that he earn this she-cat's respect, her undying admiration? Wade didn't have the time to analyze his emotions, as much as he would have preferred to sit himself down and delve into the reasons for the emotions that were playing havoc with his thoughts.

There was work to be done.

Reversing his decision, he ordered the vaqueros to construct the corrals in the same place, granting Shianne's request to keep the springs sacred to the Indians. When he glanced back at Shianne she was wearing an expression that made his skin crawl.

"Don't look so smug," he grumbled crabbily.

"Why shouldn't I? There is a certain sense of accomplishment that comes in winning a skirmish against a tyrant," she chortled as she pulled herself onto Delgado's back. "You and I have been at cross-purposes since you marched into my study to claim your throne. If you would stop to realize that I am a Texas native and that I have an ounce of common sense, we might even come to be friends."

"The kind of friendship you have with the Owl Prophet?" Wade questioned, cursing himself for allowing his tongue to translate the thought that constantly pricked his male pride.

"Must I remind you that I have known Maman-ti since I was a child? I have known you for a few weeks," Shianne said breezily. "Friendship is not given away, it is earned. Thus far, you have merely taken, offering nothing in return. Maman-ti respects me for the person I am. He regards me in high-esteem and considers my feelings. If he knew you had used me to satisfy your lust, you and whatever it is that you have stashed in the cave would not last the day."

Maman-ti this, Maman-ti that, Wade thought resentfully. If he heard that blasted Indian's name again today, he would scream! If he let his hair grow to his shoulders and painted hoot owls on his chest, he would have a better chance of winning this minx's admiration. She was in love with a man she couldn't have, erecting monuments to a renegade savage she was silently praying would whisk her away and make

168

her his *only* squaw. Damn, if Blake knew his daughter had fallen in love with a medicine man, he would be hopping up and down with irritation.

"Look yonder," Shianne murmured, gesturing a slim finger toward the rolling prairie. "My guess is that your marauding band of Indians who destroyed several weeks of hard work are located due west of here. The war chief of these particular savages wasn't Maman-ti. This looks to be one of Haden's scare tactics," she speculated. "You may have dissuaded Haden from killing you, but that won't stop him from devising ways to harass you." A challenging smile bordered her lips. "I'm so confident of my speculations that I am willing to bet our late night rendezvous that Haden was behind this Indian uprising. I doubt the warriors were Indians at all, but rather Mexican bravoes—hired guns who were garbed in buckskin and covered with war paint. Think about it, Wade. Haven't you given Haden good reason to undermine your business venture with my father? The man clings fiercely to what he believes is his, and he considers every maverick in Texas to be one of his missing stock. Haden is not accustomed to defeat, and I have no doubt that he will resort to extreme measures to ensure that you think twice before you challenge him again. The sooner you realize that, the easier it will be for you to deal with him."

As Shianne turned Delgado toward the hacienda, Wade continued to stare to the west, contemplating her words. So Haden Reems intended to play rough, did he? Well, two could participate in that game, Wade reminded himself. He would spend his spare time devising a plan to cut Haden's storklike legs out from under him.

Chewing on that thought, Wade urged his steed toward the group of cow hands who were reassembling the corrals. To his surprise Shianne reappeared on the hill forty-five minutes later, dressed as he had seen her that first day. A lariat dangled from her saddle horn, and her hands were encased in work gloves. A long braid hung over her left shoulder, and a dark felt hat set atop of her head. Her curvaceous body was draped in breeches and a shirt, but the cut and style of the garments could not disguise her shapely feminine contours. She was gorgeous no matter what she was or wasn't wearing, Wade mused as his eyes worked their way from the tip of her hat to the toes of her boots.

"Don't look so surprised, *amigo*," Carlos Santos snickered. "The señorita rarely misses a roundup. Since the day her *padre* rode off to war, she has been roping and riding beside us. I have seen to it that she is as efficient as any man."

Wade didn't doubt that for a minute. He was beginning to think he had failed to give full credit where credit was due. Shianne Kimball was no ordinary woman. She knew Texas and the various types of people who inhabited it, she could perform the gift of healing as well as Doc Winston and she was astute enough to point out the real culprit of the stampede. Admirable as those qualities were, Wade saw something else in Shianne, something that created a hunger in him. He viewed her as a passionate, desirable woman, and it ripped his pride to shreds to think she had fallen in love with that Indian medicine man.

He turned envy green each time that thought darted across his mind. Wade prided himself in being good-natured and tolerant of others, but damned if he could imagine giving this enchanting witch up to a savage who sketched owl effigies on his chest!

Carlos misread the annoyed expression that was stamped on Wade's rugged features as disapproval of Shianne's interference. "A . . . señor, it would not be

170

wise to send the lady back to the hacienda," he warned. "She has come to work, and if you deny her, you will see that beneath her beauty lies a very fiery temper."

Wade was well aware of Shianne's temperament. Although he didn't dare turn her away, he made a mental note to keep a watchful eye on her. The last thing he wanted was for her to be injured, attempting to herd skittish longhorns into pens.

Anticipating an argument, Shianne raised a rebellious chin and rode toward the swarthy cowboy who was regarding her with his veiled gaze. The look that etched her exquisite features challenged him, but Wade voiced no protest.

"No complaint?" she queried, staring down her nose at him.

"I have been forewarned," Wade responded casually. Agilely, he swung into the saddle. "When we locate a maverick do you wish to head or heel?"

"I prefer to head," she told him ever so politely. "I only pray that you will be able to hold up your end. I would be displeased to have Delgado gored by an angry longhorn because you failed to rope both hind legs and render the animal defenseless."

Wade's grin dripped with sticky sweetness. "I know my abilities are probably meager compared to yours, my lovely ward. However, I will make a sincere effort to accomplish my task *if* you manage to toss your lariat around a calf's wide-spreading horns and slow him to a gallop."

"I am anxious to see which of us needs to polish his or her technique in heading and heeling," Shianne smirked as she touched her spurs to Delgado's flanks. "But I must remind you that I cannot spend the entire day and night on the range. My guardian has commanded that I meet him tonight and every night that he is overcome by lust." She flung him a pointed

171

glance. "I cannot disobey the tyrant for fear he will blackmail me and make trouble for one of my oldest and dearest friends."

"You need not fret over your appointment," Wade told her. As usual, his true emotions were masked behind a smile. "I will not expect you to be there tonight or any other night . . . unless you want to be."

Her jaw sagged on its hinges. Had Wade suddenly lost interest in her? Damn, she had hoped to make him jealous by throwing the Owl Prophet in his face. Obviously, Wade had decided to turn elsewhere to appease his lusts. He was no longer doing the chasing.

Shianne should have been relieved, but she was disappointed. Although she had protested Wade's underhanded tactics, she could find no fault with the man himself. He aroused her, and even while her head was screaming "no" her heart was whispering "yes." The fact that Wade demanded that she succumb to his passions eased her stinging pride, but now he had taken that protective device away from her. She was left wanting him, even when she knew he was the wrong man for her. He had stripped her of any excuse for going to him. If she yielded to the temptation, she had only her feminine yearnings to blame.

Silly fool, Shianne chastised herself as they rode together in silence. She knew a man like Wade Burdett would soon tire of one woman and seek out another. She knew that from the very beginning. Wade had made it clear that he wasn't interested in lasting involvements and that he took pleasure where he found it. Yet it hurt to realize that he had quickly grown bored with her inexperience and her blunt questions. Shianne blushed, remembering how she had fired personal inquiries at him while they lay abed. Lord, what had come over her? She had freely described her experience, and Wade had laughed at her naivete.

172

Her wandering thoughts scattered when a movement in the brush caught her attention. Delgado tensed beneath her, knowing what was expected of him. Shianne grasped the lariat, mentally preparing herself for the confrontation with the maverick. She had been taught to be cautious of the wild cattle that roamed the brush country, and she took care to pay close attention to what she was doing.

When the calf sensed danger and charged away, Shianne whirled the loop of her rope above her head and edged up beside the fleeing animal. With practiced hands she flung the lariat, allowing the noose to settle on his neck. When she took the lead, forcing the calf to follow or risk having his neck stretched out like a giraffe, Wade closed in from behind. With a flick of his wrist he laid the loop beneath the calf's hooves and jerked back to snare both hind legs.

Bellowing in surprise, the calf collapsed to his knees, his back legs stretched out behind him. Shianne snubbed the end of the rope on the pommel of the saddle and bounded to the ground. At the same moment, Delgado stopped short, practically sitting down in an effort to keep the rope taut between the saddle horn and the calf's neck. Before Shianne could tie the longhorn's legs together, Wade sank down on the animal's hip to shackle all four hooves in a knot that would prevent the calf from climbing to his feet and wandering away. When Wade completed the task he reached up to lift the loop from the maverick's neck and handed the lariat to Shianne.

"My compliments," he murmured, studying her with an approving smile. "You are very adept with a rope, and Delgado has been well trained to perform his task of steadying the calf."

"I must admit I am impressed with your abilities," Shianne commented as she unhooked the rope from her stallion's saddle horn. "How did you come to be such an expert with cattle? I would not have thought you could have gained such experience in the Louisiana swamps. Does one rope and hobble alligators?"

Wade settled himself on Galahad's back. His keen gaze circled the underbrush to locate another unbranded maverick. "Your father taught me the tricks of the trade," he confessed, his attention focused on a movement in the bushes. "Before that I spent most of my time managing a sugar and cotton plantation."

Shianne followed his gaze and eased her steed toward the thicket. "Then why have you turned to gathering cattle in Texas? Surely your plantation cannot run by itself."

"I no longer have a plantation," Wade informed her, his voice quiet for fear of startling the calf. "My father was a member of Jefferson Davis's cabinet. Many of those who worked for the president of the confederacy were condemned and ostracized for their part in the rebellion. Their holdings were confiscated and their valuables destroyed. Our mansion was set ablaze and our crops were stolen. The land was then divided by the Freedman Bureau and doled out to homeless black citizens. My family was left with nothing but a memory of what once was and would never be again."

Shianne slumped in her saddle, wondering how difficult it would be to watch others take what had belonged to her family, to see her home go up in flames. Wade had every right to be bitter, to resent the world and everyone in it. Yet, he did not appear to hold a grudge. He had lost his fortune and his land holdings, and he seemed determined to acquire a new fortune.

"What became of your father?" Shianne questioned.

"When the South crumbled, Jefferson Davis and his advisors fled from Richmond. Davis was apprehended, manacled in chains and led off to prison. His cabinet members ran for their lives. Some managed to escape to England, others to the West Indies, and some even took refuge in Texas. To this day, Davis is still waiting to be released, and his cabinet members cannot show their faces until they have been granted pardon. My father . . ." His voice trailed off when a monstrous bull bounded from the underbrush, deciding to attack rather than to retreat.

Shianne came to full attention, her body taut with apprehension. She was well aware that a *cimarrone* bull, in one of his ferocious moods, was the meanest creature on four legs. The longer the animal lived, the more imposing he became. The *cimarrones* had run wild for years, giving them a toughness and vitality that was unequalled. They had withstood droughts and blizzards. They had survived the attacks of insects, wolves and often escaped the Comanches' arrows. They were known to walk as far as fifteen miles to a waterhole and could make one drink last one or two days if need be.

While a *cimarrone* bull was in an ordinary frame of mind, he merely threatened to trample anything that came near him; but when the creature was disturbed, his temper became ungovernable, and he made the most dangerous predator. Even a grizzly bear seemed a purring kitten compared to a *cimarrone* bull. He was stronger than a horse and could run like the wind, using his horns to slash holes in anything that got in his way.

When the bull charged from the thicket, Shianne wondered if she weren't staring death in the face. Savage eyes bored into her as the bull lowered his head and lunged toward his target. His horns were at least six feet from tip to tip, and Shianne shivered at the thought of being gored by this bloodthirsty animal.

As the bull thundered toward Delgado, the steed

bolted in fright. His shrill whinny pierced the air, his eyes wild with fear. Shianne yanked on the reins, forcing Delgado to leap sideways before he was gouged by those foreboding horns. There was no time to fling her rope, only time to pray.

In less than a heartbeat Wade sprung into action. Wade's loop snagged the vicious beast around the neck before he could launch a second attack against Delgado. Infuriated by the feel of the rope against his throat, the bull wheeled about to charge at Wade. Shianne hurled her lariat, catching the beast's hind legs the split second before he slammed into Galahad's broadside. Delgado instinctively pulled back, making the rope taut. The *cimarrone* bellowed in fury when his legs were yanked out from under him. The bull did not take kindly to heading and heeling. He fought with every ounce of strength to regain his legs, and it took several minutes and extra ropes to keep the monstrous creature on the ground. Finally, the bull realized escape was futile, and he slumped in the grass, bellowing for all he was worth.

When the danger had passed, Wade heaved a relieved sigh. For a long tense moment he swore he was about to watch Shianne be cut to bloody shreds. Although her expertise matched his, it didn't make it any easier to endure the ordeal. That two thousand pound bull that stood five and a half feet tall had every intention of making mincemeat of Shianne, and he very nearly accomplished his purpose. Even after several minutes had passed and Wade knew Shianne was still in one piece, he was still quaking with aftershocks.

"Lord, that was close. I hope I don't have to live through that experience again," Wade murmured. He leaned his arm on Shianne's thigh while she sat atop her steed, attempting to settle her frayed nerves. "For a minute there, I thought I had lost you. If we didn't work so well together, we wouldn't have escaped unscathed. I was there when you needed me and you were there when I needed you. I wonder if it will always be that way . . . no matter what the situation. . . ."

The intimacy in his voice and the feel of his hand gliding familiarly over her leg sent goose bumps stampeding across her flesh. Although Wade smelled of leather, horse and perspiration, he still had the power to rattle her composure, especially when she had yet to recover from her near brush with disaster. She had but to look into those vivid green eyes, and she remembered how it had been between them, how he had kissed and caressed her into wild abandon.

Afraid to speak for fear of alerting him to the unsettling effect he had on her, Shianne reined her steed around to locate yet another maverick. As she walked Delgado away, Wade let out his breath in a rush. He had hoped the wall of indifference around her heart would begin to erode, but Shianne was too proud and stubborn to see that they could be more than antagonists.

Confound it, that remarkable little wildcat was tearing holes in his philosophy that all women could be wooed and tamed. Wade was beginning to think there was at least one exception to the rule. Shianne was as wild and free as the noble savage she revered. If she could not be Maman-ti's woman, she must have decided to emulate him, Wade speculated. He might as well try to lasso the clouds, Wade thought defeatedly. He could never earn Shianne's respect, not if he had one week or one year.

Why had that become so damned important all of a sudden, Wade interrogated himself. When he came to Texas he was inventing ways to avoid the witch of the K Bar Ranch. He had even delayed his arrival, dreading their meeting. Now he was like a puppy trailing along behind Shianne, hoping for scant drippings of affection, crumbs of respect.

Damn, this witch had somehow managed to burrow her way into his heart and trigger dozens of emotions that had never disturbed him until he stared into her dark, bewitching eyes. He had a dozen tasks to attend, and all he could think about was how she felt when she lay in his arms.

"Are you coming?" Shianne called over her shoulder. "Or must I head and heel this maverick by myself?"

Grumbling, Wade swung into the saddle and followed in her wake. By the time the vaqueros had reassembled the stock pens and come to offer assistance, Wade and Shianne had hobbled a dozen calves and left them strewn across the prairie. When Wade decided they had gathered enough cattle to drive into the pens and brand before nightfall, they retraced their steps to untie the calves.

After the mavericks had spent the entire morning tied in knots they offered no complaint about being herded to the pens. They had spent several hours on their sides and it took time to adjust to having their legs beneath them. The restraining ropes had cut off circulation, making their movements sluggish. It was a technique used during roundups to ensure there would be no stampede or charging mavericks. The tactic served its purpose. The vaqueros were able to move the herd toward headquarters without difficulty.

Heaving a weary sigh, Shianne slid from the saddle to survey the cattle that were being branded. Her admiring gaze settled on the tall, lean cowboy whose lithe movements reminded her of a powerful panther.

Wade moved boldly among the skittish cattle, quietly giving orders and performing his share of the work. The vaqueros respected him and his decisions.

She had not heard one complaint since the misplaced plantation owner came to rule the roost. The hired hands had accepted Wade as one of them, and he was steadily burrowing his way into Shianne's life.

Deciding it best not to dwell on Wade's redeeming qualities for fear of becoming overly enamored with him, Shianne ambled over to concentrate on the task of branding. Unfortunately, she was not paying close attention. As she leaned against the timbers that had been placed upright in the ground, the hind hoof of a nearby calf shot through the open space to collide with her hip.

Shianne jerked back, a pained groan erupting from her lips. The fierce kick jolted her entire body. Nausea washed over her like a tidal wave, threatening to buckle her knees. Shianne hadn't meant to whimper but the pain was almost intolerable.

In an instant Wade was beside her, clutching her swaying body to his solid frame. "Are you alright?" he questioned softly.

Shianne nodded mutely, her eyes swimming with tears. She wasn't going to cry, she promised herself. Her hip hurt like hell, burned like fire, but she wasn't going to decompose, not in front of Wade. He had already seen her in a state of panic early that morning. The last thing she wanted was for Wade to see that she was vulnerable. If he thought she was capable of weakness—any weakness—it might be detrimental to her dealings with him. To her, Wade appeared invincible, and Shianne had every intention of matching him, stride for stride, even if it killed her.

His hand slid over her hip to feel the gigantic knot. Wade swore under his breath. "Dammit, you aren't all right," he scowled accusingly.

Lifting her into his arms, he carried her back to Delgado. Swinging behind her in the saddle, Wade directed the steed toward the hill, pulling the bay behind him. When they were a safe distance away from the corral he pulled Shianne down with him.

"Take off your breeches," he barked sharply.

Shianne stared at him, dazed from the blow to her side, stunned by his command. Since she made no move to obey him, Wade assumed the task. As the wool breeches eased over her hip, he cursed in disgust. A knot the size of a hoof swelled on her upper thigh.

When Shianne finally came to her senses, she blushed profusely and tugged the breeches back in place. "I'll thank you not to strip my clothes from me!" she hissed at him. "I have been bruised before, and I doubt this will be the last. I do not expect you to hover over me like a mother hen when I meet with trouble. If I want someone to inspect my injuries, I will call upon Doc Winston!"

"You are not going to call upon anyone," Wade told her curtly. "I want you to ride back to the hacienda and stay put." He shook a long finger in her face. "And I expect you to *walk* that high-spirited stallion. Don't go charging off like a bat out of hell. You could have a blood clot after suffering such a hard blow. The last thing we need is for a clot to break loose and start floating around. There is no telling where it might end up."

"I had not realized you were a practicing physician," she sniped as she fastened her belt.

"I patched up my share of men during the war," he assured her hotly, "and I have enough sense to know that if you aggravate an injury you will only make it worse. Confine yourself to the bedroom and stay off that leg!"

When he had planted Shianne in the saddle and mounted his horse, he stared her straight in the eye. "If you don't obey me, I'll turn you over my knee and give you the thrashing Blake cannot offer in his absence. Not only will you be unable to lie on your left side, but you won't be able to sit down either!"

"You wouldn't dare," Shianne sneered at him.

"Don't challenge me. I thrive on dares," he snorted. "I warn you, Shae. If you spur that horse, I'll tie his legs in knots. Delgado won't be able to crawl to the barn, much less gallop there!"

Her temper boiled over. She was not accustomed to taking orders, and it galled her to hear them spouting from Wade's lips. "You are making it easy to detest you," Shianne hissed venomously. "I told you I will not tolerate tyranny. I have been my own boss far too long to have some meddling cowboy prance in and dictate to me."

Wade was worried sick, and Shianne had her heart set on defying him, even when he was concerned about her welfare. Damn, that little spitfire. She kept him in a tailspin! Wade finally gained control of his temper, and his infuriating smile returned. "I make the laws, sweetheart, and you will obey them. You may not appreciate them, but you *will* do what I tell you or face the consequences. . . ."

How that man could smile when they were in the middle of a trenchant argument was beyond her. Shianne swore Wade grinned only to annoy her. He took wicked delight in exerting his power over her. Dammit, why had her father sent the devil's advocate to ride herd over her?

Flinging her nose in the air, Shianne aimed Delgado toward headquarters. Damn that man. He played havoc with every emotion she possessed. How could she be attracted to a man who constantly badgered her? She must be a glutton for punishment, she reckoned.

Bedridden indeed! It would be a cold day in hell before she locked herself in her room because Wade Burdett commanded it!

If the rigidness in Shianne's back was any indication of the anger within, Wade speculated that she was burning on a hot blue flame. She had scared ten years off his life when she confronted that ferocious bull. Wade sacrificed another decade when she suffered that devastating blow to her hip. My God, if that calf's hoof would have connected with her vital organs, she could have hemorrhaged. She had no business propping herself against the corral when it was heaping with spooked cattle. Shianne should have known better.

Heaving an exasperated sigh, Wade turned back in the direction from which he had come. By the time he stalked back to the pens, his irritation had dwindled. He promised himself he would sneak upstairs when he completed his tasks, ensuring that Shianne had gone to bed. If she rebelled, he would tie her to the bed post.

Hell's Bells, didn't he have enough pressing matters to attend without battling that mule-headed woman? They were constantly fighting over who was to wear his breeches, but Wade wasn't giving them up. After all, he would look ridiculous strutting around in her dress!

A wicked smile stretched across Haden Reems's lips. His bravoes had completed the first phase of undermining Burdett's plan to gather mavericks. Haden had always had a fetish about clearing the area of grass pirates whose purpose it was to brand beeves and form their own herds. He took this form of piracy as a personal threat.

The feat of destroying Wade's weeks of hard work left Haden with a feeling of smug satisfaction. Wade was no more than a corsair, working under the influential name of the K Bar Ranch. By the time Haden finished sabotaging that intruder, Shianne would think her appointed guardian to be a poor manager. Blake Kimball should have known Haden would make a meal of that arrogant cowboy. Haden had dedicated himself to the pursuit of building a cattle empire and making Shianne his wife. Nothing would stop him from having what he wanted. Perhaps he couldn't dispose of Burdett, but he could and *would* make his life hell, Haden promised himself.

Juan Mendez surveyed Haden's self-satisfied grin and frowned curiously. "What else do you have in mind for the *hombre?*"

Haden shrugged evasively. "It depends on Burdett's counterattack. If he does not suspect us of stampeding his cattle, we will continue with our same methods. If he dares to accuse me of wrongdoing, I will be forced to defend my good name." A sinister smile swallowed his features. "I would prefer it if the fool never figured out who raided the ranch. I am anxious to give Burdett another dose of catastrophe." His beady eyes swung to the hired gunman. "You do not seem pleased with my decision to bring Burdett to his knees. Why is that, Juan? It never mattered before . . . so long as you were well paid for your efforts."

Juan's dark features were fixed in a contemplative stare. "I have dealt with many men at your insistence, señor. I have only met a few who test my competency with a revolver and your clever game of wits." His gaze momentarily swung to Haden and then circled back to the sprawling range. "The man you killed last spring defied you until the end. He made a challenging opponent, but even he did not possess Wade Burdett's calculated self-control. I did not approve of what you

183

did then, nor do I now. This time I think you have roused a sleeping lion."

As Juan ambled toward the bunkhouse, Haden frowned disconcertedly. It was not like Juan to dispute Haden's orders or compliment his foe, but for some reason Juan respected Wade Burdett. Haden knew Juan was disturbed by the killing that took place the previous spring, but dammit, Haden had completely lost his temper with the man. The stranger spit in his face, even while he was staked to the ground, and Haden had come apart at the seams. By the time he regained control of his fiery temper, the stranger was dead and had to be disposed of.

Even if the unfortunate incident had put a strain on his relationship with Juan, the gunman would do his bidding, Haden reassured himself. Juan valued the prestige and wealth he had acquired as Haden's henchman. Yes, Juan would do exactly as he was told or he would face the consequences.

Feeling certain of himself and satisfied with his strategy to break Wade Burdett, Haden strode back to the hacienda. A satanic chuckle bubbled from his chest when he stepped into the foyer. Wade Burdett might be coming to call before too long. Haden was anxious to see if that cool, calm cowboy could control his temper after having his cattle scattered here and yonder. This time it would be Haden who sat casually by, watching Burdett work himself into a snit.

Burdett could make all the accusations he wanted, but he had no proof that it was Haden's bravoes who demolished the corrals and stampeded the mavericks. Besides, the longhorns Burdett and the vaqueros gathered from the bush country were half wild and easily spooked. It took very little to send those cattle into a panic, and it would have been impossible for anyone to recognize the marauders when they were wearing feathers and war paint.

A curious frown furrowed Haden's brow as he dropped into his chair. He knew Burdett had hired on extra men for the roundup, but Haden had yet to determine where Wade had acquired the money to meet expenses. Haden had gone directly to the bank when his men informed him that Burdett was offering to pay his hired hands greater sums than Haden extended to his bravoes. After Haden ranted and raved about allowing a "foreigner" to borrow from the bank in which he held the majority of stock, he was informed that Burdett had not even inquired about a loan.

Flustered, Haden had stalked around town, personally investigating every storekeeper who had done business with Burdett. He had discovered that Burdett had pawned expensive jewelry in return for supplies, and in some instances, Burdett had paid for his purchases with gold coins.

How could he cripple Burdett's business venture without cutting off his money supply? What was Burdett's source of wealth? Haden had asked himself those questions once a day for the past week. He knew the quickest way to put Burdett out of business was to drain the man's funds, but if Haden couldn't locate the source, he could do very little damage.

Perhaps it was time to send his men to do some checking on Burdett's campsite. The man had to have a pot of gold somewhere, Haden reasoned. The sooner he found it, the quicker he would be rid of the menace who complicated matters with Shianne.

Intending to do just that, Haden gathered his feet beneath him and strode back outside to speak with Juan. Haden needed Wade out of the way. He didn't trust Burdett with Shianne. She could tempt any man with that exquisite face and curvaceous body. The thought sent an aroused tingle floating through Haden's veins. Damn, he couldn't wait to get his hands on that gorgeous minx, and when he did, he would compensate for the years he had turned to other women to appease the craving Shianne instilled in him.

Haden scowled furiously when he recalled the day he had barged into the study to find Burdett holding Shianne captive. If that bastard dared to take privileges with Shianne, Haden swore vengeance, the deadly kind. No man would ever possess what belonged to Haden Reems. Shianne was his. Haden had made that decision long ago. Portraying the gentleman, he had waited for that enchanting maid to reach marrying age. Then along came that blasted war, spurring Shianne's feelings of strong will and independence.

Haden had expected her to turn to him for assistance, but she had not. Instead, she surrounded herself with the vaqueros who taught her to rule her family's holdings with a capable hand. One day he would have Shianne, he vowed to himself. He had not waited all these years for nothing. He had not discouraged her string of eager beaux, just to have her thrown into Wade Burdett's arms! If Shianne felt even a smidgen of fascination for that meddling cowboy, Haden would tear Burdett down in her eyes, and she would lose all respect for her guardian.

Shianne knew Haden could offer her everything she could possibly want—wealth and position. She could rule at his side, managing the most prominent ranch in all of Texas. What more could a woman want? He would see that she was waited on hand and foot. He would adorn her with expensive jewels and elaborate gowns.

By God, one day that attractive vixen would realize she was ready for Haden to lay the world at her feet, and Haden would control the one possession that had eluded him for five years: Shianne—the dark-eyed temptress whose voluptuous body could drive a man wild with desire and inflame his dreams. Haden wanted her, and nothing would deter him from seeing his fantasy become reality.

Chapter 9

Shianne was very nearly climbing the walls by the second day of her captivity. It infuriated her to be held hostage in her own bedroom. Wade had stormed the hacienda, discovered her in the study and toted her back to bed. Not only had he posted sentinels to guard the stock pens, but he had positioned hired hands outside her door. Then he had the unmitigated gall to summon Doc Winston who concurred with Wade's prescribed treatment of using her left leg as little as possible. When the conspirator, Jedediah Winston, left the house, Wade ordered Ramona to cater meals to Shianne and to keep her locked away until further notice.

Suffering from a severe case of cabin fever, Shianne swore she would escape her prison or go mad. Although her leg was still stiff and tender, she longed for fresh air and open spaces. Determined to flee, Shianne eased open the balcony door and crept into the darkness. The sentinel had ambled around the corner of the second story terrace and was staring absently at the moonlit countryside. Unobserved, Shianne made her escape.

Her heart pounded frantically against her ribs as she

plastered herself against the wall and inched toward the lattice. Her eyes remained glued to the guard's back as she eased her leg over the railing and groped to find footing on the lattice. Silently, she picked her way through the vines. When her foot touched solid ground, she breathed a relieved sigh. Remaining within the shadows and the thick canopy of trees, Shianne made her way to Delgado. She walked along beside the steed until they were a good distance from the hacienda.

When Shianne eased onto the black stallion's back and gave him his head, her heart soared with pleasure. She was free again! Like a spirit floating off into the night, Shianne sailed across the prairie, depending upon Delgado to guard his steps. Her destination was the cave. She knew Wade was standing watch over the cattle that night. He had told her himself. Now she was free to explore the cavern, certain he was hiding some sort of treasure in the dark, underground dungeons.

After giving the matter two day's deliberation, Shianne had concluded that Wade must have robbed a Union supply station during the war or held up every bank between Shreveport and San Antonio. That was why it had taken the varmint so long to arrive at the ranch to report Blake's whereabouts. Wade had turned outlaw to purchase the land and pay the expenses for this extensive cattle drive. How else could she account for Wade's mysterious funds? Thunderstorms didn't rain gold coins, nor did spring showers dump precious jewels in a man's lap. Wade was surviving on ill-gotten gains. Of that Shianne was certain, and come hell or high water, she was going to locate the secret treasure and satisfy her curiosity!

With single-minded purpose, Shianne aimed herself toward the cavern. Wade had warned her from following the tunnel that veered off to the left. There had to be a good reason why he didn't want her snooping in that direction. That must be where he had stashed his loot, she predicted.

As she neared Wade's campsite, Shianne beamed in satisfaction. The place was deserted, and she could go about her snooping without being caught. After rummaging through Wade's gear to retrieve his lantern, Shianne stepped into the cave to study the three winding passages that led into oblivion.

Clutching the lantern, Shianne plunged ahead, certain the left tunnel would lead her to Wade's carefully guarded secret. The passage took a sharp bend to the right and then meandered back to the left, completely confusing Shianne's sense of direction. She felt as if she were walking through a pitch-black maze. The silence was deafening, and her imagination shouted at her to turn back before she was swallowed alive, but Shianne refused to retreat until she had satisfied the curiosity that had mounted after two days of wondering and speculating.

The dust that covered the floor of the antechamber had now become thick, clinging clay. It stuck to her boots like glue and made walking treacherous. The cavern floor began to slope downward and Shianne was forced to brace one hand on the slimy wall to ensure her balance. An eerie howling echoed through the winding passage, giving Shianne a start. Her foot slid out from under her, and while leaning forward to maintain her equilibrium, she gained too much momentum.

A frightened shriek erupted from her lips when she began sliding down an incredibly steep slope. She couldn't stop. The lantern clanked against the rock wall, snagging on the mineral deposits that jutted from the cavern like thousands of coat hooks. When her light source was yanked from her hand, it dangled momentarily on the protruding rocks and then crashed to the damp floor.

The most incredible shade of darkness closed in on her. Never had she experienced anything quite like this. It was worse than she had ever imagined. Not only could she *not* see her own hand in front of her face, but she was completely disoriented. The feelings that shot through her body were terrifying. Shianne screamed hysterically as she slid downward, bumping into the jagged walls. Frantically she clutched at the slimy rocks, trying to determine which way was up when the floor of the tunnel seemed to slant in all directions, making it impossible to keep her balance.

Then the slippery rock path beneath her vanished, and she was dangling in midair. The echo of her own scream rebounded about her as she plummeted downward. This was the end, Shianne told herself grimly. Her life rapidly flew in front of her eyes . . . all of it in varying shades of black. She would wind up in a broken heap in the bowels of the earth, never to be heard from again. By the time anyone thought to look for her, it would be too late. She would be another of the restless spirits who had wandered into the cave and perished. Her voice was destined to mingle with the mysterious howls and soul-shattering echoes that belched from the darkness of this bottomless cavern. . . .

"What do you mean she vanished into thin air?" Wade scowled sourly.

Ramona stared at the tips of her shoes, afraid to meet the murderous glare in Wade's flashing green eyes. "No one saw her leave, señor. She was in her room when I served her supper, and none of the men saw her attempt to escape." Her shoulders dropped in a gesture

191

of futility. "We have torn the hacienda upside down looking for her. I cannot explain it. *No hay que darle vueltas!* She was here and now suddenly she is gone."

"Is there no one hereabout who can keep that woman caged?" Wade bellowed for the first time in years. He had rarely raised his voice, and here he was, venting his anger on the housekeeper—an innocent victim, not the doe-eyed culprit. Damnation, that ebony-haired vixen needed to have her boots nailed to the floor to make her stay put! "Has anyone ever been able to tell that girl what to do?"

"No, señor," Ramona hastily admitted, shaken by Wade's thundering voice. "She has run wild since she was fifteen. Carlos and I have tried to control the child. *Caramba,* how we have tried, but she is a headstrong, willful woman who has never taken orders from anyone. But then, why would anyone expect her to? She is the mistress of this house." Finally, the housekeeper braved a glance at the fuming *hombre* who was breathing fire down her neck. "Where could she have gone? We must find her. A girl should not be out at this hour of the night. There are savages about, waiting to abduct defenseless young women and make them slaves . . . and only God knows what else!"

Defenseless? Wade very nearly laughed out loud. That ebony-haired woman wasn't defenseless, not by a long shot. Her entire body could have been registered as a lethal weapon. Shianne could scratch, claw, bite and kick her way out of the worst disaster. It was obvious that Ramona had no idea Shianne had been traipsing off to meet the renegade savages who prowled the darkness. If Ramona knew her darling little angel had been consorting with the Indians for the past six years, she would have fainted dead away.

"I'll find her," Wade promised as he spun on his heels and stormed toward the door. "And when I do, I'm going to beat her within an inch of her life!"

"Señor, *por favor,* do not be too severe with her. Shianne is high-spirited. She cannot help the way she is. She needs guidance, a firm but gentle hand," Ramona called after him.

"And that is exactly what I intend to give her," Wade muttered spitefully. "A firm hand on the seat of her pants! When I fetch her back, make sure you lock her in her room. If she makes another escape, shoot her!"

The color waned from Ramona's dark features. "Shoot her?" she repeated incredulously.

"And empty both barrels of the shotgun," Wade muttered spitefully. "If that doesn't stop her it should at least slow that minx down!"

Ramona's wide eyes followed Wade until he became one of the swaying shadows. *Dios Mio!* The *hombre* was as wild and unruly as Shianne was, she mused disconcertedly. Ramona feared that Shianne might enter into a disastrous marriage with Haden Reems, but from the looks of things the señorita would not live that long. Her guardian would dispose of her long before she could join in wedlock to *any* man. *Ave Maria!* The señorita had made the wrong man mad!

Dammit, how could Ramona defend that impestuous whirlwind? Blind devotion, Wade muttered disgustedly. No wonder Shianne was such troublesome baggage. She was allowed to run wild, and no one dared to scold her. Ramona and Carlos made excuses for her behavior. Both of them had spared the rod and spoiled that girl rotten. Shianne was worse than any Texas tempest that left a path of destruction in its wake. She maintained her Indian heritage by prowling around in the darkness. She was swift of foot, sharp of tongue and as proud and unyielding as any warrior. In short, she was more woman than a normal man could handle, and just where the hell was he going to find an extraordinary man to hobble that feisty sprite at this late hour? Wade scowled furiously. As always, he was forced to deal with the firebrand himself. Damn that Blake Kimball. The least he could have done was inform Wade that gathering *cimarrones* and *mesentas* would be a piece of cake compared to keeping that wild minx under thumb!

Wade's angry gaze swept the corral but Delgado was nowhere to be found. Since that flighty witch had been in too big a rush to fetch her broom, it appeared that she had spirited off on her black stallion. Covering the ground in long, hasty strides, Wade returned to his horse and vaulted into the saddle as Galahad stretched out into a gallop. Wade had the sneaking suspicion that Shianne had been summoned by the Owl Prophet. Either that or she had decided to explore the cave during his absence. Damn that woman! She never granted him a moment's peace. He had both hands full and still he was required to keep tabs on Shianne.

Seeing no sign of Indians milling about the spring, Wade concluded that Shianne had made the cave her destination. He had only set one foot on the ground when he heard the terrified shrieks filtering from the entrance of the cavern. Mingling with Shianne's scream was another haunting sound, and Wade could not determine which voice seemed to be in the most pain. What the hell was going on in there, Wade asked himself. Fumbling with the other lantern, Wade hurried into the cave.

He pricked his ears, waiting for another sound to alert him to the direction Shianne might have taken. When another piercing cry echoed through the cavern, Wade's eyes soared toward the stalactites that were draped on the ceiling. "God Almighty, she took the left tunnel," he muttered in annoyance. "Didn't I tell her not to turn left? Dammit, I swear if I told that woman not to dive headlong off a cliff she would plunge ahead to spite me!"

Cautiously, Wade followed the slippery path, well aware of how treacherous it could be. He paused on the ledge where Shianne had veered off to the right and held the lantern high above him. Keen eyes squinted to survey the shadows below.

There, treading stagnant water in the underground pool, was Shianne. She looked like a drowned rat, but Wade latched onto several other phrases to describe her, all of which were less complimentary than the first one that popped to mind.

After sinking and swallowing the other half of the murky pool, Shianne burst to the surface, screaming at the top of her lungs (the bottom half was full of water). When she spied the beam of light high above her, she thanked her lucky stars that someone had heard her call.

Shianne had very nearly drowned after taking her long fall from the ledge. She had not expected to find a puddle of water at the bottom of the black pit. Before she thought to draw a breath she was surrounded by water. Frantically, she had scratched and clawed her way back to the surface, sputtering and coughing to catch her breath. At the moment, she didn't much care who had come to save her. She would have even been delighted to meet the phantom of the cave if he would retrieve her from this stagnant cesspool.

"You little fool!" Wade barked at her. "I told you not to come this way. You could have killed yourself."

Wade! Damn, what was he doing back here when he was to be standing watch, Shianne thought sickly. Never had she heard him sound so furious. She had stoked the fires of his temper once or twice, but his voice had never sliced like a knife. "You can lecture me later," she yelled at him. "But first, GET ME OUT OF

HERE!" She made the request, but she would not have been the least bit surprised if Wade decided to let her tread water until she exhausted every ounce of strength and drowned. He sounded mad as hell.

Wade inched along the ledge, shining the lantern toward the delta of sand and fine gravel that lay several yards ahead of her. "Swim over here and wait for me. I have to go back for a rope."

Swim? Shianne wasn't sure she could take another stroke. The cold water had numbed her limbs, and her left leg felt as if it had an anchor tied to it. "I'll try," she said wearily.

"Don't try. Do it, for God's sake," Wade snapped at her. "I don't relish having to contact your father to inform him that you drowned in an underground lake when you shouldn't have been there in the first place." He expelled the breath he had been holding since he heard Shianne's initial scream for assistance. "Oh hell, why am I bothering to lecture you, you never listen. Just hang on, dammit. I'll be back as quick as I can."

As the light disappeared into darkness Shianne stretched out to paddle toward the sand barge in the middle of the pond. Exhausted, she dragged herself onto the mushy delta and inhaled a ragged breath. She had endured the fright of her life. Still she had not located Wade's secret treasure, she muttered to herself. She had very nearly killed herself in the quest of Wade's mysterious treasure, but she was no closer to an answer than she had been when she was safely tucked in bed!

After what seemed an eternity, she heard footsteps from the shelf above her. She squinted as a piercing ray of light shined down on her.

"Are you still alive?" Wade called to her.

"Do you truly care?" Shianne grumbled.

"At the moment, no," he scowled. "I am so furious with you that I won't be satisfied until I whip you within an inch of your life, and when I do get my hands on you, the first thing I intend to do is shake the stuffing out of you for scaring the wits out of me!"

As he finished the last sentence, he hurled the looped end of the rope at her. The lariat fell about her as if he were lassoing a maverick.

"Shall I fasten it around my neck?" Shianne sniffed sarcastically. "Perhaps you would prefer to deliver your sermon over a corpse, though I doubt your eulogy will contain any kind words."

Wade muttered several inaudible epithets as he tied the rope around his waist and pulled himself up the slippery path. He braced his arms on either side of the narrow tunnel, grasping at bits of protruding rocks to steady himself. Finally, he heard Shianne scratching at the gravel on the edge of the ledge, and he felt the rope slacken.

Hurriedly, Wade tore himself free of the lariat and stalked back to hoist the soggy nymph to her feet. When her legs buckled beneath her, Wade scooped her into his arms, grumbling all the while. "Woman, I swear I have discovered the reason you have never married. Your daredevil shenanigans would drive your poor husband to *his* early grave. Only a self-destructive man would consider tying himself to a woman who would bring about his demise with her wild pranks."

Shianne was too weary to argue with him. Like a contented kitten she curled up against his heaving chest and laid her damp head against his shoulder. "You smell like dust and cattle," she sighed.

Wade had intended to shake her, to paddle her for her escapade, but the moment she nestled against him the fight went out of him. "You smell like a three-day-old fish," Wade retaliated, but his voice had lost its bite. It was soft and caressing. "Dammit, Shae, why do you do the crazy things you do?"

197

"I wanted to find the treasure you are hiding in this cave," she confessed drowsily. "I know it has to be here somewhere. I'm not certain what method you employed to obtain it, but I am convinced that you are protecting a treasure. That is why you refused to relocate."

"You really should take a job as a private investigator," Wade snickered, his lips brushing against her clammy forehead. "I have no doubt you could uncover every unsolved mystery that has haunted man since the beginning of time."

"You aren't going to tell me, are you?" she questioned deflatedly. "Must I continue to risk killing myself to learn the truth?"

"I think it would be wiser not to stick your nose in places it doesn't belong, princess," he advised.

Once Wade reached the opening of the cave, he set Shianne on the carpet of grass and started the fire. With that task accomplished he turned back to her, his hands braced on his hips, his feet askance. "Take off your clothes," he instructed.

Shianne eyed him warily. "Why?"

He stared at her as if she had an empty cavity between her ears. "Why do you suppose? To dry them over the fire, of course."

"You needn't talk down to me," Shianne grumbled indignantly.

A taunting smile swept across his sensuous lips. "Did you think I intended something else? Really, Shae, you cut me to the quick. My intentions are honorable. I want you out of those wet clothes before you catch your death. You suffered a shock, and you have yet to recover from the kick of an angry longhorn." Wade sank down on his haunches to unfasten the buttons of her shirt. "If you catch a chill, you could be bedridden for days. We both know how you would detest that."

The feel of his nimble fingers brushing across her skin sent her heart into a full gallop. Shianne swallowed hard, trying to ignore the warm, bubbly sensations that spurted through her veins. When Wade pulled the shirt away, Shianne covered herself, drawing Wade's husky chortle.

"You have no reason to pretend modesty." His index finger trailed along silky arms that laid protectively over her breasts. "It's not the first time, Shae. . . ." His voice was low and seductive, sending tingles trickling down her backbone. "You have an exquisite body, and I will never tire of looking at it. I swear, your image has been branded on my mind, and I can see you with my eyes closed."

One delicately arched brow lifted as she sidled over to take cover beneath a quilt. "You must have a clouded mind if you can recall every woman you have seen in indecent states of undress."

Heaving a defeated sigh, Wade grabbed her discarded shirt and stretched it above the fire. "Some are more memorable than others. Yours is more tantalizing than most."

Shianne glared at the broad expanse of his back as she wiggled out of her breeches. When she flung the garment at him it settled over his head. Shianne grinned despite herself. "I suppose I should accept that as a compliment, knowing you are a connoisseur of women."

Dragging the grimy trousers from his head, Wade tossed a wry smile over his shoulder. "I can tell by the hint of sarcasm in your voice that you do not approve. Why is that, princess? Are you jealous that you were not the first?"

Shianne glanced about her, seeking something to throw at him, something that would put a dent in his monumental arrogance, but to her dismay, she could not heave the boulder that was propping her up.

"Why should I care if you have spent more time in bed than on your feet?" she sniffed. "I am not the least bit interested in your sordid love life."

Wade burst into chuckles. "You *are* jealous," he declared.

When he had completed the task of draping her breeches above the fire he ambled back to her. "You really have no right to be, you know. After all, you are carrying a torch for the hoot owl of the Kiowas and Comanches. As for myself, I have been involved in nothing more than brief, shallow affairs. They had more to do with lust than tender passion, a mere release of pent up needs . . ."

Shianne was bruised by his insensitive remark. It felt as if he had kicked her in the stomach. She did not appreciate being referred to as a casual fling, and the only torch she carried was the one that set fuse to her fiery temper—the one Wade's comment quickly set aflame.

Shianne reacted impulsively. Flesh cracked against flesh, like the crash of thunder. Her eyes were dark and stormy when she raked him with contempt. He had that coming, she thought angrily. He had slapped her in the face with his insult, and she retaliated by leaving her hand print on his cheek.

With his jaw swinging loosely on its hinges, Wade gaped at her. His fingertips inspected the stinging welt on his left cheek. "Why the hell did you do that?" he croaked in disbelief.

"Because I do not appreciate having my first experience with passion pegged as a simple release of tension," she spewed. "If that were all it was, I should have settled for a massage!"

She looked so ridiculous standing there with a quilt draped about her, her hair caked with mud and her chin thrust out in an exaggerated pout. Shianne was the picture of stubborn pride and feisty temperament. For some reason the image she presented tickled his funny bone instead of setting fire to his temper. His merry laughter floated off in the evening breeze as he collapsed on the ground, shaking his head in disbelief. It amazed him that this spitfire could get so riled over a harmless remark.

After listening to him snicker for several seconds, Shianne was bent completely out of shape. She came uncoiled like a striking cobra. Furious that she again found herself the brunt of his amusement, she leaped on him, delivering several well-aimed punches to his midsection.

Her temper tantrum came to an abrupt halt when Wade rolled her to her back and plopped down on her belly. Before she could claw at him, he pinned her arms to the ground. His grinning face loomed over her annoyed frown, totally frustrating her.

"Enough is enough, minx," he chuckled. "I don't relish being beat to a pulp, just to satisfy your hauteur. You don't see me taking swings at you because your heart throbs for a man who wears more feathers than clothes, do you?" Wade clasped both of her wrists in one hand and removed the mop of muddy hair that clung to her cheek. "You need to learn the meaning of tolerance, sweetheart."

His method of teaching Shianne tolerance didn't work worth a damn. She detested being held down. The longer he pinned her to the ground the angrier she became. He kept smiling that exasperating smile, and Shianne was quickly becoming unglued!

"Let me up!" she hissed. Again she writhed for freedom, calling upon every ounce of strength she possessed, but Wade held her firm. "Damn you, Wade Burdett! You can't hold me down forever, and when you finally let me up, I'm going to . . ."

His mouth swooped down on hers, stealing her breath and silencing her vindictive threat. His probing tongue darted into her mouth, forcing her blazing temper to ebb into a slow, burning flame. Shianne cursed the mystical power he seemed to hold over her, the sensations he could create when there had been nothing but frustrated anger the moment before. Wade could make his will her own in less than a split second. Her traitorous body responded as he lowered himself to her, moving his hips suggestively against hers. She found herself wanting things that had nothing to do with revenge and everything to do with easing the craving that Wade's skillful techniques aroused.

"I wasn't referring to you," Wade confided when he finally came up for air. He shifted beside her. With his free hand he drew away the bulky quilt that protected what his eyes longed to caress. "There is something special between us, something that separates lovemaking from lust." His worshipping hand swam over the sea of bare flesh, fluttering from one pink bud to the other. "With you it was different. It was a warm, unique experience. God help me for admitting it but it was."

Shianne's thick lashes fluttered up to meet the glow of desire in his eyes. "You mean it isn't always the way it was between us?" she questioned innocently. Her body flinched when his roaming caresses drifted down her stomach to explore her sensitive thighs.

"No, princess. Lust feeds on primal needs, but passion only rears its head when the attraction between two people is fierce and potent. Sparks flew the moment we touched and still they could set a forest ablaze. . . ."

His sensuous lips whispered over hers in the slightest breath of a touch. Shianne was beginning to understand what he meant. Haden Reems touched her and she cringed. Maman-ti held her close and she found comfort. But when she was in Wade's sinewy arms she felt a fire boiling through her bloodstream to singe every part of her being. Her first experience with desire had become a stepping stone that led down a path to ardent passion. What she was feeling—these wild, tremulous sensations—was even more compelling than she had experienced that first night Wade had made love to her. Now she knew what awaited her, and she ached to satisfy the yearnings he instilled in her.

Her arms settled on his shoulders, drawing his raven head back to hers. Shianne kissed him without reserve, her tongue flicking against his partially opened lips. Her mouth twisted over his, increasing the pressure, savoring the taste of him.

With a frustrated groan, Wade pulled away and gulped for breath. The darkness had eyes, and he had very nearly forgotten that when he took this bewitching enchantress in his arms. Summoning his willpower, Wade came to his feet and pulled Shianne up beside him.

"I think we both could use a cold bath," he grumbled, casting a glance toward the mouth of the cave.

Hurt flashed through her eyes. It was obvious that she didn't affect Wade as severely as he affected her. He had admitted that he felt something for her, but obviously it wasn't something strong enough to overshadow any thought that filtered through his mind. When Wade held her close, her mind went blank. Perhaps he had only said those things to cool her temper. After all, she had done nothing to endear him to her, she reminded herself. Indeed, she had made it a point to remain crossways of him since the moment he strutted into the study and took over the ranch.

Shianne frowned disconcertedly. Wade baffled her, frustrated her. She knew he religiously avoided lasting entanglements. So why had he admitted that he was strongly attracted to her, if not to smooth her ruffled feathers? Why had he withdrawn from her embrace when she would have surrendered to the intoxicating taste of his kisses? A cold bath, for Pete's sake? That didn't sound like something a man would say immediately after he confessed that sparks sizzled each time they touched.

Wearing a muddled frown, Shianne tucked the quilt about her and allowed Wade to lead her around the side of the hill. On the downward slope lay strewn boulders and rocks, through which Wade carried her to prevent bruising her bare feet. The quiet murmur of the spring drew Shianne from her puzzled contemplations. She sighed at the enticing sight of the rippling pool that glowed silver in the moonlight. Like two outstretched arms, the creek diverged. One stream meandered across the K Bar Ranch, and the other drifted lazily toward the Lazy R, becoming the water source for Haden's vast ranch. The peacefulness of the night instantly reminded Shianne how much she loved this part of Texas, this ranch. The land was a part of her. Was it any wonder she had vehemently protested when Wade threatened her domain? This was her world and no one would ever take it from her.

Her drifting thoughts converged when Wade slid the quilt from her shoulders, allowing the moonlight to sprinkle over her creamy skin. A slight frown clouded his features when he noticed the huge bruise that marred her thigh.

"Is it still tender?" he questioned softly. His hand brushed across her bare flesh, inspecting the coiled knot.

His gentle touch rekindled the flames, and Shianne

nodded mutely, not trusting her voice. When his hand ascended, she shivered with pleasure, and when his moist lips skimmed her breasts, a tiny moan burst free, betraying her need for him.

Without taking his eyes off her curvaceous body, Wade retreated a step to shed his shirt, but his fingers kept fumbling over the buttons. Wade was too distracted by the enticing sight of Shianne to concentrate on what was usually a simple task. He had reached the impatient point at which he seriously considered ripping the fabric away in his haste to mold his masculine body to her soft flesh.

"Let me help," Shianne offered softly.

Her fingers worked the buttons and then her palms splayed across the thick matting of hair that covered his chest. His body shuddered in response to her light, teasing explorations. When she grasped the buckle of his belt, Wade tensed in anticipation. Laying her hands on his hips, she pushed the trousers lower, leaving a trail of fire each place she touched.

A low groan rumbled in his chest as her bold caresses investigated the hard columns of his thighs. When her hands receded to swirl over his buttocks, Wade forgot how to breathe. Lord, she had set him ablaze with her innocent touch! She was comparing the feel of his hair-matted flesh to the velvety softness of her skin, and it was driving him out of his mind. He wanted to crush her to him, to ravish her, to appease this maddening craving that sent logic fleeing from the tempest of desire.

He had taken her once, and like an arrogant fool, he thought it would be enough. But it wasn't. Shianne was tormenting his dreams and entangling his life. If he didn't guard his step he would never be able to walk away from her, not without leaving a part of himself behind. Even while he was giving himself practical lectures on the hazards of tampering with his emotions, his body was rousing with needs that tore holes in his common sense.

Oh, what the hell, he muttered to himself. He had waded into trouble scores of times, and he had always been able to swim out before he sank in over his head. Shianne couldn't tie him down. He had been born under a wandering star. He was a free spirit who came and went as easily as the wind. What could it hurt to appease his passions? They would grow tired of each other in time. That was the way it was between a man and a woman. Some men were foolish enough to marry before their time came. Then it was too late. They were tied to a woman who could no longer satisfy them. They longed for their freedom and they strayed to other arms. Wade had watched his friends make the mistake of marrying and later regret their haste. He was not about to make that mistake. He had thirty-two years of experience to call upon. It cautioned him not to trust the thoughts that seeped into his head while his mind was fogged with desire.

He and Shianne would pleasure each other until the feelings withered and died. When she became possessive of him, he would feel strangled and begin to keep his distance. Then they would drift apart without the bonds of matrimony to contain them. Satisfied that he could overcome the hazard of an affair with this tempting nymph, Wade grasped Shianne's hand and led her to the pool.

Shianne plunged into the water, unaware of its chilly temperature. When she bobbed to the surface, Wade was standing on the bank, his masculine body bathed in silver light. Shianne stared openly at him, awestruck by this raw mass of muscle and energy. She knew how his hair-roughened flesh felt beneath her touch, how the corded muscles of his back tensed when she brushed her fingertips over them. She knew the exact location of each battle scar, but she didn't know why she was feeling this odd, indescribable rush of pleasure. It wasn't desire. She had learned to decipher that sensation. No, it was something more, something she could not name.

Her admiring gaze drifted up his bare legs to his tapered waist. Her eyes lingered on the broad expanse of his chest. Then she looked into his eyes, watching the flecks of gold sparkle in the moonlight. Suddenly her heart lurched, and she could not inhale a breath.

The sensation that was hounding her was love! She stared into his craggy features, watching the crinkles spray from the corners of his eyes, memorizing the becoming dimples that slashed his cheeks. It was as if she were staring at him for the first time, and yet she was seeing *all* of him, not just his outward appearance. Here was everything she desired in a man—the irrepressible sense of humor, the strong, commanding personality that took control of every situation, the gift of gentleness.

Shianne didn't want to be in love with Wade Burdett. He was devoted to her in a certain sense, but it was an obligation to her father. The type of devotion she demanded was one that entailed fidelity. Wade didn't know the meaning of the word. He liked women—all women, not just one in particular.

She couldn't have Wade. It would destroy her, loving him, knowing his eyes would stray, and he would pursue his passionate whims. If she had any sense at all she would marry Haden Reems. She was safe with him. He would shower her with gifts, and he could never hurt her because she could never love him. There were dozens of qualities about Haden that she disliked, but this was Texas, a wild, lawless land full of hard men, not saints.

When Wade swaggered into the pool and glided through the water toward her, Shianne shrieked as if she had been snakebit. Frantically, she paddled to the bank, cutting a wide circle around Wade. He set his feet on the bottom of the pool and twirled to watch Shianne clamber up the bank.

"What is the matter with you?" he queried bewilderedly.

Shianne snatched up the quilt and draped it over her shoulders. "I want you to give permission for me to marry Haden Reems as soon as the arrangements can be made," she blurted out.

"What!" Wade hooted.

"I mean it, Wade. I want to marry him." After issuing her demand Shianne pivoted on her heels and raced back to the camp to fetch her clothes.

Scowling, Wade walked ashore. He snatched up his breeches and shoved a wet foot through his trousers leg as he followed in Shianne's wake. The woman was mad! She had dived into the water. It had seeped into her head to clog the workings of her mind. She wasn't thinking straight, Wade decided. What woman would agree to marry a man with small, beady eyes and a mouth that permanently turned down at the corners? Haden Reems had a sunken chest, no personality to speak of, and legs like a giraffe.

"Would you mind explaining why you have suddenly decided to accept Reems's proposal? I didn't think you liked the man," Wade snorted derisively.

Shianne hastily buttoned her half dry shirt and then plopped down to drag on her boots. "I don't like him and that is exactly why I want to marry him."

Wade snatched her boot away before she could slide it on her foot, forcing her to cease her frantic attempt to dress and flee. "You realize, of course, you aren't making any sense."

Jerking the boot from his hand, Shianne shoved it on her foot and reached for the other boot. "I am making perfect sense," she told him flatly.

His eyes rolled skyward. "I was afraid you would say something like that. Women!" he scowled in disgust. "Who can understand them? First you praise the Owl Prophet, protect him from harm. Then, out of the blue, you demand that I permit you to marry Haden Reems when you openly admit that you have no use for him! All this, of course, while you are swimming naked in the pool with *me!* If there was a deep end to that river bed, I swear you fell in it!"

Shianne was too rattled by her realization to take offense to anything Wade said to her. She had made up her mind what needed to be done to save herself from heartache, and she was determined to see it through.

"When we journey to the fiesta tomorrow night, I want you to tell Haden that you are going to give me away at the wedding." Bounding to her feet, Shianne aimed herself toward Delgado, anxious to put some distance between herself and the man who had managed to steal her heart.

Wade manacled her arm as she breezed by. "I'm not giving my permission. Blake would have me shot! I told you that your father was in hopes that the two of us would marry."

"That can't and won't happen," Shianne flared, flinging herself away.

"Well, you are not wedding Haden Reems," Wade shouted at her as if she were deaf.

As Shianne scampered toward her horse, Wade threw up his hands in exasperation. What devil possessed that woman? She was behaving stranger than normal, even for Shianne. Wade wheeled around to kick at a clump of grass, forgetting he was barefooted. Grumbling, he limped toward his satchel and fished out a bottle of whiskey. Sinking down by the fire, Wade made plans to drink himself insane. Then perhaps he could understand Shianne's twisted logic. It was obvious he could make no sense of her when he was sober.

"What is going on out here?" came the hushed voice from the neck of the cave.

Wade waved the bottle over his head and then guzzled his brandy. "Come join me, dark phantom. I intend to drown myself in whiskey. You may as well get into the *spirit* of things." Wade gulped another drink and chuckled at his own cleverness.

His companion trudged over to plant himself in the grass. "This cave is starting to give me the creeps," he grumbled before accepting the bottle. "You are rarely here, and I've grown tired of talking to myself."

"Then take up a hobby," Wade suggested flippantly. "I need you to defend the cave, and you agreed to it. The Indians think you are their great spirit, and Shianne swears the cavern is haunted. Without you, it would be impossible to keep our secret safe."

"There were some men snooping around here this afternoon—Haden's desperados. I gave them a performance they will long remember." The phantom chuckled in amusement. "Two of them started into the antechamber, and I let out a howl to raise the dead. By the time I crept into the tunnel, this camp had been evacuated."

A wry smile caught one side of Wade's mouth. So Haden had sent his bravoes to rummage through camp. Haden had begun to wonder where Wade had come up with the funds to hire ranch hands and purchase supplies, just as Shianne had.

It was time to repay Haden for his mischief of unleashing the mavericks and trespassing on the campsite, Wade decided. He mulled over several retaliations. Two had an appealing ring to them, and one of them would have Haden cursing a blue streak. Smiling wickedly, Wade climbed to his feet, urging the phantom to follow along behind him.

"I have a new project for you, mysterious specter. It should preoccupy you. We owe Haden Reems a dose of his own medicine, and I have just the prescription for our meddling neighbor."

A heavy sigh gushed from Ramona's lips when Shianne marched into the entryway. "You are home at last, *chica*. I was afraid something dreadful had happened to you."

It had, Shianne mused glumly. She had discovered she was in love and the revelation was depressing.

"Señor Burdett was furious when he found you were gone," Ramona rattled as she followed Shianne up the steps. "He even gave me orders to gun you down if you tried to run away again."

Shianne missed a step and came dangerously close to falling on her face. Did Wade think so little of her that he would dispose of her in such a merciless manner? She thought he cared, just a little, but obviously she was deluding herself. Becoming more depressed by the minute, Shianne trudged to bed and collapsed upon it.

Tears clung to her lashes as a pair of laughing green eyes and a charismatic grin materialized on her ceiling. She *had* to marry Haden to protect herself from Wade. Haden would not allow Wade near her after the ceremony. Wade could take control of the hacienda, and she would be safely tucked away at Haden's ranch. The memories would fade in time, Shianne reassured herself. In a few months she would not think of Wade at all. She would not remember his touch, the taste of his lips melting against hers. . . .

211

She would have surrendered to him tonight while they lay by the fire, and he would have carved another notch on his belt. Shianne laughed bitterly. How many other women found their hearts dangling about that devil's neck like trinkets of romantic conquests? He had probably slept in the arms of more women than the entire female population of San Antonio. Yet, he was the only man she had ever known intimately, would ever know until she married Haden. . . .

The repulsive thought of sleeping by Haden's side sent a wave of shivers skittering down her spine. How could she endure that man's touch? Shianne punched her pillow to relieve her frustrations. She would have to find a way. She had to marry Haden and that was the beginning and end of it!

Chapter 10

Hundreds of men and women milled through San Antonio, enjoying the gaiety of the fiesta. There was dancing in the streets and the soft serenades of violins and Spanish guitars. Laughter rang through the air, but Shianne was not one of those who had been caught up in the spirit of the celebration. Tension stretched through her body like the taut strings of the musical instruments.

The ride from the ranch in Haden's carriage had been a nerve-racking experience. Wade had planted himself between her and Haden, intentionally annoying her escort. She knew her ornery guardian was delighting in the role of the overprotective chaperone. Wade portrayed the part as if he were born to it, fussing over her as if she were a delicate flower who was sorely in need of attention. If he had been sincere Shianne might have enjoyed his company. But he wasn't and she didn't.

Shianne feared at any moment Wade would accuse her fiancé of stampeding the longhorns, but Wade merely warned Haden to beware of Indian raids, explaining that his own efforts of roundup had been wiped out by marauding renegades.

When Wade began proclaiming that a man could prosper in this lawless land of Texas if he could defend against Indians and secure a good source of water for his stock, Shianne had frowned curiously. She knew Wade well enough to know that he was up to something. What, she could not fathom, but Wade was making no idle chatter. He was a deliberate, calculating man who left very little to chance. Knowing that made Shianne all the more uncomfortable. She had the premonition that Wade was setting Haden up, and she would have given most anything to know what that cunning cowboy had on his mind.

The conversation had become strained when Haden insisted they set a wedding date. Shianne sat beside Wade on the carriage seat, willing him to hand her over to Haden, but he did no such thing. Wade firmly informed Haden there would be no marriage until the powerful cattle baron proved himself worthy of her. Wade declared he would assess Haden's behavior during the course of the evening and *then* determine if their marriage would make a suitable match.

Once they arrived at the fiesta, Shianne expected Wade to wander off to turn his dark, devil-may-care-charm on the women who were eyeing him with considerable interest, but he stuck to her like glue. Each time Haden took her arm to lead her away, Wade laid his hand to the small of her back and walked along beside them. His fingertips pressed against her skin, setting fires where they touched. To her chagrin, she found herself comparing the feel of Haden's bony fingers to Wade's practiced hands. One side of her body was warm and quivering while the other side was cold and tense. Finally Shianne could endure no more of the conflicting emotions. She aimed herself toward the refreshment table and poured down two drinks to take the edge off her nerves. When one of Haden's men appeared to confer with him, Shianne consumed another glass of spiked punch.

A concerned frown etched Wade's brow. He watched Shianne guzzle drinks as if she were a camel who had been stranded on a desert for weeks on end. "I suggest you slow down a bit, princess. You won't be able to stand up, much less dance," he chided.

Shianne reached for another drink, finding relief for the first time that night. "I am only celebrating," she defended between sips. "After all, that is what the fiesta is all about."

Wade grabbed the glass before it reached her lips. "This is brandy you're drinking, my dear ward, not a glass of courage." His green eyes probed into hers, holding her steady gaze. "You know you can't tolerate Haden Reems, and so you intend to numb yourself to his presence."

Tilting a defiant chin, Shianne downed her drink in one swallow. A silly smile tripped across her lips. The liquor had begun to take effect, and Shianne no longer had a care. Her glazed gaze slid over Wade's black wool coat and embroidered silk waistcoat. "Did I tell you how handsome you looked this evening?"

Wade did a double take. How had they landed on the subject of clothing? A wry grin caught the corner of his mouth when Shianne swayed toward him. The little imp was drunk. It was obvious she was not accustomed to the effects of liquor, and it had not taken long for the brandy to fog her brain.

His hands slid up her bare arms. His gaze dipped to the off-the-shoulder neckline of her burgundy silk gown, admiring the display of creamy skin and generous display of bosom. The gown had been made for this shapely nymph. He had known that the moment he saw it in the shop window, but the effect of Shianne's enticing figure wrapped in silk was even more devastating than Wade had anticipated. He had spent the better part of the evening trying not to notice how very lovely she was, but at this close range nothing about her went unnoticed.

His fingertips brushed across the double row of gauze lace that adorned the daring neckline. "And you, Shae, are the belle of the fiesta," he whispered against her cheek. His left hand slid down her ribs to settle on the indention of her waist. It rested there for a moment before investigating the thick folds of silk that flowed into the full, floor-length skirt. Pulling her ever closer, he let her feel his mounting desire for her. "You are stunning in your gown, but I prefer you out of it. . . ."

His mouth feathered over hers, and Shianne responded instinctively. Her lips parted to accept his kiss. She was drowning in warm, bubbly sensations, only half of which were the result of her overindulgence in brandy. Her breasts pressed wantonly against his chest, and her body inched closer. Even though they were surrounded by a crowd, Shianne could see no farther than the man who had enveloped her in his arms.

Wade made no attempt to regain his self-control. The previous night had left him frustrated, and he wanted what he had been denied. Shianne's declaration to wed Haden Reems had tormented his sleep. Now that he had Shianne in his arms, he intended to take full advantage.

Out of the corner of his eye he saw Haden approaching. The rancher's angular features were set in a murderous glare. Wade allowed Shianne to draw his head back to hers, and he returned her kiss with a mischievous grin on his lips. The fireworks were about to begin, Wade predicted, and he was going to let them. All he needed was one excuse to reject Haden's proposal of marriage. Shianne couldn't very well blame Wade for causing trouble since she was the donor of a very passionate kiss.

Haden's fingers clamped on Wade's shoulder, ripping him from Shianne's grasp. "You miserable bastard, you are to be her guardian, not her molester," he hissed furiously.

Calmly, Wade pried Haden's fingers from his expensive jacket. "I think you were too busy being indignant to notice who was kissing *whom*," Wade pointed out with an infuriating smile. His arm slid around Shianne's waist when she weaved unsteadily beside him.

Haden's fuming gaze swung back and forth between Wade's taunting smile and Shianne's droopy-eyed expression. "You got her intoxicated," he accused harshly.

"No, actually I advised her to slow down three drinks ago," Wade informed him. "But you know how Shianne is. She listens to no man. She simply does as she pleases."

"You have been trying to turn her against me since you set foot on the K Bar," Haden growled, his lips curling in a malicious sneer.

"And you have tried to undermine my business venture by dressing your bravoes up as Indians and stampeding my herd," Wade shot back. "Not to mention sending them to ransack my camp."

"I did no such thing," Haden lied through his teeth.

Mocking laughter pelleted Haden's rigid stance. "You are a liar, Haden, among your other contemptible faults."

Haden's temper exploded. Without contemplating the consequences, he doubled his fist, intending to plant it in Wade's taunting grin. Wade released his hold on Shianne and came uncoiled to block the oncoming punch to his jaw. Before Haden knew what hit him,

217

stars were spinning in front of his eyes. He stumbled back, his jaw stinging. Growling in fury, he lumbered toward Wade, determined not to be humiliated in front of the townspeople who had gathered to watch the fisticuffs.

As Haden charged like a mad bull, Wade waited until the last second and then agilely stepped aside. Looking the fool, Haden slammed into the refreshment table, slopping brandy and various assorted appetizers all over his expensive clothes. Amusement echoed in the air, causing Haden to swear viciously. He was being made to look the dolt, and he could not tolerate having his reputation soiled in front of the townspeople.

He pushed away from the table, his coat dripping with food and drink. Haden yanked open his jacket to retrieve his knife. A gasp erupted from the crowd as Haden threateningly waved the blade in front of his nemesis.

Shianne propped herself up on one elbow, and shook her head to get her bearings. After Wade had released her to take a punch at Haden, her legs had folded beneath her, and she wound up in a pile on the ground. She had tried to regain her feet, but the crowd closed in to view the tussle, and she had been knocked back down before she could stand up. With her curiosity hounding her, Shianne crawled through several pair of legs to see what had caused the shocked gasps.

The sight of Haden waving his knife at Wade spurred her to action. Sluggish though she was, Shianne scrambled to her feet and glanced hastily around her, searching for some sort of weapon.

"Apologize, Burdett, or I will slash you to pieces," Haden hissed, his beady eyes spitting fire.

"Apologize for stating that you are the one who scattered my herd of mavericks and demolished the stock pens?" Wade smirked. There was a daring recklessness in his smile, but there was a deadly undertone in his voice. "I wonder how many of your neighbors have been the victims of your skulduggery and are too afraid to admit it, Reems."

Haden was determined to cut Wade to pieces before he planted more doubt in the townspeople's heads. Like a bobcat poised to attack, Haden lunged at Wade. His worthy opponent jerked back, thwarting Haden's attempt to draw blood.

While Haden was circling Wade, awaiting the opportunity to strike again, Shianne crept up behind him. She raised the punch bowl above her head and brought it down with all the force she could muster. The pottery clanked against Haden's skull and punch splattered over him, burning his eyes. Expletives that would singe the ears off a priest burst from Haden's lips as he staggered to and fro. Then, he wilted on the ground in a senseless heap.

It took a moment for Shianne to realize what she had done. When she did, a doleful groan erupted from her lips. She stared at Haden in dismay, knowing he would be so furious with her that he would retract his proposal of marriage.

Biting back an amused grin, Wade ambled over to lift the huge bowl from Haden's head and then shot Shianne a glance. "You know what this means, don't you, my dear ward? This unfortunate incident may have serious repercussions. I hope you aren't counting upon your fiancé to forgive and forget."

Shianne spun on her heels and squeezed her way through the crowd. She pulled up short, realizing she had no means of transportation. They had come in Haden's carriage, and she knew for certain he would not invite her to share his coach, not after what she had done to him. Her eyes flew frantically about her, trying to determine what to do. Damn, if she hadn't drunk so much brandy she could assemble her thoughts. Finally an idea came to her, and she fled the crowd, running as fast as her feet would carry her.

Hoisting the limp Haden Reems onto his shoulder, Wade aimed himself toward Doc Winston's office. Jedediah had seen the scuffle and its end result. He was one step behind Wade who weaved his way through the onlookers to reach the office. Once Wade had tossed Haden onto the couch, he stepped back to survey the nasty gash the punch bowl had left on Haden's temple.

"I never expected my nurse to be drumming up business," Jedediah snickered as he opened his bag to retrieve the antiseptic. "She is supposed to be *treating* injuries, not *causing* them. . . ."

The sharp rap at the back door caused Jedediah to frown curiously. "Will you answer the knock while I tend to my patient?" he requested.

Nodding mutely, Wade fumbled his way through the small, unlit home that was attached to the back of the office. Feeling his way around the furniture Wade finally reached the back door. The moment he sprung the lock a bundle of burgundy silk flew into his arms.

"Oh, Doc, I've made a disaster of things," Shianne sobbed against the hard chest where she had buried her head.

"You most certainly have," Wade chuckled softly.

Shianne jerked back to peer into the darkness. That wasn't Jedediah's compassionate voice! "You! What are you doing here?" she demanded to know.

"I delivered your victim to the good doctor. I fear your ex-fiancé may need stitches."

Another miserable groan tumbled off her tongue.

"Dammit, this is all your fault," she muttered grouchily.

"My fault!" Wade hooted. "You were the one who was assaulting me with a passionate kiss when Haden came back to join us."

"Well, I was drunk!" Shianne defended self-righteously. "But not nearly as intoxicated as I intend to be by the time I go home!"

With that adamant declaration, Shianne pirouetted around and sailed out the back door. Wade rolled his eyes and glanced toward the ceiling, as if the solution to his problems was printed there. This was turning into one helluva a night. Shianne was making preparations to consume all the liquor to be had in San Antonio, and Haden would wake, breathing the fire of dragons. This wasn't a fiesta. It was a fiasco!

"Who was that?" Doc Winston called from the office.

Easing the door shut, Wade picked his way through the house to see Jedediah forcing laudanum down Haden's throat. "It was your nurse," Wade responded belatedly.

Jedediah glanced behind him and frowned bemusedly. "Where is she? Consoling herself in my parlor? Tell her to get in here. She had better apologize to Haden when he comes around. If not, the man is going to be more furious than he was."

"She left again," Wade grumbled.

"And you let her go?" Jedediah squeaked in dismay.

"Doc, have you ever tried to dissuade that minx when she has made up her mind to something?"

Jedediah dabbed the antiseptic on Haden's head and heaved an exasperated sigh. "I see your point. I have tried to become the father who was not here to guide her. I love Shianne dearly, but I have never been able to

221

cure her infection of stubbornness. I have not been able to understand why Blake has stayed away so long. It isn't like him to disregard his daughter."

Wade dropped into a chair and stared at Doc Winston's back. He had to tell someone the truth, just to get it off his chest. "Will you swear never to breathe a word of this to Shianne if I explain Blake's behavior? I have yet to find the courage to approach Shianne with the information because I am not sure how she is going to take it."

The remark piqued Jedediah's curiosity. "I am sworn to secrecy. Out with it!"

Wade eased back in his chair and expelled his breath. "One of the reasons Blake sent me instead of coming himself was because he was hoping I would be infatuated with Shianne. He does not want Haden Reems as a son-in-law. Blake anticipated that by throwing the two of us into a situation that would force us to work closely together, the sparks would fly."

"And so they have, haven't they?" Jedediah snickered. "You probably expected to find a meek, quiet heiress who looked exactly like her father."

Wade grumbled under his breath. The doctor was an astute old man. "As a matter of fact I did. That is why I delayed so long in delivering the message to Shianne. I knew I was walking into trouble, but it was *nothing* like I imagined."

"And the other reason?" Doc Winston prompted as he resettled Haden's dangling arm on his chest.

"Blake has gotten married," he blurted out. "He met a very gracious, charming woman during the last months of the war. Because of Blake's strong attraction to her, he tarried in Louisiana hoping she would accept his marriage proposal. Blake continued to procrastinate about writing to his daughter. He was afraid she would take the news hard and do something rash.

222

He wanted to give Shianne time to adjust to the idea that there will be another woman in his life."

"Doing something rash . . . like marry Haden?" Doc Winston chuckled. "Blake was certainly trying to play this whole affair to his advantage, wasn't he?" His expression sobered. "Blake is a dear friend, but I cannot condone his handling of Shianne. No matter what the circumstances, he has neglected Shianne and that is unforgivable."

A wry smile pursed Wade's lips. "If you resent Blake for what he did, how do you suppose his own flesh and blood is going to feel? Resentment? Bitterness? Anger?" Wade wanted to emphasize the fact that Blake considered himself to be wedged between a rock and a hard spot. "Blake regrets his lack of nerve and his cowardly approach to the situation, but he also feels very strongly about the woman who eventually married him. He could not leave her. As is true of so many families in the South, Blake's new wife found her home destroyed, her world torn asunder. From personal experience I can assure you it was an emotional blow to watch my land and possessions go up in flames."

Wade climbed to his feet to pace the floor. "Blake feels a tremendous responsibility for the woman he married, but he doesn't think the time is right to return to Texas. He thinks his second marriage deserves a chance, and he feels he has devoted most of his life to his daughter. It is not that he loves Shianne any less, but that he needs something more in life, something that has been missing for almost twenty years." His gaze circled back to Jedediah. "Can you begin to understand how difficult the past few years have been for Blake? Of course, he is concerned about Shianne, but he decided *not* telling Shianne what had become of him would be better than having her read the news in a

223

letter. It seemed too cold and impersonal. At least this way she hasn't charged off to do something drastic . . . like marry this poor excuse of a man," Wade grumbled, pointing an accusing finger at Haden who was unable to defend himself.

"Shianne is going to be stunned, no matter how delicately the matter is put to her. If she is upset it will be a normal reaction," Jedediah remarked. "Shianne feels neglected by her father because he chose to take an active part in the war." His eyes crinkled as he flung Wade an amused grin. "And she has been blaming you for stealing Blake from her, long before she ever laid eyes on you. To learn that Blake has not returned because he has married will come as a blow. I expect you to be there to pick up the pieces when she falls apart."

"The way she feels about me, I doubt that she will want me there," Wade snorted. "And as feisty and temperamental as she is, I'm not sure I *want* to be there. That is one reason I have procrastinated piling another disappointment on her until she has learned to tolerate my intrusion in her life." Wade breathed a troubled sigh. "It is enough that I have taken control of her ranch and that I have been asked to become her guardian, even when she is old enough and capable enough to make her own decisions. I am not ready to become the bearer of more disturbing news."

"It does put you in a touchy situation," Jedediah concurred as he stitched up his unconscious patient. "But you cannot delay forever. Shianne has to know about her father's marriage."

Wade's solemn expression broke into the slightest hint of a smile. "I only wish I didn't have to be the one to tell her. She doesn't have much use for me, Doc. I have become the scapegoat for her frustrations. If she is barely tolerating me now, how do you suppose she will react when she learns that I was the one who introduced Blake to the woman he decided to marry? I hesitate in giving her another reason to hate me."

Jedediah turned to survey the grim expression that was plastered on Wade's bronzed features. There was very little he could say to ease Wade's apprehensions. If Shianne blamed her guardian for everything that had gone wrong in her life thus far, any other bomb Wade dropped in her lap wasn't likely to sweeten her disposition or raise her opinion of him.

Wade raked his fingers through his hair and went back to his pacing. "Shianne holds me personally responsible for convincing her father to herd cattle to needy confederate troops. Because of me, Blake became involved in several battles. Because of his association with me, he found himself emotionally involved with a woman he couldn't forget or abandon. Then this business of arranging a new market for Texas cattle came along and time was of the essence. Plans had to be made, stock pens built. Blake could have been the one to return to the ranch with his new bride and begin the roundup, but he fears he would send Shianne right into Haden's arms, the last place he wants her to be. Blake wants no conflict between his new wife and his daughter. He wants to give Shianne time to adjust to the idea before he brings his wife back to the ranch."

"I don't envy your position," Doc Winston murmured as he grasped the needle and turned his full attention on his patient.

"Neither do I," Wade grumbled sourly, "and I cannot understand Shianne. She is a walking contradiction. One minute she defies me, and the next moment she is leveling punch bowls on Haden's head to come to my defense. I don't know what to make of her."

A wry smile hovered on Jedediah's lips. He could guess what had caused the inconsistency in Shianne's behavior. She was strongly attracted to Wade Burdett, even when she didn't want to be. She resented him and yet he stirred her emotions as no other man had.

"Would you like a suggestion from an old man?" Jedediah questioned. Working the kinks out of his back, he rose to full stature.

"I would prefer a miracle if you have one stashed in your bag, Doc," Wade snorted.

"Obey Blake's wishes and marry Shianne."

Wade's face fell like a rockslide. That was not the kind of advice Wade wanted to hear. "Even if she agreed to a marriage . . . which she won't . . . I . . ."

"Are you so certain?" One gray brow lifted as Jedediah studied the handsome cowboy who had sprawled in his chair. "Have you asked her?"

"Dammit, I didn't come here to get married, I came to settle a score with Haden Reems, to round up mavericks and drive them to Kansas!" Wade loudly protested.

"Blake didn't drive cattle to Louisiana to get married either. Sometimes those things happen," Jedediah chuckled. "There is no cure for physical attraction. Sometimes a man is forced to accept his affliction. Take an experienced doctor's advice, Wade. Marry the girl. You seemed happy enough to have her in your arms before Haden came stomping back to protest what was going on between the two of you. Shianne did come to your defense. That in itself is proof of which man she prefers."

"Marriage?" The word rattled through Wade's brain like a clap of thunder. Wade had promised himself he would never tie himself to any woman, and especially not a spitfire who had one fiancé on a leash, an Indian medicine man in the bushes and an even bigger fool as

226

her guardian!

"It isn't such a bad institution," Doc Winston argued. "I was married once, and I would not sacrifice one day, one minute of the happiness I knew with Margaret. She passed on five years ago and I still miss her. Certainly, we had our squabbles. She was much like Shianne—feisty, headstrong. But it is that spice that makes life sweet, Wade." Misty eyes focused on Wade's disgruntled frown. "Can you honestly say there has been one dull moment since you walked into Shianne's life? Marriages that go sour are those that had no sweet taste to begin with."

Wade pivoted around and strode toward the door. "I'll fetch some of Haden's men to cart him home," he grumbled.

"Please invite me to the wedding," Doc Winston enthused, reverting back to the subject Wade was purposely trying to avoid. "I would be proud to give the bride away."

"Give her away? Doc, you can have her!" Wade grunted in response to the taunt. "The last thing I need is a woman draped around my neck. I happen to be very fond of my freedom."

Marry Shianne? They would kill each other. Shianne was wild and untamed and so was he. A marriage between them would be a rocky road. Hell! Why was he even considering it? He had already decided not to become that involved with that dark-eyed enchantress. He had resolved to complete his task, have his revenge on Haden and begin a new life, but not with a wife!

Determined in that thought, Wade marched through the crowded streets toward the cantina. He knew Haden's men were in town, drinking and carousing. The moment he stepped into the tavern, he spied Juan Mendez leaning casually against the bar. A mocking grin lifted Juan's lips as Wade strode toward him.

227

"Ah, *amigo,* I hear you have been hiding behind a woman's skirts," he teased.

Wade grabbed an empty glass and poured himself a drink from Juan's half-drained bottle. "I had intended to fight my own battle," he said good-naturedly. "Indeed, the lady deprived me of the satisfaction I anticipated." Wade eyed the dark-skinned vaquero over the rim of his glass. "I expected you to come to Reems's rescue. I thought you were highly paid to finish what he starts."

Juan shrugged a shoulder. "I was curious to see if the boss could take care of himself." He downed his drink and poured another. "Besides, I like you, *hombre.* We are much alike, you and I, and I do not appreciate having another man hide behind my gun while I take all the risks. Once in a while, it is good for Reems to fend for himself. It helps remind him why he pays me so well."

Wade broke into an easy smile. "And I would guess you are not the kind who enjoys hiding behind Indian war paint when you are sent to raid the cattle at K Bar Ranch."

Juan didn't say a word, but he didn't have to. His expression said it all.

"Cowards hide themselves behind head dresses and arrows," Wade commented quietly. "It goes against your grain to perform such pranks because you are not a coward." He laid a gold coin on the bar to pay for the drink. "When you have had your fill of Haden Reems's ways, come see me. I think you and I would make better friends than enemies." Pushing away from the bar, Wade readjusted his jacket and then bent his gaze to his silent companion. "Doc Winston stitched up Haden's head and gave him laudanum to make him sleep. Perhaps you should haul him home before he wakes in a fit of temper."

As Wade ambled toward the door, Juan's voice brought him to a halt. *"Gringo?"* Cautiously Wade turned around. Juan flipped the coin back to him. "The drink was on me. And beware the Indians. I hear they are planning another raiding party. It would never do to have another roundup destroyed by a stampede."

Wade tucked the coin in his pocket. A slow smile worked its way across his lips. *"Gracias, amigo.* I will keep my eyes open for any sign of trouble."

When Wade stepped back onto the street, he breathed a frustrated sigh. Now where the hell was he to begin his search for that raven-haired wildcat? Shianne had set her sights on contracting a hangover she would never forget, and if he knew Shianne, she would waste no time in completing her task. Dammit, it was impossible to keep up with that firebrand.

Because of her the evening had snowballed from calamity to disaster. Haden Reems would be on the warpath when he roused, Doc Winston had insisted he marry Shianne, and Shianne was somewhere in the crowd making a fool of herself. Blast it, he should have gone to Springfield and left Blake to bring chaos under control!

Chapter 11

Shianne sorely regretted the sobering effect of knocking Haden unconscious. Determined to correct the problem, she aimed herself toward the refreshment table. To her relief the broken punch bowl had been replaced and an abundance of brandy-laced punch found its way to her lips.

Although she was congratulated by friends and acquaintances who delighted in seeing Haden publicly humiliated, Shianne was not drinking to celebrate her bold daring. She was drinking to forget. The way her luck had been running amuck of late, Haden would retract his proposal, and she would be unable to put a safe distance between Wade and herself. Her name would be at the top of Haden's black list, directly in front of Wade Burdett's.

Since Haden "Goliath" Reems had been struck down, a circle formed around Shianne, vying for her attention, and since Shianne was feeling no pain after consuming so much brandy, she voiced no complaint. She was passed from one eager pair of arms to another, flirting outrageously with whomever happened to be her partner at the moment. It was as if she were riding on a carousel, moving to and fro, up and down in slow motion. It didn't matter that she was making a fool of herself, she reckoned. How could she be more foolish than to club Haden over the head?

When the music ended, Shianne's tangled lashes swept up to view the smiling face too close to hers. She was in the circle of a man's arms, and that was about all she knew in her inebriated condition. The face looked faintly familiar, but she was too far into her cups to attach a name to it. The smell of whiskey filtered into her clogged senses as a pair of lips claimed hers. Shianne looped her arms about his neck, picturing a rugged face with laughing green eyes. Recklessly, she responded to the ravishing kiss, her body molding against the man who held her in his arms.

When Wade elbowed his way through the crowd to see Shianne wrapped in another man's arms he scowled in disgust. Every nerve in his body stood on end. Angrily, he watched Shianne deliver a kiss that melted her admirer into a puddle of desire. Wade should have been amused by the imp's outrageous antics, but he wasn't laughing. He was mad as hell! He had been the only man to sample that curvaceous minx's charms, and he would be damned if he would allow her to pass out free favors to every Casanova in San Antonio. He didn't give a damn if she was too inebriated to know what she was doing! If she didn't watch her step, she would find herself dragged off to be molested by a string of men who did not know how to treat a woman, especially one with such little experience in passion.

When the onlookers saw Wade standing there, his green eyes smoldering, a wave of whispers rippled through the strained silence. The crowd parted to allow Wade to stalk straight toward the chummy couple who were still in the clench.

The young swain glanced up and smiled meekly when Wade's ominous shadow loomed over him.

Without protest, the man withdrew and made himself scarce. He had witnessed Wade's scuffle with Haden Reems, and he did not relish spending the remainder of the evening in Doc Winston's office, lying unconscious on the couch.

When Shianne was passed to another set of arms she voiced no complaint. It had become habit, and she was too numb to care who was propping her up, so long as someone was. As the orchestra struck up another lively tune, Wade slid his arm around Shianne's waist and propelled her down the street.

A disappointed frown slid off the side of Shianne's face. "I want to dance," she slurred out.

Her attempt to step in time with the music ended in disaster. She tripped over the hem of her skirt, forcing Wade to tighten his grasp and hold her upright.

"You have been spun in too many circles as it is," Wade chided her gruffly. "And to make matters worse, you are drunk."

Shianne drew herself up to a proud stature (or so she thought. Actually she was tilting sideways). "I am not drunk," she denied over her thick tongue. "I'm just a mite tipsy."

Wade snorted disdainfully. "You, my dear, would have to be a damned sight more sober than you are now to be considered tipsy." He gave her a tug, uprooting her from the spot and shuffled her through the crowd. "You are going home, woman, before you get yourself into any more trouble."

A horrified expression captured her features. Shianne glanced up at the two fuzzy images that were swimming before her eyes. "Please, don't take me home. Take me anywhere but there. Wade might be there. I can't face him!"

Wade broke stride and stared at Shianne, his eyes bulging from their sockets. Hell's Bells, she didn't even

232

know who he was! "Why can't you face your guardian?" he demanded to know.

Shianne stared up at the blurred face as if he had just asked the most ridiculous question, and she was debating whether to dignify it with an answer. Finally, she glanced cautiously about her and then leaned close, as if to convey a confidential comment. "I am in love with him, but no one must know. I must guard my secret. Since I cannot marry the man I want, I have to settle for someone else. Except he won't have me now. . . ." Shianne hiccupped, covered her mouth and grinned sheepishly. "S'cuse me." A muddled frown puckered her rosy features. "How am I to sneak away at night when I am summoned if I am not living in my own house?" A contemplative expression claimed her face. "He wouldn't know where I was, and he would refuse to let me leave to be with another man." Shianne glanced up, more confused than ever. "Am I making any sense?"

Wade bit back an amused grin. "Very little," he assured her.

Shianne was so intoxicated she didn't know what she was saying or to whom she was speaking. All of the men in her life had become tangled up in her jumbled explanation. Wade didn't have the vaguest notion who the *he* was that Shianne kept referring to. Obviously, she didn't recognize Wade, and she had mistaken her guardian for her idol—the Owl Prophet. No doubt, all the men she had kissed the past hour reminded her of that confounded medicine man, Wade mused in annoyance.

Impulsively, he reversed direction and aimed himself and his stumbling companion toward Doc Winston's office. "Just stick with me, honey." He patted her limp hand. "We'll see what I can do to untangle this mess."

After propping Shianne against the bench that set

233

outside Doc Winston's office, he poked his head inside. "Doc?"

Jedediah strode from his home into the front office. A quizzical expression furrowed his brow when he noticed the exasperated frown Wade was wearing. "What's wrong now?"

"I need your assistance," Wade hurriedly requested.

The doctor grumbled under his breath. "Is someone else hurt? Lordy, I detest these festivals. They always turn into brawls."

"Just bring the smelling salts and fetch the padre," Wade ordered abruptly.

"Why?" The color seeped from Jedediah's features. "Does someone need their last rites read over them?"

"Yeah, me," Wade grunted and then glanced back at Shianne who had fallen sideways, her head dangling off the bench seat.

"But what about Haden? I can't leave him unattended," Jedediah reminded him.

"His men will be here shortly to haul him home. Just fetch the padre, dammit, I don't have all night!"

When Doc Winston came around the corner of the opened door, he froze in his tracks. "My God," he gasped. "What happened to Shianne?"

Wade scooped her into his arms and pointed himself toward the mission. "There is no delicate way to put it," he sighed. "The lady is drunk."

Jedediah reached over to pry open one heavily-lidded eye and then flung Wade a disdainful glare. "I'm surprised at you, Wade. How could you let her get in such a condition? You are supposed to be watching over her."

"I was busy talking to you and contacting Haden's men to tote him home, remember?"

Doc Winston nodded solemnly. "What are you going to do with her?" he asked as they strode through the streets.

"I'm going to marry her. It won't keep her out of trouble, but maybe it will keep her from kissing every man who asks her to dance," Wade exploded.

Jedediah smiled broadly. "I always did say if you can't find a cure for the disease, at least treat the symptoms."

Wade was not amused. He wanted nothing to do with marriage, but he was also desperate. Watching Shianne flaunt herself in front of her eager beaux turned him inside out. He was frustrated and his pride demanded some sort of compensation. Wedlock was a rather drastic measure to consider, but things had gotten completely out of hand. Bearing that in mind, Wade decided to follow through with his madness. At least it would give him a small amount of power over this bundle of trouble.

Once Jedediah had spoken with the priest, explaining Wade's intentions, they were led to the small chapel. While Shianne dozed against Wade's shoulder, the priest performed a hasty ceremony. Unfortunately, Jedediah was unable to give the bride away since she couldn't stand on her own two feet, much less walk down the aisle. When the priest paused for Shianne to repeat her vows, Wade grabbed the smelling salts and waved them under her nose.

Shianne jerked back, her lashes fluttering up to blink a blank stare. "What's going on?" she questioned groggily.

"We are getting married," Wade told her matter-of-factly.

A silly smile dangled on her lips as she braced her head against Wade's sturdy shoulder. "That's nice. . . ."

"Say I do, Shianne," Wade hastily instructed before she sank back into a brandy-induced stupor.

"I do what?" Her expression was dazed and quizzical.

"Close enough," Wade murmured as he watched Shianne slump against him and surrender to the arms of darkness.

The priest looked hesitantly at Wade. "It is proper to give the bride a ring," he reminded the groom.

Wade scowled disgustedly. He didn't have a ring. Confound it, he hadn't even intended to get married when he left the ranch earlier this evening, and here he was, hustling Shianne through a wedding ceremony that she had practically slept through.

"Can't we overlook that minor detail? I'll get her one tomorrow," Wade promised faithfully.

The priest was silent for a moment. "I suppose that will have to do," he said with a frustrated sigh. "But this is highly unorthodox."

"So is my bride," Wade sniffed caustically.

When the brief ceremony ended, Wade walked down the aisle, carrying his sleeping bride, cursing his insanity. Lord, when Shianne woke up, she would be furious to know he had deceived her. As he stepped outside, he hesitated, glancing indecisively about him. If he drove Shianne home, he would have to race back to town the following morning to purchase a ring. The best thing to do was to rent a room at the hotel, buy a ring, listen to her tirade, and *then* take her home, he decided.

"You won't be sorry," Doc Winston murmured as he clasped Wade's arm. "Shianne may be a handful, but she will make you a fine wife . . . once she adjusts to the idea." His eyes twinkled. Gently, he reached over to comb the wild strands of ebony from her creamy face. "There are many men who would gladly exchange places with you. Haden made it known that Shianne would one day be his wife and threatened any man who

236

paid too much attention to her, but there were still dozens of young men who risked life and limb to court her."

"I know," Wade grumbled resentfully. "One of them was fawning over her when I rescued her from his arms."

With that, Wade aimed himself toward the hotel. When he had rented a room for the night, he eased Shianne into bed and stared at her for a long moment. The neat coiffure of raven curls that had been pinned on top of her head at the onset of the fiesta was now in disarray. Wavy strands of hair flowed across the pillow like a sea of ebony. Her sleep-softened features drew his attention, and he sighed at the beautifully constructed lines of her face. Her sensuous lips parted slightly, as if prepared to accept a kiss. The rows of gauze lace that adorned the plunging neckline were draped low on her breasts. The soft mounds were dangerously close to spilling free as her chest rose and fell with each breath she took.

The small indention of her waist was wrapped in burgundy silk and the hem of her dress lay provocatively across her thigh, exposing the satiny flesh of her legs. Damn, but she looked tempting, Wade mused as he loosened his cravat and shed his coat. It was little wonder her eager dance partner thought to steal a kiss, and it was no surprise that Haden Reems wanted this stunning beauty . . . or at least he had until Shianne walloped him with a punch bowl.

Wade groaned in dismay. He didn't care that Haden despised him. Indeed, he welcomed Haden's contempt, but it worried Wade to think of Shianne becoming the object of Haden's fury. When Haden learned of the marriage, there was no telling what that madman might do. Wade had anticipated an all-out war against Haden, but he had made preparations for that. With

Shianne's help he would bring the treacherous rancher to his knees.

A troubled frown plowed Wade's brow. Dammit, why had he reacted so impulsively? By marrying Shianne he could well be risking her life. This wedding was not the solution. If anything it would create more problems.

When his eyes swung back to the bed, so did his thoughts. Wade peeled off his clothes and then removed Shianne's soiled gown. His touch caused Shianne to stir slightly. As Wade lay down beside her, Shianne cuddled against him like a kitten snuggling up to a cozy fire. Wade tensed, painfully aware of her soft breasts brushing against his flesh. When Shianne nestled her head against his shoulder and flung an arm over his chest, Wade groaned in torment. He was lying abed with the most fetching woman he had ever met, and he couldn't satisfy his desire to make wild sweet love to her. Wade couldn't think of taking Shianne when she could not respond, not when he knew the passion this woman possessed. There would be no pleasure in it.

Carefully, he squirmed to his side to stare into her exquisite features. "If only you were always this peaceful, vixen," he sighed whimsically. His hand gently cupped her face, tilting her lips to his. Like the prince attempting to kiss sleeping beauty from her long nap, Wade pressed his mouth to hers. Shianne responded slightly, her body instinctively moving closer to his hard length, and then she drifted off once again, lost to the hazy darkness that loomed over her like a circling hawk.

Wade expelled an exasperated sigh. Some wedding night this was, he thought bitterly. He didn't expect much from marriage, but he had at least anticipated the honeymoon to be a stimulating experience. Grumbling at his stupidity, Wade leaned out to snuff the lantern. When tomorrow came, the uneventful honeymoon would be over. Shianne would be sober and fit to be tied, and Wade would still be marveling at his idiocy.

Dammit, if Doc Winston hadn't planted the seed of thought, this never would have happened, Wade muttered to himself. Marriage? God, what a hypocrite he was turning out to be!

Closing his eyes, Wade begged for sleep to overtake him, to free him from troubled thoughts, but it was an hour before he drifted into fitful dreams. Even in sleep he was a tormented man. He kept seeing the ebony-haired temptress floating from one pair of arms to another, and he was forced to stand his ground, allowing every man to take her soft lips, to sketch her well-sculptured body with his caresses.

Wade woke in a cold sweat and glanced about him. Sighing heavily, he curled a possessive arm around Shianne and walked back into another dream, one far more arousing than the first.

A miserable groan erupted from Shianne's lips when she roused to consciousness. One heavily-lidded eye fluttered open, meeting the world through a gray haze. Expelling a woebegone sigh, Shianne eased onto her side, fighting the wave of nausea that rolled over her stomach. She could hear her pulse pounding in her head. It was either that or a bass drum, Shianne grimaced. In this condition she couldn't tell for certain. Lord, she had never felt so awful in her life! What had she done to herself? Bits and pieces of the previous night began to fall into place. Shianne massaged her aching temples, trying to sort out the events that were no more than confused, entangled thoughts.

When the image of Haden Reems collapsing on the

ground with a punch bowl on his head came to mind, Shianne groaned in dismay. God, she had invited Haden's fury. Then to forget her idiocy she began drinking heavily and . . . A muddled frown creased her features. And . . . and *what?* Shianne could not seem to remember what happened next. How had she managed to get home to bed? She was in her room in the hacienda, wasn't she?

Hating to look, afraid of what she might find, Shianne pried one eye open again. A shocked gasp flew free when she realized she was not in her own bed. She bolted straight up and then braced herself on her arm when the unfamiliar room began to spin furiously about her. Oh my God, what else had she done last night? She shuddered to imagine.

Her bloodshot eyes fell to her left hand, and she shrieked in horror. There on her ring finger set a huge diamond. Had she and Haden made amends after the incident? Had he married her in some hasty ceremony? That must have been what happened, Shianne reasoned. Why else would she be sporting a wedding ring?

Shianne glanced at the empty space beside her, one that showed evidence that she had not slept alone. Had Haden made love to her? If he had, it must not have been as bad as she anticipated, she reckoned. If it had been a nightmare she would have at least remembered that!

When the door of the hotel room creaked open, Shianne clutched the sheet under her chin and tensely waited to see who the intruder might be. Her mouth fell open when Wade sauntered into the room, carrying a breakfast tray.

It took all the self-control Wade could muster not to burst out laughing when he noticed the horrified look on Shianne's sleep-drugged features. Her waist-length hair hung about her in disarray. Her eyes were dull and

240

lifeless and streaked with red. Yet, even when Shianne was at her worst she was still enchanting. It suddenly occurred to Wade that Shianne could never look bad. Her appearance could only be measured in varying degrees of loveliness. Even a wilted rose was still a rose, though it was sorely in need of watering. After a few cups of coffee and a refreshing bath, Shianne would be herself again, he diagnosed.

"Good morning, princess," Wade greeted cheerfully. He closed the door with his boot heel and strode over to set the tray beside her. "Would you care for something to drink?" A wry smile pursed his lips when Shianne grabbed her sensitive head and covered her ears. "I hope you won't mind settling for coffee instead of brandy this morning."

The mere mention of liquor sent her tender stomach rolling in a back somersault. The sound of Wade's voice booming in rhythm with the drum that was playing in her head was too much. Shianne collapsed on the pillow, groaning in dismay. At the moment she was too miserable to tax her mind with questions such as: where was Haden and what was Wade doing on her honeymoon?

With tender loving care, Wade slid his arm around Shianne's shoulders and propped her up to take a sip of coffee. "You aren't accustomed to hangovers, are you?" he questioned in a softer tone.

Shianne shook her head negatively and allowed the warm liquid to trickle down her throat, dreading its landing on her queasy stomach. Once her innards adjusted to the initial shock, she braved another sip.

"Feeling better?" Wade inquired, frowning in concern.

Shianne touched her fingertips to her throbbing temples. "I think I would have to be dead a week before I felt better," she rasped.

Ever so slowly she began to come back to life, but she was a long way from recovery. Indeed, Shianne doubted she would ever be the same again. After munching on the warm biscuit Wade brought for her Shianne frowned curiously.

"Where is Haden?"

"At his ranch, recovering from the nasty gash in his forehead," Wade informed her blandly. "I have never seen anyone quite as effective with a punch bowl, my dear."

The taunting comment did nothing to sweeten Shianne's disposition. "I prefer not to discuss the incident," she snapped. "If he is at the ranch, what am I doing here?"

Wade strangled his amused grin. It was obvious that Shianne remembered nothing except the fiasco in the streets. "It is a shame you cannot recall what happened last night," he mocked, offering her another sip of coffee. "You were having the time of your life."

"Was I?" Shianne studied him bewilderedly.

"You were dancing on tables and clinging to every man who happened into your arms. I'm sure you were the envy of every woman in San Antonio. If you did not offer a kiss to all your eager admirers, I cannot imagine who you might have overlooked."

Shianne's eyes grew as round as her coffee cup. "I did that?" she chirped. Her gaze fell to her ring finger, and then she peered at Wade who was grinning outrageously. "You are teasing me, aren't you?" Shianne muttered under her breath. "Of course you are. If you are trying to make me feel worse than I already do, you are wasting your time. I'm sure I am going to die soon anyway." She had thought the food and drink would put her back on the road to recovery, but she was sadly mistaken. Nourishment only aggravated her condition.

"I tried to warn you to slow down, but you wouldn't

242

listen," Wade sighed. "I suppose everyone has to experience a hangover to know how dreadful it truly is."

When her eyes fell back to the ring he had slipped on her finger while she was still asleep, Wade squirmed uncomfortably. "Shianne, you were married last night," he told her quietly.

Without glancing up she nodded slightly. "At least I am not a jewel thief," she grumbled. Her eyes lifted momentarily to flash Wade an accusing glance. "Is Haden coming to retrieve me or are you playing your final role as my guardian by taking me to him?"

Wade did a double take. "Haden? Why the devil would I be delivering you to Haden? After we publicly humiliated him last night, I'm sure he holds both of us in contempt."

Shianne stared at Wade for a long, confused moment. "If I didn't marry Haden who did I marry?"

A grin as wide as Texas stretched from ear to ear. "Me."

"What!" Shianne gasped. She frantically searched her memory, trying to conjure up a thought that simply had not been recorded in her mind. "That is impossible. If you were the last man on earth I wouldn't marry you."

"Well, you must have changed your mind because that is exactly what you did last night," he told her matter-of-factly. "And there was no one twisting your arm to force you to speak the vows." When Shianne eyed him suspiciously, Wade gestured toward the ring that set on her trembling finger. "If you don't believe me, ask Doc Winston. He gave you away."

She couldn't have married Wade! He was the one man she wanted to avoid. Why, her motive for accepting Haden's proposal was to rout Wade from her life forever.

"You are lying," she harshly accused as she pulled the ring from her finger. "This is part of the treasure you are stashing in the cave—stolen jewels. You are trying to punish me for behaving like an ass last night. Well, I deeply regret the way I behaved and you needn't . . ." Her voice trailed off when Wade fished the marriage license from his pocket and dangled it in front of her face. "Oh, no . . . !"

"Oh, yes," Wade contradicted. "Not only am I your guardian, but your husband as well as . . ." Wade clamped his mouth shut, before he stuck his foot in it.

Shianne was too dismayed to insist he finish his comment. She was wrestling with the knowledge that she had married the one man she knew she could never truly have. Why had Wade consented to the marriage if he was sober? He didn't want a wife. Her lashes fluttered up, her eyes full of unanswered questions.

Wade knew what was coming. Rising to full stature, he set the tray on the night stand. "I did it to protect you." He answered her question before she asked it. "The way you were carrying on last night, I feared you would land in some man's bed. Why not mine? It isn't as if you hadn't been there before."

Shianne came straight out of bed, hangover and all. "I think you are carrying this guardianship a bit too far!" she railed at him. "You are the one from whom I need protection."

Wade wheeled around, grinning into her furious face. "So you said last night."

A wary frown knitted her brow. "Exactly what did I say last night?" she demanded to know.

Wade reached up to smooth an unruly strand of ebony hair away from her face. He met her searching gaze, debating whether or not to offer her words back to her. Feeling a bit ornery, he decided to tell her what she wanted to know. "You informed me that the reason you wanted to accept Haden's proposal was to avoid me. When I asked you why, you mentioned something about being in love with me." Well, that wasn't exactly what she had said, Wade admitted to himself, but it was close enough. He wasn't about to tell Shianne that she was mooning over that blasted medicine man!

His words took the wind out of her sails. She had said that? God help her, she would never drink again. It had wrought disaster! There was nothing to do but lie. The truth would shatter her pride. "That is the most ridiculous thing I have yet to hear!" she exploded.

"It surprised me too," Wade chuckled, watching the crimson blush work its way through her pale features. "And all this time I thought you despised me."

"I do despise you," Shianne flared, annoyed by his smug grin. "If I made such a preposterous remark it must have been the brandy talking. It certainly wasn't me."

"The words came right out of your mouth, my love," he purred in mock sincerity. "I saw and heard them."

Shianne glanced hurriedly about her, searching for her clothes. She was not about to stand here and allow this arrogant cowboy to taunt her for her foolishness. With no consideration for modesty, Shianne tossed the sheet aside and pulled the gown over her head.

"I am going to have this marriage annulled," she told him harshly. "I will not be married to a libertine."

"Don't you think you are woman enough to hold my fascination?" he tossed at her rigid back. Wade was being cruel and he knew it. But dammit, she deserved it after she forced him to watch her melt in other men's arms the previous night and to listen to her babble about her infatuation with Maman-ti.

Shianne whirled on him, eyes flashing. "No woman on God's green earth could satisfy you. I have known your kind before, and I have purposely taken a wide berth around them. You pride yourself in conquering women. You gloat over every conquest." Shianne squared her shoulders and tilted a proud chin. "Well, I will not stand by and be humiliated while you hop from one bed to another."

Now why had he expected Shianne to take the news about their marriage and accept it as fact? He should have known she would put up a fuss. But by damned, she was not getting an annulment. They had spoken the vows, and they were legally married. She may not like it, but she was going to live with it!

As Shianne stormed toward the door, Wade stepped in front of her, his smile vanishing. "You are going nowhere," he told her sternly. "This is our honeymoon, and I intend to reap the rewards from speaking the vows." He grabbed her hand, forcing the ring back on her finger. "We may not have had our wedding night, but we *will* enjoy the morning after."

"I am not wearing this stolen ring," Shianne hissed, futilely attempting to remove the diamond.

"Dammit, I didn't steal it. I bought it!"

"With stolen money!" Shianne hurled at him. "And I do not want a hand-me-down who has bedded more women than I have even *met* in my lifetime. . . ."

Wade was finished arguing. He yanked Shianne's tense body to him to deliver a kiss that would melt her resistance. Shianne silently cursed his technique. He bent her backwards, forcing her to cling to him or fall in a heap on the floor. Then, to make matters worse, he didn't ravish her. The miserable varmint assaulted her with a tenderness that was more potent than any forceful embrace. His sensuous lips whispered over hers, gently coaxing her, subtly inviting her to taste the kiss he offered.

Shianne hated herself for responding. She certainly hadn't meant to. Lord, he was the devil's own temptation. Wade knew how to touch a woman and make her body respond. He knew how to offer a kiss and leave her craving a dozen more just like this one.

When Wade lifted his head, his emerald eyes were glowing with unmistakable desire. His hands glided over her shoulder, sending the gathered neckline of the silk gown drifting down her arm. "You give yourself very little credit sometimes, Shae," he murmured as his lips strayed down the swanlike column of her neck. "You are aware of your ability to manage your ranch, but you are much too modest when it comes to realizing what dramatic effects you have on men. Why would I want to wander if you made it your intent to satisfy me, to willingly offer those things a man needs and craves from a woman? Show me what it could be like between us if you truly did love me," he challenged her.

For a long, silent moment Shianne stared into his rugged face. Yes, for once she would come to him without her protective armor of pride. She would find a way to assure him that what was between them would drain every ounce of his strength and discourage him from seeking out another woman. She would make him remember this day, she promised herself. Wade didn't love her, but she vowed never to let him forget her.

Casting pride aside, Shianne stepped back to push the gown over her breasts and hips. She watched him watch her as she sent the yards of silk fluttering into a pool around her feet.

Wade caught fire and burned the moment Shianne unveiled her beauty to his all-consuming gaze. He wasn't certain what he expected when he issued his challenge, but whatever it was, it wasn't this!

A provocative smile traced her lips as she mapped the landscape of his chest. "Our marriage may not last but a day, my handsome husband, but for a time, I will not allow the vision of another woman to cross your mind. . . ."

Her fingertips fluttered over the buttons of his shirt. Almost as if by magic the garment fell away, revealing the bronzed flesh of his chest. Her lips skimmed his skin, melting muscle into mush. Wade could feel her long lashes tickling, her lips arousing, her caresses doing incredible things to his sanity. A sigh of pure pleasure tripped from his lips as her roaming hands glided around his ribs to assault his spine. Her soft breasts brushed across his hair-matted chest, driving him mad with unfulfilled desire, and when she opened her lips to him, he drowned in a sensation that shook the roots of his soul.

Her kisses and caresses were unhurried, achingly tender, holding intimate promises of things to come. Wade allowed her to have her way with him, and he made no protest when she urged him to the bed. Never had removing a pair of breeches seemed so arousing. He would never shed his trousers again without remembering the inventive technique Shianne had employed. Every inch of bared skin was subjected to a rash of moist kisses and light caresses. Wade swore he had sunk into the feather mattress by the time this spellcasting witch had completed her task. Every nerve and muscle in his body had wilted beneath her exploring touch. Wade doubted if he could climb to his feet, even if his life depended on it.

Shianne amazed herself with her bold seduction, but she could not seem to satisfy her desire to touch him, to learn every inch of his hard masculine flesh. Although she was giving pleasure she was receiving pleasure in return. She loved touching him, making him respond, evoking moans that had nothing to do with pain and everything to do with passion. As if her hands possessed a will of their own, they flooded and then receded over his hair-roughened flesh. She sketched the sinewy tendons of his thighs and calves, monitored the accelerated beat of his heart. She feasted on him, worshipping him with soft kisses.

Only when she had tasted every inch of him did she seek out his lips. When she did, Wade moaned in sweet torment. His arms came around her, crushing her to him, even when he had promised himself he would display no forcefulness. He could not seem to help himself. There was no time to think, only time to respond, to ease this insane craving she had instilled in him.

"My God, woman, do you have any idea what you have done to me?" he breathed against lips that melted like rose petals beneath his.

"Do you want me, Wade?" Her expression was questioning. Lovingly, Shianne reached out to trace the chiseled lines of his face, to trail her finger over his clean-shaven cheek. "Or will any woman do to satisfy your longings? If we remain married, no matter what reasons have brought us to this, I have to know you care enough about me not to hurt me, to shame me. It's all or nothing with me, Wade."

A tender smile caressed his lips. Shianne was the epitome of pride, the essence of beauty. At the moment Wade couldn't think past her bewitching face, even if he had wanted to make comparisons. When Shianne made love to him she filled up his world and his mind, erasing the memory of every woman who had come before.

"If we are going to make vows to each other, I expect one in return," he insisted, his voice heavily disturbed with passion. "No more midnight rendezvous with Maman-ti."

Shianne pressed closer, refusing to debate the

subject, at least not now. She had explained about the Owl Prophet but Wade just didn't seem to understand.

Wade gripped her upper arm and held her away from him. "I want your promise, Shae. I want you to . . ."

Her head tilted to study his determined frown. Her adventurous hand slid across his thigh, rediscovering the feel of his muscular flesh. "Do you want to talk or make love?" she questioned point-blank.

When she put the question to him in that manner and supplemented it with an arousing caress, Wade lost all interest in conversation. She touched him and his brain malfunctioned. "Make love to me, vixen," he growled seductively.

She did. Shianne held nothing back. She came to him in wild abandon, letting her heart rule her head. Her quiet sighs encouraged him. Her softly spoken words lured him closer. She whispered her need for him, assuring him that he pleasured her.

Wade forgot all about his envy of the Owl Prophet. He had Shianne in his arms, and she was taking him on the most splendorous of voyages through a sea of rapture. Her feminine body arched eagerly toward his, accepting him, possessing him. They moved together in perfect rhythm, soaring higher and higher still. Wade caught his breath when the first wave of ecstasy crested upon him. He could feel himself losing control, feel himself surrendering to each rapturous sensation that toppled over him. He wanted to cherish this magnificent moment, to make it last forever, but the feelings gave way to even more splendid sensations. Something was very wrong, Wade thought deliriously. He didn't remember lovemaking being quite like this all-consuming emotion that he sensed was about to swallow him alive. Something was tugging at the strings of his heart. . . .

Then it came to him, that devastating, soul-shattering sensation that made him clutch at Shianne and hold on for dear life. Wade felt as if he had been knocked sideways by a tidal wave, swamped and buffeted by an ocean of turbulent sensations. His heart was racing so furiously he swore it would beat him to death. His body shuddered in sweet release, and he slumped against Shianne.

A contented smile rippled across her lips as she combed her fingers through his raven hair. That first night when they had made love Shianne had been apprehensive, but this time there had been nothing but the quintessence of pleasure. If they never enjoyed another peaceful moment at least she would have this memory to call upon, she reassured herself.

Wade eased down beside her, returning her smile. With a sigh, he traced the line of her jaw. For a moment no words formed. He was content just to gaze into her dark eyes and to remember the exquisite magic between them.

They lay there in silence, each vividly aware of the other, sharing a serenity that words could not express. In that time in space, the obstacles that stood between them faded, and they were satisfied just to gaze into each other's eyes. Their absent caresses wandered freely, and when Wade smiled intimately, Shianne smiled back. It was a quiet time, unlike anything she had ever known, and she was most reluctant to give it up.

Chapter 12

The sound of footsteps in the hall roused Wade from his pensive deliberations. Instinctively, he reached down to retrieve his pistol and tucked it beneath the sheet. When the footsteps paused in front of their door, Wade cursed himself for not locking it behind him. There should have been nothing unusual about traffic in the hallway, but Wade recognized the heavy-footed sounds and speculated that he and his new bride were about to receive an unwelcomed visit.

He was right. Haden Reems kicked at the door, causing it to sag on its hinges. The moment the intruder barged inside, Shianne grasped the sheet to cover herself and colored seven shades of red, but the shade of embarrassment that crept to her cheeks could not match the crimson fury that attacked Haden's bony features.

"You little slut!" He spat at Shianne as if the words left a disgusting taste in his mouth. "I heard you and this worthless bastard had checked into the hotel, but I had to see for myself that you had stooped that low."

Wade was propped against the headboard of the bed, watching Haden like a hawk. Behind him was the small army that made Haden think he was the ruling king of San Antonio. Wade shot the cluster of men a discreet glance, but most of his attention was on the fuming rancher. In Haden's fit of temper, Wade wasn't sure how far the man would go to satisfy his thirst for revenge.

"That's the second time you have burst in without announcing yourself, Haden," Wade remarked, his voice deadly calm. "I overlooked your rudeness once, but not this time." Reaching over with his left hand, Wade tugged on the sheet beside him, displaying the revolver that rested in his right hand. "Where I come from, a man takes offense when another man makes slanderous remarks about his wife."

Wade may as well have shot Haden right through the heart! The words were just as painful. "Your wife?" he bellowed in disbelief. Wild eyes swung to Shianne, noting the ring that encircled her finger. "Damn you!"

When Haden took an impulsive step forward, Wade cocked the trigger and lifted the revolver. "I wouldn't if I were you, Haden. I need very little coaxing to blow holes in your expensive clothes. Your next step may be your last. . . ."

Haden went rigid with fury. "Kill him!" he screeched at his vaqueros. "Drop him where he lies. . . ."

The silence was so thick it could have been chopped with an axe. No one moved. Juan had already tossed his men a warning glance. Shianne lay there, her body quaking with apprehension. She had never seen Haden so furious, and she had never found herself in such an uncompromising position.

"I said kill him!" Haden raved.

"Señor, this is not the time or the place," Juan assured the outraged rancher. "None of us wishes to be strung up for murder. If you want no witnesses, you will have to kill the girl and everyone in the hotel as well. Even then there is the matter of the *gringo's* letter that lies in the lawyer's office."

Haden didn't want to be reminded of Wade's forethought. It only served to fuel his blazing temper. He had intended to forgive Shianne for what had happened the previous night. Her acceptance of his marriage proposal would have soothed his pride, and the townspeople would have realized that her over-indulgence of liquor had caused her to react as she had. But this new twist was unforgivable. Now he could never regain his respect in San Antonio. He would be the laughingstock of Bexar County. Damn them both to hell and back!

His hand trembled as he raised it to shake a long finger in their faces. "You have openly invited my wrath. Be warned, Burdett. I will show you no mercy. And you . . ." His vengeful gaze pelleted over Shianne. "I would have laid the world at your feet. I have waited far too long for you, woman. I granted you the time you wanted. You have betrayed me and I will never forgive you for that. I swear I will find a way to ruin both of you!"

The door slammed shut behind Haden, and Wade listened to the receding footsteps until they died in the silence. He watched curiously as Shianne bounded from the bed to fetch her clothes. "Where do you think you are going?"

"To try to talk some sense into Haden," she threw over her shoulder.

Wade rolled from the bed to stand before her. "You would be asking for trouble. The way he feels at the moment he would as soon shoot you as talk to you."

"Well, I have to try!" Shianne insisted. "He'll destroy us and everything I have scratched and clawed to hold together during the war."

Wade grasped both of her arms and held her away from him, staring grimly into her wide eyes. "It's too late to talk. What's done is done. Besides, by the time Haden receives the reports from his range hands, he will be even more furious with us than he is now."

Shianne regarded him warily. "What did you do?"

A sly smile pursed his lips. "I rerouted the channel of the spring. Before I came to the hacienda last night, I put on the finishing touches. Haden's creek will be dry by evening, and he will have no source of water. The mouth of the spring is on *my* land, and I have no intention of allowing his cattle to drink my water."

"Now who is asking for trouble?" Shianne sniffed.

Wade shrugged a bare shoulder. "Haden asked for it when he stampeded our cattle. I figured I owed him one, and you are going to help me give him another dose of misery tonight."

The dubious frown that clung to Shianne's features deepened. She didn't like the look on Wade's face. It spelled more trouble. "Just what is it you expect of me?" She wasn't certain she wanted to know, but she had to ask.

"When the Owl Prophet summons you, I'm going to come with you. He and I are going to meet face to face," Wade informed her.

"Are you mad? You can't just waltz into council with the war chiefs of the Kiowa and Comanche! Maman-ti hates all white men. He might torture you," Shianne gasped. "Dammit, Wade, sometimes I don't know if you are incredibly brave or downright crazy."

Sporting a confident smile, Wade lifted her hand and brushed his finger over the ring. "I feel reasonably protected. The Owl Prophet wouldn't harm a hair on your head, nor would he have the heart to threaten *your* loving husband. But he just might be willing to give Haden a taste of trouble . . . if *you* insist."

Shianne jerked her hand from his grasp and glared holes in his broad chest. "So that is why you married me. I knew there had to be an ulterior motive. You are planning to use Maman-ti against Haden. You use everyone to suit your purposes, don't you, Wade? You intend to start a chain reaction, and when all the pieces fall, you will walk away with whatever it is you have plotted to possess."

Hurt registered in her eyes. At last she understood why Wade had made her his bride, why he purposely provoked Haden Reems. He didn't want just the mavericks he could gather from the Texas range. Wade wanted Haden's cattle as well, she speculated. Haden couldn't win. If he disposed of Wade he would face a hanging, but if Wade disposed of Haden it was winner take all. That conniving bastard! He was as bad as Haden Reems, and now she was married to him. Wade intended to use her as a mediator to get to Maman-ti. Well, she would not be a party to treachery, and she would not put the Owl Prophet's life in jeopardy!

"If you want Maman-ti's help, you confront him yourself," Shianne snapped brusquely. Angrily, she tore the ring from her finger and hurled it across the room. "I'm going home. If you want to get yourself killed, that is fine with me, but I am not going to lift a hand to assist you."

As Shianne stomped toward the door, Wade grabbed his breeches and grumbled at her stubbornness. While Shianne stormed out of the hotel to rent a carriage Wade got down on all fours to recover the ring. Damn that woman! One minute he was counting her saving graces, and the next moment he was cursing her faults. Why was she so contrary, and why did she always think the worst of him? Someone had to put a stop to Haden Reems's skulduggery. He had threatened and stolen from every rancher in the county. Someone had to rid the area of that sidewinder, and Wade was the likely candidate since he had more than one score to settle with Reems. If Shianne couldn't see he and Haden were bound to clash since the beginning, she was more naive than he thought. By damned, she *had* to help him. She wouldn't be safe until Haden Reems was behind bars for strong-arming every rancher in the county, not to mention stealing cattle and horses and placing the blame on the Indians. The Comanches weren't the true culprits on the range, Haden was. The Indians took what they needed to survive, what they felt they deserved after the government stripped them of their lands. The homesteaders had tilled the Indians' hunting grounds and insisted that all red men be rounded up and corralled on reservations.

Wade knew what it was like to watch others take over land that had been in his family for generations. He did not approve of the Indians' methods of retaliation, but he understood their frustrations far better than Shianne would ever give him credit.

Haden Reems was different. He didn't take only what he needed. He was a greedy man who wanted his brand on every head of cattle and horse in Texas. He had an obsessive craving to become the most powerful man in the state. Men like Haden Reems were a threat to every decent citizen who tried to make an honest living after the interruption of the war. Had Haden offered a hand to aid the South? No, he was too damned selfish to consider anyone but himself.

Hell, he should have delivered this lecture to Shianne, Wade thought as he pulled on his shirt and boots. Maybe then she would place part of the blame on Haden instead of carrying around her yoke of guilt. So what if she had pounded him over the head with a punch bowl? Haden would have cut Wade to pieces, given the chance. Haden wasn't to be pitied; he was to be condemned. What would Wade have to do, get himself killed before Shianne realized Haden Reems deserved no mercy?

Heaving an annoyed sigh, Wade stalked down the steps. Maybe it was time he took Shianne into his confidence. He would appease her curiosity about the cavern, he decided. Then perhaps she would not be so mistrusting of him. Well, it was worth a try. Nothing could be worse than having her despise him, having her think he was a calculating thief.

The moment Shianne stepped into the entryway of the hacienda, Ramona bombarded her with questions. When Shianne had finished explaining the disastrous events of the fiesta, ones that had led to her subsequent marriage, Ramona clasped her hands in delight.

"You have found a man worthy of your love," Ramona sighed happily.

"Wade Burdett is many things, but *worthy* is not among them. Manipulative and deceitful make a better description," she muttered sourly.

"You are only pouting because the wedding was not your idea," Ramona assured her. "Once you adjust to having a husband, you will realize you could not have made a better choice."

Shianne was in no mood to hear Ramona praise that treacherous varmint. All she wanted was a hot bath and solitary confinement. She had to decide what to do. The day had put her emotions in turmoil, and she needed time to sort them out and deal with them separately. Once she had regained her perspective she could choose her course of action.

Determined to do just that, Shianne requested a bath and retired to her room. Expelling a weary sigh, Shianne sank down on the edge of the bed and stared at the wall. It hurt to know that she was no more than a device to Wade. He had convinced her father to join in a partnership, and he had seduced Shianne, using her in his scheme to devastate Haden. Not that Haden was a saint, she admitted. Why was Wade so determined to spite him at every turn? It made no sense. She could understand Wade's craving to repay Haden for staking him out and stealing his cattle, but there was something else driving him, she speculated. It couldn't have been the fact he and Haden were after the same woman. Wade didn't really want her. He had only married her because Haden had made a claim on her. Wade wasn't fighting for her love. Of all the things he wanted from her, love was not among them. Dammit, why was Wade so hellbent on destroying Haden?

Oh, why was she trying to analyze Wade Burdett? The man was a paradox. If she had any sense at all she would avoid him like the plague, and that was exactly what she was going to do, she vowed to herself. She would have this ridiculous marriage annulled and forbid Wade from entering her home. He could manage his roundup from his campsite and protect whatever it was he was hiding in the cave. What did she care?

Shianne squeezed her eyes shut when a tormenting memory flashed through her mind. She could see Wade lying beside her, smiling at her with what she mistook for true affection. No doubt he was grinning in smug satisfaction, gloating over his scheme to wed her and then use her for his purpose. Shianne tossed the thought aside, refusing to allow her physical attraction for the man influence her. From now on she would be objective when she considered Wade Burdett. He was going to get himself killed. The man was self-destructive. She had thought he had put the war behind him, but he hadn't, not really. He had made Haden Reems his crusade, simply because he was frustrated by the defeat of the South. Yes, maybe Haden Reems needed to be cut down to size, but Wade was a foreigner to Texas. It wasn't Wade's battle.

Shianne massaged her aching head. She had promised not to give Wade another thought and here she was analyzing him again. Whoever and whatever he was, he was not the man for her. Ramona was wrong on that count. Shianne certainly wasn't indignant because the wedding hadn't been her idea. That was the most ridiculous thing she had ever. . . . Shianne gulped hard. Was she truly that stubborn and contrary? Was she defying Wade because he was as strong-willed and determined as she was? Was she truly annoyed with him because she couldn't twist him around her little finger? Well, maybe she was, Shianne begrudgingly admitted, but dammit, how was she supposed to feel when the man marched in and took over her life and her ranch? It wasn't easy to step down after she had been in complete control. Oh, why hadn't her father come home? She needed him. Didn't he care about her? How could he have dumped her in Wade's lap? Damn men everywhere. They were nothing but trouble!

As nightfall descended on the hacienda, Shianne heard the quiet call of a distant owl. Damn, she had prayed Maman-ti and his warriors would stay away. If Wade heard the call, he would know where she was going. She had to warn the Owl Prophet that there was trouble brewing. If Wade had his way he would have the Comanches and Kiowas involved in a war that was none of their concern.

Frantically, Shianne climbed into her breeches and boots. Fleeing through the terrace doors, she made her way down the lattice and out to the corral. A surprised gasp burst free when Wade emerged from the shadows.

"I'm going with you," he told Shianne, his expression stern.

Shianne ignored him. When she attempted to pull onto Delgado's back, Wade wedged in front of her. "I am going alone," she hissed at him.

Once Wade had settled himself on the black stallion, he lifted Shianne's resisting body up behind him. When he gouged Delgado, Shianne had no choice but to hang on or be dumped on the ground.

"Damn you," she spewed, resenting the fact that she had to clasp her arms about his waist.

"Lord, woman, I wish just once I could hear a compliment pass your lips," he smirked. As Delgado thundered across the prairie, Wade slipped the ring back on her finger for the third time that day. It was worse than keeping a bit in the mouth of a green-broke colt. "If you will pretend to portray my loving wife when I meet the Owl Prophet, I will explain the secret of the cave."

Shianne simply could not resist the temptation. For weeks her curiosity had been eating her alive. If Wade was finally willing to explain himself, she would see that Maman-ti granted him amnesty . . . at least for one night. "We have struck a bargain," she declared.

Wade breathed a relieved sigh, but it was short-lived. His gaze focused on the looming figure who emerged from the underbrush. Even in the moonlight the Indian made a proud, foreboding figure. Although Wade could not see the expression on the Owl Prophet's face, he could feel the piercing scrutiny directed toward him. Reining Delgado to a halt, Wade returned the bold stare. When he had set Shianne to her feet, she flew into Maman-ti's arms. Wade watched the touching scene with eyes that turned a darker shade of green. It annoyed him that Shianne went so easily into the

261

Indian's arms while Wade was forced to coax her into his. What would it take to earn Shianne's devotion, he wondered bitterly.

"Why have you brought this man with you?" Maman-ti questioned, never taking his eyes off the tall, muscularly built stranger. "Is he the one I have seen in my dreams?"

Shianne felt the Owl Prophet's body grow taut as he held her in the protective circle of his arms. "He is. . . ."

Wade had fully intended for Shianne to lead him to the Indian, but he carried too much pride to allow her to speak for him. The fact that Maman-ti continued to hold Shianne aggravated Wade and he wanted it known that he did not approve.

"My name is Wade Burdett. I am Shianne's husband." Wade walked boldly toward the bare-chested oracle. The faintest hint of a smile hung on one corner of his mouth. Deliberately, he sized up the Indian, noting the wild nobility that was stamped on Maman-ti's features.

Shianne could feel the tension mounting as the two men stared each other up and down. They were built much alike, both exuding a strength that made others sit up and take note. It was obvious both men were not quite certain what to make of each other, and it was a long moment before Maman-ti spoke.

"Shianne has told you about me?" the Owl Prophet queried.

"I know of her ties to your people, of her devotion to you," Wade informed him casually. Then his tone changed, growing firm and insistent. "I have no quarrel with you or your people. In many ways I am like you. I understand the resentment you bear because the white man has come to claim the land that has been your home for generations. My home was in Louisiana until the Civil War pitted brother against brother. Because of my family's firm beliefs and strong stand our home was destroyed, and our land was divided and given to others.

"I have learned to tolerate what I cannot change, but I have also come to cling fiercely to possessions that are mine." Wade's gaze shifted from the Owl Prophet's stern features to Shianne's bewitching face. "She is my woman, Maman-ti. She wears my ring as a symbol of the promise I made when I spoke the vows. I want no other woman, and I will not give her up to any other man."

If Shianne hadn't known this was all an act she might have been touched by Wade's words, but she knew better. Wade was playing upon her strong attachment to the Comanches and Kiowas to gain favors, but if wishing would make it so, Wade would have meant every word that tumbled from his tongue.

The semblance of a smile rippled across Maman-ti's bronzed features. "Do you threaten me, Wade Burdett? You know who I am, and yet you come to stake your claim on this woman? You must know how I feel about her. Do you expect me to stop loving her because you have taken her for your wife?"

Shianne flinched. Maman-ti had never spoken the words, at least never so openly. He had shown his affection in his tender touch and his protective attitude. Discreetly, she glanced at Wade, wondering if he knew what the devil he was doing by challenging a man with the Owl Prophet's influence.

One dark brow climbed to a mocking angle. "Do you expect me to stop loving Shianne because she leaves my arms to answer the call of the owl?" Wade took a bold step forward. His callused hand folded around the raven tendrils that cascaded over Shianne's shoulder. "I know of her admiration for you, and I envy it. I wish I possessed the gift of magic. I would rout you from her thoughts and keep her all to myself." His eyes lifted to hold Maman-ti's unblinking gaze. "But since I do not, I chose to confront the man who cherishes her as much as I do. I have also come to warn you that there is another man, an evil white man, who wants to take her from both of us and do her harm."

"Who is this man?" Maman-ti demanded to know.

"His name is Haden Reems. He has vowed revenge because I have made Shianne my wife. He has sworn to destroy both of us because he cannot have what has become an obsession to him. I will fight him to the death before I will give Shianne up to the man who dresses his army in Indian buckskins and war paint to steal my cattle. He delights in laying the blame on the Comanches and Kiowas."

The Owl Prophet's dark eyes circled the sprawling range. He suddenly understood the dream that had tormented him the past few weeks. In his visions, he had perceived trouble for Shianne, and for that reason he had often come to her ranch to ensure she was not in danger. Premonition had persuaded him into another raid, a raid that would bring his people much prosperity.

"The evil white man's land lies beside Shianne's home. His fate was decided when the feathered oracle sent me a vision," he murmured, as if in a trance. "It is his land we will raid this night."

Wade eyed the prophet warily. If he didn't know better he would have sworn the Owl Prophet *did* possess some supernatural gift.

"He has many cattle and horses, but he will have fewer numbers when the sun climbs into the morning sky. My braves will catch his bravoes unaware, and they will be no match for us. In the raid we will loose no warriors, but two of his men will fall. There is one among them who will bravely fight against us, but it is

264

not his time to die. He has some other purpose. . . ." Maman-ti's voice faded, and in the distance a screech owl's eerie song shattered the silence.

For a moment Wade simply stood there staring at the Owl Prophet. He had heard Shianne praise Maman-ti's ability to foresee the future, but he had been skeptical . . . until now.

When Maman-ti's dark eyes drifted back to Wade, he produced a challenging smile. Boldly, he drew Shianne closer and, after tossing Wade another smug glance, proceeded to press an affectionate kiss to her brow. Releasing her, he nudged her toward Wade who had gritted his teeth in an attempt to retain self-control. He knew the warrior was purposely taunting him, trying to prove his power over Shianne, but Wade was as mischievous as Maman-ti, even moreso perhaps.

Determined to make his point, even if it increased the friction between them, Wade slid his arm around Shianne's waist. With the Owl Prophet as witness, Wade planted a passionate kiss on Shianne's lips.

Shianne did not appreciate being tossed back and forth between these two proud men like a yo-yo. Maman-ti's show of affection was meant to annoy Wade, and Wade's devastating kiss was a premeditated display of defiance. Shianne had a good mind to kick them both for taunting each other.

Propping Shianne upright, Wade kept a possessive arm about her. That notoriously infuriating smile crept across Wade's shadowed features, and white teeth gleamed in the moonlight. "*My* woman, Maman-ti," he told the Indian matter-of-factly. "Body and soul."

The Owl Prophet strode over to scoop Shianne in his arms and set her atop the black stallion. Long, lean fingers lingered on her thigh, and Wade glared at them. "*Our* woman," he corrected with a gruff snort.

Not to be outdone, Wade swung onto Delgado's

back and reached around Shianne to grasp the reins. He molded his chest to her back and crowded his thighs against her legs, forcing Maman-ti to remove his hand or risk having it slide onto Wade's knee.

"You have two wives, Maman-ti. I will settle for one. *This* one. I think I would like you better if you and I were not compelled to the same woman."

Maman-ti broke into a reluctant smile. He could not help but admire the daring white man. There was a challenging glint in Wade's eyes, an aura of raw strength and stubborn pride exuding from him. "I think I would like you better, Wade Burdett, if you were not determined to steal Shianne from me."

A slow grin worked its way across Wade's handsome face. "I forebade her to come to you when you summoned her, but I know this woman well. She takes orders from no man, at least not with any consistency. You may dare to take her in your arms, but know this, Maman-ti, I won't like it."

For another long moment the two men raked each other with calculating scrutiny. Shianne ached to shout at the both of them. When Wade reined Delgado away, putting distance between himself and Maman-ti, Shianne unleashed her tongue.

"I swear, you both reminded me of two rutting stags who were debating locking horns," she muttered disgustedly. "Men! I'm not sure there is one in the species I would defend with words or deeds."

"You have certainly spouted your loyalty to Maman-ti often enough," Wade snorted derisively.

"You don't have to pretend you care about me," she snapped harshly. "Maman-ti is not here to listen to your glowing accolades. You love me? You want no man touching *your* woman?" Shianne scoffed sarcastically. "With your broad background, I am beginning to think you were also a member of some theatrical group. The touching performance you gave certainly deserved a standing ovation."

"Do my ears deceive me?" Wade chuckled softly. "Was that a backhanded compliment?"

Shianne compressed her lips, refusing to be taunted. She had been used quite enough for one night, and she would not become Wade's source of amusement. When they reached the stables, she threw one leg over Delgado's neck and hopped to the ground, intending to part company without uttering another word.

"Shae?"

Wade's hushed voice slowed her footsteps. Hesitantly, she pivoted to face his quiet smile. Despite her firm resolve, she felt herself melt. His all-consuming gaze flooded over her, intimately touching her just as surely as he had reached out to caress her.

"Yes?" One perfectly arched brow lifted in question.

"Tomorrow I will take you into the cave and answer all the questions I have purposely avoided. Now that we are in this together, you have a right to know my motivation." His gaze shifted to the shadows. "I know I have given you no reason to care, but just once . . ." Wade sighed heavily as his penetrating eyes slid back to Shianne. "Just once in this ill-fated marriage of ours, I would like you to run *toward* me instead of *away* from me . . . in the same manner you eagerly greet the oracle of the Indians."

When Wade pushed away from the edge of the barn and ambled toward his horse, Shianne stared thoughtfully after him. Didn't he know she would fly into his arms like a homing pigeon returning to its roost if she were certain he wanted her there? Oh, how her heart wanted to believe the words Wade had spoken to Maman-ti, but she had become suspicious by habit. Shianne was afraid of being hurt more deeply than she already had been. What she felt for Wade was difficult enough to bear. If she truly opened her heart to him, confessed how she felt, he could slash her pride to shreds, and then what would she have? Wade had already taken away her ranch, her freedom. If he took possession of her soul, she would have nothing left.

Shianne tilted a proud chin and made her way up the lattice. She thought times had been difficult during the war, but the readjustment period was far worse. Radicals had taken control of the government. Outlaws terrorized the citizens of Texas and then sneaked back into Indian Territory to count their loot. Soon there would be a range war between Wade Burdett and Haden Reems. If she had any sense she would pack her belongings and seek out her father.

Who was she kidding, Shianne asked herself as she padded across the terrace to her room. She had always been in the thick of things. She couldn't leave the ranch when trouble was brewing. She was a Kimball, and like her father, she couldn't sit out a war. It just wasn't her nature to sit idly by. No, she would wait out this conflict between Wade and Haden. Besides, she couldn't leave until her curiosity had been appeased. She had to know why Wade had not buckled beneath Haden's pressure. Was it a matter of pride or was it something more? What was driving Wade to provoke Haden into a full scale battle?

Damn, she wanted to hear the answers to her questions, and they couldn't come soon enough to suit her. Mentally listing every question she intended to fire at Wade, Shianne sank into her bed. A smile bordered her lips, remembering the way Maman-ti and Wade had tormented each other. They were both little boys at heart, fighting over her only because neither of them wanted the other one to claim her. Such foolishness, she thought with a tired sigh. Without the challenge, both men would probably lose all interest in her.

Maman-ti had been content with friendship until Wade showed up, and Wade was only protecting his possession because she was a means to an end. Wade wanted to join forces with the Indians. If Wade could have recruited an army to aid in his plan to ruin Haden and amass a cattle drive to Kansas, he wouldn't need her *or* Maman-ti. But he did, and she was left loving a man who had lied about caring for her just to get what he wanted.

She was so frustrated she wanted to vent her anger. Impulsively, she punched her pillow, sending a cloud of feathers billowing about her. What she ought to do was line up the men in her life and have them shot. Then she could resume management of her ranch . . . Wade's ranch. . . . Dammit, he had branded everything he touched since he set foot in Texas. He was as wicked as Haden Reems, but Wade couldn't see that. His worst fault was his inability to recognize his own peccadilloes, even if they marched up and slapped him in the face!

Haden Reems glanced hastily around him, ensuring that his men were listening for their final instruction. He faced a tribe of would-be warriors, each garbed in buckskin and toting a pouch of arrows . . . all except Juan Mendez who refused to hide behind war paint. For some reason his most competent hired gun had become contrary of late. Haden wasn't certain what had caused Juan's sudden burst of conscience, but it was damned annoying. If Haden had known Wade's subtle remarks had begun to take their toll on Juan, he would have been more furious than he already was.

"Tonight I intend to break Wade Burdett once and for all," Haden declared to his bravoes. "He has managed to capture and brand more than two thousand head at last count. When we finish with him, I want him left with a herd of one, compliments of Haden Reems." He straightened in the saddle and clutched the reins in a stranglehold. "I intend to have the last laugh on Burdett. As soon as we have herded his cattle to the north edge of my ranch, we will begin a trail drive up the Chisholm Trail. Half the profit from this drive will be equally divided among you." A low chuckle rumbled in his chest. "No doubt, all of you will want to thank Burdett for saving you the trouble of rounding up the cattle and branding them before we put them on the trail."

As the men filed through the gate of their headquarters to raid the K Bar Ranch, Haden touched his heels to his mount's flanks and followed at a slower pace. Tonight's plunder would help to ease the fury Haden had felt when Wade secretly married Shianne and dammed up his water source. Haden had been in a fit of temper when one of his men returned that afternoon to report the creek had suddenly run dry. He didn't have to investigate to know what had stopped the flow of water. Burdett knew exactly what he was doing. He had hinted at it the previous night during the fiesta. All too late Haden realized it was a forewarning of what was to come. Now Haden intended to retaliate against the counter-attack. When Haden was finished with Wade Burdett, the pesky varmint would have a deep pond on his newly purchased property and only one calf to drink from it.

Chuckling devilishly, Haden urged his steed into a faster gait. How he hoped Wade would play the martyr and come charging out to prevent a stampede. Nothing would please Haden more than to watch that grass pirate trampled by the herd he had gathered from the brush country. Burdett wouldn't be the first defiant cowboy to find himself battered and broken after

270

daring to confront Haden.

Only last spring Haden had run across a man who was almost as fearless and rebellious as Wade Burdett, but Haden and his men had made fast work of the belligerent *gringo*. Haden never even bothered to learn the man's name. Not that it mattered, the *hombre* hadn't lived to seek revenge, and neither would Wade Burdett. Haden swore he would find a way to bring about that foreigner's demise without leaving himself suspect. Accidents happened frequently, and Wade would find himself a victim of one, somehow or other. Then Burdett would be another forgotten face in Bexar County, just like the drifter who had passed through after the war, toting his valuables. The drifter had no use for gold when Haden finished with him, and Haden was all too happy to transfer the gold coins and jewels into his safe.

Haden would have preferred to handle Wade Burdett in the same manner, and he would have if someone hadn't come along to see Wade staked out. Another day and Wade would have been a dead man. It was a pity a good Samaritan happened by that day. Wade Burdett could have suffered the same fate as his predecessor, and Haden wouldn't be forced to tolerate Burdett's annoying presence.

Chapter 13

A cloud of dust drifted into the night sky, making Haden frown curiously. He and his men had crossed the boundary that separated the Lazy R from the K Bar Ranch. The thought of unidentified men traveling across his range disturbed him. He was left to wonder if Wade Burdett and the vaqueros had decided to pay an unexpected visit to the herd of cattle grazing on the Lazy R.

Disgustedly, Haden called his men to a halt and directed their attention to the west. Then another thought skipped across Haden's mind, causing him to grin fiendishly. Wade may have played right into his hands. If Haden could catch the bastard stealing Lazy R cattle, there would be a lynching as quickly as they could locate a sturdy tree. With Wade out of the way, Haden could have Shianne *and* her ranch.

Smiling in satanic anticipation, Haden wheeled his horse around to give chase, but his smile vanished when he realized he was not confronting K Bar vaqueros but rather a war party of Comanches. The skilled horsemen were running circles around his cattle and remuda of mares. Although the bravoes thundered across the prairie, the marauders were not easily persuaded to abandon their raid.

Horrified by the disastrous turn of events, Haden urged his steed toward cover. Indians brought out the coward instinct in Haden. He hated the Red man, and he had padded many a politician's pocket to see that the troublesome heathens were rounded up and confined to a reservation.

Crouching in the underbrush, Haden watched the battle taking place on his range. To his dismay his men were unable to subdue the Indians. They rode all over their ponies—on the side, lying down, under the steed's belly—every which way at full speed. It was impossible for the bravoes to hit a target that was crawling all over a pony in the dark. By the time the dust had cleared and the shooting had stopped, the raiders had made away with more than a hundred head of horses and cattle, and Haden had lost two good men.

"Damn," he scowled as he climbed from the brush and swung into the saddle. His raid on the K Bar would have to wait until another night. His men would be in no condition to encounter more resistance after their harrowing experience with the savages. If Haden didn't know the Indians raided at will, he would have accused Wade of putting them up to it, but no white man in the area dealt with the Indians, except the Comancheros. They were a lawless breed of Mexican-Indians who were as merciless as their red-skinned cousins.

Haden and his men had fought against them at various times during the Civil War. The Comancheros were yet another reason Haden surrounded himself with an army. The mixed breeds ravished Texas while most of the men were away battling the Union army. Although the Comancheros no longer posed as great a threat, there was trouble on all fronts. If a man wasn't prepared he could find himself stripped of everything he owned, but Haden had prepared himself for all sorts

273

of confrontations. His name struck just enough fear in his neighbors and the roving bands of outlaws to protect him from devastation. Only Wade Burdett and the Comanches dared to seize Haden's personal property.

Grumbling over his losses, Haden ordered his bravoes back to the ranch to regroup and tend the wounds they had sustained. The past two days had proved to be nothing but disaster. Things had gone from bad to worse since Wade Burdett arrived, but Wade wouldn't be here much longer, Haden reassured himself as he stalked into his study to pour himself a drink. Burdett would become another ghost, just like the one his men claimed haunted the cavern near the foreigner's campsite. Phantoms indeed! Haden snorted disdainfully. What superstitious nonsense!

Ramona poked her head around Shianne's bedroom door to inform her that her new husband had come to pay her a call. Ignoring the smug smile on the housekeeper's face, Shianne grabbed her hat and strode into the hall.

"It will not be long before your new husband comes to take his place in the hacienda. *Si?*" Ramona was delighted about Shianne's marriage, but she was ever so curious to know why Wade insisted upon camping out on the prairie when he could have been sharing Shianne's bed. "Surely you have not prohibited him from living here with us."

"My husband does as he pleases," Shianne informed Ramona, her emotions masked behind a carefully blank stare. "And you should mind your own business."

Ramona muttered under her breath. Shianne had always been a private person, but her condition had worsened since Wade Burdett came to disrupt her carefully organized life. "I think you care much more for the man than you are willing to admit. You want him with you, but you are too proud to ask him to take his place by your side."

Shianne heaved a perturbed sigh and glared at the plump-faced housekeeper. "Yesterday you lectured me for being too stubborn and today it is my pride that is the brunt of your criticism. Sometimes I wonder why you haven't gathered your belongings and sought work elsewhere. Have I not one redeeming quality?"

A merry chuckle erupted from Ramona's lips as she waddled alongside Shianne. "*Si,* you possess one or two," she confessed. "But it is your *faults* that prevent you from having what you want most." She gestured a stubby finger toward the foot of the steps where Wade was standing in wait. "It is the *hombre.*"

"I accept your free advice for what it is worth," Shianne smirked, determined not to let Ramona rankle her before she confronted Wade. "I will be gone most of the day so don't expect me until late."

"I have come not to expect you at all," Ramona sniffed. "You disappear for hours at a time and no one knows what has become of you."

When Ramona stomped away in a huff, Shianne bit back a smile. It seemed Ramona wanted the newlyweds underfoot so she would know exactly what was going on between them. The woman thrived on having her finger on the pulse of the ranch. Ramona was, in most respects, a meddling mother hen, but Shianne loved the housekeeper dearly, despite her faults. Ramona had been the only mother Shianne had ever known.

The moment Shianne focused her attention on Wade, her meandering thoughts dispersed. His smile was intact and those hypnotic eyes were freely roaming over her. Shianne's gaze flicked over her torso and then flew back to Wade.

"Do I have my boots on the wrong feet?" she mocked dryly. "The way you are staring at me leaves me to wonder if something is out of place."

Wade's grin broadened to encompass every craggy feature. "Everything is very well placed," he assured her in a velvety tone. His attention lingered on the curve of her hips that was outlined in her tight-fitting breeches and then ascended to survey what lay temptingly beneath the thin gauze shirt. "I trust you slept well *without* me last night, my lovely bride."

Shianne impatiently waited for his pointed gaze to lift to her condescending frown. When it didn't, she walked down the steps to confront him face to face. "I slept like a log, thank you," she said flippantly. "And you, my dear husband?"

"I slept *on* one," he chuckled as he took Shianne's arm and steered her toward the door. When they were outside, he assisted Shianne onto her steed and then climbed onto Galahad's back. "I have learned Haden's ranch was raided last night." The quick change of subject caused Shianne to jerk up her head and pay close attention. "He lost more than a hundred head of stock, besides two of his hired guns."

As they rode across the pasture, Shianne kept the silence. Finally, Wade expelled his breath in a rush. "Well, aren't you going to say 'I told you so'?" he muttered acrimoniously.

"I am in no mood to gloat," she insisted, urging Delgado into a trot. "I have long been aware of Maman-ti's ability to foretell the future before it happens. Your secret is what fascinates me most. I cannot wait to discover how you manage to fish gold coins from midair."

When Shianne galloped away, Wade held Galahad to a walk to study her departing back. Why had she bypassed the opportunity to needle him? It was out of character for her. She thrived on chopping his pride to bits.

Wade breathed a frustrated sigh. Even if he lived with this woman for the next hundred years, he wasn't certain he could learn to predict her moods. As soon as he anticipated her next response and prepared himself for it, Shianne would do something totally unexpected, and Wade was forced to reevaluate her.

Oh hell, why was he picking that firebrand apart and attempting to put her back together? He had attempted it several times the past few weeks and had received nothing but a headache for his efforts. Shianne was a walking contradiction. She always had been, and she always would be, he decided.

Casting aside his contemplations, Wade spurred his steed to catch up with the shapely beauty who galloped ahead of him. When Shianne heard the thunder of hooves behind her she urged Delgado into his swiftest pace. It had been ages since she had enjoyed a challenging race.

When Shianne glanced back in Wade's direction, he caught the challenging gleam in her eye. Wade nudged his steed, and Galahad stretched out to cover the ground at lightning speed. As the bay stallion edged closer, Wade stood up in the stirrups to snatch Shianne from the saddle and drag her onto his lap.

"That wasn't fair! I was winning," she grumbled, begrudgingly clasping her hands around his neck to prevent toppling off the blood-bay stallion.

"You had a head start," he argued with a grin. His smile faded when he stared too long into her ebony eyes. The mysterious darkness in their depths lured him closer. "Shae . . ."

She knew what was coming, and her lips parted to accept his kiss. His musky fragrance surrounded her senses, making her painfully aware of the man who held her close. She could feel the hard length of his thighs beneath her hips, taste the hunger in his kiss. For a moment pride and pretense fell away, and Shianne moved closer to the flame that was burning her inside and out. God help her, she would never get over this insane craving for this man. He held her in his arms, and she melted like snow on a roaring campfire. He kissed her, and she whimsically wished it could last forever.

When the cloud of desire finally parted, Shianne's eyes fluttered open to see that Galahad had arrived at his destination without guidance. Wade had dropped the reins to fold both arms around her waist. Feeling a little ashamed of herself for giving in so easily, Shianne blushed. She tried to slip from his lap, but his grip tightened, refusing to release her.

"Shae?" Wade's husky voice drew her unblinking glance. He could make her nickname sound like an intimate caress, and she shivered in response. Wade smiled again when her body quivered in his arms. "That's all I wanted to know."

She flushed in annoyance. Damn that man. He was only testing her reaction to him. Was that all she was to him? A game? A challenge? Did he toy with all women the way he toyed with her?

Gently, he reached up to smooth away her frown. His fingertips sketched her delicate features as if memorizing them by touch. "You affect me the same way, you know. There is no need to take offense."

"Isn't there?" Shianne stilled her fluttering heart and wrestled her way to the ground. "I have not made you my conquest, and I do not appreciate being treated like a gambit. Just once I wish you would look at me and see me as a person who has feelings. I am not an object, a toy that a man takes in hand to amuse himself.

Sometimes you make me so angry I could . . ."

Wade hopped to the ground. Hastily he pressed his index finger to her lips to shush her, but Shianne was not to be put off. She was just gathering steam, and she wasn't to be stifled until she gave him a good piece of her mind.

Angrily, she flung his hand away and glared at his infuriating grin. "And that's another thing. Will you please stop smiling all the damned time. It drives me insane!"

Wade broke into a comical expression. His face was puckered and his eyes crossed. "Is this more to your liking, my love?"

In frustration, Shianne pounded him on the chest. How could she stay angry with him. He had the uncanny knack of draining her irritation and making her forget why she was spouting at him.

"Come on, princess," he murmured, guiding her toward the entrance of the cave. "I promised you an explanation, and I am a man of my word."

"Today, perhaps," she hurriedly tacked on. "Tomorrow I will probably learn it was all a concocted lie."

"Oh, ye of little faith," he sighed defeatedly. "A man could fall to his knees and spill his heart to you, wicked woman, and you would mop the floor with him."

Shianne pulled up short. Her dark eyes locked with those unnerving pools of emerald green. "I want to trust you, Wade," she told him solemnly. "Just be honest with me for once. Please."

"If I do, will you stop taking Haden's side?" he queried softly. "If you are harboring even a smidgen of guilt about the way you treated the man, you are wasting sentiment. Haden Reems deserves nothing but contempt. There is no need to feel ashamed because you kept him dangling for years, never accepting or declining his marriage proposal. He is a ruthless man, and before the day is out, you are going to understand why I carry this personal vendetta against him."

Shianne clamped her mouth shut and allowed Wade to lead her into the antechamber of the cave. He retrieved the lighted torch that was braced between the jagged rocks on the wall. Shianne found herself shuffled toward the narrow tunnel she had yet to explore in her search for the treasure or whatever it was Wade was hiding in the cave.

Her hand clamped into his arm as they trekked through the winding passage into oblivion. Shianne shivered uncontrollably. Although the torch splattered light a few feet ahead of them, she was apprehensive about placing one foot in front of the other. After taking that terrifying plunge into the underground lake, Shianne had gained new respect for darkness.

"I know where I am going," Wade reassured her when he felt her deathlike grip on his elbow.

Shianne tried to ease her grasp but her fingers remained clamped into his flesh, and her body clung to his. It was difficult to overcome the apprehensions that hounded her when she was surrounded by solid rock and cramped darkness.

A gasp of surprise burst free when she rounded the corner and peered over the ledge. There, fifty feet below inside a huge cavern, were elaborately decorated rooms filled with elegant furnishings. Several torches had been hung on the walls that glistened like gold in the flickering light. Stalactites and stalagmites formed the semblance of walls that separated each expensively furnished chamber from another. Blue velvet chairs, carved oak tables, and bedroom suites were placed throughout the cavern. Draperies of frozen rivers cascaded down the walls, accenting the splendor of this underground fairyland. Along the far west wall lay a crystal clear spring. It formed an inviting pool before it swirled around the massive, glazed boulders and disappeared from sight. In the distance she could see the faint hint of sunlight spraying into the cavern. This must have been the water source that fed what Maman-ti referred to as the speaking springs, Shianne surmised.

Her gaze recircled the elegant underground home and then swung to Wade's amused smile. "Where did all this come from?" she questioned bewilderedly.

Wade urged Shianne along the sloping path that descended to the floor of the cave. "We hauled every stick of furniture here from our plantation in Louisiana and then transported it into the cave on the back of our mule." Wade led Shianne toward what looked to be a parlor and gestured for her to plant herself on the tuft sofa. When he had dropped into the high-backed chair across from her, he began to unfold the events of the past.

"During the last year of the war it became evident that we faced impending doom. A black cloud hung over the South, one that forewarned of devastation. The entire region was being ravished and laid to waste. My mother was apprehensive about losing our valuables and the imported pieces of furniture that had been in our family for generations. She felt a strong sentimental attachment for those things symbolizing a way of life that was about to be lost forever.

"Each time we journeyed back to Texas to trail another herd of cattle to the Confederate troops, Blake, my brother Chad and I loaded wagons and transferred the furniture to this cave. Because this cavern contained everything that was held dear to my family, Blake sold me the land surrounding the cavern." A quiet smile pursed Wade's lips. "In a way, Maman-ti is right. This cavern is brimming with spirits—ghosts of generations past. It boasts the memories of a lost time, a time before the gracious elegance of the South fell, never to rise again."

A faraway look crossed his rugged features, and the smile dissipated. "Although we were prepared for the worst, none of us expected such devastation. I have already told you that my father's position as a member of Jefferson Davis's cabinet worked against him in the end. The Union army ensured that his land and home were completely demolished. It was only part of my father's punishment for taking a strong stand against the Union."

Wade leaned forward, resting his elbows on his knees, staring at the lavish carpet beneath his feet. "Blake and I had just returned with a cattle herd when we found ourselves ambushed by Union soldiers. The herd was confiscated, and Blake and I were both wounded before we could escape. I took your father to my plantation, hoping we could recuperate there. When we arrived, more dead than alive, my mother had already received news that Union troops were moving in our direction. She and a few of the remaining servants loaded us in a wagon and hauled us to safety. From a thick clump of trees we watched the army swarm onto the plantation. The crops in the fields were set ablaze. After our horses were confiscated to become mounts for the Union soldiers, torches were hurled into the stables. Then the mansion itself was set afire. What the soldiers could not carry away was spitefully destroyed, leaving nothing to feed the inhabitants of the plantation. Even the pastures were strewn with dead livestock, purposely denying any rebel fresh meat.

"For months we lived like rodents, searching for crumbs to survive. We nursed our wounds and slowly regained our strength. Chad had not accompanied Blake and I during our last trek to Texas, nor was he involved in the ambush that left Blake and me wounded. Chad had agreed to scout for a rebel infantry. Four months after the war ended, he finally managed to return home, but he did not bring encouraging news with him."

Wade eased back in his seat to stare at the mineral deposits that formed rows of spikes on the cavern ceiling. "The day we were gathering mavericks you asked me what happened to my father. With all the commotion, I was unable to finish relating the story," he reminded her grimly. "Chad came back to what was left of our plantation to inform us that Davis and his cabinet had abandoned Richmond and had been chased through the South. My father was not one of the advisors who was fortunate enough to escape. He stayed with Davis. When an argument broke out between the Union troops and the rebels, my father was shot to death.

"Blake was the stabilizing force during that critical time in our lives. Although he felt he should return home to you, he stayed to comfort my mother. Her world was no more than charred ashes, and she had lost her husband. Blake felt a strong obligation to remain with us after he had watched the destruction of our home and the mutilation of our livestock. Micara had nursed your father back to health, and he had come to care deeply for her, as well as the rest of the family." His eyes swung to Shianne, holding her gaze as he emphasized his point. "Blake didn't have the heart to leave us, Shae. Not when we needed him to lean on. My mother was ridden with conflicting emotions and guilt, none of which you can fully comprehend since you were not there to endure the hell we lived through. You may resent your father's absence and lack of communication, but we were fugitives behind enemy lines and the situation was impossible. Even if Blake could have escaped with his life, he couldn't turn his back on a family who had lost one of its members, its home and its property."

Wade frowned pensively, debating whether to tell Shianne the rest of it. No, he decided. He had set the stage, explained the circumstances. He would allow her to digest the information, to turn it around in her mind. When she was fully aware of the crisis in his family's life and Blake's strong sense of obligation to those who had become his second family, Wade would describe the events that followed those last months of the war.

Shianne shuddered uncontrollably, wondering how she would have reacted if she found herself standing aside to watch her home smolder and collapse into ashes. Wade's mother had undoubtedly clung to her spirits, thinking things might have been worse, but when Micara lost her husband as well as her home, she must have thought the world had come to an end. Shianne sat with her head bowed, staring at her clenched hands that lay in her lap. She was ashamed of herself for resenting her father's delay in returning home. How selfish she had been. Blake was consoling his friends and helping them pick up the pieces of their shattered lives. She would not have expected her father to turn his back when the Burdetts needed him so desperately.

"During the dreadful months that followed, we had to decide where to go and how to begin again," Wade went on to say. "When we heard about Joseph McCoy's venture to fill the Yankee demand for beef with Texas cattle, we decided to pool the profits we had gained by selling cattle to the South. It was our intention to build the railroad to Abilene and construct pens for cattle. Blake and I had been paid in gold coin, not worthless Confederate currency. Blake took part of the gold to Springfield to invest in the new cattle market. The rest has been my source for purchasing necessary supplies for the cattle drive and paying salaries for extra ranch hands," he explained. "I also sold a few pieces of jewelry that were part of my inheritance."

Restlessly, Wade unfolded himself from the chair and ambled over to toy with the dainty figurine that sat on the table. "Blake thought it best to take my mother with him while he finalized the arrangements with McCoy. He hoped the change of scenery would help Micara put the tragic past behind her. Since I was the younger and stronger of the two of us, Blake requested that I come to Texas to supervise the roundup. I tried to convince my brother, Chad, to invest in the enterprise, but he wanted no part of it. Chad had been soured by the murders and desolation in the South. He was not prepared to forgive the Yankees for what they had done. He refused to be a party to any business venture that might feed the North. Chad decided to take his part of the inheritance and move west."

Wade sighed heavily and set the figurine back in its normal resting place. "I suppose Chad needed the wide open spaces and the opportunity to sort out the events of the past. Mother was in capable hands, Blake had persuaded me to set up headquarters at the K Bar and Chad was free to begin his new life . . . away from all the tormenting memories."

His features turned as hard as the rock walls that surrounded them. "Chad came through Texas in the early spring, bound for New Mexico and points beyond. He gathered enough valuables to support him until he decided what he wanted to do with the rest of his life."

The sound of Wade's voice grew so cold and harsh that Shianne glanced up at him. A quizzical frown settled on her delicate features. She could see the smoldering fury surfacing as Wade paced back and forth in front of her. Something dreadful had happened to Chad Burdett. She could sense it. Tensely, she waited for Wade to regain control of his emotions and continue.

"There is a man in Texas who has appointed himself king. He rules his empire with an iron hand. Any drifter who is unfortunate enough to cross paths with him and his bravoes risks life and limb. This self-righteous bastard rids his land of drifters and homeless war veterans alike. He lays the blame on outlaw gangs and renegade Indians to protect the ruthless culprit who kills and frightens off so-called *foreigners*. Haden Reems has taken it upon himself to deal severely with any man who might think to take advantage of the millions of wandering cattle that roam the county. Haden is too selfish to share with those who fought the Civil War for him. He wants all the riches of the cattle market for himself."

Wade drew in a deep breath and expelled it slowly, fighting to contain the hatred he had so carefully controlled in Haden's presence. "Chad crossed paths with Haden last spring. The bravoes used the same tactics on Chad that they used on me. The only difference was that Haden happened to be traveling with his men the night they found Chad traversing across the northern boundaries of the Lazy R Ranch.

"Haden decided to make an example of Chad. His henchmen staked him out in the cold and taunted him unmercifully." He bent his gaze to Shianne for a moment and then focused on some distant point. "You know how fond Haden is of flashing his knife. He began carving on Chad to emphasize his point, demanding that Chad tell everyone he ran across to steer clear of the ranch or risk bearing the scars for the rest of his days."

Wade sank back into his chair to stare at the carpet. "Chad was already embittered by the atrocities of the war. He grieved for our father and cursed the devastation of our home. The losses had crippled him emotionally. At the time, he hated the world and everyone in it. Haden's abuse only intensified the frustrations Chad harbored." Wade's jaw clenched, his eyes dark with his own brand of fury. "When Chad spit in Haden's face, defying the brutal treatment, Haden lost his temper. He took out his bull whip and drew more blood after he had slashed Chad with the knife.

"Instead of whimpering for mercy, Chad cursed Haden with every breath he took. In his own mind, I suppose Chad was fighting a war he couldn't win, but he was determined to die trying. The lashings continued until Chad was overcome with pain and fell unconscious. Haden ordered his men to take the mutilated body and hurl it into the river, thinking he had seen the last of the nameless drifter who had dared to defy the mighty king of Texas. The cold water brought Chad to his senses, but he pretended death until Haden and his men rode away. When they were gone, Chad dragged himself ashore and crawled back to the cave. He had lost his clothes, his valuables and his horse. All he had left was a burning hatred that ran so deep it has poisoned him. He hates Haden even more than Maman-ti despises Texans."

Heaving another agitated breath, Wade peered into Shianne's peaked face. "When I arrived at the cave, I expected Chad to be long gone, but he was here, recuperating from his injuries. Chad lived like a creature of the night, hunting wild game to survive, waiting for me to come and help him avenge the brutality. Haden thinks Chad is dead, and because of my brother's experience, I took the precaution of naming Haden as the prime suspect in case I should suffer a worse fate." Wade ambled toward Shianne to tower over her. "Now do you understand why I want to break Haden? Yes, I'd like to kill him, to wipe him off the face of the earth, but that isn't enough. I want to torture him first. I want to strip him of everything he holds dear, to torment him for what he has done to me, my brother and everyone else."

Shianne sat there trembling, unable to believe Haden could be so cruel and ruthless. All these years when Haden had complained about the lawless hoards who swooped down on Texas, he had been using others as a cover for his bloodletting. Haden had resorted to threats and violence to discourage anyone from crowding in around him.

"You may take pity on Reems if you wish, but I despise the man and his cruel treatment of those who want to make new lives for themselves in Texas. I hold Haden in contempt for attempting to murder my brother. When his men staked me out, I pushed them just as Chad had, but I did not press them far enough to provoke them into killing me. I was fortunate Haden was not riding with them. He is more ruthless than any of his men, but I did want Haden to know there was one man who posed a threat to him, one he couldn't kill without bringing suspicion on himself. When Blake made me your guardian, it doubled the threat, and when you and I married, his dream exploded in his face." Wade's eyes glazed over with thoughts of revenge. "Haden is going to hang himself. By the time I finish with him, and Chad appears to testify, Haden will not only lose his ranch, but his life as well."

Shianne finally understood why Wade had used her. The hatred he felt for Haden Reems was his underlying motivation. Wade was willing to do most anything to repay Haden for his brutality. God, to think she might have married that despicable bastard. Only too late she

288

would have learned of his ruthless tactics and his demented obsession of ridding Texas of "grass pirates"—the name he used when referring to those who had migrated west after the war.

Curiously, Shianne glanced about her. Wade had been talking about his brother, but as of yet, she had not met the man who had obviously been haunting the cave these past months. It must have been *Chad's* voice she heard each time she ventured into the cavern, *his* footsteps she heard echoing behind her.

Reading her quizzical gaze, Wade turned toward one of the many dark tunnels that led from the main cavern. "Chad? Come out here. There is someone who wants to meet you."

Shianne's lashes fluttered up to see the tall, young man emerge from one of the passages. Her gaze flickered over his stern features. When Chad strode into the light, Shianne was assured that this was indeed Wade's brother. There was a definite resemblance between the two men, but Shianne was quick to note Chad's piercing blue eyes. Although their hair color and features were similar, there was no hint of laughter in Chad's expression, no smile playing on his lips. Chad looked to be two or three years younger than Wade, but it was difficult to tell for certain. The years and tragedies of the past had etched severe lines in Chad's face, not to mention the pale complexion caused by spending the daylight hours in the cavern.

There were several other differences between them, Shianne noted as she assessed Chad. Wade was darkly tanned and finely muscled after spending hours working with wild cattle. Chad was well-built, but he had not taxed his strength these past few months. Wade had also mastered the art of self-control and tempered patience, while Chad seemed a mass of nervous energy. Shianne speculated that Chad would have sooner walked up to Haden and shot him than strip the man of his pride and crumble his cattle kingdom around him.

To Shianne's surprise, the slightest hint of a smile touched Chad's lips. His deliberate gaze wandered over her trim figure, one that was wrapped in a linen shirt and tight-fitting breeches. "So this is the daring young minx I have been haunting the past few weeks." The resonance of his voice carried a faint undertone of amusement. "You are not easily frightened, Shianne. I have sent better men than you scrambling from the jaws of darkness with greater ease than I persuaded you to evacuate the cave when you were searching for treasure."

Shianne was greatly relieved when Chad's features softened. He did not seem so foreboding when he smiled. "Perhaps I was a bigger fool than most," she admitted. "My curiosity has always been one of my worst faults. It leads me into trouble more often than not."

Chad shot his brother a sideways glance. It was obvious to Wade that Chad liked what he saw. Approval was written on his younger brother's face. Chad had been soured by his past experiences and nothing fazed him these days . . . or at least it hadn't until he laid eyes on this sultry beauty. A dose of Shianne might be just what the doctor ordered, Wade diagnosed. Perhaps Chad's fascination with Shianne would smooth the wrinkles from his soul.

"Why don't you show Shianne our legacy from the South," Wade suggested. "Since her insatiable curiosity very nearly got her killed when she took the wrong passage, she deserves to see the treasure, don't you think?"

Nodding agreeably, Chad gestured for Shianne to follow after him. Grabbing a nearby torch, Chad led her down the winding tunnel, leaving Wade to wonder if he might have been overly generous in sending his wife off with his brother. A contemplative frown creased Wade's brow. Damn, he was getting possessive with Shianne, even to the point of harboring suspicions about his own brother, but he had good reason not to trust Chad these days, Wade reminded himself. Chad was a colder, harder man than he had once been. The past weighed heavily on Chad's mind, and he was even less the gentleman than Wade was.

Giving way to that thought, Wade decided to give his brother a mere ten minutes alone with the curvaceous vixen. Any more time could lead to trouble. Wade knew that for certain. After all, Wade could barely keep his hands off Shianne. After Chad's forced celibacy, there was no telling what he might do when he found himself alone in a dark niche with a beautiful woman.

When Wade's imagination began to stampede he checked his watch and then plopped into his chair. He would give Chad ten minutes and not a second more, he told himself.

Chapter 14

Chad set the torch aside and directed Shianne's attention toward two large trunks that had been stashed in the narrow cubicle. Shianne gasped in amazement when Chad lifted one of the lids to display hundreds of gold coins, priceless diamonds, emeralds, ornate silver dishes and miniature statues.

"Wade has always been modest, never boasting of his wealth," Chad declared while Shianne stared bug-eyed at the heaping treasure. "Both sides of our family were wealthy plantation owners. My father had money and married money. These priceless trinkets adorned our forty room mansion, all gifts from wealthy friends and relics from generations past."

Shianne's jaw gaped when Chad fished into the trunk to retrieve a necklace of diamonds and rubies. "We were fortunate that Wade had the foresight to abandon the sinking South when he did. If not, we would have lost everything of value. The Union troops intended to leave those with the most wealth with nothing except their crumbling pride. The war left us destitute because all our valuables were here in the cave. We lived like paupers for several months while Louisiana lay in ruin, but we could buy out Haden

Reems without sacrificing the sentimental pieces Mother refuses to sell." His facial expression hardened, and his voice turned as icy as the arctic wind. "I would have preferred to take Haden's own knife and carve him into bite-sized pieces after what he did to me, but Wade insisted on using his own methods to destroy Reems. Wade is not so vindictive. He does not have to live with this. . . ." Chad unbuttoned his shirt. His cobalt blue eyes gauged Shianne's reaction to the scars that marred his chest and belly. "I would exact a pound of flesh for each pound Haden cut from my hide," he snarled vengefully. "But Wade thinks there has been enough violence in the war-ravaged South, and he insists on slashing Reems in places that leave no visible scars."

Bitter laughter resounded about him when Shianne grimaced involuntarily. Her heart went out to Chad. His chest and stomach were a mass of crisscrossed scars caused by the blade and whip. She knew how much it must have slashed the vanity of a man who possessed the virile masculinity of his brother.

"It isn't a pretty sight, is it?" he muttered as he refastened his shirt. "I may as well be a ghost. What woman would want to make love to a man whose body looks like a human road map?"

His blunt remark caused Shianne to blush up to the roots of her hair. Determinedly, she rewound her unraveled composure and peered at the acrid expression on Chad's face. "I think you have failed to take into account the man himself," she countered. "A woman wants certain things from the man she loves. It isn't the scars that matter. It is what's inside that counts."

Chad tossed back his raven head and laughed, but there was no humor in his voice. "Ah, the idealistic woman," he mocked. "How pure and sweet is your philosophy, little dark-eyed nymph. If you had found yourself in bed with me the morning after your marriage, would you have been eager to touch, or would you have requested that we make love in the dark?"

The man did not mince words. Although Shianne sympathized with Chad's plight, she resented his sour attitude and crude remarks that were meant to embarrass her. He was sorely testing her patience, one that boasted a notoriously short fuse to begin with. Her compassion evaporated, and she reacted impulsively. Her hand circled through the air and collided with his cheek. Chad's jaw fell from its hinges, and for a moment he could only gape at Shianne, watching black sparks leap from her eyes.

"Maybe you did marry the wrong man, sweetheart," he smirked as he brushed his knuckles over his stinging cheek. "My brother is slow to anger while you and I are far more alike. We are hot-blooded and hot-tempered." He took a bold step forward and roughly yanked Shianne against his scarred chest. "Let's see if my embrace repulses you after you have claimed my marred body makes no difference to women."

Shianne found herself the recipient of a devouring kiss. She was certain Chad had no other intention except to make her dislike him. He had been rude since the moment they were alone, and now he was forcing himself upon her. It was obvious that Chad had lost his self-respect when he was slashed and left for dead. That, compounded with his bitter feelings about the war, had transformed him into a spiteful creature. Instead of trying to make friends with her, he was trying to put a wall between them, but Shianne was stubborn and most contrary. Wade could have testified to that if Chad would have thought to ask before he tangled with this high-spirited minx. Instead of fighting his bruising kiss, Shianne melted in his crushing embrace. Her lips opened beneath his, turning Chad's bitter anger into smoldering desire.

A look of utter astonishment passed across Chad's face when he withdrew. His eyes fell to the tapered fingers that had loosened his shirt to make bold contact with the scars that disfigured his chest. He had every intention of shocking Shianne speechless with his bold affront, but she had countered his assault, surprising him out of his boots!

"As I said before, Chad, beauty at best, is only skin deep." Without batting an eye, she traced her fingertips over the jagged scars, fascinated to find his flesh almost as rock-hard as Wade's. "You have allowed these scars of the flesh to disfigure the man within. A pity that." She sighed regretfully. "I happen to like bold men like you and Wade, and I found no fault with your kiss, except for the fact that there was no sincerity in it." Brazenly, Shianne stilled her right hand against his thudding heart and curled the other hand around his neck. Holding his bewildered gaze, she pulled his head back to hers. "Kiss me again, Chad, with feeling. I don't want to feel the bitterness, only the touch of a very attractive man who has a great deal to offer a woman. Let's see if there is something here that is worth a woman's affection."

Chad needed little in the way of coaxing. He had been without a woman for months on end. The feel of this shapely goddess in his arms was like tossing a torch on a stack of dry kindling. He gave Shianne what she requested—the tenderness that had been locked deep inside him, the gentleness that bitterness and hatred had very nearly destroyed.

When Chad finally found the willpower to drag his lips away from her intoxicating kiss, he noticed the soft smile playing on the corners of her mouth. It only took a moment for Chad to realize he had been *had*. He had meant to wedge a wall of ice between him and his brother's attractive wife. It was to have been a protective device of sorts, but Shianne had successfully managed to melt every icicle that might have formed between them. She had become the victor in this tender battle, and Chad could not dislike a woman with Shianne's spunk, even though he wanted to.

Chad had been attracted to this ebony-haired enchantress from the first moment he saw her flawless features silhouetted in the torch light. He didn't want to feel anything for his brother's wife, and that conflict of emotion caused him to behave like a forceful brute. Only Shianne hadn't allowed it. She had used her feminine wiles, a technique that was far more potent than masculine force.

"I don't think any woman would find fault with that type of kiss, Chad," she assured him. Her hand wandered over his laboring chest. "There really is no need for you to carry that chip on your shoulder, and if I was not in love with your brother. . . ." Shianne bit her bottom lip, wishing she hadn't blurted out that confession. Her long lashes swept up to stare Chad square in the eye. "If you breathe a word about that to Wade, I'll bob your tongue," she threatened.

An easy grin hovered on his lips. "I gather you haven't mentioned the fact to him as of yet," he snickered. "Kimball pride, I suppose?"

"An armload of it," Shianne admitted sheepishly. "Your brother is very adept at hiding what he feels. Only today I learned of his hatred for Haden. He masks his emotions well. I knew he had no use for the man, but Wade has been toying with Haden, infuriating him with taunting jibes. Haden doesn't know how deeply he is loathed, and *I* am not certain if I am loved."

Damn that Wade, he had all the Burdett luck, Chad

mused as he trailed a lean finger over Shianne's exquisite face. "If he doesn't, he is a fool." A defeated sigh escaped Chad's lips. "Alright, lovely lady, I will keep your secret, and I promise not to behave like an ass when you are about. You won this round, and I know when I have been beaten."

One delicate brow lifted as she regarded the muscular rogue who could be every bit as seductive as Wade if he put his mind to it. "Whatever are you talking about?" she questioned in mock innocence.

Chuckling, Chad flicked the end of her upturned nose. "Don't play naive with me, honey. You proved your point." He was irresistibly drawn to those heart-shaped lips that felt like rose petals beneath his. His kiss was light, almost reverent. "It would have been easier on me if I had instantly disliked you. . . ."

"What the devil is going on in here?" Wade demanded to know. His accusing gaze pelleted over his brother who looked a damned sight happier than Wade had seen him in two years.

Boldly, Chad draped his arm over Shianne's shoulder and refastened his shirt, a movement that was intended to put even more suspicious ideas in Wade's head. It did. "The lady and I were only getting better acquainted," he defended nonchalantly. "There is no harm in that, is there?"

From the look of things, not to mention the kiss Wade witnessed when he stepped around the corner, there was a helluva lot of harm in throwing Chad and Shianne together even for ten minutes! Wade begrudgingly admitted that Shianne was a fetching beauty, the kind a man could not ignore, but dammit, Chad could have had the decency to remember whose ring encircled her finger!

"Maybe you got a little carried away in your attempt to become better *acquainted* with *my* wife." The words were as pointed as the sharpest of daggers.

The smile evaporated from Chad's features. In silence he stared at the angry frown that was stamped on Wade's face. Chad removed his arm from Shianne's shoulder and then cupped his hand beneath her chin. For a long moment he stared into those fathomless pools of ebony.

"She gave me back my self-respect, Wade. Don't begrudge me that." He winked down at Shianne. "And I gave her directions to a pair of open arms . . . just in case she finds herself in need of them."

Wade glanced back and forth between Chad and Shianne. They seemed to be sharing a secret that neither of them intended to divulge. God, Wade felt a growing jealousy for his own brother, and if anyone needed patience and understanding, Chad did, Wade reminded himself. So why did he feel this insane urge to shake the stuffing out of Chad?

While Wade was wrestling with a riptide of disturbing emotions, Chad made no pretense about his affection for the sultry temptress. He planted another kiss on Shianne's soft lips and then swaggered away, beaming like the morning sun.

"She's all yours, big brother, but to tell you the truth, I'm not sure either of us is man enough to handle her. There is a lot of woman wrapped in that petite body." Chad breezed by Wade, flinging him a broad smile. "I'll go out to camp and stir up supper while you show Shianne around our spacious underground mansion."

Wade watched his brother strut down the tunnel before turning to glare at Shianne. Wasn't it enough that Maman-ti had staked his claim on this tempting minx? Lord, now it was his own brother who insinuated that there was a line forming behind him. Wade did not appreciate watching other men use Shianne's lips as if they were community property.

298

Dammit, she was *his* wife! Didn't anyone around here have any respect for the limitations on the institution of marriage?

"Would you mind explaining what the blazes was going on in here?" Wade demanded sharply. "I sent you in here to appease your curiosity about the treasure, *not* your curiosity about Chad!"

It did her heart good to know the jealous green monster had taken at least one bite out of Wade's male pride. Maybe he didn't love her, but he felt a smidgen of possessiveness. It was a start, Shianne reassured herself.

Shrugging nonchalantly, she knelt down to rummage through the treasure chest. "Chad tried to make me dislike him by insulting me and forcing me to endure a bruising kiss," she explained matter-of-factly.

"And what did you do?" Wade prodded, frowning warily. Judging by Chad's behavior, Shianne must have done the unexpected.

"I kissed him back. Then I told him he needn't carry a grudge. He is not a freak who belongs in a circus because he bears a few scars. Your brother had convinced himself that he would no longer appeal to women because he has been disfigured by Haden's dagger and whip, but he is every bit the man you are, and he needed the kind of reassurance that can only come from a woman."

"You seem very conscious of my brother's needs," Wade snorted sarcastically. "I wish you were as concerned about mine."

Shianne glanced up to note Wade's sour frown and then stared down the dark passage Chad had taken moments earlier. "Until today, I also carried a grudge. It was easy for me to identify with Chad. He resents Haden's abuse and the tormenting memories of the war. I resented my father's absence in my life." Her eyes slid back to Wade, and a wry smile skipped across her lips. Slowly, she rose to her feet and moved to stand directly in front of Wade. "Now that Chad feels better about himself, and he no longer believes women will find him repulsive, what can I do to ease your frustrations?"

A provocative grin dangled on the corner of his mouth. Wade hooked his arm about her, pulling her full length against him. "Although I do not approve of your methods, I appreciate the end results. In case you have forgotten, you are a married woman. If anyone around here needs kissing it is your husband. Have you any idea how frustrating it is to watch an assortment of men, my own brother included, embracing you?"

Shianne raised an eyebrow, her smile slightly mocking. "Is it anything like knowing your husband has done far more than kiss the many women he has invited into his arms?"

Voicing the thought spoiled Shianne's mood. The moment Chad kissed her, Shianne knew there was only one man who could set her afire. Yes, there was potential attraction between her and Chad, but he could never touch the strings of her heart when they were tied to Wade.

Didn't a man have that same built-in mechanism that made him feel a need, a craving for one woman and one woman only? Could a man surrender to passion's pleasure even if there was no love involved? If Wade could, why couldn't *she?*

Shianne tried to imagine herself in Chad's bed. The very thought made her feel like a traitor unto herself. She knew who and what she wanted, even if Wade didn't want her in the same ways. She still had her pride, and she was not willing to settle for Wade's passion if he could find the same satisfaction in someone else's bed. If he didn't care about her, *truly* care about her, they had nothing at all, and Shianne was not willing to settle for a one-sided love. She didn't want to be hurt more than she was already hurting.

When Shianne pivoted on her heels, Wade followed her. The moment they stepped into the cavern he caught her to him. His face was dangerously close, his eyes intently focused on her lips, as if he found their delicate curve intriguing. "Dammit, woman, don't you know the others don't matter to me. Hell, I don't even remember their names, and I didn't marry any of them, did I? Does that count for nothing?"

If that was supposed to make her feel better it didn't. Shianne focused on a distant point, fighting like hell to keep the mist from clouding her eyes. "I know why you married me, Wade. You needn't pretend. You wanted to use me to get to Maman-ti and to add more fuel to Haden's fiery temper. Haden has been your motivation from the beginning. He preoccupies you, provokes you to do what you do. Not that I can blame you for wanting revenge for what he did to Chad and who knows how many other innocent victims," she added.

Her lips quivered as she forced herself to meet Wade's emerald gaze. "But I need to be more than a man's device for extracting revenge. If our marriage was nothing more than another provocation aimed at Haden, I want it annulled. I am not something to play with between skirmishes with Haden. I will not be a mere physical release for your passions, Wade. You can appease your lust in any number of beds, and I refuse to live with pretense."

"Does this feel like pretense to you?" His sensuous lips courted hers with heart-stopping tenderness. "I don't blame Chad for feeling the same attraction I felt the first time I laid eyes on you," he confessed huskily. "But I don't want you to become an obsession with him, the way you have become an obsession with me. I

301

touch you and I want more than a moment of physical satisfaction. I want the assurance that when my hunger for you begins to gnaw at me again you will be there . . . today, tomorrow and the day after."

His breath whispered over the pulsations on her throat, and his hands wandered at will. He rediscovered the feel of her shapely body beneath his caress, erasing the memory of every other man's touch, and the fire burned hotter.

"No, Shae, this is definitely not pretense. You make me ache with the wanting of you, and there is only one remedy for this kind of pain."

Wade grasped her hand to weave through the incredibly breathtaking rock formations of this secluded fairyland. "Come with me, princess. I'm anxious to show you the spring. It is far more fascinating than the dark dungeon you fell into during your last visit."

The smile on his rugged features promised more than a stroll along the underground river. Shianne knew she should protest before he made a move toward her. She knew she would melt all over him. Wade had that effect on her when other men didn't. She had kept her head with Chad, but Wade had the uncanny knack of sending logic flying. Yet, her heart was ruling her head, and she followed Wade without complaint.

When she spied the clear spring, an appreciative sigh tumbled free. This was like some fantastic dream, she mused as she watched the spring water glide over the river bed of mineral deposits and then swirl into the inviting whirlpool. As Wade's hand slid beneath her blouse to make arousing contact with her flesh, she surrendered to the multitude of sensations he evoked. This might be the last peaceful moment they spent before Wade devoted himself to Haden's downfall. She wanted to cherish this memory, and she vowed to make this moment one that would linger in Wade's thoughts for days to come. She could not bring herself to speak the words, but she would prove her love for him in the way she touched him, the way she kissed him.

When his expert hands ascended to savor the softness of her breasts, her temperature rose by degrees. Shianne felt the familiar sensations begin to unfurl deep inside her, blossoming and growing until they consumed all thought. She arched toward him, wanting him in ways words seemed helpless to explain. She returned his ardent kiss, sharing the same ragged breath, feeding the fire that was coming dangerously close to blazing out of control.

Shianne couldn't seem to remember whether she had shed her clothes or if Wade had assumed the task. She was only aware of the sinewy muscles that pressed against her, those emerald eyes that shimmered with awakened passion. They stood waist deep in the whirlpool of cold water, but Shianne felt no chill. His all-consuming gaze warmed her, promising her pleasure that compared to no other moment.

"Do you know how incredibly beautiful you are, Shae?" he rasped. His gentle fingers traced along her jaw and then followed her collar bone. Her olive skin glowed in the flickering light, compelling him to continue his featherlight caresses. "You are truly striking with your dark hair and dark eyes." His free hand lifted, and his fingers threaded through the waterfall of ebony tendrils. He twisted the lustrous strands around his wrist, gently tilting her head so that he might stare into those fascinating pools that were as black and mysterious as midnight. Her long, thick fringe of lashes added to her mystique, a lure no man could resist. "I am bewitched. You stir a craving in me that I can't seem to talk myself out of, even if I were the world's greatest orator. Feed this hunger, sweet witch. . . ."

His kisses cherished her soft, responsive lips. His exploring hands worshipped her satiny flesh. A groan echoed in his chest as he curled his arm around her waist to mold her slender form to his hard, trembling contours. What had begun as a slow, languid embrace suddenly transformed into a breathless tempest of desire. When Shianne answered each ardent kiss and caress, his body caught aflame, burning with compelling desire.

"I want you," she whispered against his warm mouth. A tiny moan bubbled in her throat when his fingertips traced along her inner thigh to intimately caress her. "Wade . . . please make love to me. . . ."

His lips abandoned hers to drift down the slope of her shoulder. "In time, princess," he assured her huskily. Wade made certain she not only heard his words, but felt them vibrating on her quivering flesh. "When I have satisfied my craving to touch and caress, I will surrender to the need to possess. You are my wife, and I have the right to make love to you in all the ways lovers explore when they are giving and sharing the pleasures of passion. . . ."

Shianne was sure she would die of wanting before he got around to appeasing the sweet, tormenting ache that uncoiled within her. His tongue flicked and then gently suckled each throbbing peak. His hands weaved seductive designs across her belly. His fingers delved into her feminine softness, making her gasp with agonizing pleasure. When he cradled her in his arms and allowed his lips to trace the same maddening path his practiced hands had followed, Shianne felt shock waves roll down her spine.

Finally, Shianne could endure no more. He was doing impossible things to her body, things that aroused fierce needs. Shianne wanted him, wanted to feel his raw, masculine strength consuming her. She wrapped her legs around his hips, and her arms encircled his shoulders. Her fingers curled into his thick hair, bringing those warm, sensuous lips to hers.

When her mouth slanted across his, Wade's mind went blank. He could feel her flesh brushing seductively against his, taste the dewy sweetness of her lips. She was like an uncontrollable addiction, an incessant craving that wouldn't go away. Each time he made love to her it left him wanting more. He could appease his hunger for her for a time, but the need flowed like an eternal spring that had grown into a monstrous craving.

Suddenly, his priorities were out of sinc. Wade had intended to arouse her to the limits of sanity, but her provocative movements made him painfully aware of his own unfulfilled needs. Male instinct assumed command of his malfunctioning brain. It was no longer *her* pleasure that was foremost in his mind; it was the giving and *sharing* of pleasure that would lead them beyond the boundaries of passion that concerned him most.

Wade kissed her with all the pent up emotion that rioted inside his male body. His footsteps led him from the swirling pool to the massive four poster bed that was situated only four strides away from the spring. He tumbled with her onto the soft mattress, his long legs intertwining with hers. His taut body slid over hers, and he marveled at the exquisite sensations of having her so wonderfully close with nothing but flesh melting against flesh.

He braced his arms on either side of her shoulders and stared into those dark, spellbinding eyes. "I need you, princess," he breathed hoarsely. "Only you can ease the ache. No other woman but you, Shae. . . ."

Shianne asked herself how many times Wade had

murmured such confessions to the woman in his arms, but there was no time to contemplate an answer. When he peered down at her with the expression that seemed to say he hungered for her alone, Shianne allowed herself to believe it, at least for the moment.

His body surged toward hers, his knees gently guiding her thighs apart. As he bent to steal her breath and scatter her thoughts, Shianne yielded to the ecstatic pleasure of giving herself up to him, wildly, freely, without an ounce of feminine reserve.

His hard, driving thrusts triggered quakes that tumbled through every nerve and muscle in her body. Sensations spiraled through her bloodstream like the leaping flames of a forest fire, leaving her soul to burn. As he drove into her, seeking ultimate depths of intimacy, she felt a mountain of emotions erupting and spilling over her like hot lava.

Shianne bit her lower lip to prevent crying out. The pleasure was so intensely sweet she feared she could not survive it. This was rapture in its purest form, a reckless sensation that left her uncaring if she lived to see tomorrow. Shianne clung to him, her nails biting into the corded muscles of his back. She was falling through time and space like a shooting star, knowing this white-hot fire would quickly consume her. It was the most fantastic of feelings, Shianne thought deliriously. It was as if she were soaring in motionless flight, journeying through a sea of twinkling stars without leaving the circle of Wade's sinewy arms.

Then sublime ecstasy poured through her, para-lyzing her mind. Her body was numb from the ineffable pleasures of his lovemaking. Shianne had often told herself it was all wrong to love a man like Wade, but when they were of one body and soul, it seemed so right, so perfect. He brought her to life, filled her with rapture. There was nothing more precious than these moments that seemed to last forever.

When the haze of passion faded, and she could see the perimeters of reality, Shianne peered up into the ruggedly handsome face that was so close to hers. The roguish grin that clung to his lips caused Shianne to arch a quizzical brow.

"Rainbows," Wade rasped and then chuckled softly. "I saw a sky brimming with them."

Shianne giggled giddishly and then gave her head a contradicting shake. An impish smile alighted her face as she traced her index finger over the crinkles that fanned from the corners of his emerald eyes. "No, it was stars, a sea of them, each shining with a brilliance to match the sun."

Lovingly, his hand followed the ebony waterfall that spilled across his pillow. "One would think that when a man and woman were making love they would be lost in the same fantastic dream."

"Perhaps it is the same dream, only that the scenery is different," Shianne speculated. A wondering frown settled into her flawless features. "Is there any rhyme or reason to this fascination between us, Wade? Has it some long enduring purpose, or will it be another of your shallow affairs?"

Wade chuckled at the thoughtful expression that clung to her face. "Why is it that everything must have an explanation for you, sweet nymph?" His smile evaporated as he traced his finger over her kiss-swollen lips. "It is good between us, Shae. It always has been. Can't we just leave it at that? Must we attach names and descriptions to the pleasures we find in each other's arms? Must we attempt to make promises we might be unable to keep? Today is all that matters. Why not allow tomorrow to take care of itself?"

Shianne glanced away, refusing to be trapped in the captivating pools of green. Wade was no longer speaking of stars and rainbows. He was insinuating that they should enjoy what they had together, that they should allow their passion to spread its wings and fly where it would. He had married her because it suited his purpose, but Wade in no way implied that what they shared would last forever. Wade didn't believe in forever, and he didn't want to be tied down. It seemed an unnatural inhibition for this restless tumbleweed.

Yes, she loved him, but she was not beneath turning the tables on this libertine. Two could play his game, and perhaps what was good for the gander could be even better for the goose. After all, she had gotten nowhere by insisting that they make a commitment to each other, she reminded herself. It was time to veer off in another direction since the one she had taken had reached a dead end.

Slowly, her gaze drifted back to his. "Very well, Wade. We will do it your way. There will be no strings attached to this marriage of ours if that is what you wish. Our marriage will serve your purpose and mine as well. There will be no double standards. If I find someone whose touch arouses me, I will disregard the vows. After all, I do not even recall speaking them. Since you insist that there should be no restricting limitations, I will also enjoy the wide boundaries of this marriage. It might prove enjoyable, and I may even find that I was too old-fashioned in my thinking," she added with a reckless shrug. "It is done. I will make no demands of you, and you will hold no binding commitment to me." Let him chew on that thought and see how he liked it, Shianne thought spitefully.

Now why had he expected her to debate the issue? Hadn't he learned that she was impossible to predict? Dammit, he had been baiting her, testing her devotion. While other women would do the predictable thing and utter soft confessions of love, Shianne threw challenges

308

in his face. The thought of Shianne responding to another man as wildly and passionately as she responded to him tied Wade in knots.

What they shared was special. Dammit, she had to know that, didn't she? Just because she was young and innocent didn't mean she needed to dillydally with a score of other men to test her reaction to Wade. Lovemaking was good, no matter who lay in his arms. Lovemaking at its *worst* was good, but it was at its best with Shianne.

Wade very nearly strangled on the thought! My God, he had stumbled onto a revelation, and it was not one that pleased him. Sweet mercy, was he in love with this dark-eyed vixen? Was that why he was so blasted possessive of her? Was that why the thought of another woman had not wedged itself into his mind of late?

No, he could find pleasure elsewhere, he assured himself confidently. He was just rushing his conclusion. It was as he had prophesied a hundred times before. The feelings between a man and woman faded with time. A man had only to outwait his emotions. Once Wade had put his feelings in proper perspective, he would realize he was not in love with this woman but in love with the fascination she held for him.

What a relief it was to know he had caught himself the split second before he fell into that age-old trap, Wade thought with a sigh. Of course, Shianne intrigued him. She fascinated every man who laid eyes on her. That was just the way it was with a woman who possessed Shianne's stunning beauty. The fact that she was a wild, free spirit was yet another enticement, but she was still a woman and feelings changed. In a few months she would lose her mystique, and he would grow restless. He always did.

Shianne frowned as she watched surprise fade into rationalization and then into complacency with the situation. Damn that man! What must a woman do to make Wade Burdett fall in love with her, not just for the moment but forever?

Employ the same nonchalance, Shianne told herself. Hound him with his own idiotic philosophy until he discards it. Deciding to test her theory, Shianne eased onto her side and propped her head on her hand. An amused smile bordered her lips as she watched the spring-fed river ripple along the floor of the cavern.

"I rather like the idea of indoor running water," she said casually, allowing the previous subject of conversation to flit away as if it carried little importance.

A wary frown gathered on Wade's brow. Why had she suddenly discarded their debate? Had she decided to let him go, just like that? Had she already fallen out of infatuation with him? An hour ago she was demanding that it had to be all or nothing, and now she behaved as if she couldn't care less. Lord-a-mercy, he couldn't figure this woman out. She had him stymied.

Wade wasn't quite sure why he was feeling so exasperated, but he was. Shianne had somehow managed to puncture his male pride. Perhaps they did need to talk this matter out, here and now. There had to be some sort of working compromise. The last thing he wanted while he was setting Haden up for the fall was to fret over this high-spirited nymph.

His hand clamped on her bare shoulder, forcing her to her back. "Shianne, I think . . ."

Playful laughter echoed about the cavern as Shianne wiggled away to bound from the bed. "I totally agree," she enthused. "We should seek out Chad. I'm starving."

With his jaw sagging, Wade watched Shianne scoop up her discarded garments and shrug them on. Dammit, he wasn't thinking about nourishment. How could she be hungry at a time like this? They had to

310

decide where they stood with one another, determine how they would respond to each other in private and in public.

When Wade didn't make an effort to collect his clothes, Shianne cast him a mock innocent smile. "Aren't you coming? We have kept Chad waiting much too long as it is."

"I . . ." Wade held up his hand to detain her, but she was spiriting off through the partition of rocks, humming a lighthearted tune.

Grumbling over this unsettling state of affairs, Wade swung his long legs over the edge of the bed and snatched up his breeches. Damn, women were supposed to be sentimental creatures who cherished those quiet moments of lying in bed when the loving had ended. Shianne sentimental? Wade smirked at the thought. *He* was supposed to be the one who left her arms before she was prepared to release him. *He* should have been the one to suggest that when one hunger had been appeased it was time to satisfy another. Somehow, things had been turned around backwards, and Wade couldn't determine how and when he had lost control.

Shaking his head, he thrust his arm through the sleeve of his chambray shirt. Who could understand that woman? Not him. Shianne had totally confused him.

The sound of merry laughter drifted from the ledge above. Wade glanced up to see Chad smiling down into Shianne's upturned face. Lord, now she had set about to bewitch his own brother, Wade predicted. Was that why Shianne was so eager to vault from bed after their romantic romp? Was she intrigued by Chad's dark charm? She had certainly made a new man out of Chad, Wade thought sourly. The change was for the better but look who was paying the price!

"Chad snared a rabbit," Shianne called enthusiastically. "And it isn't even burned! Come join us, Wade. It is delicious!"

"Isn't even burned," Wade mimicked, annoyed that she was mocking him for the night he had allowed their meal to be cremated.

Pouting like a spoiled child, Wade plopped down at the table to chew on the succulent meal. The meal tasted a great deal like sour grapes to Wade, but he didn't say a word. Not that he could have wedged one in, he mused acrimoniously. Chad and Shianne were so deeply involved in conversation that they barely acknowledged Wade's presence. Shianne was relating incidents from her past, things she had never bothered to mention to Wade. Amusement danced in Chad's blue eyes as he surveyed her expressive face and listened to her unfold tales of her childhood and her experiences with the renegade Comanches who roamed the area. It ground on Wade's temper that Shianne confessed her association with the Owl Prophet to Chad, especially since Wade had to pry the information out of her. While Wade had been forced to wait weeks to gain a smidgen of her trust, Chad had immediately been taken into Shianne's confidence. Damn that woman. She was giving him fits!

When they completed their meal, Shianne scooped up the plates. "I'll wash the eating utensils and leave them in camp before I return to the hacienda," she offered.

"I'll escort you back to the ranch," Wade announced, rising from his chair.

"There is no need," Shianne insisted. "I have been fending for myself for years."

As Shianne sauntered away, a light spring in her walk, Wade grumbled under his breath. He had definitely lost control. Chad was now the object of

Shianne's attention, and if the look on Chad's face was any indication of what was dancing in his head, Wade would have had every right to take a punch at his own brother. Chad was mentally performing the same arousing techniques Wade had employed while he and Shianne were alone in the cavern.

That realization turned Wade's mood black as pitch. For several minutes he sat there brooding, amazed by his insane urge to wipe that wry smile off Chad's face. Damn that witch. She could have been more discriminate. There were thousands of men in Texas. Why did she have to turn her charm on his own brother?

Chapter 15

Chad eased back in his chair, contemplating the contents of his brandy glass. A sly smile grazed his lips. Damn, he hadn't grinned so much in years. Shianne's presence had worked like a magic potion. Although she had come and gone like a cyclone, the lingering fragrance taunted Chad's senses. He glanced at his sour-faced brother, thinking they had suddenly exchanged roles. In the past it had been Wade who masked his irritation behind a casual smile. Now it was the other way around. Wade was the one who read like an open book, not Chad, and Chad found himself liking his new role, the one Wade had always portrayed so easily—the carefree rogue who was not easily provoked to anger.

"Shianne tells me that the two of you have finally come to a satisfactory arrangement where your marriage is concerned," Chad remarked, discreetly assessing the expression that claimed Wade's craggy features.

Wade grunted in response and swallowed down his drink, hoping it would cool his irritation. It didn't.

"I rather like the unlimited freedom you have granted each other. It sounds like something a dedicated bachelor might invent when he finds himself shackled in wedlock. I'm sure this arrangement will perfectly suit your purposes." Chad took another sip of brandy and stretched his long legs out in front of him. "When you married the woman Haden wanted, you gave him all the more reason to detest you, provoking him to react without thinking matters through. You have even managed to form an alliance with the Comanches, not to mention the personal privileges you gained by making that lovely firebrand your wife." Chad sighed enviously. "I have to hand it to you, Wade. You are a cunning strategist."

"Since when did you become such a conversationalist?" Wade snorted sarcastically. "I thought you preferred to keep to yourself."

Chad shrugged a broad shoulder. "It's the isolation of this cave, I suppose," he speculated. "I've spent months alone, rehashing the past, talking to myself. It has begun to take its toll. Occasionally, a man needs to talk . . . as well as satisfy his other needs to be with someone."

"Like a woman?" Wade's narrowed green eyes riveted over his brother's wry grin. The transformation in Chad's behavior was incredible, Wade thought to himself. If that sultry temptress was not the cause of Chad's new lease on life, Wade might have been delighted with the change.

"Exactly like a woman," Chad concurred. His gaze focused on the fascinating rock formations that clung to the walls and ceiling of the cavern. "It has been a long time, Wade, too long."

Wade didn't utter a word. He just sat there, becoming more agitated by the second. Chad had learned to live with his celibacy, surviving on his craving for revenge. After Shianne's appearance, Chad's thoughts had turned to more arousing matters,

315

ones that had nothing to do with spiteful retaliation.

"Is she good in bed?" Chad questioned out of the blue.

The glower Wade sent his brother would have melted a lesser man in his boots. "That is none of your damned business!" he snapped hatefully. Wasn't that just like Chad? If he wanted to know something, he just came right out and asked, and he had no qualms about asking anything, no matter how delicate or personal the question.

Chad was undaunted by Wade's furious glare and fiery tone of voice. Indeed, Chad was delighting in ruffling his brother's cool, calm facade. It didn't happen often.

"Why not? Since when has it bothered you to speak of your passionate conquests?"

Chad was loving this. Never had he seen Wade threaten to reduce himself to a pile of smoldering ashes. Wade's self-control had cracked. It assured Chad that the brother he had long admired was human . . . at least in some respects. The logical, calculating machine who could smile through the worst of disasters was beginning to malfunction. Wade had an Achilles's heel—a sultry temptress named Shianne.

"It appears to me that Mother neglected to teach you courteous manners," Wade growled, his eyes throwing off hot green sparks. "That is not the kind of question you ask a man about his wife."

"Mother told me to be honest and straightforward," Chad argued, strangling a chuckle. Lord, Wade looked like a ticking bomb waiting to explode.

"*Not* to the point of being rude!" Wade blared, vaulting to his feet. "I am not going to discuss my encounters with Shianne as if she were some common whore who has lain with every man in Bexar County!"

Wade was so puffed up with indignation that Chad

was certain his big brother was about to burst the seams of his shirt. "My, but you are sensitive about this line of questioning," he mocked dryly. "We all know your reasons for marrying Shianne. Even *she* has accepted her purpose in your scheme of revenge. If you don't love her, there is no reason why we can't share her. She seems willing enough, and I know I certainly am!"

Wade had not considered clobbering his little brother since the days of their childhood spats, but he was contemplating it now. His temper, already sorely put upon several times during the course of the afternoon, was coming close to erupting.

"What the devil are you getting so upset about?" Chad inquired. "You are the one who granted her the right to sleep wherever it met her whim."

Wade was beginning to despise himself for marrying Shianne in the first place. Yes, the wedding had served several practical purposes, but he had failed to anticipate that Shianne might suddenly decide she wanted the same freedom Wade demanded for himself. The boot was on the other foot, and the pinch was excruciating. Wade didn't like this overwhelming feeling of possessiveness where Shianne was concerned. It made him uncomfortable and put him out of sorts.

"Dammit, I have no intention of sharing her," Wade burst out. "Not even with you, deprived though you have been of late!"

Chad chuckled at Wade's explosive tone. It was apparent that his older brother was suffering an upheaval of emotions. Yet, Wade was too stubborn to accept the metamorphosis he was undergoing. What Wade felt for Shianne was more than a passing fancy. His behavior was proof enough that he was in love, but Wade refused to allow himself to believe that. Chad

317

was well aware of Wade's philosophy that time cooled a man's fascination with a woman, and he was prone to believe it himself until he witnessed his older brother's reaction to that shapely nymph. Shianne had turned Wade wrong side out, exposing his innermost feelings. Not every man and woman could fall in love forever but there were exceptions. Chad was willing to bet his fortune that he was viewing one of those special relationships in the making. In a way, he was jealous of it. He had the feeling that *any* man could crumble beneath Shianne's charms. She was high-spirited, unpredictable and obviously passionate. If Chad hadn't known Shianne's deep feelings for Wade, he would have been doing far more than taunting his brother.

"Are you saying I am to keep my hands off that gorgeous creature?" Chad questioned.

"That is exactly what I'm saying. I will not allow her to come between us," Wade growled. Heaving an angry sigh, Wade attempted to regain his self-control.

Chad stared pensively at his brother from over the rim of his glass. Then he set it aside. "You are a fool, big brother," he told him matter-of-factly. "A sensible man does not half tame a wild mare and then turn her out to pasture. The next time you summon her, she might not return, and would you like to know what else I think about this affair you're having with Shianne?"

"Not particularly," Wade muttered as he plopped down in his chair to guzzle another drink. "But I suppose I am about to endure another of your long-winded lectures."

"No, I intend to be blunt and to the point," Chad assured him. "I think you are in love with the lovely lady, but you are too mule-headed to admit it."

"And I think I liked you better when you kept to yourself and wore a permanent frown instead of that

318

smirking smile," Wade grumbled grouchily.

Chad laughed out loud. "My God, now that I know love turns a man into a sourpuss, I will most surely try to avoid it. I always admired your ability to grin, even in the most critical of situations, but it is obvious that there are some things a man cannot smile through. Love seems to be one of them."

"I am not in love!" Wade blared.

"If you say so," Chad drawled. "And since you have loudly declared it, I see no reason why I can't share Shianne's affection. You must know how it is when you take that curvaceous minx in your arms. One kiss only whets a man's appetite." The amusement evaporated from Chad's eyes. "I've been hungry a long time, Wade. You gave Shianne her freedom by declaring this to be a marriage of convenience. I only hope you can live with the bylaws because I intend to follow them to the letter. . . ."

"Dammit, I told you I will not share her," Wade scowled.

Chad didn't cower. He only chortled at Wade's harsh glare. "You made the rules, big brother. Now you must abide by them."

Wade was a condemned man, he realized as he sat sulking. How did this matter become so entangled? Somewhere along the way he had contradicted himself. He had not wanted to feel the confining chains of matrimony, and he had made that clear to Shianne; but when it came right down to it, he didn't want her to exercise the same privileges. Shianne had first insisted that the marriage be dissolved if it could not be all or nothing between them. Like a blundering fool, Wade had proclaimed that they save the marriage, observe loose limitations and avoid attaching names to emotions. That was fine and good until Shianne accepted the arrangement on *his* terms and then proceeded to enjoy herself in other men's company—Chad's in particular.

Chad was intrigued. That was obvious. He had not made such ado about a woman since he stood on the threshold of manhood. Chad was not going to back off after Wade threw open the door. They were bound to clash, and as usual, Shianne stood directly between them—just as she had with Haden and Maman-ti. She had become like a chain link between every facet of his life, Wade realized. There was no way to get around it. Shianne was either the obstruction or the go-between in every purpose in his life. She was his link to her father, the obsession that would help place the noose around Haden's neck and the mediator between him and the reinforcements of Comanches. Not only that, but she had become the conflict between Wade and his own brother. No matter which way Wade turned, Shianne was there, adding more complications in his life.

This wasn't love. This was lunacy, Wade scowled to himself. No woman should cause a man such headaches. But Wade had one—a five-foot-one-inch headache with midnight hair and dark, entrancing eyes!

A smug grin settled on Shianne's features as she made her way along the winding tunnel that led to the mouth of the cavern. She was going to make Wade love her or force him to dissolve their marriage. She had been foolish to make demands on him, she had realized. Her only hope was to beat Wade at his own game. If he cared for her, he would retract his remarks about no strings attached, and if he felt no jealousy when he found her in the company of other men, she would know she was fighting a lost cause.

Shianne chided herself for scheming. That had never

been her way, but the situation demanded it, she rationalized. She had to force Wade to let her go if he didn't love her. Chad had encouraged her to have patience, to give Wade time to sort out his feelings. Reluctantly, Shianne had agreed, but she was not willing to wait more than a month. If Wade hadn't decided that she meant more to him than a means to an end in that span of time, he never would. She might go on loving him, but she would not remain married to him, she promised herself. . . .

Shianne was jostled from her pensive deliberations when she rounded the corner of the antechamber to see Haden and his men blocking the exit to the cave. The sinister smile that clung to his bony features sent a shiver of dread racing down her spine. What was he doing here? He should have been out trying to recover the cattle Maman-ti had stolen from him the previous night.

"What perfect timing," Haden chuckled fiendishly. "We are in need of a guide to lead us to the treasure Burdett has to be hiding in here."

"What are you talking about?" Shianne questioned, masking her apprehension behind an innocent stare.

"You know perfectly well what I mean," Haden snarled. "Burdett has mysteriously come up with the funds to hire ranch hands and purchase supplies for his cattle drive. The money has to come from somewhere. I know for a fact that the bank has lent him no money." He stalked closer to glare into Shianne's carefully blank expression. "I intend to investigate his money source. One never knows if these grass pirates who have infiltrated Texas have stolen money to pay for their business ventures unless one investigates."

Shianne wheeled away when Haden lunged at her, but he grabbed her hair, yanking her against him. "Show me where Burdett keeps his loot or you will

321

never see the outside of this cave again," he threatened maliciously.

Frantically, Shianne wrestled with her choices. The feel of Haden's dagger lying against her throat had considerable influence on her decision. When she nodded reluctantly, Haden eased his grasp, but he refused to remove the knife from the side of her neck.

Her eyes darted toward the three tunnels, and she gestured to the left. "There. His treasure lies in the cavern at the end of that passage," she assured him.

Haden clamped his arm around her waist and handed the torch to Gustavo Ruiz. "If you are lying to me, you will sorely regret it," he hissed. "Don't think you aren't coming with us. If I fall into a bottomless pit, so will you."

Shianne swallowed with a gulp as Haden herded her along beside him. She had hoped he would be so eager to confiscate Wade's gold that he would charge blindly ahead, leaving her to dash down the other tunnel to alert Wade to Haden's presence. As the footsteps echoed through the passage Shianne grimaced, wondering what Haden would do to her when he realized she had taken him on a wild-goose chase. After seeing what he had done to Chad, she had the sickening feeling she would suffer the same fate . . . or worse.

When Gustavo rounded the corner and found nothing but air beneath his feet, a piercing scream resounded about the gloomy chamber. As Gustavo Ruiz fell into the underground pond, dousing the light, eerie darkness settled about them.

"Damn you, you little bitch!" Haden growled furiously. He pricked his ears to the sound of his henchman thrashing in the pool below. Angrily, he struck out in the darkness, his fist colliding with Shianne's cheek.

"I didn't lie to you," Shianne insisted. She shielded

322

her face from another painful blow. "The treasure lies along the narrow, winding path that edges along the wall."

Haden didn't know whether to trust her, so his only choice was to feel his way back to the opening of the cave and retrieve another torch. He was not about to risk losing all his men in this treacherous dungeon. After ordering his bravoes to retrace their steps, he braced one hand on the wall and clutched Shianne to him.

Shianne swore her heart would beat her to death before they managed to make their way through the darkness and return to the antechamber. Lord, what was she going to do next? She had to think of something and quickly!

The sound of voices drifting from the underground mansion had her cursing under her breath. Haden pricked his ears and then chortled devilishly. "Perhaps I should allow your husband to lead me to his hidden treasure. He is in one of the other tunnels, isn't he, Shianne?"

Shianne did not respond. Her body was rigid, wondering what Haden would do if he should happen to get a look at Wade's brother. She could guess Haden's reaction when he came face to face with a man he had long presumed dead.

Before she could think of a suitable reason not to follow the passageway, Pedro had lit another torch and aimed himself toward the voices that bubbled up from the lower levels of the cavern. Panic gripped her as she was propelled through the tunnel. If she screamed, Wade and Chad might come running, only to be shot down, never to be seen or heard from again. If she kept silent Haden would have the element of surprise on his side. Dammit, was there no solution, Shianne thought in exasperation.

As they neared the opening that overlooked the Burdett's underground home, Shianne went limp in Haden's arms. The moment he eased his grasp, she threw herself away and burst toward the ledge to warn Wade. Scowling, Haden grasped his bull whip. With one snap of his wrist he flung the whip, catching Shianne around the waist before she could flee down the path.

The commotion on the upper rim of the cavern caused Wade to bolt to his feet. "What the hell . . ." His voice trailed off when he saw the portal fill with Haden's small army. He swore under his breath when he spied Haden using Shianne as his shield of protection.

Wade shot his brother a quick glance, watching the glaze of hatred shadow Chad's eyes. The painful experience came back to torment Chad the moment he spied Haden. Killing fury was stamped on Chad's pale features. Instinctively, Chad reached for the pistol that was strapped on his hip, but Wade's hand closed over his wrist before his brother could satisfy his thirst for revenge.

"Haden has Shianne," Wade reminded his brother. "Use your head, man. You could get her killed."

Although Chad had not taken his eyes off Haden, his hand fell limply by his side. "That son of a bitch," Chad hissed venomously. "He either hides behind his henchmen or a woman, but never is that bastard alone."

Spiteful amusement glistened in Haden's eyes as he dragged his writhing bundle closer to the edge. His composure cracked momentarily when he noticed the man who was standing rigidly beside Wade Burdett. It only took a second to recall where he had seen that face. Haden glanced back and forth between the two men, noting the family resemblance. Suddenly he understood why Wade had continued to press him. It was to avenge the incident that should have left his brother dead. Damn, Haden had been so certain there was not a breath of life left in the man he tossed into the river. Now he knew what ghost haunted the cavern. It was Wade Burdett's brother, a man who was waiting for the opportune moment to reappear and point an accusing finger at Haden.

The repercussions of allowing either man to live would be disastrous, Haden realized. He had to dispose of both of them. Clinging to that thought, he called for Juan to toss him the rope he had intended to use to retrieve the hired gun he had left floundering in the other tunnel.

The instant Juan approached the ledge, the color drained from his dark features. He recognized Chad Burdett, and the shock of seeing a dead man standing below him caused him to stagger back. "What are you going to do?" Juan questioned, his gaze swinging from Haden to the Burdett brothers.

"Give me the rope," Haden growled impatiently.

When Juan did not respond, Haden snatched it away and bound one end around Shianne's ankles. After shoving her face down, he pushed her over the edge, leaving her dangling upside down in midair. Once he had secured the free end to a nearby boulder he crouched on the ledge and laid the sharp-bladed dagger against the lifeline that kept Shianne from plunging to her death.

Wade stood paralyzed. A fear, the likes of which he had never known, washed over him. He knew Haden was capable of murder, and he was well aware that Haden felt desperate after learning that Chad had survived his ordeal. Wade had no choice but to comply with whatever demand Haden decided to make. If he didn't Haden would kill Shianne. Dammit, he should never have dragged her into this, Wade cursed himself.

"Your treasure for her life," Haden called down to Wade.

"Don't give it to him," Chad hissed, never taking his eyes off his nemesis. "He'll kill her anyway. You know damned well he's going to dispose of all of us the moment he has the money."

Wade didn't need to hear his thoughts voiced. The implications were grim enough when they were rattling through his head. His keen gaze settled on Juan, trying to determine if he could elicit aid from Haden's hired gun. The look on Juan's face revealed nothing. Juan was staring at the knife Haden held against the rope, and he hadn't moved a muscle since he recognized Chad as the man who had been cut, whipped and left for dead.

While Wade was wrestling with his troubled thoughts, blood was rushing to Shianne's head. The rope was biting into her ankles, and she could do nothing to relieve the pain; but her apprehension was for Wade, not for herself. Oh, how she detested this feeling of helplessness, the utter exasperation of waiting to see if Haden unleashed his hired guns on Wade and Chad.

The tension was growing thicker by the second. Wade had despised Haden since he found Chad in the cave, nursing his injuries, but Wade could not hate Haden more than he did at this moment. The thought of watching Shianne plummet to the rock floor of the cavern sickened him.

Finally he expelled the breath he had been holding. "I'll bring out the gold when you pull Shianne back to the ledge," Wade bartered.

Haden gave his head a negative shake. "She stays where she is until you produce this mysterious treasure of yours, Burdett." To make his point, Haden slashed

326

one side of the rope. "I am not a patient man. . . ."

"Chad, fetch the chest," Wade ordered quietly.

"I told you we should have ambushed the man," Chad scowled sourly. "If we had we wouldn't be in such a scrape."

"Get the money," Wade ground out.

Growling, Chad stalked toward the passage to retrieve the chest. When he returned, dragging one trunk behind him, he glared at the man who was crouched on the ledge.

"Open it," Haden demanded. "I want to ensure you haven't tried to trick me. It seems the two of you are adept at treachery."

Begrudgingly, Chad kicked open the trunk and then lifted a handful of coins, letting them drop back into the pile. "There is a curse on the treasure. I cannot think of a more deserving man to lay claim to this gold."

Haden's satanic laughter rang through the cavern. "I have faced better men than you, Burdett. There is no curse on this treasure. The curse is on you and your brother. You should have veered around me. No man who dares to confront me has ever won."

After Haden ordered his men to carry the trunk up beside him, he pulled Shianne back to the ledge. To ensure that she didn't escape him again, he laid the blade against her throat.

"Take your last look at your husband and your brother-in-law, my dear. You will never see them again."

Shianne risked cutting her own throat when she heard the click of the revolvers behind her. "No!" she screamed at the top of her lungs. Her elbow rammed into Haden's midsection.

Her tussle with Haden gave Chad and Wade time to dive for cover before the pistols exploded, but Shianne

327

could not determine if the gunmen had missed their targets. Haden's blow sent her reeling backwards. The moment her head slammed against the rock floor she fell into the haze of darkness.

Cursing a blue streak, Haden ducked away from the volley of gunfire that came from the lower level of the cave. Ordering a few of his men to keep his victims pinned down, he dragged Shianne's limp body over his shoulder. While four of his men wrestled with the treasure chest, Haden took up the torch to hurry through the tunnel. Once outside, he dropped Shianne's unconscious body on the ground and glanced frantically about him.

A wicked smile caught the corner of his mouth when he spied the gunpowder Wade had used to reroute the creek channel. He would set off an explosion in the mouth of the cave, entrapping both men. Since there would be no bodies, no one could accuse him of murder, he speculated.

Hastily, he scooped up the barrel and carried it into the antechamber. After sending Juan to retrieve the rest of the men, Haden spread a fuse of gunpowder on the ground. The moment his men stepped outside he lit the fuse.

Juan ground his foot into the gunpowder and glared at Haden. "One of your own men is in that cavern," he snapped.

Haden drew his pistol, forcing Juan to stand aside or be blown to bits. "That can't be helped. If Wade and his brother do not meet their demise, I am a dead man. There is no time to determine if Gustavo can swim out of that hell hole. I have no choice but to make the sacrifice."

Gritting his teeth, Juan watched the smoldering trail of gunpowder inch closer to the barrel. He knew Gustavo was a dead man. The man had never been able to swim a lick, and Haden was too anxious to dispose of the Burdetts to fret over one of his gunmen.

Juan's eyes darted toward Shianne, knowing she would be crushed when the rockslide began. Hurriedly, he scooped her in his arms and carried her a safe distance away.

The deafening explosion caused the earth to shake beneath his feet, but Haden didn't care. He had locked the Burdetts in their underground tomb. Demented laughter echoed about him as he watched the dirt and rocks collapse, leaving no exit from the cave. With the Burdetts out of the way, he could properly punish Shianne for betraying him. She would become his captive whore, his object of pleasure. Haden intended to lock her in his home and pleasure himself with her body when it met his whim, but she would never become his wife, not after she had bedded Burdett.

If Blake Kimball ever returned to search for his lost daughter and business partner, Haden would simply speculate that Shianne had been with Wade when the disastrous rock slide trapped them in the cave.

Haden glanced over to see Juan cradling Shianne in his arms. Angrily, he stalked over to retrieve the limp bundle. "You seem to be losing your nerve, *amigo*," he snorted. "Have you considered where you will find work if I decide you are no longer of any use to me?"

The muscles in Juan's jaw tightened as Haden snatched Shianne away. He watched as Haden tossed her across his saddle and turned his steed toward home. Damn, Juan muttered under his breath. He should have taken Burdett's offer when he had the chance. Haden was becoming more vile and ruthless by the day. Juan had killed his share of men at Haden's request, but he was losing his taste for killing, even if he had been well paid to ignore his conscience.

Fearing Haden's intent for Shianne, Juan swung

into the saddle. He had long admired the feisty young beauty of the K Bar Ranch, and he did not relish the thought of Haden taking his knife to Shianne. There was nothing he could do for his friend who had been trapped in the cavern or for the Burdetts, but he could spare Shianne a fate worse than death.

Wicked satisfaction radiated from Haden's face as he aimed himself toward the hacienda. He couldn't wait to have his revenge on this defiant minx. Before he finished with Shianne, she would beg for his touch. He would have made her his queen, but now she would become his slave, he promised himself.

Relief washed over Haden. A great burden had been lifted from his shoulders now that Wade Burdett was out of the way. Haden had been a tormented man since the day Wade showed up at the K Bar Ranch, but now the ordeal was over, and Haden was free to round up his cattle and those Wade had collected. The irony of the situation delighted Haden. Wade had saved him the trouble of collecting more cattle to send north. With the cattle Haden had gathered, plus the huge number Wade had branded, he would make a fortune in Kansas.

The thought caused Haden to laugh out loud. It was a pity Wade wouldn't live to see Haden convert the cattle into cash, but Wade got exactly what he deserved after he tried to outfox Haden. Let the man rot at the bottom of the cavern, Haden thought spitefully. Never again would the Burdetts see daylight. They would die a slow, tormenting death, and nothing could have pleased him more.

Chapter 16

A groggy moan tumbled from Shianne's lips. Her lashes fluttered up to stare around the dark, unfamiliar room. A muddled frown furrowed her brow. When fragments of memory came back to her, Shianne tried to sit up, but she found herself strapped to the bed.

"Haden. . . ." she hissed, cursing his name and the dreadful thought of what he might have done to Wade and his brother after she had lost consciousness. Unable to free herself from the restraining ropes, Shianne slumped back against the pillow. Her misty gaze focused on the ceiling. Had the hired guns found their mark? Were Wade and Chad lying in the cavern bleeding from their wounds? What was to become of her? What fiendish death had Haden planned for her?

The sound of footsteps in the hall caused Shianne to tense. She waited, wondering if she would spit in Haden's face as Chad had done or if she would defy the scoundrel with one of Wade's infuriating smiles. The moment Haden set foot in the room, Shianne realized she did not possess Wade's remarkable self-control. She detested Haden on sight, and she itched to claw that triumphant grin off his face.

"What did you do to them?" she ground out between

331

clenched teeth.

Haden plopped down beside her to investigate the discolorations on her cheeks. It was a pity he was forced to mar such a lovely face, but Shianne had left him no choice. When his straying hand trailed down her shoulder to rest familiarly on her breast, Shianne winced as if she had been burned. God, how she detested his touch.

"Where is my husband?" she demanded to know.

"Ah, yes, you would be curious about that, wouldn't you," Haden smirked caustically. "I had forgotten you were unconscious when disaster struck." Rising, Haden stuffed his hands in the pockets of his breeches and strolled over to peer out into the night. "I'm afraid I have some bad news for you, my dear Shianne. After all the commotion and gunfire in the cavern, the entrance of the cave crumbled, sending rock and debris everywhere." He turned back to survey the horrified expression that claimed Shianne's bruised features. "Your husband was buried alive . . . or dead. I cannot say for certain, but it would take an army two weeks to remove the mammoth boulders that block the entrance of the cavern. By then it would be too late."

Shianne felt her heart wither and die. She had been so certain Wade would conquer Haden, but it seemed Haden had found a way to emerge the victor. Who could lay the blame on the owner of the Lazy R if an act of God had brought about Wade's demise. . . . Or was it a freak accident of nature? After learning of Haden's ruthless techniques of ridding the area of unwanted "foreigners," Shianne could not help but wonder if Haden had been the cause of the rock slide.

"You used explosives, didn't you?" she accused, her voice dripping with venom.

Haden snickered at her hateful tone. "You are jumping to conclusions, my dear. There is no way to prove such an accusation. Besides, one of my own men perished in the avalanche of rock. Surely you don't think I would have purposely closeted my ranch hand in that cave."

"I wouldn't put anything past you," Shianne growled bitterly. "Not after I learned what you did to Wade's brother."

"That is all in the past," he told her harshly. Haden stalked back to the bed to glare at Shianne's murderous frown. "From this day forward I will be taking care of you. I will enjoy the same privileges you extended to your late husband."

Shianne flinched. The thought of surrendering to Haden after what he had done to the Burdetts and countless other victims repulsed her. "I would die before I allowed you to touch me," she sneered at him.

Defiantly, Haden bent to cup his hand around her breast, making Shianne cry out when his fingers bit into her soft skin. "You will live, and I will take you each time it meets my whim," he insisted with a satanic smile.

"I detest you," Shianne spat at him. "You may rape me, but I will curse you with every breath."

Haden's temper boiled over. Impulsively, he back-handed the stubborn spitfire. "You will treat me with the respect I deserve, damn you. You played me for the fool, making me wait years to possess you while you gave yourself to Burdett like a shameless whore. You will pay for your sins . . . every day, Shianne."

Now Shianne knew the full extent of Chad's hatred for this man. It was a pity Wade had insisted upon doing the decent thing. Chad *should* have barged into Haden's hacienda and shot him. It would have spared them all a great deal of misery.

Haden retrieved his knife and cut away the rope that bound her ankles. "Get up woman and strip from your

333

clothes. I wish to pleasure myself with your body."

Shianne swung her legs over the edge of the bed and tilted a rebellious chin. "I will not give you the satisfaction of thinking I want your touch."

Furiously, Haden manacled her arm and yanked her to her feet. Grinning maliciously, he used his dagger to carve away the buttons on her shirt. With the handle of the knife still clamped in his hand, he slid his arm around her. Shianne was forced to endure his touch or risk having his initials etched in her spine. When his mouth opened on hers, Shianne writhed for freedom, only to have the point of the dagger embedded in her flesh. Haden took advantage of her painful gasp, ravishing her with his bruising kiss.

The taste and feel of his body pressing intimately against hers was nauseating. Shianne knew she would go mad if she was forced to succumb to this bastard's clumsy lovemaking. Her heart cried out for the one man who had taught her the pure essence of pleasure. She could have no other lover, not after she had known Wade. Her soul belonged to him, even if he had perished.

When Shianne bit at Haden's lip, he withdrew, cursing her name. "You little bitch!" he roared.

"Let her go."

Haden's arm hung in midair. He had fully intended to send her senses reeling with another blow. Scowling, he swiveled his head around to see Juan Mendez's bulky figure looming in the doorway.

"I said let her go," Juan repeated deliberately.

"You are paid to take orders not give them," he snarled at his hired gunman.

When Juan made the mistake of taking his eyes off Haden to appraise the fresh bruises on Shianne's face and the gaping shirt that exposed the inner fullness of her breasts, Haden sprung like a striking snake. Before

Juan could fire the revolver that was clenched in his fist, Haden hooked his arm around Shianne's waist and thrust her between them.

"Drop the pistol, Juan," Haden commanded sharply. When Juan refused, Haden laid the dagger to the side of Shianne's neck, allowing the sharp blade to draw blood. "I said drop it, or I will let you watch me carve designs in her throat."

Begrudgingly, Juan tossed the revolver aside. For two days he had stood like a posted lookout, keeping close tabs on Haden's activities, wondering when Haden would make his move toward Shianne. The moment he saw Haden's silhouette against the window of Shianne's room, Juan had sneaked inside, but like an arrogant fool, he thought he could persuade Haden to keep his distance from the girl by waving a pistol in his face. He should have known the coward would hide behind Shianne, just as he had done in the cave. Cowards never stood alone. They always hid behind armies and employed all means of protection within their grasp.

Juan cursed himself for not shooting Haden in the back when he had the chance. There could never be such a thing as a fair fight where Haden was concerned. His burst of conscience had cost him dearly, and now he was the one at the disadvantage.

"Step aside, Juan," Haden barked. "I am no longer in need of your services."

"Where are you taking her?" Juan questioned, his eyes on the trickle of blood that lay on Shianne's neck.

"That is none of your concern. Pack your belongings and get off my ranch!"

Haden edged toward the door, deciding it best to take Shianne with him on the cattle drive. He could no longer depend on his servants to follow orders. No doubt, Juan would sneak back to the hacienda to free the girl after Haden had gone.

As Haden inched past him, Juan lunged to knock away the knife. But Haden anticipated trouble. A shriek of pain erupted from Juan's lips as the knife slashed across his arm. Instinctively, he clutched at the bleeding wound and shrank away.

Shianne took the opportunity to attempt to claw her way to freedom. Her nails dug into Haden's features, ripping the hide from the side of his face. Her assault only served to enrage Haden. An infuriated bellow resounded about the room when Juan came at him again. Haden struck out wildly, slicing the dagger across Juan's belly. Frantically Haden clung to the squirming bundle in his arms. He was determined not to let her escape, leaving him vulnerable to Juan's attack.

When Juan doubled over to protect his wound, Haden kicked him in the groin. Juan fell to his knees, gasping for breath. Blood stained his shirt, and he fought the wave of nausea caused by Haden's punishing blow. Blindly, Juan fumbled to reach for the discarded pistol. A pained growl bubbled from his chest when Haden ground his heel into Juan's hand, crushing the bones in the fingers of his gun hand. Before Juan could recoil and stagger to his feet, Haden swung his sharp-edged blade, leaving a wide gash in his challenger's back.

Shianne was sickened by what she saw. It reminded her of the account Wade had given of the incident that had left Chad's body a mass of scars. Wildly, she thrashed in Haden's arms, but the man suddenly had thrice the normal amount of strength. Haden's fingers clamped into her ribs, and the knife returned to her throat to draw another drop of blood.

She grimaced when she saw Haden lift his foot and plant the toe of his boot on Juan's chin. With a pained groan, Juan collapsed on the floor, leaving Haden free to make his escape. Shianne found herself shuffled down the hall and out the door. Although she resisted every step, Haden slung her onto a horse and tied her to the saddle. When he had swung onto his steed, he grabbed the trailing reins and led Shianne across the pasture.

Her body slumped defeatedly. Wade and Chad were dead, and Juan was in no condition to lend assistance, she thought dismally. How was she to fight Haden alone when he had tied her wrists to the pommel and her feet to the stirrups?

Haden's victorious laughter rang through the night. Urging his steed into breakneck speed he raced toward the army of men who had made preparations to begin the cattle drive. The day after the incident at the cave, Haden had sent his bravoes to steal the cattle Wade had penned in the corrals. With Burdett's two thousand head and the matching number Haden had collected, he intended to put the herd enroute to Abilene, Kansas. Shianne's presence would ensure he had a buyer, Haden mused. If Blake Kimball wanted to see his daughter again, he would pay whatever Haden demanded for the cattle herd, but that would not be the end of it, Haden assured himself. He had other plans for Shianne. Blake would consent to Shianne becoming Haden's whore, and he would not lift a hand to intervene . . . not if he wanted to ensure Shianne's safety. At last Shianne would be his, Haden promised himself. Blake Kimball would bow to the stronger force, or he would lose his daughter forever.

Mulling over that delightful thought, Haden made his way to the campsite. Once they were on the trail he would appease his hunger for this defiant beauty. By the time they reached Abilene, Shianne would obey every command he gave. There were ways to tame this feisty, headstrong woman, Haden reminded himself arrogantly. Captivity and the feeling of hopelessness would break her spirit. Soon she would submit without a fight, and he would erase every memory of Wade Burdett from her mind.

Wade massaged his aching left arm and stared angrily at the mass of boulders that blocked the exit of the cavern. "There has to be another way out of this damned cave," he muttered.

Turning away, Chad held the torch in front of him to make his way back to the lower levels of the cavern. "If there is, I have yet to find it. I have searched every nook and cranny. Every passage leads to a dead end."

Frustrated, Wade fell into step behind his brother. "Then we are left with one choice. We will have to attempt swimming through the underground river that leads to Speaking Springs."

Chad wheeled around, staring at Wade as if he had taken a leap off the deep end. "My God, man, you would have to be able to hold your breath like a fish! And there is not enough daylight between the rocks and the river for a man to wedge himself between them."

"Would you prefer to sit here and do nothing?" Wade snorted disdainfully. "I have no intention of waiting around until we have exhausted our meager food supply and fuel to keep the torches burning. After staring into the darkness for days on end we'll go blind!"

Wade had a point, Chad begrudgingly admitted. They had been buried alive, and any alternative was better than waiting for starvation and blindness to overtake them.

Once they had made their way to the elaborately

furnished chamber, Wade walked into the underground river to inspect the narrow passage where the waning sunlight sprinkled onto the water. God, how he wished he *was* a fish, he thought whimsically. It would not be difficult to swim to freedom if he were no bigger than his boot, but the riverbed of rock and jutting boulders that blocked the small tunnel could snag a man and drown him before he could wedge his way free.

Damn, if he hadn't been so preoccupied with Shianne, he would not have allowed Haden to take him by surprise. He should have anticipated Haden's arrival. But no, Wade had been stewing over that unpredictable woman.

A twisting knot formed in the pit of his belly when he thought of Shianne. What had become of her? Had Haden decided to appease the last of his vindictiveness by carving on her the way he had cut on Chad? Or had he devised another form of torture for her? Wade scowled at the thought of Haden touching Shianne, forcing her to succumb to his amorous advances. If he survived being buried in this underground sepulcher, Wade vowed he would make Haden pay retribution with his life.

"I'm sorry, Chad," Wade apologized as he sank back against a slippery boulder.

A puzzled frown set upon Chad's brow. "Sorry for what?"

"If I would have granted you your whim, you would have walked up and shot Haden. Maybe then we wouldn't be sharing the same grave," Wade sighed heavily.

"And maybe that fiend wouldn't be doing whatever it is he is doing to your wife at the moment," Chad snorted disgustedly. "I'm not sure which of us has suffered the worst fate, but if I were a woman, I would hate to endure Haden's touch. I'd rather be dead."

"She very well could be," Wade grumbled bitterly.

The dismal thought left both men lost to their troubled musings. After Wade had inspected the riverbed, he requested that Chad locate something that would serve as a measuring stick. Chad glanced about him. Spying an object that might suffice, he stalked over to lift one of the chairs over his head. When the piece of furniture collided with the rock floor it shattered to bits.

"Mother has always been fond of that dining room suite," Wade smirked as he watched Chad rummage through the debris to grasp what was left of the chair leg.

"I thought she was rather fond of us too," Chad parried. "If we live through this ordeal, I'll buy her a whole damned set of chairs."

The faintest hint of a smile touched Wade's lips as he accepted the chair leg from his brother. "Does this mean you have forgiven Mother for marrying Blake Kimball?"

Chad heaved a heavy sigh and walked into the water beside his brother. "I guess I knew all along that things had never been right between our parents. It was even more obvious when Mother did not travel to Richmond when Father took the position in Jefferson Davis's cabinet. For them, I suppose the separation was a blessing." Chad's somber gaze swung to his brother. "But you know how I felt about Father. I looked up to him, tried to be like him. It hurt when Blake wedged his way into Mother's life, and it has taken time for me to accept the change." A curious frown plowed Chad's brow. "How does Shianne feel about the marriage between our mother and her father?"

Wade didn't look up. "I haven't told her yet," he mumbled.

"Why the hell not?" Chad croaked in disbelief. "I thought that was one of the reasons Blake sent you in his stead . . . to pave a smooth path." He surveyed their underground sepulcher and then sent Wade a withering glance. "I'll say one thing for you, big brother. You have certainly gone to drastic measures to avoid telling Shianne about the marriage. And from the look of things, you may never be able to tell her at all, even if you could find the nerve to explain she had unknowingly married her stepbrother."

"I wanted to break it to her gently," Wade defended. "I was afraid Shianne would take the news as badly as you did, but no matter what you think of the marriage, I believe Mother and Blake needed each other and that they have been good for each other." Wade squatted down to gauge the depth of the water between the high riverbed and the low ceiling of rock. "I also think they deserve a little happiness."

Wade grumbled under his breath when he measured the depth of the tunnel and realized it was much longer than the length of his arm and the chair leg. There was an obstruction blocking the river channel, one that would force a man to turn sideways if he ever hoped to squeeze through it. And once he did, there was no telling what lay beyond.

"Someone on the outside deserves to enjoy life; I'm not sure we will ever see daylight again. Save your money, little brother. You may not be required to replace Mother's dining room suite because you may never be anywhere near a store again."

"That bad?" Chad questioned deflatedly.

Wade shook his head in dismay. "It doesn't look hopeful." His eyes shot around the cavern. "Fetch a rope. I'm going to try to swim through the channel. If I am wedged between a rock and a hard spot, you may have to drag me back out."

After wading ashore, he returned with the rope

341

Wade had requested. "I hope the hell you can hold your breath," Chad muttered.

"It can't be much of one," he snorted. "I'll never get through that narrow niche with my chest swelled up with air."

Apprehensively, Chad watched Wade secure the rope around his waist. He speculated on the tiny portal that rippled with water and then surveyed Wade's bulky form. It was like trying to cram a boot in a thimble, Chad thought to himself. The only way for Wade to slither through the opening was if he disassembled his parts and then reassembled himself when he reached the outside.

"I don't think this is such a good idea," Chad grumbled.

One dark brow raised acutely. "Do you, perchance, have a better one?" Wade queried.

Wade's eyes strayed to the crumpled bed where he and Shianne had made love two days earlier. When she had been in his arms, responding in reckless abandon, Wade swore he was in heaven. Now he was certain he had been trapped in hell. Not knowing what had become of Shianne was tearing him to pieces, bit by excruciating bit. He could envision Haden holding Shianne captive in his arms, forcing her to tolerate his kiss, his caress. The thought turned Wade inside out.

A wry smile slid across Chad's lips when he followed Wade's pensive gaze. "It must have been good," he speculated aloud. "But I had already suspected as much."

Wade glared at his brother. "Your mind has a way of dropping into the most sordid caverns," he grunted sarcastically.

Chad replaced his grin with a frown. "I do wish you could make your comparisons without referring to *caves* in my skull. It is dreary enough, thinking I'm to spend the rest of my days, numbered as they are, in this underground pit."

Releasing a sigh, Wade focused his attention on the narrow path ahead of him. "You're right, Chad," he admitted quietly. "It has always been good with Shianne, even the bad times. . . ."

Inhaling a deep breath, Wade submerged in the river and pulled his way around the jutting boulders that sought to entrap him. As he made the third turn in the river channel, his cumbersome body snagged between the rocks. Suddenly, Wade felt as if the solid walls were closing in on him. He couldn't move. Rock and water surrounded him. He opened his eyes to see the dim sprinkling of light a few feet above him. Maneuvering his arm upward, he located the tiny pocket of air between the river and the low rock ceiling.

Wade swore his lungs would burst before he could wriggle free and pull his knees beneath him. The split-second before he depleted his oxygen supply, he managed to free his shoulders. Still wedged between the boulders, Wade thrust his head upward and gasped for breath.

A shudder of fear shot down Chad's backbone when he heard his brother sputtering and coughing somewhere in the distance. "Wade? Can you hear me?"

Taking a soggy but thankful breath, Wade pried his hips free and sat up in midstream (or as close as one could come to sitting when one's knees were wrapped around one's neck). "Follow the rope, little brother. It is a tight squeeze, but you can reach the air pocket before your lungs collapse."

Chad sank into the river, frowning warily. "And just what are we going to do when we both exhaust that precious pocket of air?" Chad queried, uncertain which he preferred, death by drowning or starvation. Neither alternative sounded appealing.

"Hell, I don't know," Wade growled. "We'll sit here and decide whether to turn back or risk crawling the rest of the way through this damned tunnel!"

"Don't encourage me," Chad shot back. "I'm not sure I can wedge through this hell hole while I'm inflated with enthusiasm."

"Dammit, hurry up!" Wade barked impatiently. "We haven't got all night. If we lose the source of light, we'll never find our way out of here."

"As if we could anyway," Chad scoffed before inhaling a breath and rattling off a quick prayer.

Wade waited, his arm braced between the narrow crevice that separated the boulders, hoping any moment Chad's head would collide with his hand. After what seemed forever, Wade felt his brother struggling to maneuver his bulky frame through the opening. He knew the panic Chad was experiencing. In an effort to grant his brother a breath of air, Wade clamped his hands around Chad's neck, forcing him steadily upward.

Chad snorted and choked. Finally, he replenished his oxygen supply and then wormed around to glare at his brother. "You needn't have twisted my head off my shoulders," he sputtered in annoyance.

"Would you rather I let you drown?" Wade tossed back at him.

The two grown men were wedged in the tiny cubicle, their arms and legs wrapped around each other, unable to move without gouging the other. Wade spared a quiet chuckle when he realized how petty their arguments were in the face of such a grave predicament.

Chad rolled his eyes in disgust. "You are wasting precious breath," he scolded. "And half of that air was mine." He dragged in a breath to ensure he was granted his equal share. Dammit, how could Wade laugh at a moment like this? No matter how dire the straits, Wade could always produce a smile. Confound it, that was unnatural!

"Well, little brother, now what do you suggest? Shall we forge onward or return to the cavern?" Wade inquired.

Chad turned his attention to the cavity that was growing darker by the minute. "Did you remember to bring along your chair leg to measure the width and depth of the tunnel?"

"I thought you had it," Wade grunted as he wormed around to relieve the cramp in his coiled leg. Sighing melodramatically, Wade swiveled his head around to survey the dark passage that was running level full of water. "I have always found myself leading the way for you. The complications of being the first born, I suppose."

"Your sense of humor is dripping wet," Chad pointed out, his tone carrying a caustic clip. "Besides, Mother always liked you best. She granted you every whim."

"Oh? Then how do you explain the fact that she spoiled *you* rotten?" Wade smirked just as sarcastically.

"There you go again, taking more than your share of the air." The childish rejoinder was supplemented by a fond smile. "Wade, in case we don't get out of here alive, I want you to know how glad I was to have you for my brother. . . ."

Wade wiggled around to face in the direction of the unexplored tunnel. "Don't go getting sentimental on me, Chad," he cautioned. "It doesn't suit your personality."

Drawing in a deep breath, Wade sank into the river and felt his way along the winding spring bed. The light had evaporated, and there was nothing but pitch black darkness ahead of him. The route was as treacherous as before, but Wade was determined to follow the channel to the end . . . or die trying. At least then Chad would know to turn back.

When Wade felt his brother's hand against his leg, he scowled to himself. Dammit, Chad had not waited to ensure the way was clear. He could perish alongside Wade, never having the opportunity to turn around and swim back to safety. Again, Wade feared his lungs would explode. He had very nearly depleted his oxygen supply, but he had yet to feel air above him when he lifted his hand over his head. There was nothing above him but solid rock and nothing surrounding him except a wall of water.

Even in the dark cramped space that Wade feared was about to become his tomb, he could see a bewitching face. Shianne was always there, haunting the corners of his mind, burrowing her way into his thoughts. He was about to meet his maker and still she preoccupied him, Wade mused sourly. He should be repenting his sins, not lamenting the loss of a woman who had caused him nothing but trouble.

Damn, Shianne had taken up permanent residence in his mind. But not for long, Wade reminded himself as he thrashed on his last bit of breath. In a few more seconds, the waterway would be clogged with two bodies, and the spring would run dry.

In that instant, when he realized he was fighting a hopeless battle, Wade refused to give up. He heard Shianne's name echo through his mind, vibrating through his head until he lost consciousness. His body slumped in the confining tunnel, failing him when he would have scratched and clawed his way to freedom. . . .

Chapter 17

A muddled frown plowed Maman-ti's brow. Again he cupped his hand around his mouth, his voice taking on the lonely sound of the owl. He had been plagued with an unsettling dream that Shianne needed him, and he had come to ease his apprehension. The fact that Shianne had not answered his first call greatly disturbed him.

Maman-ti grumbled under his breath, wondering if the green-eyed white man had forebade her to answer the call, not that Maman-ti could blame Wade for keeping his enchanting woman at home, he admitted to himself. But Maman-ti had delighted in challenging Wade, testing him to determine if he were man enough for a woman like Shianne.

Finally, Maman-ti heaved a disappointed sigh and swung onto his pony. He had hoped to see Shianne one last time before he and the other braves moved north to trail their herd of confiscated livestock to the village. Resigning himself to the fact that he would be forced to wait several months before he spoke to Shianne, Maman-ti aimed his steed toward the Speaking Springs. He would consult the great spirits that dwelled in the river before deciding if another raid would prove profitable to the Comanche and Kiowa.

When Maman-ti rode upon the group of waiting Indians, a concerned frown claimed his bronzed features. Several of the war chiefs hurried toward him, horrified that the gushing springs had become a trickling stream. Curious about what had caused the disturbance in the river, Maman-ti strode along the bank.

"The gods are angry with us," one of the chiefs surmised. "Not only have they stopped speaking, but they have dammed up the water, refusing to quench our thirst."

For a long, silent moment, the Owl Prophet peered at the narrow opening between the rocks. He had no explanation for this odd occurrence. A surprised squawk burst from his lips as a wall of water belched from the ground. To his disbelief, he watched Wade Burdett and another man of similar size and stature ride the wave that replenished the river.

When the limp bodies washed aground, Maman-ti rushed to Wade's side. Ignoring the gash on Wade's temple, Maman-ti pushed the white man to his stomach and sank down on top of him. One of the warriors followed the procedure on the other unconscious man. Maman-ti shoved the heel of his hands against Wade's back and forced the water from his lungs. After several tense moments, Wade's chest heaved, and he sputtered for breath. Over and over again, Maman-ti worked to bring Wade back to life, singing chants to the screech owl and the great spirits of the spring.

Maman-ti gained new respect for the two white men who had somehow ventured into the earth to parley with the great spirits. It was obvious to the Owl Prophet that these white men had been blessed. If the gods had not smiled on them, the men would not have been delivered up from the bowels of the earth.

When Wade and Chad began breathing on their own, the Owl Prophet sank back on his haunches to stare at the waterlogged victims. Reasonably certain the men would live after being allowed time to recuperate, Maman-ti turned his thoughts elsewhere. If Shianne's man was not with her, preventing her from answering the call of the owl, why hadn't she come?

An eerie sensation drifted down Maman-ti's spine. Something was wrong, he could sense it. Never had Shianne refused an audience with the Owl Prophet, not once since the day they had first met.

Wade's groggy groan stirred Maman-ti from his troubled contemplations. Maman-ti grasped Wade's shirt and rolled him to his back to shake him awake.

"Where is your woman?" the Owl Prophet demanded to know.

Wade heard Maman-ti's voice, but he could not seem to comprehend the words. It was as if someone were calling to him from a long, echoing tunnel. The sensation triggered a memory and Wade thrashed wildly, attempting to free himself from the maze of water and rocks that sought to entrap him. His flailing arm rammed against Maman-ti's chest, sending the startled Indian sprawling on his back. Wild, tormented moans erupted from Wade's lips as he fought the terrifying memory. His eyes flew open in a sightless stare, and he thrashed on the ground, muttering inaudible words and syllables that Maman-ti could not decipher in any tongue—white *or* Indian.

With his jaw gaping, Maman-ti climbed to his feet and backed away. "The great spirits have taken command of the white man's body," he told the war chiefs. "The Indian gods have taken human form to lead us."

A wave of murmurs rippled through the congregation of braves. In awe, they stared at Wade and the other man who had also begun to flop around on the ground like a fish out of water. After several minutes, both men fell into an exhausted sleep. Cautiously, Maman-ti edged up beside Wade to ensure that he was still breathing.

"The spirits have left their bodies to return to the Speaking Springs," Maman-ti informed the gaping chiefs. "Come, we will chant our praises to the spirits while the white men recuperate from their experience of walking with the sacred ghosts of our ancestors."

When Wade and Chad had been covered with blankets, the council of chiefs circled the great medicine man, waiting for him to speak to the owl oracle. The ceremony was a most inspiring one. The superstitious Indians listened intently to the words that floated from the Owl Prophet's lips as he fell into his trance. They heard and vowed to obey the commands they were given.

Chad was the first to awaken from his harrowing experience. His eyes fluttered open when he heard the eerie chants of the Indians. He flinched when he realized he and Wade were lying not fifty feet from the camp.

"Wade, for God's sake, wake up," Chad whispered, giving his brother a sound shake. When Wade did not respond immediately, Chad shook him again.

Wade's body shuddered from the chill. Groaning miserably, he willed his heavily-lidded eyes to open. The silhouettes dancing around the campfire, and the low chants of the Indians invaded his senses. Shaking his head to get his bearings, Wade focused on the blur that he surmised to be his brother. When he had propped himself up on one elbow he stared across the creek to see the tribe conducting their ceremony.

"We have to get out of here before they decide to lift

our scalps!" Chad insisted.

Wade wasn't certain he had the strength to sit up, much less stand on his own two feet and dart off into the night. The sight of the Owl Prophet eased his apprehension. He gestured his throbbing head toward the tall, muscular shaman who was shaking his medicine stick toward the sky.

"That is the Owl Prophet, Shianne's devoted Indian," he informed his brother.

"I would feel a helluva lot better if Shianne were here," Chad grumbled.

Suddenly, the ceremony came to a halt, and silence shrouded the night. The tribe fell back to allow the Owl Prophet to stride toward the two men who were propped on their elbows.

"You are most fortunate, Wade Burdett," Maman-ti commented as he came to tower over them. "You have visited the great spirits and have lived to tell of it."

Chad slid his brother a discreet glance, waiting for Wade to say something. To Chad's way of thinking, facing a tribe of renegade Indians was almost as bad as being snagged in an underground river.

"Our experience has given me great respect for your people," Wade assured the Owl Prophet. Slowly, he pushed to an upright position. "My brother and I sought the advice and assistance of your powerful gods."

Maman-ti sank down crosslegged, peering cautiously at Wade. "What has disturbed you, Wade Burdett?"

"Haden Reems, the rancher whose cattle you stole during your raid, the man who swore vengeance, has taken Shianne," Wade explained. "I sought to parley with your gods to determine how to defeat a man who possesses powerful, but evil spirits."

Wade was laying it on a mite thick, but he was

351

desperate. He had been trapped in the cavern for several days, and he didn't have the slightest notion what Haden had done or what the bastard was planning. One thing was for certain; Wade needed the assistance of the Comanches and Kiowas if he was to defeat Haden.

Drawing Maman-ti's attention, Wade reached over to yank open Chad's shirt. "See for yourself how cruel and ruthless Haden Reems can be when he is provoked." While Maman-ti stared at the scars that slashed across Chad's chest, Wade continued, "The white man is malicious. I cannot bear to think what will happen to my woman. . . ."

Maman-ti felt rage boiling through his veins. The thought of Shianne enduring torture and disfigurement infuriated him. "If Haden Reems has laid his knife to Shianne, I will cut his heart from his chest," he spat vindictively.

That was exactly what Wade wanted to hear.

"We will catch up to the white man and his herd, and we will slaughter them all!"

"Catch up to them?" Wade repeated incredulously.

Maman-ti nodded affirmatively. "We saw the dust billowing into the air. The cattle that were penned on this ranch and those that belonged to the vicious white man were taken north," he informed Wade.

The news had Wade cursing under his breath. If he intended to steal back his herd, and he most certainly did, he would have to gather the necessary supplies and equip the chuck wagon. All that would take time and money, neither of which Wade had at the moment. What was left of his treasure lay beneath several tons of rock, and each second he delayed put a greater distance between him and Haden and Shianne.

The thought further soured Wade's curdled disposition. How could he be certain Haden had taken

Shianne with him? How could he even be certain she was still alive? There was no way of knowing what Haden had done to her in his demented fit of temper.

Wade struggled to his feet, indecision etching his brow. He could not leave the area until he knew exactly what had happened to Shianne, nor could he go thundering off until he had rounded up the ranch hands and supplies to outfit a trail drive. Yet, he felt the need to pursue Haden as quickly as possible.

His eyes swung to Maman-ti, staring pensively at the harsh scowl that was embedded in the warrior's angular features. "I need your help. There is much at stake here. I fear for Shianne's safety, but I do not know for certain that Haden has dragged her along with him. There is also the matter of the cattle that belong to me and Shianne's father."

"I will slaughter the men who ride with Haden and spare the cattle," Maman-ti offered, his voice heavy with vengeance.

As the Owl Prophet spun away, Wade grasped his arm to detain him. A wry smile surfaced on his face. "I have another method of torture in mind, Maman-ti, one befitting of the man and his malicious deeds."

A skeptical frown etched Maman-ti's features. In the past he had been one to contemplate raids instead of plunging recklessly ahead, but after hearing that Shianne might have been held captive by the vicious white man, he was prepared to ride off with a hatchet in one hand and a rifle in the other. If he did not believe Wade and his brother had been granted the blessings of the great spirits, he would not have stayed to listen.

"Speak, Wade Burdett. I will do your bidding," the Owl Prophet promised.

Relief washed over Wade's tense body. He had no intention of involving Maman-ti in a massacre. Such actions would draw more attention to the conflict between the Indians and whites. Wade refused to instigate an all out war the Comanches and Kiowas could not hope to win, and that was exactly what would happen if Maman-ti attacked the trail herd and slaughtered the men, worthless though they were. The government would send a well-equipped army to annihilate the Indians for the atrocities. There were bitter feelings between the Indians and whites, and Wade was not about to add more fuel to an already smoldering fire.

What Wade had in mind was allowing the Indians to badger Haden without drawing Maman-ti's people into a major conflict. Shianne would never forgive him if he put her Indian cousin's life in jeopardy, Wade reminded himself. After all, Shianne cared more for the Owl Prophet than she did for her own husband.

Carefully formulating his thoughts, Wade unfolded his plan, and Maman-ti nodded in compliance. Once the Owl Prophet regained control of his temper, he realized that what Wade prophesied could come true. A massacre of such great proportion would provoke the white leaders in Washington. Maman-ti had no love for the white man, but he was not a fool. He did not wish to face more cavalry troops. There were already thousands of them stationed on the outposts of civilization. The Indians would be doomed if they confronted a full-scale war with the whites.

Maman-ti promised to do Wade's bidding and then ordered his warriors to round up the horses and cattle they planned to take north to their village on Medicine Creek. Chad watched the Comanches disappear into the darkness, shaking his head in disbelief. It amazed him that Wade could keep his head when those around him were flouncing about like decapitated chickens. Chad would have been perfectly satisfied to go galloping off in pursuit of Haden Reems, thoughtless of the consequences, bent on pure revenge, but Wade was calm and calculating, considering his actions and the possible effects they might have on the future.

There were times when Chad cursed his brother's careful forethought, but this wasn't one of them. Although Chad hungered for his revenge on Haden Reems, he realized that sending the Owl Prophet to slay a herd of trail hands would cause even more trouble.

As Wade strode toward the mounts Maman-ti had left for them, Chad stared at his brother's departing back. "Wade?" When his brother turned to lift a quizzical brow, Chad smiled at him. "I know you told me not to go mushy with sentimentality, but I do admire you. I always have."

A puzzled frown puckered Wade's brow. "What brought that on?"

Chad strolled past his brother to swing onto the Indian pony. "I would have gone off, half-cocked, just like Maman-ti," he confessed. "And I would have later regretted my rashness. I admire your ability to think matters through before you set destiny in motion."

Wade pulled himself onto the steed and tossed his brother a quiet smile. Chad *had* changed, Wade realized. They had always been competitive, and rarely had Chad spared him a compliment. In a round about way, Shianne had brought them closer than they had ever been, as well as giving Chad a new lease on life. Shianne. . . . Her name echoed through his mind and penetrated his soul. God, he hadn't realized how painful their separation would be. Not one thought crossed his mind without her name pinned to it. Was she alive or dead? Had Haden violated her in his demented attempt for revenge?

A shiver as cold as the icy waters of the spring ran through him. Chad had praised him for contemplating his actions before putting them in motion. Nevertheless, Wade itched to confront Haden so he could tear him apart with his bare hands. If Chad could read the vengeful thoughts that were buzzing in his brother's head, he wouldn't be dishing out compliments. Wade was envisioning a violent, torturous death for Haden Reems. He swore the day would come when both he and Chad could enjoy the satisfaction of watching Haden perish by his own grizzly methods.

"Let's go back to camp," Wade said quietly. Touching his heels to the steed's ribs, Wade cantered away, leaving Chad to stare thoughtfully after him.

When they returned to the shattered remains of their campsite, Wade reined his mount to a halt. His jaw swung from its hinges when the moonlight splattered across the fallen rocks to reveal that someone had been digging away the rubble blocking the mouth of the cave. A lone steed was tethered in the brush, and a single figure was crouched by the campfire.

The intruder heard the approaching horses and wearily came to his feet. His face registered surprise and then a relieved smile. "*Hombre,* you are alive!"

Wade slid to the ground, confused by Juan Mendez's appearance in camp. His gaze narrowed on the bandage that was wrapped around Juan's gun hand and the dark bruises on his face.

"What happened to you? What are you doing here?" His rapidly fired questions erased Juan's smile and turned his expression to granite.

"Those of us who have suffered from Haden Reems's wrath should unite," he muttered as he stared at his broken hand. Juan unbuttoned his shirt with his left hand to reveal the bandages that curled around his belly. "I tried to prevent Reems from harming your woman. He kept her locked in the hacienda until he was ready to begin the cattle drive. When I intervened, he used her as his protection from my pistol." A bitter laugh erupted from Juan's swollen lips. "After he finished breaking my hand and carving on me with his dagger, he kicked me in the face with his boot and took the señora with him on the drive."

"What did Reems do to her?" Wade gritted out the question.

Juan's eyes lifted to meet Wade's unblinking gaze. "He beat her when she defied him, but my intrusion prevented him from having his way with her . . . at least for a time." Juan glanced toward the pile of rocks and dirt that obstructed the mouth of the cave. "When I regained consciousness and tended my wounds, I came to the K Bar to enlist the aid of your vaqueros. We were trying to dig you and your brother out of this death trap. Reems also left one of his own men in this hell hole. . . ." His voice trailed off as he swung his attention to Wade. "How did you escape? Is there another way out of the cavern?"

"My brother and I swam through the tunnel formed by the underground spring," Wade explained. "But we very nearly died trying. Unless we can clear the opening of the cave, we can never rescue your friend."

"The vaqueros will return at daylight to continue digging," Juan murmured. "I sent them back to the ranch to eat and rest." He paused, his eyes downcast. "I regret I did not take your offer earlier, *hombre*. The money Reems was paying me does not matter so much anymore. I despise myself for working for that bastard. He grows more evil with each passing day."

"Do you know what Reems has done with the treasure?" Chad questioned.

Juan shrugged evasively. "It must be somewhere in the hacienda. I have not seen the trunk since Reems toted it back to the ranch."

"Damn," Wade scowled. "Unless we find it, we have

no means to purchase supplies for the trip north. Everything we had gathered for the drive lies at the bottom of the cavern, and it will take weeks to dig through this wall of rock."

"The money I have saved is yours," Juan offered. "As well as my assistance . . . if you have use for a man with a late-blooming conscience and a broken gun hand," he added bitterly.

Wade laid his hand on Juan's shoulder. "You have paid retribution, *amigo*. I appreciate your attempt to aid Shianne. Perhaps together we can put an end to Haden Reems's brand of evil."

"When I get my hands on that bastard, I intend to repay him for his dastardly crimes, even the ones you and your brother know nothing about," Juan hissed venomously.

"You will have to take your place in line," Wade snorted as he took up the reins to his mount. "Chad and I are still debating which one of us is to be the first."

"We could chop him into three equal pieces," Juan suggested with a disdainful grunt. "Then none of us would have to wait our turn."

"Four," Wade amended, his tone so frosty that it dripped with icicles. "If I know my wife, she will protest if she is not allowed her fair share of Haden's hide."

The remark brought grim silence, each man venturing a guess as to how Shianne was faring in captivity. Wade could not wait to search the hacienda to retrieve the stolen treasure. He was anxious to gather the vaqueros and journey north; but there was much to be done, and every moment they lingered could mean more hideous torture for Shianne.

Wade's heart twisted in his chest. The thought of losing Shianne forever evoked a sensation like nothing Wade had ever experienced. She had often accused him of using her to get what he wanted. Maybe he had used her in the beginning, but each minute he had spent with her had become a savored memory. The thought of her kept driving him, even when he was certain he was fighting a hopeless battle for survival. The image of her bewitching face tormented him each time he closed his eyes and prayed for sleep to overtake him. She was far more than an obligation or a means to an end, Wade admitted to himself. Shianne had become his reason for living, and without her, the days seemed as dark as the nights. . . .

Shianne stared up at the starlit sky and breathed a dismal sigh. They had been on the trail for more days than she cared to count. Twice she had attempted escape, but with no success. Now Haden watched her like a hawk eyeing its prey. He kept her beside him while they moved the cattle across the Colorado River near Montopolis. The large, strungout herd had grazed slowly northward. Haden kept a constant surveillance behind them, assuring that some unforgivable miracle had not spared the Burdett brothers and allowed them to give chase.

Shianne had watched the huge herd of longhorns trample the prairie, putting more distance between her and her home. They had passed by the rolling range land and fields of cotton that lay to the east. To the west, beyond the Balcones Escarpment, were the hills of Edwards Plateau. The countryside had been green with oak, mesquite and cedar until the darkness had settled, leaving the world in gloomy shadows that sent Shianne's spirits plunging.

Shianne expelled another heavy-hearted sigh. Life no longer seemed as precious as she remembered it. She felt empty and dead inside. When Wade had been stripped from her arms, the sunshine had evaporated.

Shianne had not realized how she had lived for Wade's laughter until she was deprived of it. Now she was faced with Haden's leers and hateful sneers.

Certain she could not endure one more minute of Haden's looming presence, Shianne had attempted her first break for freedom when they forded the muddy red Brazos River. It had proved a difficult crossing, and Shianne had taken advantage of Haden's preoccupation with herding the cattle across the swift, flowing channel. When the cattle balked and began to scatter, Shianne gouged her heels into her steed's flanks and darted back in the direction from which she had come.

Haden had caught up with her, growling and snarling at her like Satan himself. Because of her daring attempt, Haden had struck her with his bull whip, laying open the skin on her back. It had taken several days before Shianne could move without wincing in pain.

When she had recovered from her tender wound, she began to make plans for another escape. Since Haden had made a rather hasty exit from Bexar County, he found it necessary to stock up on supplies for the journey north. The frontier town of Fort Worth had been Haden's destination. There, he purchased six-shooters, staple groceries and other needed supplies. Some of the items he bought were for Shianne—garments that would camouflage her shapeliness from the other drovers who were also moving their herds toward the Kansas market.

Upon his return from Fort Worth, Haden demanded that Shianne garb herself in the clothes he had bought for her. Shianne had insisted on privacy while she donned the baggy clothes, swearing she would make no attempt to flee. Reluctantly, Haden had consented, but he refused to do more than turn his back for two minutes. Shianne had snatched up the clothes and darted through the brush on foot, determined to find a safe hiding place until Haden lost his patience and continued his drive northward.

Unfortunately, Haden had summoned every man he could spare to search out the runaway. If Shianne would have had the time, she would have dug a hole and crawled into it. But she was not granted her wish. One of Haden's men spotted her as she nestled between the rocks and underbrush.

It was then that Shianne learned hell had no fury like Haden Reems when he completely lost his temper. After enduring several punishing blows, her unconscious body was tossed over the back of a horse and tied in place. She had ridden like a feed sack for more than two days, and the fight had very nearly gone out of her.

Shianne had begun to realize she faced a losing battle. Each night, Haden bedded down beside her, forcing her to sleep beside him. She was thankful he had not raped her . . . at least not yet. Fearing she would escape him again, Haden positioned himself and his captive in the middle of camp, certain she could not step over two dozen men without waking at least one of them.

Since her futile escape attempts, Shianne had kept to herself, deciding it best not to infuriate Haden. Her body ached from the rough abuse he had inflicted on her. The long hours they spent swallowing the dust of four thousand head of cattle left her with not one breath of hope. With disinterest, Shianne had watched the herd graze the open prairies and ford the streams they encountered along the way.

Another feeling of hopelessness had engulfed her when they journeyed into the valley of the Red River. The rising water and quicksand made the crossing perilous, but Shianne experienced no fear as she swam her mount through the swift channel. Haden was putting impossible distances between her and the familiar countryside where she had been born and raised. Fording the Red River was yet another bitter reminder that she had left the life she loved far behind.

Although she was surrounded by rolling prairies, skirted with blackjack oak, willows and cottonwood trees, Shianne found no satisfaction in drinking in the scenery. She was still mourning her loss, wondering what had been running through Wade's mind while he was trapped in the bowels of the earth, wondering if he were even alive.

God, she had been such a fool not to make the most of every moment she had spent with Wade. If she had it to do over again she would not have wasted a second of their time together. Their squabbles seemed so senseless now.

Shianne laughed bitterly, remembering how she had proudly declared it had to be all or nothing to satisfy her vanity. Well, now she had nothing, and she would have settled for even one scrap of Wade's affection, no matter how insincere it might have been.

Oh, why was she rehashing the past? It only depressed her. Now there was only cattle, rolling hills and Haden. That was even more depressing, Shianne thought wearily.

The rumble of thunder echoed about them, making the longhorns fidget uneasily. The sound of Haden grumbling beside her reminded Shianne that her captor was still holding the reins to her steed. These days Haden made doubly sure she could not escape. She was bound to the saddle, hand and foot, and her horse was tied to Haden's steed. They had become like Siamese twins these past weeks, and Shianne would have given most anything if she could sever the tie that bound her to Haden. She had but to glance in his direction and hatred poisoned her blood. To think she had not thought him to be such a bad sort, she scoffed. All these years he had pretended to be the gentleman in her presence, but there was a devil lurking beneath his expensive garments. Only now had he exposed himself for what he was, and Shianne despised him with every breath she took. Too late, she had realized Haden Reems was rotten to the core. The acquisition of power and vast wealth were his obsessions. He hungered to break men down to build himself up. He thrived on striking fear in the hearts of those who defied him.

A glaze of hatred covered Shianne's eyes as she stared straight ahead, seeing nothing. She shared that deeply embedded desire that had driven Wade and motivated Chad. Haden made her life hell, and there would be no greater satisfaction in life than to watch that miserable bastard die an agonizing death.

Shianne scolded herself for allowing her feelings for Haden to poison her, but she couldn't seem to help herself. Every time she looked into those small, dark eyes and watched that smug, triumphant smile swallow his homely features, she wanted to scratch and claw at him, to hiss curses in his face.

Someday, somehow, Haden would reap his just rewards, Shianne promised herself. God forgive her for being so vindictive, but she would not shed one tear when Haden Reems met his demise. He was vicious and evil, and she hated him with every part of her being. But it would be only small consolation to watch him die. Haden had killed the man she loved. Her heart cried out for retribution. If Haden made one mistake, if he gave her the slightest opportunity, Shianne swore she would snatch his knife and bury it in his chest.

Haden frowned at the expression that was etched in Shianne's tired features, and a chill ran down his spine.

Hatred was printed on her brow in bold letters. "Don't think I'll give you the chance to stab me in the back, bitch," he jeered at her.

"Every man makes an occasional oversight, Haden," she told him, her voice deadly calm. "Even you." A spiteful smile traced her lips as her gaze raked over him with contempt. "You may have killed my husband, but I will never allow you to forget your abominable sins. One day you are going to make a mistake while you are preoccupied with your duties. To someone else it might appear inconsequential, but for you it will be the error that will send you to your grave. . . ."

Haden scowled at her threat and raised his hand to strike her as he had so many times before, but Shianne didn't cower or whimper when his knuckles collided with her cheek. Even while the right side of her face stung with the force of his blow, Shianne stared him down.

"You may hide behind your army and tie me to a horse so that I cannot defend myself against you, but I would expect no more from a lily-livered coward." A mocking smile touched the corners of her mouth. "You are such a little man, Haden," she scoffed at him. "My hell on earth comes from being forced to tolerate your detestable companionship. In a way, I suppose I am the fortunate one. *Your* private hell is living with the kind of man you are. Thank God I do not have to live with that. I can think of nothing worse!"

Haden snarled at her belittling remarks. Just once he would like to see this feisty hellion cower from him and reduce herself to tears when threatened with violence. When he had the chance, he was going to humiliate her by forcing her to become his whore. Then she would lose that damnable self-respect of hers. Haden vowed when he finally got this firebrand alone, he would not be gentle with her. He would use her body for his pleasure, and she would rue the day she defied him. He would prove to her once and for all that he was the master of her soul. She may hate him, but he would still take what he wanted from her.

Giving Shianne's mare a rough yank, Haden led her away. "We'll just see who emerges the victor, little bitch," he hurled over his shoulder.

Shianne's taunting laughter nipped at his heels. "Indeed we will," she spat at him. "But do not expect me to stake a marker upon your final resting place. For when you have come and gone, there will not be one soul to grieve your passing."

"Shut up!" Haden hissed furiously.

Although Shianne fell silent, it was by her choice, not because of his hateful command. She had said everything she intended to say to that despicable excuse for a man. She may have not made any progress with Haden, but she felt ever so much better for voicing her thoughts. His torment would come from spending the rest of his days looking over his shoulder, wondering when and how Shianne would repay him for his maliciousness.

Chapter 18

A cold, drizzling rain settled about Shianne's shoulders, sending a chill rippling across her skin. Since her hands were tied to the pommel of the saddle, she could not pull the collar of her shirt against her neck. Her eyes shifted to the rapid flowing channel of Beaver Creek, fifteen miles north of the Texas border. As Haden shouted orders to ford the stream, Shianne peered at the high banks that waited on the other side. Just beyond, silhouetted in the fog was a flat-topped mesa, strewn with slabs and huge boulders of sandstone.

A gasp of surprise burst from Shianne's lips when a tribe of Indians appeared atop Monument Hill. Her heart leaped when she spied Maman-ti riding at the front of the band of warriors. Although he could not recognize her in her baggy garb, Shianne felt a sense of well-being just knowing the Owl Prophet had returned to Indian Territory.

When Haden spied the awesome warriors perched above them, he growled under his breath. Thus far, he had been fortunate, but it seemed his luck had run out. After swimming the herd across the creek, Haden turned the reins to Shianne's mount over to Pedro and approached the waiting band of Indians.

Maman-ti's eyes were fastened on Haden's harsh features. With great difficulty, he resisted the urge to lift the white man's scalp then and there. He had made a promise to Wade Burdett, and he was obliged to keep it. Drawing himself up in the saddle, Maman-ti gestured an arm toward the herd that grazed before him. His keen gaze circled the riders, wondering what had become of Shianne. Since he saw no trace of her, he assumed Haden had left her in Texas.

"You have many head of cattle," Maman-ti observed. "In Indian Territory you must pay a tax for driving and grazing your herd on our land."

"How much do you want?" Haden questioned impatiently. He was anxious to be on his way, and he did not intend to sit there all day, haggling over the tax.

Maman-ti frowned thoughtfully as he resituated himself on his pony, one that appeared oddly familiar to Haden. If he were not in such a touchy situation, Haden would have accused the renegade Indian of stealing that particular horse from the remuda, as well as a good number of his cattle.

"I think one dollar and seventy-five cents a head will be enough," Maman-ti said with a thoughtful nod.

Haden very nearly shot out of his saddle. "A dollar and . . ." he croaked in disbelief. He had expected to pay perhaps forty to fifty cents a head. This was robbery! My God, these renegades had already raided his ranch, Haden thought furiously. He was not about to pay them such an outlandish tax. "I will give you forty cents a head and not a penny more."

A challenging smile slid across Maman-ti's lips. "These are heavy beeves, white man, and their numbers are many. They will each eat much grass and frighten off game. We will take only the price I want, no less."

Haden glared holes in the Indian's gloating grin. He

had little use for the red man. They were nothing but marauders and thieves who swarmed into Texas and then scampered back into Indian Territory where they were not subject to law and order. It got his goat to be forced to pay such outrageous prices to this herd of savages.

"Fifty cents," Haden bartered.

Maman-ti's smile broadened, his eyes glittering with deviltry. "One dollar and seventy-five cents," he insisted, delighting in watching the vicious white man squirm in his clothes. "If you do not pay the tax the Comanches and Kiowas levy on your herd, we will take them all." His gaze swung over his shoulder to draw Haden's attention to the number of warriors who rode behind him and then focused his attention on the trail herders. "Your men cannot match the skills of my braves. Make your choice. We will collect the tax or take the herd."

Damn, Haden muttered under his breath. How could he make a profit if he was stopped every other day by some renegade tribe who expected payment for crossing their lands? Finally, Haden heaved a defeated sigh and nodded begrudgingly.

"Very well, we will pay. Pick out the beeves you want to compensate the amount of the tax," he instructed.

Maman-ti gave his dark head a negative shake. "We do not need the beef. Our tribe has its own herd."

Haden didn't doubt that for a moment. These renegades had already raided ranches in Texas, and Haden would have bet his left arm that half the steers in the Comanche nation carried the Lazy R brand. "Then what is it you want in payment?" he questioned, his tone carrying an unpleasant edge.

"We wish to be paid in cash," Maman-ti insisted. "The money will purchase many supplies from the army posts."

"Cash?" Haden hooted in disgust.

He hurriedly calculated the fee and cursed under his breath. It would put a serious dent in his funds if he paid the Indian in cash! But he had no choice unless he wished to have his cattle stampeded and sacrificed to these red-skinned highwaymen. Grumbling, Haden unstrapped his money belt. When he counted out enough cash to satisfy the thieving tax collector, he stretched out an arm to offer the sum to Maman-ti's extended hand.

As Haden reined his steed away, the Owl Prophet's mocking voice settled about him. "It is only the first of many taxes, white man. The Chickasaw nation will also demand payment when you reach the border of their land."

Haden's back went rigid. He had the uneasy feeling this conniving Comanche would ride ahead of them, alerting his red-skinned cousins to the approach of a cattle herd. No doubt word would spread like wildfire, and Haden would be penniless by the time he reached the Kansas border.

The smug grin that crept to Shianne's bruised features had Haden scowling again. Angrily, he jerked the reins from Pedro's hand and glowered at Shianne. "You delight in watching my money supply dwindle to nothing, don't you?"

Shianne raised her head so Haden could see the vindictive sparkle in her eyes. "You have stolen from every man who crossed the boundaries of your ranch, Haden. It does my heart good to know there is some justice in the world. You have dressed your own bravoes like Indians to raid other ranches. It is small consolation that the Comanches receive what they have been wrongly accused of stealing these past few years."

Haden raised his hand to slap the insolent smirk off

her face, but he caught himself the split-second before he delivered the painful blow. If Shianne cried out, the departing Indians might detect the female voice and come to investigate. Haden couldn't risk losing Shianne. He needed her to barter with Blake Kimball. Cursing the entire predicament, Haden let his arm drop to his side and then called to his men to move the herd north.

As the cattle lifted their heads from the sea of plush grass beneath their hooves and began the next leg of their long journey, Maman-ti watched the procession with narrowed eyes. He had seen Haden Reems lift his hand to strike the young boy who was tied to his saddle. A curious frown knitted the Owl Prophet's brow. He wondered what the boy had said to provoke Haden's anger.

When the trail herders filed past him, Maman-ti's body went rigid with fury. The lad lifted his head as he rode past the congregation of Indians. Two dark, expressive eyes focused on Maman-ti. He stared at the hideous bruises that marred Shianne's cheeks and cursed the white man that had put them there.

How he itched to clench his fingers in Haden's hair and remove it with the aid of his knife, but he had given his word to Burdett and knew he must bide his time. The malicious white man would pay with his life, Maman-ti promised himself. Haden had dared to lay a hand on the cousin of Black Kettle, great chief of the Cheyennes. He had dared to beat a woman, the woman Maman-ti cherished.

Summoning his self-control, the Owl Prophet sat like a stone statue until the herd disappeared over the rolling hill. Then he wheeled his steed around to thunder off to alert the Chickasaw chief of the coming herd. He would trail Haden Reems day and night, Maman-ti vowed to himself. Although he could not massacre the trail hands and their vicious leader, he could keep a watchful eye on Shianne until Wade and his caravan reached Indian Territory.

Disappointment etched Shianne's brow. She could see the strained expression on the Owl Prophet's lips when he recognized her that morning. Although she knew Maman-ti's hands were tied, she had prayed he would do something, *anything* to free her from bondage.

Her shoulders slumped, and she stared at the leather straps that were tied around her wrists leaving her skin raw. Someday, somehow she would repay Haden for his abuse, she vowed to herself. He could not keep her bound to him forever.

When the sky opened to pour buckets of rain about her, Shianne felt her spirits drowning. Haden had offered her no protection from the inclement weather, and her clothes were dripping wet. Try as she may, she could not stop shivering. Shianne wasn't certain if it was the chill that affected her or simply the depressing sense of hopelessness.

Listlessly, Shianne rode along as the cattle trailed over the open prairie. Through the foggy mist she followed the herd across Rush Creek and wound through the jack oaks to reach the Washita River that was lined with willows and slick, red clay banks. By the time they bedded down for the night, Shianne couldn't stop shaking. Her entire body ached, and she longed to curl up on something soft and warm. Even the feel of Haden's bony body was comforting, she thought with a dreary sigh. He was good for little else except a wind block and a blanket.

Just as Shianne was about to drift off to sleep, she heard the cry of a distant owl. It was screeching a vindictive song, and Shianne smiled to herself. At least she knew Maman-ti was not far away. Perhaps he couldn't steal her away from her captive, but he was there, watching from the distance, ensuring that she would come to no more harm.

"What the hell is that?" Haden grumbled when the noises shattered the silence for a second time.

"I would guess it is the Indians," Shianne insisted as she curled into a tighter ball. "No doubt they are watching you and your herd, Haden. Perhaps they have decided to take the cattle after all."

The remark brought Haden to his feet. Squinting, he studied his surroundings, wondering if the renegades were thinking of sneaking in to startle the herd. Since he was not about to risk losing the cattle, Haden kicked several of his men awake, demanding that they post extra sentinels on the herd. Wearily, the men dragged themselves from the bedrolls and saddled their horses.

The events of that night were to begin a ritual that had Haden scowling longer and louder with each passing day. In the distance, the Indians kept constant surveillance over his herd and disturbed Haden's sleep with their mimicking cries of owls and coyotes. After four days and nights of living on little sleep and pushing the herd to its limits, the men were exhausted and grumbling.

Haden very nearly had a riot on his hands, not to mention his frustration of living with an Indian escort. The men were grumbling that they were not receiving enough pay for the amount of extra hours they were forced to spend guarding the herd. Even a share of the profit from Wade Burdett's cattle was not enough to satisfy them. Haden found himself promising higher wages, only to pacify the grumbling desperados.

To add insult to injury the Comanches crept into camp to steal the remuda of horses from the trail herders. After leaving the men afoot during the morning hours, Maman-ti and his band of warriors appeared, offering to *sell* Haden his own horses. Not once but twice the Owl Prophet rode into camp, wearing a challenging smile. Maman-ti was offering the vicious white man the chance to go for his throat with his knife, but Haden refused to be baited into a skirmish he knew he couldn't win. Muttering in disgust, he continued to buy back his own horses and then cursed the renegade Indian each time he trotted out of camp.

While Haden was stomping about in exasperation, Shianne was spitefully gloating over his misery. Earlier that morning Haden had been approached by couriers from the Chickasaw nation. The Indians had demanded another outlandish price for crossing their land, and Haden had been forced to pay it or risk losing his herd to yet another band of thieving Indians.

"It seems to me you would have been money ahead if you would have remained at your ranch," Shianne taunted, even though her throat was raw, and she felt as if she were frying with fever. "You could have massacred a flock of homesteaders and stolen their valuables. It would have proven more profitable than handing over all your cash in Indian taxes and fees for gathering your *runaway* remuda of horses."

Finally, Haden could endure no more. Her last taunting remark snapped his temper. Haden reached across the distance that separated them to backhand Shianne. The blow sent her senses reeling. She was already ill from exposure to the chilly weather, and it took little to make her collapse. When she wilted against the horse she was tied to, Haden scowled irritably.

This little bitch had become more trouble than she was worth. He had yet to find the opportunity to pleasure himself with her body, and he had been incensed by her barbed tongue. If he didn't need her for his purpose, he would have given her to the savages and let them take their turn molesting her. . . .

Haden's thoughts scattered when he glanced from Shianne's slumped body to the congregation of men who appeared on the hill ahead of them. His shocked gaze focused on the three men—Wade, Chad and Juan—who stood apart from the human fence of vaqueros blocking the path. Wade sat atop his blood-bay stallion. In one hand he held a rifle, and in the other clenched fist lay the reins to the riderless black stallion that belonged to Shianne.

How the devil had Wade Burdett and his brother escaped from their underground tomb? What was Juan Mendez doing with them? To further complicate his frustrations, Haden caught sight of the flank of Indians approaching from either side of timber that skirted the prairie. Panic gripped him. It was obvious that Wade had come to retrieve his wife and that Haden was about to lose his herd and his life.

Wade felt his body tense with outrage when he saw Haden level the rider beside him. Maman-ti had already informed him that Reems kept Shianne dressed as a boy and tied to her mount, never allowing her out of his sight. After Haden struck Shianne, knocking her senseless, Wade gouged his steed and charged straight ahead. Although he had pushed himself and his men to the limits to catch up with Haden, he was itching for a fight. Watching Haden abuse Shianne was the last straw. There was vengeance glowing in Wade's eyes, a vengeance that smothered logic.

When Haden realized Wade's intentions, he clutched

the pistol that dangled at his side. Frantically, he ordered his men to stampede the herd over the top of the human blockade. Gunfire rang through the air, startling the cattle, sending them charging forward in a dead run.

Scowling, Wade circled the thundering herd, trying to turn them back on Haden and his band of desperados. When Maman-ti gave the signal for his warriors to block the herd from the east side, Haden grew even more frantic. The cattle were confused. They circled and then began to scatter. When the horn of a nearby steer gouged him in the leg, Haden was gored by cowardice. The horse stumbled, very nearly throwing Haden into the path of the panicked herd. Riders and steers were coming at him from all directions. Haden glanced wildly about him, searching for a means of escape. Grasping the reins to Shianne's steed, Haden nudged his horse toward the thicket of trees that lined the nearby creek.

The world had suddenly become mass chaos, and Haden wanted no part of it. He saw two of his bravoes fall into the stampeding herd and two more topple from their saddles amidst the arrows and gunfire. Haden pressed his body against his steed, making it difficult for Wade and his men to spot him within the milling cattle. Slapping his laboring steed on the rump, Haden continued toward the underbrush with Shianne's unconscious body in tow.

When Wade finally spotted the fleeing coward, he cursed under his breath. He was trapped by a wave of oncoming cattle. His apprehensive gaze flew to Maman-ti who was on the far side of the herd. The Indian had yet to spot Haden, and he was too far away to give chase. Wade twisted around in the saddle to locate Chad and Juan. They were suffering from the same difficulties that hampered Wade. The milling herd pinned them back, threatening to trample or gore anyone who dared to attempt to cut his way through the frightened mass of longhorns.

Wade gritted his teeth and raised his revolver to fire over the longhorns. He would risk life and limb if he must, but he was not allowing Haden to steal off with Shianne, not again! She had suffered enough at Haden's hands. Wade's persistence paid off. The herd split, one group circling north and the other south. Although Wade felt the scrape of a twisted horn against his thigh, he did not bother to inspect the wound. His eyes were on the clump of trees where Haden had disappeared. Nudging his steed with his good leg, Wade thundered across the range to follow in Haden's wake. Galahad objected to riding blindly through the brush, but Wade forced the stallion onward.

When Wade appeared in the clearing along the creek bank, Haden swore under his breath. Frantically, he yanked on the reins to encourage Shianne's mount to a swifter gait, but the mare was limping badly and refused to quicken her pace. Haden stared at the high banks of the arroyo that was thick with underbrush. If he could climb the steep incline, he could gallop away, putting more distance between him and Burdett.

Glancing over his shoulder, he saw Wade galloping his stallion through midstream. Shimmering green eyes were boring into Haden. Spurred to action, Haden slapped his steed, forcing him to clamber up the steep slope. A disgusted scowl erupted from his lips when Shianne's mare balked. In frustration, Haden tugged on the mare's rope, demanding that she make the climb or have her head twisted off her neck.

Reluctantly, the wild-eyed mare lunged into the side of the hill, but her tender leg folded beneath her. With a frightened whinny the mare scrambled to maintain her footing on the rocks. Her front legs pawed at the air as she reeled sideways.

Haden was forced to relinquish his grasp on the reins when the mare tumbled back down the side of the rocky creek bank. There was no time to urge the fallen mare back to her feet. Wade was thundering after him like Satan racing up from the fires of hell.

Snarling over his misfortune and the lack of bullets in his revolver, Haden urged his steed up the incline. When the steed set foot on solid ground, Haden gouged him again, sending him racing across the prairie.

Wade leaped from Galahad's back the moment he reached the fallen mare. Panic blazed through him when he sank down beside Shianne's unconscious body. Her leg was pinned beneath the horse, and her body was contorted in a broken heap. Wade's heart flip-flopped in his chest as he laid his head to her breast. She lay so still, so lifeless, that he began to wonder if she was still alive. Her faint pulse gave him hope, but not enough to smooth the worried frown from his taut features.

Grabbing the reins, Wade softly encouraged the mare to gather her feet beneath her. The mare, unfortunately, had other ideas as to where she should be after suffering a broken leg. Standing seemed to be out of the question.

Muttering at his futile attempt to rouse the injured mare, Wade snatched the knife from his belt to free Shianne's hands. Reaching over the sprawled mare Wade cut away one leather strap that held Shianne's left ankle to the stirrup. Since he could not crawl beneath the mare to free Shianne's right leg, Wade unfastened the girth and attempted to drag both the saddle and Shianne away from the fallen steed. The task was impossible. Shianne was still unconscious and the mare held the right side of the saddle against the creek bank.

In frustration, Wade scooted himself down beside Shianne and braced his boot heels against the mare's shoulder. With a forceful shove he coaxed the mare into an upright position, but still he could not free Shianne's foot from the stirrup.

The sound of another rider splashing through the creek caused Wade to jerk his head up. He expelled a sigh of relief when Maman-ti rode up beside him. "Help me with this confounded mare," he requested. "She refuses to stand on her broken leg, and I can't free Shianne."

Maman-ti bounded from his mount and took up the reins. While the Indian tugged, Wade pushed with both feet. Snorting, the mare wobbled onto three legs and curled the broken one beneath her. Once Wade had cut away the leather strap that held Shianne to the stirrup, he hoisted her limp body into his arms.

A black scowl covered his features when he stared into her expressionless face. What had once been flawless beauty was marred by red welts and bruised cheeks. Lovingly, Wade bent his head to skim his lips over her forehead and then jerked back as if he had been scorched.

"My God, she is burning up with fever!"

Maman-ti laid his palm to her forehead. His eyes widened in concern when he felt the heat radiating from her body. Instinctively, he curled his arms beneath her. "Give her to me, Wade Burdett," he ordered sharply.

Wade pulled back, fiercely clinging to his limp bundle. "She is my wife," he reminded the Owl Prophet. "I will take care of her."

"You have done a poor job of it since you thrust your ring on her finger," Maman-ti snorted disdainfully.

"You need not remind me I am the cause of all her misfortune," Wade grunted as he stalked toward his horse.

"Will you keep her from me, only to spare your pride?" Maman-ti growled sarcastically. "If you do not allow me to work my medicine she will die."

Wade broke stride. He had practically ridden his stallion into the ground to find Shianne. He had watched Haden beat her, and he had lived with the tormenting dread that the malicious bastard had taken Shianne for his own pleasure. The thought of handing Shianne over to the Owl Prophet after all Wade had been through to retrieve her was exasperating. Yet, Wade desperately wanted her to live.

His somber gaze dropped to Shianne's puffy lips. His heart twisted in his chest. She seemed so vulnerable, so helpless. Wade had always been quick to react to disaster, but suddenly he found himself immobile. He cared deeply for this feisty sprite who had been stripped of her pride and subjected to Haden's cruel abuse. To see her lying so still in his arms was nearly his undoing.

Noting the tormented frustration that claimed Wade's features, Maman-ti moved silently toward him. When the Owl Prophet slid his arms beneath Shianne, his dark eyes locked with Wade's. For a long moment they stood there, staring grimly at each other, neither refusing to relinquish his grasp on Shianne's fevered body.

"I have loved her longer," Maman-ti murmured. The faintest hint of a smile found the corner of his mouth. "She is your woman now, but if we do not break the fever you will live on nothing but her memories. . . ."

It took every ounce of willpower for Wade to let go. When Maman-ti shifted her weight against his chest, Wade's shoulders slumped. In utter amazement he watched the Owl Prophet spin on his heels and walk into the creek, singing a doleful chant to the great spirits.

"Are you mad?" Wade shrieked incredulously. "She will catch her death in the cold water." Dammit, the Indian was trying to kill Shianne instead of bring her back to life!

"We must stop the fever," Maman-ti insisted. Gently, he laid Shianne in the water, cradling her in his arms. Again he began to chant to the gods, pleading for their mercy. When Maman-ti was satisfied with the first phase of his healing ceremony, he scooped Shianne against his chest and emerged from the creek. "Bring my saddle blanket."

Mechanically, Wade hurried over to make a pallet on the ground. A skeptical frown plowed his brow when Maman-ti reached into the pouch that hung around his neck. Hell's Bells, Wade thought sourly. Shianne needed emergency medical attention, not some superstitious ceremony performed over her. While Maman-ti was sprinkling his magic potion around her, Wade peeled off his jacket and laid it over Shianne. Glancing quickly about him, Wade located some fallen limbs to start a campfire. He was not about to allow Shianne to lie on the cold, damp ground. She was already chilled to the bone after being baptized, Indian fashion.

When Maman-ti completed his ritual he unfolded himself from his crouched position and climbed up the steep bank to fetch wild quinine and jewel weed. Wade muttered under his breath while the Indian selected his assortment of weeds. Dammit, Shianne needed Doc Winston not this superstitious medicine man. The Indians might have put great stock in the Owl Prophet's magic, but Wade didn't. It all seemed a waste of precious time to him.

Impatiently, Wade waited for Maman-ti to gather herbs and concoct his potion. When the shaman lifted

Shianne's head to pour the poison down her throat, Wade rolled his eyes in disgust. Why was he allowing this, he asked himself. He should have scooped Shianne off the ground and headed straight for . . . Where? he asked himself. There was not a doctor in a hundred miles. They were in Indian Territory and physicians were scarce.

As Maman-ti danced about his unconscious patient, Wade paced back and forth along the edge of the creek. Finally, Wade had enough. He was going to fetch a wagon to make a proper bed in it. There was naught else for him to do but send Chad and Juan with the herd . . . if and when they managed to round them up. He would remain behind with Shianne, praying she would recover.

A startled expression passed Maman-ti's bronzed features. His eyes followed Wade as he sprung to his steed. "You are leaving your woman before you know if she will live or die?"

Wade stared down at the medicine man and then swung his attention to Shianne's ashen face. "I'll be back as quick as I can," he murmured absently. "I want to put her in the wagon bed. The thought of Shianne lying in those damp clothes on the wet ground is enough to give *me* the grippe! You have had your chance to revive her. Now it's my turn."

With that, Wade urged Galahad in the direction from which he had come. To his relief, Haden's bravoes had abandoned the herd and scattered in all directions, leaving Wade's men and the Comanches to gather the cattle and confiscate the supplies.

A stricken look settled on Chad's face when his brother returned alone. "What happened to Shianne?" he questioned in concern. "And where the hell is Haden?"

"Haden showed his true colors by turning tail and

381

running. Maman-ti is performing his healing powers on Shianne," Wade explained resentfully. "Shianne is too sick to move. You will have to take the herd north while I remain behind with her. I am not leaving her with that Indian. It is no wonder entire tribes were wiped out by disease. These superstitious Comanches feed their patients weeds and roots, none of which are worth a damn as medication."

A wry smile flitted across Chad's lips as he surveyed the scowl that was plastered on Wade's face. "You are being a mite hard on the great medicine man, big brother. Shianne believes the Owl Prophet to possess supernatural powers."

Wade was in no mood to be taunted. Fretting over Shianne had shaved ten years off his life expectancy. "Take the herd and follow the markers," Wade ordered gruffly.

After Wade had gathered the necessary food staples and blankets to tend his patient, he climbed onto the wagon seat and aimed himself toward the creek. Damn, he wanted to pursue the bastard who had left Shianne for dead, and he longed to push the cattle herd to Abilene; but most of all, he wanted to cradle Shianne in his arms and ensure she was still alive after Maman-ti fed her poison.

To his dismay, Shianne had yet to rouse from motionless sleep. After a heated argument with Maman-ti, Wade carried Shianne up the creek bank and eased her into the back of the wagon.

Angrily, Maman-ti stared at his sleeping patient and then glared at Wade. "You are taking a great risk, Wade Burdett," he warned.

"I am assuming full responsibility for her welfare," Wade growled back. "If Indian medicine is good, then a mixture of white and Indian will be better."

"If she dies, you die with her," Maman-ti vowed

vindictively. "I will see to it that the Cheyenne and Arapaho take your cattle. Your brother will not reach the Kansas border."

"Why don't you go coddle your two wives and let me take care of mine?" Wade grumbled, undaunted by the threat. "You seem to forget that I have walked among the great spirits that dwell in the springs. My healing powers are as great as yours."

The reminder left Maman-ti with a sagging jaw. In his anger he had forgotten about Wade's experience near Speaking Springs. The gods had given the white man powers, and Maman-ti had sworn not to interfere. If he had not been so concerned about Shianne, he would have been able to reason more clearly, he assured himself.

Offering a peace treaty smile, Maman-ti extended his arm to clasp Wade's hand. "I will leave you with your woman for a time," he relented. "But you must watch over her for the both of us."

The frustration drained from Wade's strained features. Returning the smile, he offered his hand in friendship. "I owe you a great deal, Maman-ti. We may be in constant conflict because of Shianne, but I respect you. Without your help she may have perished. Haden would have forced her to remain in the saddle until she breathed her last breath."

Maman-ti's gaze strayed to the clump of cottonwoods that lined the creek. "His evil will not ride forever. My warriors will search him out, and when we find him, he will learn the Indian's method of torture."

"He is mine," Wade insisted, his stern green eyes clashing with Maman-ti's narrowed gaze.

A vengeful smile clung to Maman-ti's lips as he swung onto his pony. "You can have the evil white man," he consented and then added, ". . . *after* I finish with him."

Wade stared at the tall, muscular warrior until he disappeared in the distance. His gaze fell to Shianne, and he forgot every spiteful thought that was buzzing through his mind. God, she looked so pale and fragile lying there.

Tenderly, he traced his index finger over her swollen cheek. "Don't leave me, Shae," he whispered as he pressed his trembling lips to hers. "I have brought you a lifetime of misery in the course of a few months. I want to make it up to you. . . ."

Her unresponsive lips were warm against his, too warm. Wade hopped from the back of the wagon to fetch a bucket of water. When he returned, he dabbed a cold cloth across her fevered brow. Every few minutes he repeated the procedure, praying Shianne would rouse enough to sip a drink.

Wade sat beside her throughout the afternoon, regretting that he had involved Shianne in his feud against Haden Reems. God, if she died, Wade wasn't certain he could live with himself. He had taken this wild, feisty beauty and transformed her into a lifeless corpse. He was just as guilty of dealing her misery as Haden was, Wade lectured himself. If Shianne survived and refused to speak to him again, Wade wouldn't blame her. It was what he deserved after he had put her through hell.

As darkness overcame them, Wade curled up beside Shianne to share his warmth. It seemed an eternity since he held her in his arms. The sensation stirred a sea of memories, and Wade cursed himself again. What a beast he was. Shianne was hovering between life and death, and he longed to lose himself in the passion she evoked from him. He should be feeling nothing but compassion at the moment. But he had never experienced just *one* emotion at a time since he laid eyes on Shianne, he reminded himself.

A gentle smile hovered on Wade's lips as he closed his eyes and cuddled closer to Shianne. Being with this vixen was like riding on a carousel. She could cause all of his carefully guarded emotions to spin simultaneously, and before he knew it, he was feeling things he didn't want to feel, experiencing sensations that were foreign to him.

Was this love? Wade asked himself just before he drifted off to sleep. This didn't feel like the kind of emotion a man experienced when he was intrigued with a beautiful woman. Something had a hold on him, something he was at a loss to explain.

Why the hell was he fretting over this unnatural sensation when Shianne was tripping over the borderline between life and death, Wade chastised himself. He should be praying for all he was worth instead of contemplating his strange reaction to this mere wisp of a woman. Determined in that thought, Wade requested divine assistance—an armload of it. For that was what it would take to get Shianne back on her feet. Haden had done his damnedest to kill her, and Wade would never forgive that vicious viper for that!

Chapter 19

As the haze of unconsciousness fell away, Shianne opened her eyes. It seemed as if she had been asleep forever, and she could not remember where she had been the moment before the world turned black. Suddenly it struck her like a bolt of lightning. The scene flashed before her eyes, and she whimpered slightly. She could see Haden's hand coming at her, feel the blow that had knocked her unconscious.

A muddled frown puckered her brow. If he had struck her on the face, why did her entire body feel as if it had been squashed flat? Shianne tried to move, but her muscles refused to cooperate. It was then that she became aware of a presence beside her. Haden! Her tormented mind screamed. The figure squirmed in the darkness, and Shianne grimaced, knowing at any moment Haden's harsh, avenging features would loom over her.

To her amazement, it was Wade's face that hovered directly above hers. But that couldn't be. She was imagining things, Shianne told herself. Wade was dead, buried beneath tons of rock.

That explained it. She was dead too, Shianne told herself as she peered into those dark, craggy features.

They were both trapped in purgatory, waiting to learn which direction they would take to reach their final destination. Only now Shianne didn't care which way they were going. Wade was there beside her, and that was all that mattered. Where she found the strength to lift her arms, Shianne didn't know, but they flew around Wade's neck. She clung to him as if she meant to never let him go.

Wade braced himself above Shianne before she caused him to collapse on her frail body. That she didn't need, Wade reminded himself. Shianne had already been squashed by her horse.

His heart lurched when he heard her muffled sobs on his shoulder. "Shh . . . shh . . . Don't cry, love," he murmured compassionately. "It's all right now."

"How did I die, Wade?" Shianne questioned in ragged spurts. "Was it by Haden's hand or was I trampled in a stampede?"

Wade frowned bemusedly. Shianne was talking out of her head. The fever must have fried her brain! Crouching beside her, Wade pulled her arms from his shoulders and stared at the befuddled expression on her bruised features. It finally occurred to him that Shianne had no way of knowing what had happened. She had been unconscious for three days. She was oblivious to the fact that he and Chad had escaped from their tomb and confiscated the treasure Haden had stashed in his cellar. Nor was she aware that he had thundered across Texas to catch up with her. She had missed the stampede, the argument with Maman-ti, not to mention the nightmare he had endured, wondering if she would survive her injuries and illness.

"You are not dead and neither am I," he assured her with a soft laugh.

He was teasing her again. He had always teased her, Shianne mused. "I certainly feel dead," Shianne breathed weakly. "I can't move anything but my arms, and even that takes incredible effort."

The color drained from Wade's face. Had she been paralyzed during her fall with the horse? Would she ever walk again? God, what had he done to this feisty nymph? Crippled her for life? This was all his fault. He should never have interfered in her life. Until he came along she had been safe, free to come and go as she pleased without fear of Haden's wrath. She had been pure and innocent, an untamed spirit who thrived like a wild flower on the open prairies of Texas.

Wade sank back to stare at the thin form that was wrapped in blankets to preserve warmth. A smile of relief washed over his taut features when he diagnosed why Shianne could not move her legs. Carefully, he drew away the quilt to reveal the splints that ran from her thighs to her ankles. He wasn't sure if her right leg had been broken or merely strained and bruised during the fall. Both her legs were covered with scrapes and punctures, and Shianne had been in no condition to tell him where and how severely she was injured. Fearing the worst, Wade had bound both legs to ensure that they healed properly.

"Can you wiggle your toes, princess?" he questioned.

Shianne lifted her head to stare at the contraptions of bandages and tree branches that were strapped around her legs. Concentrating on the task, she moved her feet and then flinched when a searing pain shot up from her right ankle.

"It's still a mite tender, I see," he murmured thoughtfully as he inspected her swollen foot.

"What happened?" Wide eyes lifted to survey Wade's weary features. "How did you get here and where are we?"

"Juan, Chad and I, accompanied by the vaqueros from the K Bar, rode onto the hill just as Haden knocked you unconscious. Then he started a stampede to run the herd over the top of us. With Maman-ti's help, we cut off the longhorns and circled them back on Haden and his men." Wade paused to dip up a cup of water and then lift it to Shianne's ashen lips. "Haden exposed the yellow streak that runs down the middle of his back when he fled into the clump of cottonwoods by the creek . . . with you in tow of course. He was trying to lead you up the steep bank to make a dash for freedom when your horse fell on top of you."

Shianne digested his explanation along with the sip of cool water. "How did you escape from the cave? Haden told me you were buried alive, and he was making no attempt to rescue you."

"Chad and I crawled through the spring channel," Wade informed her, shuddering at the thought of how close they had come to death. "Maman-ti and Juan Mendez agreed to help us retrieve the herd and rescue you from Haden." A tender smile grazed his lips. "You have been terribly ill. I was beginning to wonder if you would wake at all. You've been babbling in your sleep for three days and nights."

Exhaustion settled about her, and Shianne yawned tiredly. "Thank you, Wade. I am indebted to you for saving my life. Haden's maliciousness had dashed every ounce of hope. When I was with him, I didn't care if I lived or died. . . ."

As Shianne surrendered to sleep, Wade trailed his index finger over her discolored features. Had Haden raped her? Is that what she implied when she admitted she had given up hope? Damn that bastard to hell and back. How he prayed Maman-ti would locate Haden and employ every form of torture known to the Indians.

Wade vowed never to let Shianne out of his sight until he delivered her to her father. She was a good woman, the best, he thought as he peered into her bruised but exquisite face. He was going to repay her for every painful experience he had forced her to endure. He was going to take her to Blake and do her the greatest favor any man had ever done for her. Wade was going to get the hell out of her life. After all, he was the one who put the *hell* in her life in the first place.

Until that day came, he would become her constant shadow, protecting her from harm. Determined in those thoughts, Wade reached down to draw the quilt over both of them. His arm slid around her waist, drawing her petite form against his. Unknowingly, Shianne moved toward the warmth and rested her head against his shoulder.

Wade was overwhelmed by the most baffling emotion. It was akin to desire, and yet it was a stranger to passion. These were not the kinds of feelings he was accustomed to experiencing when he laid with a woman. It reminded Wade of the tormenting nights when he had cradled Shianne's unconscious body in his arms. He didn't want to let go. He wanted to hold her and go on holding her. It was as if she were a part of him. He could almost feel her pain and exhaustion. He loathed Haden Reems in ways he had never detested the man before—the way Shianne must have despised him and his cruel abuse.

"Haden will never harm you again," Wade whispered against her lips. "If Maman-ti doesn't hunt him down and make short work of him, so help me I will track that bastard until I find him, and when I apprehend him, I will have his apology for mistreating you before I spill his life's blood."

For the next two days Wade catered to Shianne like a servant attending a queen. She had but to look as if she wanted or needed something and Wade ensured that she had it. He refused to allow her to do anything for herself, insisting that she save her strength. Shianne appreciated his concern for her welfare, but she was not accustomed to being smothered with this sort of attention, especially from Wade.

Propped against the stack of saddles, Shianne watched Wade pace back and forth across camp, checking on the meat he was roasting over the fire. Her eyes swept from the top of his raven head to the toes of his boots. His broad shoulders were covered with a faded blue shirt and a tan leather vest. His tight brown breeches hugged his masculine frame, accenting the hard tendons of his legs. Shianne swore she had never seen a more handsome specimen. Strength and power exuded from him as each long stride he took caused his form-fitting clothes to strain sensuously across his steel-hard muscles. Shianne was content just to sit and admire the man who was so easy on the eye and so hard on a woman's blood pressure.

How could she be falling deeper in love with Wade, Shianne quizzed herself. If there were indeed varying degrees of love and admiration, she had reached the pinnacle of that emotion. Shianne had suffered through those torturous weeks, chained to Haden, living without Wade's laughter. That experience intensified her feelings for the man who had stolen her heart.

His contrasting philosophy of love didn't seem to matter anymore. Shianne had begun to understand what Wade had been telling her from the very beginning. It was time she began to live for today and allow tomorrow to take care of itself. She had come dangerously close to losing Wade forever, and she was not about to waste the precious moments they spent together . . . no matter if they had one day or one month. Never again would she press him for a commitment. She would take what Wade could offer her and be satisfied with it.

Shianne set aside her idealistic dreams of a love that would endure eternity. As Wade had once said, there were no dashing knights and enchanted Camelots. This was the frontier where men were men, and a woman had to accept a man for what he was without trying to mold him into something he could never be or truly wanted to be. Wade was a tumbleweed, and the time would come when he longed to explore new horizons, face new challenges. Until it was time for him to go, she would offer him all the love that had been tucked inside her heart, all the love that her foolish pride had refused to release.

She would not speak the words because Wade had no use for them, but she would love him, just the same. Every kiss, every caress, every smile would be embroidered with the deep affection that bubbled just beneath the surface. She would be his until he no longer wanted her. When he was gone she would survive on the sweet memories, but she would never beg him to stay, Shianne promised herself. Wade wanted no ties and there would be none.

While Wade was preoccupied with the meal, Shianne peeled off the stained shirt and scooted from her breeches. The rumble of thunder in the distance caused her to glance upward, noting the rolling clouds that were swallowing the stars. Shianne smiled to herself as she rearranged the quilts into an inviting pallet in the grass. It didn't matter if they endured a downpour this night. The storm of passion that would billow between them would be far more devastating.

Fussing over his meal, Wade lifted the quail from the fire and set it on a plate. When he had cut a leg of meat and dipped up a scoop of beans, he turned toward

Shianne, prepared to offer her his attempt at cooking. The metal plate very nearly tumbled from his fingertips while the call to dinner died on his lips.

A streak of lightning darted across the stormy sky, spraying a stream of silver across Shianne's shapely body. The flickering light of the campfire added a golden hue, making her naked flesh glow like honey long after the flash of lightning evaporated. Her long hair was laying about her in disarray, giving her a reckless, bewitching appearance. The dark shadows of the night camouflaged the bruises and scrapes she had sustained, but they were of little consequence at the moment anyway. Wade was viewing a wingless angel who hovered just out of reach, and all he could think about was how enchanting she was.

Shaking his head to shatter the spell, Wade frowned at her provocative smile. What the hell was she doing, he asked himself when his senses cleared. She was weak and injured. If she didn't crawl back into the blankets before the storm struck, she would catch her death all over again.

"Woman, I swear the fever burned a hole in your brain," Wade grumbled as he stalked over to offer her the plate. "It was bad enough that Maman-ti tried to dunk you in the stream while you were so critically ill. If Doc Winston could get a look at you now he would swear you remembered nothing of your training. You are supposed to feed a fever, not expose it to inclement weather!"

Shianne was unaffected by his stern lecture on proper medical practices for the sick and ailing. All she could see was the man who had become her world. All she could hear was the whispered longings of her heart.

"There are some things that medication cannot cure," she assured him, her voice low and seductive. Her gaze swung from the plate he held in his hands to the hard male length of him.

One dark brow shot straight up. Wade watched her expressive eyes sketch his masculine form with undisguised interest. "Are you sure you are feeling up to this?" he chuckled.

"Come here and I will show you. . . ." she invited as she patted the empty space beside her.

Wade was torn between his concern for Shianne and his lusty passions, ones that he had held in check for more weeks than he cared to count. Damn, she was tempting, but she was also weak and frail after her bout with the grippe and the strains and bruises sustained during her fall. If he wasn't careful, he might hurt her when he crushed her to him, overwhelmed by his unfulfilled needs. He would have to portray the tender, patient lover. Wade wasn't sure he possessed that much self-control. He had denied himself for so long that it would be difficult to be gentle, but then, it had always been impossible to control himself with Shianne, he mused as his eyes consumed her curvaceous figure. She brought out the savage male instincts within him, ones that could never be controlled until passion had run its windswept course.

Wade squatted down beside the delicious temptress who lay provocatively before him. "Eat your dinner before it gets rained on," he ordered gruffly. "I don't think it would be a good idea to feed the *other* form of hunger at the moment." If Wade could have gotten his hands on a medal, he would have pinned it on his chest. He certainly deserved one for resisting this tantalizing bundle. It was for her own good of course. It damned sure wasn't for his. He would be forced to soak an hour in the creek to cool the fires of desire.

Damn that stubborn man! Since when did this rogue decline such a blatant invitation? Well, she was every bit as headstrong as he was, Shianne told herself proudly.

Shianne came up on her knees, careful not to put much weight on her tender ankle. With deviltry dancing in her eyes, she took the plate from his hand and set it aside. Her gaze never left his face as she unbuttoned his chambray shirt and pushed it from his broad shoulders. When her roaming caresses trailed along the band of his breeches, Wade choked on his breath.

"Stop that, minx," he commanded, catching her adventurous hands in his. "I said *no.*"

Shianne wormed her hands free to work the buttons on his breeches. Again, Wade manacled her hands and stared straight into her mischievous eyes.

"Don't you know what *no* means?" he grumbled. "You aren't well. Dammit, I could hurt you!"

Undaunted by his harsh rejection, Shianne drew nearer, even though her wrists were shackled in his unrelenting grasp. Her lips feathered over his chest in the lightest breath of a touch.

"How could I be hurt any worse than I already have been?" she whispered against his hair-matted flesh.

Wade's resistance was crumbling like a poorly constructed dam besieged by turbulent flood waters. Shianne was doing impossible things to his defenses, ones that were not too sturdy to begin with. When her kisses hovered along the slope of his shoulder to assault the sensitive point beneath his ear, a herd of goose bumps stampeded across his skin. Dammit, she was making this incredibly difficult!

"I've been without you for weeks," he rasped in belated response to her question. "I'm not sure I can control myself."

A sly smile played on her lips as she spread kisses across his cheek. Her breasts brushed wantonly against his chest, teasing and taunting him until his sanity threatened to shatter in a million pieces.

"I'm not sure I want you to. . . ." she murmured against his full lips.

Lightning sizzled across the sky, followed by a loud clap of thunder. A gust of cold wind whistled through the camp, assuring Wade that the approaching storm was less than five miles away—the exact distance this Texas temptress had flung his willpower.

Somehow her hands escaped his grasp. They were dipping beneath the band of his breeches, tying every nerve and muscle into tangled knots.

"Shianne . . . don't. . . ." he ordered, but his heart wasn't in it. He wanted to drink his fill of her like a thirsty traveler quenching his needs after being stranded on a desert for days on end. He wanted to devour her like a starving man craving a feast. But dammit, she was in no condition to be ravished, and that was exactly what would happen if he surrendered to the smoldering passions that had lain dormant these past weeks.

"Don't what?" she chuckled seductively. Shianne pushed away his trousers, exposing the muscled columns of his legs. "Don't stop? I don't intend to. . . ."

Her sweet mouth drifted over his. Her bold caresses sensitized his quaking flesh. Wade groaned in unbearable torment. Her touch was driving him insane. Her kisses were setting him on fire. Finally, he could endure no more of this sweet agony. She had pushed him past resistance and primal instincts took hold of him.

"You asked for it, vixen," he warned her, his voice heavy with barely controlled passion. His hands cupped her face, tilting her head to accept his kiss.

"I did," she agreed, her eyes brimming with heart-felt emotion. Her arms slid around his shoulders, pressing closer to his sinewed contours. "And for a moment I wondered if you truly intended to deny me that which I crave more than food and drink. I want you, Wade . . . nothing else. . . ."

Wade knew he was crushing her when he clutched her against him. He knew he was hurting her when his lips swooped down on hers. But God, he was like a wild, savage beast, and he couldn't restrain himself. There was no logic in this kind of passion. It was raw emotion, so fierce and potent that nothing could contain it. His firm body strained against hers. His heart thundered against his chest. He was stealing her breath, devouring her. His hands were upon her, touching her in the most intimate of places, arousing her to this same fervent pitch of passionate frenzy.

His taut body covered hers, aching to become a living, breathing part of her. He could feel her pulse racing in rhythm with the frantic beat of his heart, hear her gasp for breath when he thrust into her. His hands slid beneath her hips, lifting her to him as he drove into her. He was like a wild man driven by some maddening inner force. The emotion refused to relinquish its claim on him until he had satisfied the tormenting need.

As his body shuddered upon hers, granting release of the fierce, untamed emotions that had engulfed him, Wade felt the driving rain on his back. The huge drops were like impatient fingers tapping at reality's door, forcing him to grasp his scattered thoughts.

As much as he would have preferred to remain where he was, Wade drew Shianne to her knees. Together they gathered the saddles and blankets. Under Wade's instruction they moved beneath the bed of the wagon to protect themselves from the raging storm. Once Wade had secured the tarp, making a tent over the wagon, he crawled inside the dark niche. He could hear the hailstones pounding against the roof of their crude abode, but his ears were tuned to Shianne's soft, inviting laughter.

"It's a perfect night for making love," she murmured, reaching out to bring his head to hers.

Wade chuckled at the provocative temptress who continued to amaze him with her bold daring. "Perfect? In case you haven't noticed there is a violent storm raging around us."

Her fingers combed through his damp hair and then wandered at will, stroking his flesh, enticing him all over again. "As I said, it's perfect. There is little else to do but listen to the wind and rain. . . ."

Her lips skimmed his and then descended to follow the arousing path her hands had taken. Wade felt himself melt into a puddle of desire as she brazenly caressed him.

After her near brush with death, a change had overcome Shianne. She showed little signs of self-restraint. Not that he minded, but in the past he had been forced to battle his way through her firm defenses. Now it was the other way around. He was trying to be sensible, and *she* was as reckless as the thunderstorm that was swirling about them.

"Shianne, you are going to wear yourself out," Wade chided, squirming away.

Her hand roamed over the curve of his hip and then followed the thick matting of hair that covered his chest. "I can't think of a more delightful way to wear one's self out."

Wade expelled an exasperated sigh. He was fighting the battle of self-conquest and failing miserably. "If you don't save your strength, you will get sick again. I don't want to live through that twice. I worried ten years off my life."

Her titillating kisses swept over his collar bone to monitor the accelerated beat of his heart. "Passion will add years to your life expectancy," she parried.

"You have an answer for everything, don't you?" he muttered and then caught his breath when her wandering caress glided over his lower abdomen.

"An answer to every question except one," she assured him, her voice like soft velvet.

"I cannot imagine what it might be. . . ." Wade breathed raggedly.

"I cannot understand why you are putting up such a fuss," Shianne chortled softly. "It's out of character for you. I didn't realize 'no' was in your vocabulary."

Damn, what a gentleman he was turning out to be, Wade thought as he endured the sweet torment of her caresses. He had come to care about Shianne more than anyone else in the world, and that changed everything. He was aware of her needs and her frailty. He was concerned about her physical well being, even though it was costing him every iota of willpower.

Lightning tore jagged holes in the sky. Another wave of hailstones hammered against the wagon, and the wind howled like a parade of banshees. Wade could think of a dozen reasons why they should crawl beneath the quilts and huddle together to wait out the storm, but Shianne's assault on each of his senses had warped his logic. He could only think of one reason why he should cast caution to the hailstorm—Shianne. She had filled up his world, weaving her spell of black magic about him.

"To hell with it," he grumbled as he pressed her to her back, his body half covering hers. "You win, sweet witch. Transport me to that paradise that boasts of rainbows. . . ."

As his lips slanted across hers, Shianne arched to mold her soft curves to the hard length of him. She surrendered to the bubbling passions that churned within her. She didn't care if they were uplifted by the fierce wind, as long as she was in the circle of Wade's

399

arms. No thunderstorm could be as devastating as this need to love and be loved.

As the raging storm continued on its course across Indian Territory, Shianne and Wade catapulted across rainbows, basking in the warmth of passion. It was much later when they returned from their intimate journey to paradise. They roused from their dreamlike trance to find the world laying in that mystical serenity that follows the wake of a storm.

Shianne lifted the tarp to peer across the rain-soaked prairie and sighed contentedly. A smattering of stars on the northern horizon cast a faint light upon the clump of trees near their wagon. Ah, it was good to be alive, to nestle in the warmth of Wade's embrace.

"Do you suppose Chad and the vaqueros were forced to endure this same storm?" she questioned curiously.

"If they did, I doubt that they were occupied in the same fashion," Wade chuckled as he propped himself beside Shianne. His gaze swept the peaceful meadow. "But I'm sure my brother would have given most anything to exchange places with me."

A devilish twinkle flickered in her eyes as she tossed him a hasty glance. "He has mentioned something to that effect to me before," she said breezily.

Wade jerked up, forgetting he was beneath a low ceiling. His head clanked against the underside of the wagon. "Knowing my brother, he was undoubtedly plain-spoken about what he wanted from you." Rubbing his aching head, Wade sank back beside Shianne. "Would it have mattered who had been available tonight?" he queried, his tone carrying an unpleasant bite.

"What do you think?" Shianne put the question to him, accompanied by a mischievous smile.

"If I knew I wouldn't have asked," Wade muttered crabbily.

Why was it that the thought of sharing Shianne always put him in a snit? It had been over two months since he had seen her, but his fascination for her had not dwindled, not even a smidgen. In the past, he had lost interest in women after that same span of time, but with Shianne every moment was like the first moment—an intriguing adventure. There was nothing predictable about the way she reacted to two similar situations, and that continued to mystify him.

Frustrated by this riptide of emotions that tormented him, Wade struggled into his breeches and crawled outside to determine if the horses had thundered off during the storm. It almost came as a relief that they had bolted and run. It offered the perfect excuse to be alone with his perplexing thoughts.

"Where are you going?" Shianne called after him.

"To round up the horses," he threw over his shoulder.

"Wait! I'll come with you," Shianne offered as she reached for her discarded clothes.

"No, you stay put," Wade ordered sharply. "You have done quite enough for one night. The parts of your body that you haven't yet exercised don't need it!"

As he trudged off to locate Galahad and Delgado, Wade muttered under his breath. He had decided to walk out of Shianne's life when he returned her to her father. So why was he disturbed by the thought of another man taking his place?

Wade was no fool. He knew there would always be a man in Shianne's life. She had never been without eager admirers. But each time he envisoned her lying in someone else's arms his body burned with jealousy.

This wasn't normal, Wade lectured himself. He had always been a rudderless individual who cruised from one affair to another without looking back. Women flocked to him, and he had never been alone when he desired female companionship. He sorted through the long list of women he had known, attempting to latch on to a memory that burned as bright as the one Shianne had created. To his chagrin, he came up empty-handed.

Wade broke stride when he haphazardly stepped into a puddle. Good God, was he in love with this feisty temptress? Really in love? What an ironic twist of fate that would be, he mused as he shook the mud off his boot and continued on his way. He had resolved to remove himself from Shianne's life. He had been howling about no strings to bind them together since the beginning. Now, here he was on the verge of eating crow. Undoubtedly, he was going to choke on his words.

He had convinced Shianne to take passion where she found it, making no demands on him. Now that she had accepted his philosophy and responded accordingly, Wade didn't like it one damned bit. Hypocrite, he shouted at himself. He had made all the rules, and now he felt the urge to retract them. Well, maybe he was getting what he deserved, he thought sourly. He had finally stumbled into a romantic affair that snared him like quicksand trapping an unsuspecting traveler. He was bogged down with thoughts that contained the words tomorrow, lasting ties, and forever.

"You're a bigger fool than I thought, Wade Burdett," he preached to himself.

"What makes you such a fool, Wade Burdett?" came a voice from so close behind him that Wade nearly leaped out of his skin.

Wade wheeled around to see Maman-ti standing as motionless as a shadow on the fringe of darkness. The swarthy warrior was garbed in doehide, looking every bit the wild renegade he was.

"Where the hell did you come from?" Wade snapped, annoyed that his natural instincts were clogged with frustrating thoughts of Shianne.

Maman-ti strode up in front of Wade. Amusement glistened in his dark eyes. "Indians creep up out of nowhere, and when they go, they vanish into nothing. Have you not heard that the Comanches amuse themselves by sneaking up on unsuspecting white men?"

"Spare me your Indian wit," Wade grunted sarcastically. He was in a sour mood, and Maman-ti's appearance only served to remind him that here was yet another man who had designs on Shianne. "I suppose you have already seen Shianne." Grumbling, he pivoted to pursue the two horses that were grazing in the distance.

"I have seen her," the Owl Prophet admitted as he fell into step behind Wade. "My medicine brought her back to life."

When Wade pulled up short, Maman-ti slammed into his backside. "Is arrogance a priority for becoming a medicine man?" Wade snorted caustically. "If it is, I can certainly see why you were elected the resident shaman. You possess enough conceit to equip the entire tribe."

"Your tongue is sharp, Wade Burdett," Maman-ti growled. "You seem to forget that it is only because of Shianne that I tolerate you."

"And you have neglected to mention that it is only because of Shianne that we clash. We might even come to be friends, if not for our mutual interest in that she-cat," Wade countered.

"There are few pale faces I would dare to call friend," Maman-ti shot back. "White men are the Indians' enemies, and they always will be."

Wade expelled a frustrated sigh. Why was he picking a fight with Maman-ti? There was enough dissension between them without searching out thorns to stab in one another.

"Did you find Haden?" Wade questioned, allowing the previous subject of conversation to die a quiet death.

Maman-ti gave his head a negative shake. "My warriors have carefully searched the area. His tracks led into the South Canadian River. We scouted the cottonwoods and plum thickets, but he was not to be found. Haden Reems has more cunning in the wilderness than I thought. We were too many hours behind him to track, and he was clever enough to cover his horse's hoof prints and travel rocky paths that left no trail."

Wade scowled at the discouraging news. He had slept easier the past few nights, thinking Maman-ti had initiated Haden into the Indians' brand of excruciating torture.

With Maman-ti's help, Wade retrieved the stallions and the two geldings that pulled the wagon. When the men returned to camp, Shianne was limping about, fishing dry kindling from the back of the wagon. While Shianne and her devoted Indian conversed, Wade gulped down his coffee and stared at some distant point. His troubled thoughts made him restless. He was anxious to seek out his brother and preoccupy himself with moving the herd.

When Shianne invited the Owl Prophet to bed down with them, Wade's mood turned a darker shade of black, especially when the Indian flung him a gloating smile. Shianne was well aware of Wade's remote attitude, but it did her heart good to see him sulk. At least it assured her that he cared enough to be a mite jealous of the undivided attention she was receiving from the Owl Prophet.

Chapter 20

Shianne stared into Maman-ti's weathered features. A rueful smile rippled across her lips. Her hand found his, giving it a fond squeeze. "Will you be wintering in the reserved lands?" she questioned softly.

Maman-ti nodded affirmatively. "The Comanches and Kiowas will go to our tepee village near Medicine Creek. It will be many months before we return to the hill country." His gaze strayed to Wade who sat stiffly on the wagon seat, impatiently waiting for Shianne to bid adieu to the Owl Prophet. "Are you certain you do not wish to come with me while *he* drives his cattle north? You are still weak, Shianne. I will see that you are treated well among our people. The Cheyenne are camped to our north. I could take you to Black Kettle. He has long awaited to see the woman I . . ."

"I'm taking her to her father," Wade interrupted, casting Maman-ti a stern glance. "And we are wasting daylight."

Shianne went into the Owl Prophet's arms, offering a farewell embrace that had Wade grumbling under his breath. When she stepped back, Maman-ti curled his hand beneath her chin. Although she still bore the bruises of Haden's anger, she was bewitching with her hair laying in two long braids, and her dark eyes misty with sentiment. Maman-ti could not control his envy for the bold white man.

"Part of my heart will go with you," he murmured affectionately. "When Mother Earth again grows green and blossoms with wild flowers my people will venture south to Speaking Springs."

Wade gnashed his teeth when Maman-ti dared to kiss Shianne, right on the mouth. Damn that Indian. He had twice as many wives as Wade had, and still Maman-ti would not keep his hands off this dark-eyed enchantress!

When the Owl Prophet finally lifted Shianne into the wagon, Wade popped the reins over the horses and sent them cantering down the trail. For several minutes Wade sat in silence, attempting to recover from his two day visit with Maman-ti. The Indian had parked himself in camp and bedded down beside them each night. It had been a constant battle to see which one of them would wait on Shianne hand and foot. Wade sorely resented Maman-ti's intrusion while Shianne delighted in his companionship.

Once the medicine man deemed Shianne strong enough to travel, Wade had gathered their supplies in record time. He couldn't wait to part company with Maman-ti. As far as Indians went, Maman-ti commanded Wade's respect, but the bronze-skinned warrior had one annoying flaw—his overt interest in Shianne. It still galled Wade that the shaman had no qualms about pursing a woman right under her husband's watchful eye.

"Do you intend to sulk all the way to Abilene?" Shianne taunted. "You have made a poor host the past few days. There were times I feared Maman-ti was contemplating scalping you, and I wouldn't have blamed him if he had. You have had the disposition of a

406

wounded lion, growling and snarling over little or nothing."

Wade forced his token smile, even though he felt more comfortable with a frown these days. "Your hospitality compensated for my lack of warmth," he insisted, his voice carrying the slightest trace of sarcasm.

"I should think you would be far more appreciative. After all, Maman-ti kept surveillance over the herd until you arrived to retrieve it," Shianne countered.

"For *that* I thanked him," Wade declared. "But I am not about to express gratitude for the way he doted over you when I would have preferred he didn't go near you at all. You can hardly expect me to praise a man who delights in kissing *my* wife!"

His voice rose sharply, and Shianne struggled to keep from snickering when Wade puffed up like an indignant rooster. "We made a bargain, you and I. After my near collision with death, I realized how important it was to reap the pleasures each day offers." Shianne nodded thoughtfully. "And you were right, Wade. The events of each passing day cause us to undergo changes in the way we think and behave. After my harrowing experiences, I am not the same reserved, naive young girl I was the day we met." Her gaze circled the landscape, enjoying the beauty of the rolling hills and the thick canopies of cottonwoods and pecan trees that shaded the meandering creeks. "I view life much differently than I once did. I owe my transformation to you, and when you've gone your own way, I will smile occasionally and remember the moments we shared, just as I will recall the times I spent with Maman-ti."

"Who said I was going anywhere?" Wade snorted disdainfully.

Shianne studied his sour frown. Wade certainly didn't smile as much as he once had, she noted. He had once been the epitome of good humor, and now he was as ill-tempered as the *cimarrones* that roamed the brush country of Texas.

"I presumed you would pack up and leave after you made profit from the cattle drive," she said with a lackadaisical shrug. "You really hadn't planned on settling on your acreage to raise cattle the rest of your days, had you? I could have sworn this whole affair had more to do with obliging my father and seeking revenge on Haden Reems than putting down permanent roots in Texas."

Wade fell silent. He had honestly intended to make a fresh start in ranching. That was until he felt the obligation to extricate himself from Shianne's life. Since Haden was still on the loose, Wade couldn't think past settling the score, no matter how many months or years it took to do it. Yet, in the back of his mind, he knew he would return to Texas to retest his reaction to Shianne, to determine if she still created this turmoil of emotions within him.

Shianne bit her tongue, refusing to voice the thought that was humming in her head. She wanted to ask Wade to stay, to tell him that he was the sunshine in her days, but she couldn't. He was the kind of man who thrived on the freedom to come and go as he pleased. It had to be his strong affection for her that made him want to return to Texas to build his own herd and make a new life as her husband. In the end she would have her way, Shianne vowed to herself. It would be all or nothing. She would play this charade, pretending it didn't matter that their marriage strings had loose ends, but she could not hang in limbo forever. When she returned to Texas, she would be prepared to get on with her life—with or without the man who had taught her soul to sing.

* * *

After they crossed the Cimarron River to camp for the night, Wade grabbed his Winchester rifle and set out to hunt their meal. Shianne limped around camp, making preparations. Once finished with gathering wood for the fire and setting it to blaze, her gaze strayed to the inviting river. It had been months since she had been allowed the privacy of a leisurely bath. Riding on the bumpy wagon and pacing around camp had caused her ankle to swell, and she yearned to relieve the dull throb in her leg.

With her soiled garments tucked under her arm, Shianne waded into the river. Vigorously, she scrubbed her only set of clothes. With that task accomplished, she sank down in the cool water, sighing in the pleasure of solitude. Although she played the masquerade for Wade's benefit, Shianne was still hurting in her own quiet way. She loved Wade with all her heart and soul. Pretending she didn't care if their romantic interlude came to an end was her own private hell. Perhaps she would have been better off if she had gone with Maman-ti. At least he would have kept her preoccupied.

Ah well, it was too late to turn back, she mused as she stretched out to glide across the river. Maman-ti was long gone, and Shianne would keep on pretending there would not be a hole the size of Texas in her heart when Wade rode off into the sunset.

Wade laid the wild turkey beside the campfire and glanced curiously around him. Where the devil was that woman? He had left her alone for an hour, and she had vanished into thin air. His first thought was that Maman-ti had decided to retrieve Shianne. Wade might have worked himself into a frustrated frenzy if he were allowed to grapple with that unsettling thought, but Shianne's cry of alarm shattered his contemplations and brought him to immediate attention.

Wade dashed off in the direction of Shianne's bloodcurdling scream. But, too late, he realized he could have selected a better route for his rescue attempt. Before he could plow his way through the thick underbrush to ascertain what had frightened Shianne, he stumbled onto a skunk. The startled varmint turned tail, but it refused to run before leaving Wade with a foul-smelling reminder of their encounter.

The sickening aroma settled over Wade like a dense fog. It clung to his clothes and attacked his nostrils, making him gasp for breath. As the creature scampered off to seek shelter in the brush, Wade scowled to himself and fought his way through the thicket to reach the stream bank. There, on the opposite side of the river hiding in the brush, was Shianne, wearing nothing but her gaping shirt.

"What the sweet loving hell are you screaming about?" Wade grumbled disgustedly.

Shianne's head swiveled around to peer wide-eyed at the man who stood in the mud, his feet askance, his rifle cocked and ready to fell whatever monstrous beast had startled her. Shianne's gaze swung back to the convoy of water moccasins that slithered down the stream. She pointed an accusing finger at the fleet of vipers.

Wade rolled his eyes and inhaled an exasperated breath, only to be reminded that he smelled exactly like a skunk. "If you can come out of hiding long enough to fetch me another set of clothes, I would appreciate it. I stink to high heaven."

When Shianne was assured the snakes had not conspired to wind their way out of the water and slither up the bank to attack her, she rose from the bushes and swam across the river. The closer she came to Wade the more aware she became of the putrid aroma that hovered around him.

"Whew," she exclaimed, holding her nose. "I suggest you find some other fragrance of cologne. The one you are wearing is most offensive."

Wade muttered under his breath, unaffected by her attempt to humor him. This was not what he anticipated after finding Shianne barely clad, looking as delicious as any feast. After three nights of celibacy, Wade ached to be as close to Shianne as two people could get.

The enticing sight of Shianne's shapely legs protruding from the long hem of her shirt was hard on Wade's blood pressure. The gaping garment revealed the full swell of her breasts, and Wade ached to touch what he had been forced to ignore while Maman-ti was underfoot. But she would never allow him near her when the only creature he could possibly attract was one that smelled just like him.

When Shianne hurried off to retrieve fresh clothes, Wade shook off his garments and hurled them as far away as he could throw them. Grumbling, he waded into the river, hoping the water would cleanse away the offensive smell that clung to his skin and hair. Although he very nearly scrubbed off one layer of his hide, it didn't help. He still reeked of skunk.

Shianne appeared on the bank and draped his clean clothes over a nearby bush. When she had peeled off her wet shirt, she approached Wade, carrying the soap she had fished from the supply sack. Lathering her hands, she threaded her fingers through his hair, leaving his head capped with bubbles.

"I'm sorry to cause you such distress," she apologized as she worked the soap into his scalp. "The snakes startled me. I was paying little attention, and they were upon me before I realized it."

Wade glanced up, his eyes glued to the soft mounds of flesh that begged for his touch. His fingertips

411

investigated each taut peak, causing Shianne to jerk away.

"How am I to concentrate on my task?" she chided him. Her voice cracked, providing evidence that he was having a disturbing effect on her.

"Find a way," Wade murmured seductively. "You concentrate on your chore, and I will dedicate myself to mine. . . ."

A soft gasp bubbled in her throat when his warm lips made arousing contact with one pink bud. His feather-light kisses drifted between the valley of her breasts to pay the same tantalizing attention to the other taut peak.

"Wade, you are sorely in need of a bath," she reminded him as his arms fastened about her.

"I have other needs," he grumbled as he be-grudgingly released her to sink back in the shallow water. "At the moment, they are more potent than sitting back to soak off the smell of skunk."

"First things first," Shianne declared.

The feel of her hands roaming over his bare flesh reminded Wade of the first day they had met. She had massaged his baked flesh with her tender touch, arousing more in him than she could have possibly known; but now she had become a skillful seductress, and she knew full well how potent her caresses could be, even when she pretended to bathe him. In no way could this experience be compared to the ordinary ritual of cleansing skin!

While she continued her gentle ministrations, Wade eased back on his elbows. His emerald eyes were fixed on her curvaceous figure, one that was impossible to ignore when she was hovering over him as naked as the day she was born. A man could tolerate only so much excitement before he lost all interest in bathing, and he was at the frayed end of his rope. It seemed Shianne had twice the normal number of hands, and they were spreading tingles of pleasure everywhere they touched. He may not have smelled like some perfumed dandy, but he deemed himself clean enough. This bath was officially over, he decided.

The expression on his craggy features was one of blatant hunger. His eyes flamed with unmistakable desire. With one lithe movement he hooked an arm around Shianne's waist, flattening her against him. "You are going to have to stop what you're doing to me, woman, or you'll have to keep doing it all night long," he rasped, his voice thick with disturbed passion.

Shianne propped herself up on his chest to trace the sensuous curve of his mouth. "Which would you prefer?" she inquired, her eyes dancing with wicked delight.

His gaze burned over her while his roving hands settled on her hips, moving her so that she was fitted exactly over him. "I think you know the answer to that, vixen. . . ."

Her head came to his. She nibbled at the corners of his mouth until he groaned in torment. Lord, he was drunk on the taste of her, mesmerized by the sight and feel of her. God help him, he could never seem to get enough of this woman. Even when the fires of passion burned themselves out, there was always a lingering flame in the embers. It took so little to fan the fire into a blazing inferno, Wade mused as her caresses became bolder. She had him dancing like a puppet on a string, and his body roused to her touch. Wade swore his galloping heart would trample him to death before he could satisfy the maddening longings she stirred in him.

Breathlessly, he answered each soul-quaking caress, returning each stroke of splendor, each kiss of rapture.

413

Desire fogged his mind, and primal needs assumed control. Wade turned on his side, pressing intimately against her, holding her to him.

The sweet hypnotic cadence of their lovemaking sent them into reckless abandon. Shianne reveled in rapturous bliss, one so sublime that tears of pleasure swam in her eyes. Her body was a mass of tremors. Pinpointed sensations assaulted her, leaving not one part of her untouched. Heaven was the unending circle of Wade's arms, that boundless dimension in time and space that fanned out in all directions. There was nothing but one incredible sensation of ecstasy piling atop another.

Then it came, that wild, indescribable feeling that splintered into the core of her being. Shock waves of rapture crested upon her, draining every ounce of strength and scattering rational thought. Shianne clung to him, paralyzed with the quintessence of pleasure she always found when they made sweet, savage love.

It was a long breathless moment before her eyes fluttered open to see that the world was not pitch black. Indeed, it was cloaked in the pastels of sunset. When she realized they had made their bed of passion in the shallow neck of the river on a blanket of sand, she giggled softly. There had been a time when she had thought only a bed would suffice when a man and woman surrendered to their desires, but when Wade tugged her into his arms, it didn't matter where they were . . . at least not until they had satisfied their fervent cravings for each other.

Wade raised a heavy brow and glanced at the radiant smile that clung to Shianne's kiss-swollen lips. "Dare I ask what you find so amusing, minx?"

Shianne dug her fingers into the riverbed and dropped a glob of sand on his hip. Wade snickered when he realized what she implied.

"It's not exactly the honeymoon suite at San Antonio's luxurious hotel, is it?" he questioned, his voice still husky with the aftereffects of their ardent lovemaking.

"A far cry from it," she concurred. "But I am not complaining." Struggling, Shianne sat up to wash away the sand. "I found no fault with the pallet beneath the wagon during a hailstorm either."

Wade braced himself on an elbow. His lean fingers tunneled through the damp strands of ebony that cascaded down her back. "You deserve better than this, princess," he murmured apologetically.

Shianne swiveled her head around, her chin resting on her shoulder. Mischief flared in her dark eyes. "How can it possibly be better? It seems inconceivable to improve on perfection. You are a very skillful lover."

Wade slid her a roguish smile. Using her hair as a tow rope, he pulled her down beside him in the river. "Flattery will get you everywhere, my sweet. Make a wish, and I will ensure that it comes true."

The words were on her lips, aching to fly free, but Shianne refused to give the thought to tongue. She would have wished for his confession of love, but she had vowed never to press Wade. After dropping one last kiss to his mouth Shianne sprang to her feet to fetch her clothes.

"No whims, Shae? Not even one?" Wade persisted, staring thoughtfully after her.

"No," she lied through her carefree smile. "I am content with the way of things. Indeed, I am just happy to be alive."

As she disappeared into the underbrush, Wade gathered his feet beneath him. Damn, he was at a loss to understand Shianne these days. She had become a seductive gamine who took pleasure when and where she found it. He could not help but wonder if she would have succumbed to her need for passion, no matter what man had been convenient. Confound it, he had been the one to introduce her to the world of passion. *He* had been the one who made her aware of her needs as a woman, and he had been correct in assessing this high-spirited sprite. Her passions for love and living were unmatched by the other females he had known.

Things had not unfolded as he had anticipated, Wade thought with a pensive frown. Shianne offered him such incredible freedom that it was strangling him. Did that make any sense, Wade asked himself. Why did he feel so tightly bound to this vixen when she had made no demands on him? She had flung the door open wide, granting him the opportunity to come and go whenever he pleased. Yet, even when she offered him an out, Wade was hesitant in overstepping the threshold of marriage. If he had a mind to make his bed in a bordello, he had the feeling Shianne would not object.

Knowing this unchained freedom of theirs was a two-way street, Wade could not think of touching another woman for fear that Shianne would turn to another man. And, no doubt in this part of the country, Shianne would be the first to find a replacement for *his* arms. All that temptress had to do was cast an interested glance in Chad's direction, and he would come bounding toward her like an eager puppy.

Wade expelled an exasperated breath. Life would be much simpler when he walked out of Shianne's life. Then he wouldn't be around to know where she was and with whom. Hell, she might even succumb to Maman-ti when he returned in the spring. . . . The thought cut through Wade like a sharp-edged knife, slashing his disposition to shreds.

When he wandered into camp a half-hour later, he

found that Shianne had dressed the turkey and was in the process of preparing their meal. A lighthearted smile bordered her lips as she limped around camp, humming a soft tune. Each time Wade glanced in her direction he found himself resenting her high spirits and her carefree attitude.

Damn, she was taking this all too well, he thought disgustedly. In less than a month they would arrive in Abilene. He would set out for parts unknown in search of Haden, and Shianne would still be smiling when she bid him adieu. Well, that was the way he wanted it, wasn't it? Wasn't it, Wade asked himself again when the answer did not immediately pop to mind.

Disgruntled, Wade uncorked the liquor bottle he had stashed in the wagon and gulped a drink. A curious frown knitted Shianne's brow as she watched Wade guzzle another generous portion of brandy.

"Is something troubling you?" she questioned, sipping her coffee and staring at Wade over the rim of her cup.

Plenty, but Wade wasn't about to admit it to little miss cheerful. "I only hankered for the taste of whiskey," Wade hedged. "Would you care to join me?"

Shianne extended herself to turn the fowl over the blazing fire. "No thank you." She gestured toward her coffee cup. "I will stick to less potent drinks. I only resort to liquor when something is disturbing me, and I want to forget what it is. But I am sitting on top of the world at the moment. One cannot climb much higher than that, even with the assistance of brandy."

Wade downed another swallow and rolled his eyes heavenward. All this cheerfulness was depressing him. Where were all the whimpering, pleading women he had left behind in days gone by? The ones who had begged him to stay after he lost interest? Damn, Shianne was hard on a man's pride. She knew their days were numbered. She knew they would enjoy very little privacy when they caught up with the trail herd, and still she kept smiling.

Confound it, Shianne had become too much like him. It frustrated him that she was taking this all in stride, wearing that sugar-coated smile that was giving Wade a toothache just staring at her.

When the meat was cooked Shianne sliced off a drumstick and offered it to Wade. Nodding mutely, he chewed on the poultry and washed it down with brandy. By the time he finished his meal, his eyes were glazed and his movements were sluggish. It was the first time Shianne had seen Wade intoxicated, and she could not help but giggle when he staggered to his feet to fetch another drumstick.

"Perhaps *I* should retrieve the food, lest you fall face-down in the fire," Shianne suggested, stepping in front of him.

Wade picked her up and set her aside. "I am perfectly capable of seeing to the task myself," he boasted over his thick tongue.

"Wade, watch where you are setting your feet. . . ." Shianne warned too late.

His pained shriek sent the birds fluttering from their nests in the overhanging branches. Wade's reactions were slow but his numbed brain assured him that he was standing on live coals. Dancing a jig, he attempted to extinguish the smoldering soles of his boots.

When Wade had put out the fire and collapsed on the ground, Shianne strode over to help him remove his boots. Clasping her hands on his left foot, Shianne stepped over his leg and tugged. After the second boot had been removed in the same manner, Shianne cleansed her hands and brought Wade his second helping of turkey.

A silly smile was draped on the corner of his mouth.

418

His fuzzy gaze worked its way across the baggy shirt that camouflaged her shapely contours. "Damn, you're gorgeous," he complimented in his slurred voice.

One delicate brow raised acutely. How could he find her attractive when she looked like a wild witch? Her hair was a mess of tangles and, her clothes were befitting a scarecrow.

"Damn, you're drunk," Shianne scoffed at him.

"Maybe," Wade admitted with a guilty smile. "But you are still the prettiest female I ever laid eyes on."

A becoming blush crept into her cheeks. Shianne sank down beside him on the pallet. Her eyes searched his for a long moment. Why was he paying her compliments when he had spent the past two hours gulping brandy and sulking as if he were drowning in troubled thoughts. What was bothering him, she wondered.

"Wade, what is the matter with you? You have been behaving strangely, even for you."

He tipped up the bottle and threw down another drink before responding to her question. "Is there something wrong with a man admitting that he has a lovely wife?" he snorted.

"Yes, when that particular man would prefer not to have one at all," Shianne parried.

The shrill whinny of the horses interrupted their conversation. Muttering, Wade climbed to his feet to investigate the ruckus in the bushes. With his rifle clutched in one hand, Wade disappeared into the brush.

Shianne wrung her hands in front of her, concerned about Wade's welfare. He had been drinking heavily. Considering his intoxicated condition, Shianne feared Wade would wind up shooting himself. Finally apprehension overcame her. Snatching up her pistol, Shianne followed the direction Wade had taken.

Again she heard the horses whinnying in the distance, and a rustling in the bushes behind her. Shianne wheeled around, simultaneously cocking the trigger of her revolver. A gasp of fear gushed from her lips when a bobcat leaped from the shadows. The creature's eyes glowed in the darkness, and his piercing cry shattered the night. Shianne's finger squeezed against the trigger just as Wade's rifle exploded from somewhere in the underbrush.

Suddenly, Wade appeared from the thicket. His temper exploded when he spied Shianne standing only a few feet away from the lifeless bobcat. "Dammit! I could have killed you!" Wade roared. He wasn't as inebriated as he had been the split second before. Realizing he could have easily shot Shianne by mistake had a sobering effect on him, one he was anxious to remedy. "What are you doing out here?"

"I came to look for you," Shianne defended. "You were drunk, and I was afraid you were going to injure yourself in some foolish accident."

His free hand bit into the tender flesh of her arm. With quick, impatient strides Wade hauled Shianne back to camp. He thrust her away, growling more ferociously than the bobcat that could have made a meal of her.

"The next time I go off to investigate strange noises, you stay put!" he thundered. "Dammit, Shae, I didn't even see you in the shadows. If I would have missed my mark, you could have been dead!"

"Well, I'm not," Shianne sassed, annoyed by his poignant glare and his biting tone of voice. "And even if I were, what would it matter to you? I'm sure you see me as a necessary inconvenience. If not for me you would be with your herd of longhorns."

"Is that why you think I have been behaving strangely?" he shot back. "Do you think I begrudge

420

waiting for you to mend from your injuries, that I would prefer to be surrounded by four thousand head of cattle and a throng of vaqueros?"

"Well, don't you?" Shianne questioned point-blank. "You've been playing up to me since the beginning, using me to suit your purpose, but if the truth is known, you are more concerned about reaching Abilene and boasting that you conquered the challenge of a trail drive under the most difficult of conditions. You hold *any* challenge that tests your abilities more dear than *any* woman."

Wade kicked at the clump of grass beneath his feet and then stalked over to plop down on the pallet. "I am in no mood to argue," he muttered. "I have yet to recover from the shock of seeing you standing in the direct line of fire."

Huffily, Shianne stomped across camp to retrieve Wade's whiskey bottle. After choking down a drink she glared in Wade's direction. Angrily, Wade picked himself up and stormed over to snatch the bottle away before Shianne drained the flask.

"Oh no you don't," he growled. "The last time you started pouring down liquor the night turned into a fiasco."

Shianne lunged at him, grasping the bottle before he could put it out of her reach. "Since liquor got me into this preposterous marriage, maybe drinking will get me out of it."

After Shianne had downed another generous helping, Wade dragged the bottle from her hands and gulped a drink. "Fine, madam, we shall see which one of us will be the first to forget about this *preposterous* marriage as you so aptly refer to it."

Sending him a challenging glower, Shianne took the brandy and helped herself to another drink. She had vowed never to partake so much liquor again, but she broke her own promise in the face of Wade's daring smile. When they had taken turns tipping the bottle and draining it dry, Wade weaved over to the wagon to fish out another flask.

Silently brooding, they passed the bottle back and forth until the flames in the campfire died into glowing coals. By that time, Wade could barely keep his eyes from slamming shut. He had drunk far too much liquor earlier that night. The effects of the second bout with brandy were saturating his brain.

"Shae?" he called sluggishly. Wade was reasonably certain the ornery chit was there somewhere, but he was long past being able to see her. His eyes were glazed with a blurry haze.

Shianne recklessly set the bottle aside. Her gaze circled to see Wade half-propped against his saddle, his legs sprawled out in front of him.

"Do you still remember my name?" she questioned slurrishly. When Wade nodded affirmatively, Shianne retrieved the brandy and tucked it in his limp hand. "Then you have not had nearly enough to drink."

A muddled frown puckered her relaxed features when Wade began chuckling to himself. Her eyes widened when the bottle moved toward his lips and then halted in midair. His arm suddenly dropped straight down, sloshing liquor on the front of his shirt.

Shianne leaned over to prop the bottle upright and then glanced down to see that Wade had fallen into a drunken stupor. She would have been gloating over her ability to outlast the big brute if she could have pulled herself into a sitting position, but her body refused to move. So there she stayed, her head resting on Wade's belly, her hand flung around his waist.

Her tactics had proved successful, she thought as her eyes drifted shut. She couldn't remember what they had been arguing about, and she didn't care to contemplate it, knowing it would cause a more severe headache than the one she was going to have when she woke.

When the sun climbed into the sky to announce the dawning of another day, Shianne lifted her head and groaned silently. Her heavily-lidded eyes surveyed the sleeping body she had used as a pillow. With an effort, Shianne pushed into an upright position and rose unsteadily to her feet. Lord, Wade had driven her to drink again, she thought miserably. This had to stop. Her body could not tolerate this kind of abuse. It had only begun to mend from her last illness and injuries.

Forcing one foot ahead of the other Shianne trudged to the river, hoping the cold water would revive her—at least partially. When Wade roused, she vowed to be her cheerful self again. He would never know that she was nursing a throbbing headache. Let him think she had survived their drinking contest better than he had. That should put another dent in his male pride, she thought spitefully.

After a hurried bath, Shianne weaved through the brush to return to camp. Wade was still sprawled on the ground, his chest rising and falling in methodic breaths. Shianne set the coffee pot to perking and then propped herself against the wagon. When Wade began to stir, Shianne pasted on a pleasant smile, even though she feared her face would crack under the pressure.

"Good morning," she greeted more cheerfully than she felt.

Wade groaned in reply. Suddenly, he remembered his intent to behave as if he were fit as a fiddle when he roused. Tacking on a lackadaisical grin, he rolled to his knees. That was as far as he could go before the world began to spin furiously about him. Fighting for composure, Wade put one stocking foot on the pallet and hoisted himself to full stature.

"Good morning, princess," he responded. "Did you sleep well?"

"Splendidly," Shianne assured him enthusiastically. When she turned away to check on the coffee, she grimaced at the sharp pain that shot across her temple. Lord, she had slept like a rock—hard and unmoving. Her body was a mass of aching muscles and quaking nerves.

As soon as Shianne pivoted away, the smile slid off Wade's pallid features. God, he felt awful. No one should feel this bad and be alive, he thought sickly.

"So did I," he enthused. "Ah, I never felt better."

"Coffee?" Shianne offered him a steaming cup and another sunny smile.

Wade willed his hand not to shake when he accepted the cup. "Thank you, princess. I think I will just take it along with me to the creek while I bathe. I want to ensure that there are no lingering fragrances from the skunk before we pack up and take to the trail."

Liar, Wade chided himself as he meandered through the thick brush. He couldn't wait to be alone to wallow in his self-inflicted misery. Breathing an agonizing groan, he peeled off his clothes and fell into the river, praying the shock of the cold water would revive him. Something had to. He could not spend the day pretending to be the picture of health when his head felt as if it were swollen to the size of a pumpkin.

God, how could Shianne be so bright and energetic after all the liquor she had consumed? She should be the one sporting this atrocious headache, he thought miserably. But he was not about to be bested by that rambunctious nymph. Shianne would never know he could barely contain his nausea. He was going to behave as if he were feeling perfectly fit, even if it killed him.

After Wade walked out of camp, Shianne slumped against the wagon to sip her coffee, praying it would settle her churning stomach. Damn, she thought Wade would have been too sick to stand on his own two feet after guzzling so much liquor the previous night. The man was incredible! He had felled a bobcat while under the influence of liquor and then drank himself to sleep. How he managed to rise and shine like the sun was beyond her.

But Shianne was not to be outdone. Wade would never know that their childish game had left her with a dull headache and a queasy stomach. However, Shianne made a mental note never to enter another such ridiculous challenge, ever again. This one, like the last one, had been devastating.

As they loaded the wagon and made their way back to the trail, Wade and Shianne pretended to suffer no ill effects of liquor. Their conversation was sparse. They simply sat side-by-side on the wagon seat, smiling through their misery. There was no consolation that day. Neither of them knew the other was dying on the inside.

Shianne was sure she had gotten what she deserved for resorting to such childish vindictiveness. She only wished Wade was receiving his just desserts. She would have felt one hundred percent better had she known Wade's eyes were squinted in a smile, only to counteract his blinding headache.

Chapter 21

Shianne sighed appreciatively when they rode up the hill to see the string of cattle that filed through the valley below. After a week of long hours on the trail, they had finally caught sight of Chad and the vaqueros. The herd was preparing to cross the Salt Fork of the Arkansas River. The treeless meadow stretched out for miles, and it was dotted with hundreds of prairie dog towns. Yet, it was also treacherous territory for a cattle herd and range hands. A horse could step into a hole, break its leg and throw a rider before either of them realized what had happened.

When Wade hopped from the wagon onto Galahad's back, Shianne took up the reins. Her admiring gaze followed Wade as he galloped off to assist in the river crossing. He was like a part of the blood-bay stallion he rode, a centaur who sailed across the prairie in what Shianne deemed mystical precision.

Tension replaced her dreamy smile when the cattle balked at crossing the wide, swift flowing river. The sun was shining in their eyes, and they were most reluctant to forge forward when they could not determine exactly what lay ahead of them.

The trail herders popped bull whips over the

longhorns' heads and hollered at them, encouraging them to take the plunge. Quicksand along the banks made the cattle even more skittish. When one of the calves floundered and bellowed, the herd threatened to bolt back in the direction from which they had come.

Shianne watched nervously as Chad lassoed the struggling steer and dragged him into midstream. Wade flung his noose to haul another longhorn into the river, giving it the choice of having its neck squeezed in two or stretching out to swim. Although several steers became bogged down in quicksand, the vaqueros pulled them to safety and urged the rest of the herd to trek across the river.

Pensively, Shianne stared at the scene that lay before her. All she could make out was the heads of hundreds of longhorns, their eyes wide with fear, their nostrils flaring. The far-reaching horns of the cattle that were practically submerged reminded Shianne of thousands of rocking chairs floating across the sparkling water.

Once the herd reached the far bank, the strays were rounded up and persuaded to graze with the rest of the cattle. Improvised rafts were hastily constructed to ferry the wagons through the swift moving channel. As Shianne swung onto Delgado's back, Chad trotted up beside her. His welcoming smile was as wide as the river they were about to cross.

"You are a sight for sore eyes, pretty lady," he murmured affectionately. "Juan and I had begun to wonder if we would ever see you again."

As Chad's all-encompassing gaze wandered over her, Shianne flung him a withering glance. "It is obvious you have had little association with women of late." She tugged on her baggy clothes. "I look as appealing as a feed sack. Pretty lady indeed!"

"Feed sack or not, I find you wildly attractive," Chad growled seductively.

Impulsively, he leaned out to pull Shianne onto his lap. "Come here, woman. I haven't had my hands on anything so soft and shapely in months. . . ." His voice trailed off when Wade appeared out of nowhere to breathe down Chad's neck.

"I expected you to be happy to see my wife," Wade snorted disdainfully. "But I didn't expect you to be so overzealous!"

"Aw, come on, big brother," Chad chuckled. "What happened to your good disposition?"

"I sent it out to have it starched and pressed," Wade snapped caustically.

Chad grinned down into Shianne's exquisite features. "I didn't hear Shianne complain, and *you* are beginning to sound like a hypocrite." Wearing an ornery grin Chad glanced back and forth between the lady in his lap and his sour-faced brother. "I still don't see any strings between the two of you. So what's the harm?"

Chad couldn't have annoyed Wade more if he had slapped him across the face. Wade had called himself a hypocrite on several occasions, but hearing the thought voiced turned his mood pitch black. By damned, he *was* a walking contradiction, Wade scowled at himself.

Jerking on the reins, Wade wheeled Galahad around and trotted off to oversee the ferrying of wagons across the river. Chad watched his brother's huffy exit with marked interest.

"It appears there is a new wrinkle in Wade's old philosophy of share and share alike. It seems to have him flying off the handle over little or nothing." Chad observed and then cast Shianne a sly wink.

Shianne stared after Wade, frowning thoughtfully. "Do you suppose he has begun to care just a little?"

Chad eased his horse into the river, keeping a tight hold on his shapely bundle. "He's showing all the signs of a man who cares more than he wants to admit, *especially* to himself," he assured her. "A few days of taunting, and I predict he'll buckle." His blue eyes settled on Shianne's bewitching face. "Even a man of Wade's firm convictions can't hold out forever. I'd say my big brother is hooked, and he's fighting like hell. He cares, Shianne. If you keep accepting my attention, you will have that big brute tied in a Gordian knot."

"I think you are being overly optimistic," Shianne declared.

"Believe me, honey. If I were in my brother's boots I would have ceased fighting the feelings long before now."

Her upturnd face and heart-shaped lips were all too tempting. Chad may have been plotting to assist Shianne in her quest to hog-tie Wade, but he had no qualms about portraying the eager admirer. Indeed, it could prove to be a most intriguing role. When his head came to hers, he found himself drowning in the taste of her, aching for things that had nothing to do with making Wade jealous.

Wade had the misfortune of glancing up while Chad and Shianne were engaged in what appeared to be a confidential conversation, and when Chad planted a very passionate kiss on Shianne's lips, right in midstream, Wade came unglued. Snarling, he snapped the whip over the horses, forcing them to hastily ford the stream. Wade couldn't wait to get the herd moving and find something to occupy that love-starved brother of his. Chad had only been under Shianne's spell for ten minutes, and already he was making bold advances!

With wry amusement, Shianne watched Wade sulk in his saddle for the remainder of the day. She prayed the steamy scene with Chad was the cause of his sour disposition. After all, one had to live on hope, Shianne reminded herself.

When a huge buffalo herd was spotted in the distance, it eroded what was left of Wade's tolerable disposition. Frantically he and the vaqueros surrounded the herd, attempting to hold them while two thousand shaggy beasts thundered over the rolling hill, heading straight toward the milling herd. If not for the cowboys' skills in herding and riding, they would have faced stampede, but experience and a helping of luck were with the trail riders. The buffaloes crossed the prairie, veering east to follow the creek.

After the buffaloes disappeared into the timber and Wade was satisfied the cattle had calmed down, he gave orders to move north. The drive proceeded with only the usual amount of difficulties until they prepared to cross Polecat Creek and enter Kansas. Half the herd had taken to the stream when swarms of disturbed hornets dropped down from their nests in the cottonwoods and thick brush to assault both man and beast.

Shianne yelped in pain when the buzzing pests attacked her. The vicious stings were causing huge welts to pop up all over her. The cowboys were crawling out of their shirts to rid themselves of the hornets. They waved their garments in the air, discouraging the second squadron of hornets from sinking their stingers in human flesh. Shianne considered the men's defense the most practical way to deal with the pain-inflicting pests, and she didn't care how indecent she appeared. This was an emergency, and she was in need of quick relief!

When Shianne tried to peel off her shirt, Wade was beside her in an instant. "Dammit, keep your clothes on!" he growled harshly. "Isn't it enough that you encourage Chad's advances without baring yourself to every man here!"

While Wade was clutching the front of her shirt to keep her in it, Shianne was tugging on the hem to worm out of it. The horror of having these malicious yellow jackets climbing into her garments with her set her into panic. When Shianne tore the shirt free and swatted at her buzzing assailants, Wade gasped in outrage. Instantly, he positioned himself between Lady Godiva and the rest of the cowboys.

"Confound it, woman, have you lost every ounce of modesty?" he hissed furiously.

"Yes," Shianne snapped back and then pounded another yellow-winged predator flat. Satisfied that she had given the vicious hornet exactly what she had gotten, she glanced up at Wade's flushed face. "My modesty flew off when the hornets descended."

When Shianne finally clutched her shirt around her, Wade's head swiveled around to see that they were sitting on the perimeter of chaos. The moment the bawling cattle set foot on solid ground they broke into a run to elude the swarming pests. Longhorns were tearing off in all directions, forcing the cowboys to give chase instead of nursing their wounds.

Shianne watched Wade, bare-chested, cursing a blue streak, bound off in quick pursuit. It seemed that it took very little to set off a herd of half-wild longhorns. Thunder and lightning could frighten them. A covey of quail flying up in front of them could start a stampede, not to mention a descending hoard of hornets.

It was several hours before the raucous herd was brought to heel. Finally, they began their quiet march across the open prairie that was splotched with sunflowers and golden rods. While Shianne hung back with the chuck wagon and supply wagon, Chad eased his mount up beside Wade who was riding point in front of the herd.

"I never thought I would be praising the appearance of hornets," he chuckled, his blue eyes dancing with deviltry.

Wade shot his brother a skeptical glance. "What the hell is that supposed to mean?" he grunted.

"She is gorgeous," Chad said point-blank. "From the top of her head to the tantalizing curve of her waist . . . and every luscious, well-sculptured inch in between."

Wade's hand snaked out to decrease the distance between him and his grinning brother. His clenched fists curled into the front of Chad's shirt, twisting it tightly around Peeping Tom's neck. "You were supposed to be keeping a close surveillance on the herd, *not* Shianne," he spat furiously.

Chad's grin was as wide as the Kansas prairie. Even though Wade was threatening to choke the life out of him, Chad remained undaunted. "I always keep one eye on the lady, just in case she might need to be rescued."

"You may be my brother, but by God, I won't stand aside and watch you seduce my wife. She's mine, Chad, and I'll fight you if I must to keep her!"

One by one, Chad unfastened Wade's fingers from the collar of his shirt. His gaze grew somber. "Then you better decide whether the feelings between the two of you are just another passing fancy or something permanent," he told Wade bluntly. "Occasionally, I have found myself in bed with a woman *before* you've had her, and sometimes I've wound up with a wench *after* you've had her. It didn't bother either of us then, and it shouldn't be bothering you now, not since you entered the institution of marriage and braced the doors wide open." Blue eyes clashed with smoldering green ones. "You better make up your mind what you are going to do with Shianne . . . and soon. That woman excites me, and before long I'm not going to care *who* I have to fight to sleep with her."

Snarling like a grizzly bear, Wade gouged his heels in

432

Galahad's ribs, sending him lunging into his swiftest gait. When Wade flew over the hill to scout out the trail ahead of them, Chad slumped back in his saddle. He was no longer certain if he was playing the role to aid Shianne's cause or if he meant every word he said. The plain-spoken remarks just seemed to trip off his tongue. Chad was beginning to wonder if he was suffering from the same affliction that was plaguing Wade.

Pensively, Chad twisted in the saddle, squinting to make out the trim form of the woman who rode beside the chuck wagon. Chad had no difficulty understanding why Wade was so fascinated with Shianne. She defied everything Wade *thought* he knew about women, and to make matters worse, Shianne had Wade stymied. Wade was of the belief that his interest in the dark-eyed beauty would fade, Chad thought to himself. But the many trials Wade and Shianne had faced had only strengthened the bond between them. Wade was like a man trapped in quicksand. He couldn't rescue himself; he could only sink deeper. Although Wade was as bullheaded as they came, he couldn't seem to forget Shianne or permit another man to charm her.

Just where did that leave him, Chad asked himself. When he had kissed Shianne, he hadn't been pretending to enjoy it. He delighted in every minute of it. A perplexed frown clouded his brow. Was he going to gracefully bow out if Wade decided he was playing for keeps? Or was he going to fight to take what rightfully belonged to Wade? Hell, he had seen so little happiness these past years that he found himself clinging to every pleasure-filled moment he spent peering into Shianne's expressive eyes. Chad knew Shianne didn't love him, not the way she cared for Wade, but that didn't keep him from wanting her the way a man longed for a beautiful woman.

Damn, he wasn't certain if he was in love with her either, but he was willing to bet that if he wasn't, it was one hell of an imitation. Given time and the right circumstances, his and Shianne's relationship might evolve into something special. . . .

"What's the matter with Wade?" Shianne questioned, dragging Chad from his contemplative deliberations. "He certainly looked as if he were riding off with the devil nipping at his heels. Is he anticipating trouble?" Her eyes shifted to Skeleton Creek, noting the bleached bones of the Wichita Indians who had perished from cholera. Did Wade expect what was left of the Indian band to harass them for driving cattle near the burial ground?

Chad smiled faintly, still wrestling with his own emotions. "I do believe he is, but I don't think it is what lies ahead of the herd that frustrates him. He is hounded by the torment a man faces when he is running from himself."

Shianne tossed Chad a muddled glance. "If that is your idea of an explanation, I'm afraid you've failed to *un*confuse me."

His tanned features wore a mischievous grin. "I said something to upset him," he confessed.

"Exactly what *did* you say?" Shianne prodded. Chad had that devilish look about him. She was prepared to bet her share of the profits from this cattle drive that Chad was intentionally needling his older brother.

His shoulder lifted nonchalantly. "Only that I looked at you with far more than brotherly affection," Chad told her flatly. "I insisted that he decide what is to become of this marriage and to do it quickly. I also reminded him that I have never been long on patience and informed him that I have even less where you are concerned." Chad stared straight into her wide eyes. "I

434

want what my brother has, and I don't really much care who knows it."

Shianne dragged her gaze away, focusing on some distant point. Chad's comment rattled her. The man never did give a whit about diplomacy. He said what he meant. Although Shianne was fond of Chad, even to the point of tolerating his straightforward remarks, he could never replace Wade in her eyes. Shianne was a one-man woman. If she couldn't have what she wanted, she would settle for nothing. She was not about to confuse the issue by encouraging Chad. The rough-edged cowboy, who had endured more than his fair share of misery, deserved a woman's love, but Shianne knew she wasn't the right one for him. In her eyes, Chad would always be standing in his brother's shadow, but she didn't have the heart to tell him that.

When Shianne did not respond, Chad chuckled softly. "Stubborn woman, you are as bad as my brother." His hand drifted across the pensive frown that puckered her exquisite features. "Don't worry, sweetheart. I won't force you into anything you don't want to do, not even for the sake of making Wade jealous. He'll come around after we light a few fires under him." His expression changed to a rakish grin. "I'll supply the fuel, and you provide the flame. He can't hold out forever." Chad paused, waiting for Shianne to lift her eyes to his. "But if by some miracle he doesn't, you know where you can turn for consolation. Make no mistake, it won't be compassion that compels me to hold you in my arms. I won't lie to you, pretty lady. You arouse me. I want you in my bed, and if I ever get you there, I'll take my time loving you the way you deserved to be loved, slow and easy . . . all night long."

As Chad eased his steed away, Shianne gulped hard. There were times when she didn't care to know what

435

Chad was thinking, and this was one of those times. The man never hesitated to speak his mind, and it flustered Shianne to hear his thoughts put to tongue.

Her gaze flew to the silhouette of the man who had just reappeared. Shianne was overwhelmed by the insane urge to gallop into Wade's arms, whether he wanted her there or not. She ached to tell him how she felt before she did something crazy like turning to Chad. Oh, why had she fallen in love with a man whose heart was encased in ice?

Even at a distance Shianne could feel Wade's penetrating gaze. What was he thinking, she wondered. Had Chad's ultimatum annoyed him or had it actually come as a relief? Dejectedly, Shianne dropped her head, refusing to be held captive by Wade's probing green eyes. If she had any sense at all, she would ride west to find Maman-ti's village and beg a potion from the medicine man that would rout Wade from her mind forever. It would take powerful medicine, Shianne thought glumly. Wade's taproot ran so deep that it would probably require surgery to extract him from her thoughts.

As the days dragged on into a week, Shianne had serious reservations about Chad's overzealous ploy to make Wade jealous. She was sure Chad's overt display of affection was doing more harm than good. If the end result was to bring Wade closer, the tactic had failed miserably. Wade had shut her out of his life and avoided her like the plague. He seemed too preoccupied with the cattle to give her notice. Either that or he had decided to back away and allow Chad to take his place with her, Shianne concluded. That wasn't helping matters one iota. Chad was becoming bolder by the day, and Shianne was becoming uneasier by the minute.

Wade was always the first to rouse in the morning. He woke the men who had not been on night watch. Before the breakfast meal was served, Wade would ride ahead to scout the distance to the next water hole. Although he pushed himself to the limits, going without food and sleep, he didn't press the longhorns. He had managed the feat of keeping the cattle under restraint without allowing them to know it. Each step the steers took was voluntary. They never knew they were being guided in the direction Wade wanted them to go.

From his position as point rider, Wade would signal the men with the wave of his hat, giving them direction to water or away from the skirting of timber where the cattle might wander and delay a day's drive of twelve miles.

While Wade distracted himself with the cattle, Shianne dedicated herself to helping with the cooking. The chuck wagon was heaping with a five gallon keg of sourdough, sacks of flour, cans of coffee, beans and dried fruits. Her day centered around preparing and cleaning up after meals, and Shianne worked from sunup to sundown. However, her remedy of distraction was not entirely effective. She still found herself staring after Wade, watching the way his shirt strained across his broad shoulders, admiring the way his chaps hugged the sinewed columns of his legs, listening to the methodic jingle of his spurs when he ambled across camp. Occasionally she found herself wishing to take the red bandana that was tied around his neck and strangle him with it for being so distant and remote, but mostly she wanted to remove the kerchief and every other article of clothing and embark on a sensuous journey into starry worlds.

When the herd traversed swollen streams, Shianne

always tensed with concern, fearing Wade's bold daring would bring him catastrophe. The day he was dragged under by a swift flowing current in his attempt to rescue floundering cattle, Shianne very nearly lost her composure and chased after him, aching to blurt out her confession before he drowned, but Chad had grabbed her arm and held her firm, cautioning her not to smother Wade with affection. It took every ounce of self-control to stand her ground. When Juan pulled Wade to safety, Shianne collapsed in relief and vowed never again to watch one of Wade's death-defying feats.

Since Shianne had experience in nursing, Wade put her in charge of the medicinal supplies, which he had packed in the wagon. Yet, Wade scowled each time one of the cowboys came to her for liniment to ease the aches and sprains. When she massaged away the sore muscles, Wade would stalk off, not to return until Shianne had removed her healing hands from a man's aching back or sprained knee.

One evening after the men had confined the herd to a compact circle and bedded them down, Wade strode up to Shianne. All expression was disguised behind his businesslike facade, the same one he had been wearing since they had caught up with the herd.

"There seems to be a rash of strains and sprains of late. I doubt there is any liniment left, but if there is, I could use some," he announced.

Shianne strode over to retrieve the supplies and offered the soothing salve to Wade. Although the task was difficult, she managed to remain as calm and collected as he was, but on the inside she was a bundle of frazzled nerves, wanting him so desperately that it made her ache.

A disappointed frown clung to his brow. "Don't I get to enjoy the same treatment the rest of the men have been receiving from those miraculous hands of yours?" he snorted sarcastically. "Chad and Juan have beaten a path to the chuck wagon every night. I have yet to see you slap the liniment in their hand and shoo them away to nurse their own aches and pains."

One delicate brow arched. Shianne regarded the brawny cowboy for a curious moment. "They were eager for my services. I didn't think you would be. You have taken a wide berth around me for more than a week. I had begun to fear I had contracted leprosy, and you were attempting to avoid affliction."

The gold flecks that rimmed his green eyes glittered in the waning light. Wade had been testing himself, attempting to control his instinctive need for Shianne, allowing Chad the chance to win Shianne's affection since the man seemed so starved for it. The week-long experiment had been the worst seven days of his life. His self-denial had done nothing to sweeten his disposition. His dark mood seeped into his tone when he spoke.

"I thought you were too busy flaunting about your court of eager beaux to notice what the hell I was doing, princess," he smirked.

Shianne tossed her head, sending the wave of ebony rippling down her back. "A woman learns to tell who wants her companionship and who doesn't. You, Wade Burdett, have been as unapproachable as a coiled rattlesnake."

When Shianne wheeled around to march away, Wade hooked her around the waist, pulling her back against his hard chest. The feel of his masculine body meshed into hers unchained sensations that had been carefully held in check for more days than she cared to count. Shianne swore she would have wilted at his feet if he had not clamped an arm around her.

"There was a time when you confessed that you

439

resented being a woman," he growled against her ear. "Obviously you outgrew that phase when you progressed from maidenhood into womanhood. Now you seem to delight in being the queen bee in this buzzing hive of men. If I have kept my distance it's only because I keep finding myself at the back of your long line of admirers. This is *not* where a husband likes to find himself."

Slowly, Shianne turned in his arms, braving a glance into those jade green eyes. "I didn't make the rules, Wade. You did. I only adapted to them and attempted to make the best of a difficult situation. This marriage has served its purpose for you. If you want it dissolved, then do so." She inhaled a deep breath and plunged on before she lost her nerve. "I promised you that afternoon in the cave that I would no longer cling to my old-fashioned beliefs. You wanted your freedom, and I gave it. If you want even more freedom, take it."

Her chin tilted to a proud angle. It hurt to voice the lie, but Shianne masked the pain of having her heart twist in her chest. "I am a survivor, Wade. I held our ranch together when other young women my age were primping and prancing about, their heads filled with nothing more than whimsical dreams. They were fretting about what they would wear to the next social affair, while I was laboring over my father's ledgers, wondering if and when he would ever come home.

"Then I found myself pushed aside when you waltzed in to assume command of the K Bar, and I endured hell on earth when Haden took me captive. I feared he would rape me, and I would not be able to live with myself. At least I was spared that humiliating disgrace." Shianne could not resist trailing her index finger over his bronzed features. It had become habit with her, one not easily broken. "Although I thought you and I had something special, something strong and

440

enduring, I do not intend to fall apart and beg you to stay when you decide to go."

"If I should decide to go, will you run to Chad?" Wade laughed bitterly. "God knows you won't have far to run. He's been your constant shadow. You know as well as I do that he would prefer to be as close as two people could get when it comes to you. As blunt as he is, I doubt that a day has gone by without Chad inviting you to do more than while away your idle time in conversation."

The faintest hint of a smile traced Shianne's lips. Her brow tilted slightly. "I don't think I married the wrong Burdett," she murmured. "I care for Chad, as if he were the brother I never had, but I'm not right for him. I'm not exactly certain what kind of woman he needs, but I don't think I could make him happy because I can't give him my heart. Chad needs to be reassured with deeds and words after the ordeals he has suffered. He needs someone who will love him with every breath she takes, the way . . ." Shianne clamped down on her tongue before she said: *the way I love you*.

"The way . . . what?" Wade questioned, his eyes probing hers.

"The way a woman should love the man she cherishes more than life," she said quietly. "Chad deserves that. I only pray one day the right woman will come along."

For a moment they stood there, inches apart, staring at each other. Shianne willed him to clutch her to him and kiss away the aching loneliness that tormented her, but Wade set her aside and walked off, leaving her heart to shatter like fragile crystal.

Mechanically, Shianne went back to her task of preparing the evening meal of sourdough biscuits, meat and gravy. To her surprise Wade returned ten minutes later, smelling of liniment and wearing the

441

same poker faced expression that had claimed his features since he took control of the herd.

"Chad and Juan are going to tend my duties for a few days. We are going to Wichita to purchase you some decent clothes," he announced abruptly. "Blake would be furious to find that you have been traipsing about in these baggy rags for nearly two months."

Shianne's mouth dropped open. Wade was taking her away, granting them privacy? For what purpose? She had the feeling a new wardrobe was not Wade's only motive. The man was too complex not to have at least a dozen reasons for doing whatever it was he was contemplating. Was this to be their hour of reckoning? Was he going to insist that they go their separate ways as soon as they set foot in Wichita? Or did he intend to put her on a stagecoach and ship her to Abilene while he accompanied the herd?

Since Shianne had nothing to take with her it was a simple matter of climbing onto Delgado's back to prepare for their journey. She sat tensely in the saddle as they rode northeast, wondering if she could control her composure when Wade announced his intentions of letting her go—permanently. If Wade's rigid position on the back of his horse was any indication of how a man looked before he sent his wife away forever, she was as good as gone. The tension between them was so thick it couldn't be cracked with a bull whip, Shianne mused despairingly. Soon it would be all over but the crying, and Shianne would have to find a private place to fall apart.

Juan sank down beside Chad, steadying his plate in his mending gun hand. His amused grin followed Shianne and Wade until they disappeared over the hill. "The *hombre* has had a burr under his saddle all week. I

442

wondered how long he was going to allow you to fawn over the señora."

"Me?" Chad hooted. "*You* are the one who stuck to her like a bee to honey. You never had so many aches and pains until Shianne showed up in camp. Suddenly a massage became one of your nightly rituals."

Juan did not rise to the taunt. What could he say in defense? He cherished Shianne's attention, and he didn't much care what excuse he employed to get it. She was the one bright spot in the mundane days of herding the cattle north.

"I greatly admire the señora," he admitted. "When I was working for that bastard, Haden Reems, I stood aside, hesitating to defy him. The day Haden dropped the lady over the ledge of the cavern, I wanted to shoot him down in his tracks, but I didn't." His voice was laced with self-resentment. "Shianne fought him, even against impossible odds. She is a woman of incredible courage and inner strength." Juan sighed heavily and stared at the contents of his plate. "She made me feel half a man when she valiantly attempted to save you and Wade that day. After Haden dragged her back to the hacienda and threatened to do her bodily harm, I could no longer tolerate the man I had become. All of Haden's money could not soothe my conscience.

"I had turned my back when Haden beat you within an inch of your life, and I stood paralyzed when he used the señora to get to you and your brother." He glanced up at Chad and then returned his attention to the heaping plate of meat and gravy. "But I could endure no more of the man's dastardly deeds. When Haden vented his wrath on Shianne, I couldn't step aside, not again, not when I, too, loathed Haden Reems. He had gone too far too many times." Juan flexed his crippled hand. The bitter memory came back to torment him. "I tried to stop Haden from abusing the señora, but he used her as his armor and got the best of me.

"When the señora returned to the trail herd she came to me to thank *me* for trying to rescue her from Haden's grasp." Juan sadly shook his head. "I was too humiliated to approach her, but *she* sought me out, voicing her appreciation, calling me friend."

Chad stared into the sunset, remembering the day Shianne had given him back his pride. He had been a man poisoned by bitterness and void of self-esteem, but Shianne had endeared herself to him when he would have built an indestructible wall between them. "There is something special about her," he agreed softly. "My brother is a lucky man. Shianne has—and will always—defend him, even with her life. I just hope Wade comes to his senses and realizes what he stands to lose before Shianne gives him up for a lost cause. Because I will make damned certain he won't have a second chance with her."

Juan chuckled quietly. "You are not the only man who would be eager to satisfy that high-spirited *ninfa.* I'm sure the *hombre* will long live to regret giving up his rights to her. *Caramba!* He would be every kind of fool."

Chad snickered at Juan's emphatic tone. *"Sí, amigo.* He would become the world's biggest imbecile, and I have made it a point to mention the fact to him on more than one occasion."

"I shall inform him that I agree with you, just as soon as he returns from Wichita," Juan decided. "I have come to feel great respect for the *hombre* but sometimes he can be mule-headed."

"Amen to that," Chad chimed in. "There are times when my big brother makes *me* look the saint, even when I can do no better than tattered wings and a tarnished halo."

As they settled down to their meal, Chad could not

help but wonder what Wade intended by this trip to Wichita. Part of him was rooting for his brother to commit himself to Shianne, and another part of him wished Wade would let her go. Shianne was a remarkable young woman. All she had endured was proof of her incorrigible strength and willful determination. He had never met a woman quite like this sultry beauty, and if Chad ever had visions of settling down, he knew exactly where he would wish to pitch his tent. Right smack on Shianne's doorstep.

Why the blazes did Shianne have to be his big brother's wife, he asked himself resentfully. If it were any other man besides Wade, Chad would never have waited this long to take what he wanted, even if Shianne were reluctant. Well, he could say one thing for his brother, Chad thought as he munched on his meal. Wade had a hell of a lot more self-control than Chad possessed. If Shianne were Chad's wife he would have seen to it that she had done more than sleep when they bedded down for the night. There were far more arousing things to do when one was lying beneath a blanket of stars, and those things had nothing to do with closing one's eyes and drifting off in dreams. Chad would have been *living* his dreams, not conjuring them up in his sleep!

Chapter 22

The ride into Wichita was a silent one. Shianne was mentally preparing herself for Wade's announcement that there was nothing left worth saving in their marriage. She had the premonition that was what this journey was all about, even if Wade claimed it was to purchase a new set of clothes.

As they trotted into the town that was strung out along a bluff on the Arkansas River, Shianne sighed appreciatively. If nothing else, she could anticipate a warm bath and a soft bed. Never again would she take the simple luxuries of life for granted.

Wichita set on the sight of what had been the village of the Wichita Indians before they were relocated in Indian Territory. Shianne could not help but wonder if this boom town that was established to accommodate cattle drovers hadn't been a mite hastily thrown together. Her gaze surveyed the grocery and hardware shops. Then she assessed the saloons, restaurants and two modest hotels. As of yet, the town had very little lure, but it was a welcomed change after crossing Indian lands.

Wade smiled when he noticed the way Shianne was surveying her surroundings. "The town lacks sophistication," he admitted. "But before long it will be a thriving community. Once the railroad arrives, Texas cattle will make this a prosperous town. Although you are accustomed to more luxuries, I don't think you will find complaint with the room."

"I have grown accustomed to little or nothing," Shianne promptly reminded him. "I'm sure the hotel will seem a palace compared to sleeping on the ground beside the creatures that crawl about in one's sleeping bag." She gestured toward her battered garments. "And I will not quibble over fashion as long as my new set of clothes does not resemble these oversized breeches."

When they dismounted, Wade took Shianne's arm to guide her into one of the crude log buildings. Shianne found little selection in the way of clothing. Ready-made clothes to fit her voluptuous figure were rare if not nonexistent. Even in San Antonio she found it necessary to take alterations. In Wichita there were even fewer garments her size, and no one available to ensure proper fittings. When she reappeared from the dressing room in one of the two garments she found to fit her petite figure, Wade's eyes bulged from their sockets.

"Is that the best to be had?" he croaked. His gaze flooded over the diving neckline that exposed so much bosom that he feared Shianne would spill from the confines of gingham if she dared to inhale a deep breath.

"The other garment is no better," Shianne declared, tugging self-consciously at the lacy pink bodice.

"I never thought I would hear myself say this, but I wish you were a little less endowed," Wade grunted.

Shianne clenched her fists on her hips and glared at him. "I apologize that I do not come with detachable parts that can be removed and stashed in a trunk," she

447

sniffed sarcastically. "I cannot help the way I am constructed!"

"And that is the bittersweet irony of it," Wade muttered and then choked on his breath when Shianne drew herself up and nearly split the seam of the bodice. The way she looked was almost sinful. It would make a man want to commit the crime of groping! Heaving a peevish sigh, Wade unfolded his tall frame from the chair. "You could cause a riot in that gown. I fear I will spend the entire evening wondering how many hooligans are contemplating stealing you away from me."

"Oh, for heaven sake!" Shianne snapped irritably. "You talk as if every man in the territory has his sights set on me."

"Don't they?" Wade snorted derisively. He stared at the provocative display of bosom. "You attracted a mob of cowboys even while you were garbed in men's clothes. I hate to venture a guess at the disturbance you will cause when the rest of the men see your ample assets."

When they purchased the two dresses and strode outside, Wade expelled another agitated breath. The man who passed them on the street nearly wrenched his neck to gape long after he had crossed paths with Shianne. "You see? What did I tell you," he grumbled grouchily.

When Shianne flung him a withering glance, Wade shook his head in dismay. "Dammit, woman, sometimes I wonder if you are unaware of how attractive you truly are. Men don't gawk at you because you have an unsightly wart on the end of your nose. You have a body that would halt a stampede and a face that is . . ." Wade paused to locate a word to describe her beauty. "Well, to tell the truth, you are positively enchanting. You are all too easy on a man's eye, which is fine and dandy for you and your leering admirers, but it is damned hard on me!" he exploded.

Shianne scoffed at the compliments he had begrudgingly offered. She was certain that the long days Wade had spent in solitude had warped his brain. "How is it that you manage to blame me for all your misfortune? If you would look deeper you would realize that the only strain on you is the direct result of your own irascible disposition."

When Shianne inhaled an angry breath, the bystanders in the street waited an anxious moment. Wade, noting all the attention Shianne was receiving, did an about-face. Without another word of debate he stormed back to the store to purchase a shawl. In less than a minute he returned to drape it over Shianne's shoulders—backwards—thereby covering the daring display of bosom.

"There," he said with a satisfied nod. "And don't take it off until we are in our hotel room. I would prefer to enjoy my evening meal without having to gun a man down for ogling you."

As Wade hustled her down the street, Shianne rolled her eyes in disbelief. She was in love with a maniac! Wade didn't want her, but he didn't want another man looking at her. If he knew how ridiculously he was behaving, he might have laughed at himself. No, Shianne decided, giving the matter second consideration. Wade no longer laughed, and he rarely smiled. He had turned into a sourpuss. She could only conclude that the strain of having her underfoot for so many months had finally worn on him. He was out of sorts, and he probably would be until he deposited her on a stagecoach and sent her north to Abilene.

Deciding it best not to argue with a lunatic, Shianne kept the shawl on backwards during their meal, but when they secured a room for the night, she doffed the shawl and ambled over to the mirror. She gasped at the

449

reflection that stared back at her. Her hair lay about her in wild tangles, and her face was deeply tanned from the long hours she had spent in the sun. To make matters worse, she could have passed for one of the Calico Queens in a saloon with her form-fitting gown.

She looked a sight! Wade was concerned that men were staring at her with lust in their eyes? Shianne laughed at the absurdity. No doubt, the stares directed toward her were provoked by her wild appearance.

Wade was of a different opinion. To him, Shianne appeared recklessly radiant. He never had much use for prim and proper women who would not dare to set foot outside for fear the wind might muss their coiffure. Shianne never had to fret about her hair or her appearance. Her natural beauty always shined through, whether she was at her best or worst. There was no way around it. Shianne was simply bewitching with those dark, expressive eyes, shiny raven hair and curvaceous figure.

"Come sit down, princess," he ordered, gesturing toward the vacant chair.

Shianne tensed. This was it—the beginning of the end. Wade was going to suggest that they dissolve their marriage. Mutely, she walked across the room and parked herself in the seat across from him. Her long lashes drifted up to peer into Wade's somber expression. She felt as if a collection of butterflies were rioting in her stomach. *Calm yourself,* Shianne ordered sternly.

Holding Shianne's absolute attention, Wade drew in a deep breath and formulated his thoughts. The time of reckoning had come, and he was having difficulty selecting the right words. "Shianne, I have not been satisfied with the way things have been going between us," he declared. "There comes a time in a man's life when he has to decide what he wants and to determine

450

what he must sacrifice to have it."

Shianne waited, her nerves taut. Wade was trying to let her down gently. Her downcast eyes were pinned to her hands, which were clenched so tightly in her lap that her knuckles were turning white.

Suddenly, Wade was on his feet, pacing the confines of the room. "I have been struggling with many conflicting emotions since I made you my wife. To be honest, I never considered myself the marrying kind. I have been skeptical of lasting love. Consequently, I wouldn't have bet a plugged nickel that any emotion between a man and woman could withstand the test of time. For the past month, I have awakened each day, becoming more and more dissatisfied with the man I am . . . or at least the man I *was* before you came along."

A muddled frown furrowed Shianne's brow. This conversation was not veering in the direction Shianne had anticipated. Indeed, it seemed Wade was talking in circles. My, but he had suddenly become long-winded. Shianne was too impatient to allow him to ramble on all night. She wanted to hear him say there was nothing about her that enticed him to remain within the confines of marriage, no matter how loose the ties between them. When he had blurted out the announcement, she would wait until he walked away to cry her heart out. She was going to feel much better when she had vented her pent up emotions. Wade was prolonging the agony, and Shianne was not certain she could endure the wait.

"If there is some point to this soliloquy, I wish you would spit it out," she grumbled.

Wade's shoulders slumped. "Dammit, Shae, don't rush me. This isn't easy!"

When Shianne piped down, Wade regathered his thoughts and stumbled on, feeling more uncomfortable by the minute. "This stormy relationship between us has evoked feelings in me that I have had difficulty dealing with. I feel as if I never really lost you, even when other men have been vying for your attention. Yet, I don't feel as if I ever really had you either." Wade shook his head, wondering if Shianne could comprehend what he was trying to say. "It is as if you belong to me in the physical sense, and yet, I have no right to make any demands on you. Each time I have tried to exert my position as your husband, I feel the hypocrite."

Shianne shot Wade an aggravated glance. For all his talking he still was getting very little said, she thought acrimoniously.

"My parents had what I considered to be a tolerable marriage. Love may have entered into it in the beginning, but in the end there was little left except a habit neither of them felt they had the right to break. They merely shared the same space and very little else. Because of that cool, sometimes strained relationship, I believed it was better to remain free and unattached. I took pleasure where I found it and then turned elsewhere when the feelings I felt for a woman began to dwindle to nothing more than bland tolerance."

Now Wade was going to compare *their* marriage to that of his parents, Shianne speculated. Stiffly, she sat on her chair, vowing not to decompose right before his eyes. She would hold out until Wade left her alone. Then she would spill the sea of tears that was mounting behind this collapsing dam of self-control.

"I believed that, in time, you and I would drift apart. I thought the fascination would wither and die." Wade stuffed his hands in his pockets and strode back to tower over Shianne. "Well, it hasn't," he blurted out, almost as if he resented the admission. "Every time Chad or Juan go near you I want to strangle the both of

452

them, especially Chad because he cares too much for you to even grant his own brother space!"

Her lashes swept up. A stunned expression captured her features. "Are you trying to say you do care about me, Wade?"

"Care?" Wade tossed back his head and laughed at her modest description. "Woman, you occupy the very core of my heart. If I had you surgically removed, I would be left with a hole the size of Texas. Blast it, Shae, are you still so naive that you can't tell when a man loves you? I'm frustrated by my own philosophy, one that has become grossly outdated in the light of the potent emotions that sizzle between us." Wade threw up his hands in a gesture of futility. "For the love of mercy, woman, if I *cared* any more than I already do, I'm not certain I could survive it! These loose strings on our marriage are very nearly choking me!"

Shianne blinked, and her mouth fell open wide enough for a pheasant to roost. This was not at all what she had expected. Indeed, she had been sitting in her chair, prepared to hear the exact opposite.

Frustrated by her silence, Wade went back to his pacing. "Ironic, isn't it? I offered you free reins in this marriage, and you delighted in your freedom. Suddenly, *I* am the one resenting the independence I have no desire to exercise. I want no other woman. I could have killed Haden in cold blood for abusing you. I detest my own brother for fawning over you, and I want to punch Juan in the nose every time he melts beneath your disarming smiles. I hate myself for being so cussed possessive, but damned if I can stop what I'm feeling when another man looks at you with something akin to lust!"

Wade wheeled around and stomped toward his speechless wife. "Well, go ahead. Laugh. Get it over with. You don't want any strings. You're satisfied with the way things are, and *I'm* the one who sounds like a simpering fool, begging you to remain loyal to one man—the very man who has been harping about no strings from the beginning." Wade let his breath out in a rush. "I stuck my foot in my mouth, and I have yet to adjust to the taste of leather. I deserve exactly what I'm getting," he finished deflatedly.

"You most certainly do," Shianne concurred, beaming in satisfaction.

She was offering not one ounce of sympathy for his plight, Wade thought resentfully. Not that he expected any. He had encountered the one woman he couldn't forget. He had met his match and had emerged the loser. This tender battle with this Texas temptress bruised his heart, and Wade doubted that the wound would ever heal. Why shouldn't Shianne gloat? he asked himself. She had taken a reckless rogue and turned him wrong side out. No other woman had been able to accomplish that feat.

Turning away, Wade called her attention to his backside. "Go ahead, kick me. Ridicule me. You owe me for the hell I've put you through."

Shianne gave her head a negative shake. "No thank you. I think we have hurt each other enough. I have a less violent form of punishment in mind."

Then it came, that flareup of mischief in those fathomless eyes. What form of torture had she conjured up for him? No doubt she had an endless repertoire to call upon, considering her association with her Indian cousins. After all, that was what Indians did for a living—sit around and dream up the most unusual and effective brands of torture. Wade didn't much care what she did to him. He wasn't going to feel better until he paid his penance.

"Name it," he ordered courageously. "And I will subject myself to it."

One delicate brow shot up. "You will submit to my wildest whim, no matter what it is?" Shianne taunted unmercifully.

Wade was becoming impatient. "Hell, I said I would, didn't I? Now what the devil is it to be? The suspense is killing me."

"Take off your clothes," Shianne demanded abruptly.

Wade did a double take. "What?"

"You heard me. Drop 'em."

A wary frown puckered his thick brows. Hesitantly, he unbuttoned his shirt. "What is it you intend, witch? Do you plan to tie my garments together and lynch me? A mite drastic, even for you, isn't it?"

Shianne crossed her arms under her breasts and tapped her foot. "You are sorely testing my patience...."

Sighing heavily, Wade shrugged off his shirt and cast it aside. When he had unfastened his breeches, he stepped out of them and tossed them atop his shirt. Wearing nothing but a quizzical frown, he watched Shianne point a dainty finger toward the bed.

Another dubious expression clouded his features. "What the hell do you ..."

"Now lie down," Shianne cut him off before he could voice another question.

Begrudgingly, Wade did as she commanded, but he was befuddled. He didn't have the foggiest notion what fiendish thought was whipping through her mind.

"I truly am disappointed," he mocked. "I expected more originality from you. This is one of Haden's tactics—staking a man out stark naked...."

His voice trailed off when Shianne unfastened the dainty buttons on the front of her gown, exposing even more bosom to his hungry gaze. Wade was all eyes. He watched in pained torment as Shianne left the top of her gown gaping in a most provocative manner.

So this was to be her brand of torment, he realized dismally. Having and having not was a fate worse than death. Shianne was going to reveal bits and pieces of her curvaceous body to him, allowing him to behold what she would not allow him to caress.

Her index finger followed the placket of the dress, taking his eyes on the most arousing of journeys. While Wade held his breath, Shianne shed the upper portion of her gown, allowing him to devour her with his eyes and nothing more. When she placed her hands on her waist to push the drooping garment over her hips, Wade's heart tore loose and galloped around his chest.

Lord, how much of this maddening provocation did she think he could endure before he was overwhelmed by the urge to ravish her? That was it! Shianne intended to tempt him beyond resistance, and when he made a move toward her, she would snatch up his pistol and blow him to smithereens. What torture could be worse than dying while he was aching to have her, knowing he would never be able to satisfy this craving before he breathed his last breath?

As the dress drifted into a pool at her feet, Wade groaned in unholy torment. "I would prefer a dagger through the heart to this. It would be less painful."

She walked gracefully toward the night stand to snuff the lantern. Her sylphlike movement created a spell of seduction that excelled any experience Wade could name. When Shianne floated toward the window to pull back the curtains, Wade strangled on his breath. Her enticing silhouette was bathed in the silvery light that sprinkled through the pane. Moonbeams danced like diamonds in the flowing waterfall of hair that lay about her like a dark cloak. Her skin appeared as smooth as satin, and Wade moaned as the gnawing hunger overcame him. She was the image of the arousing, elusive goddess every man longed to possess, if only for that one sublime moment.

Shianne came to stand beside the bed. Her dark eyes skimmed over the sinewed mass of muscle and flesh, admiring the hard, well-proportioned length of him. A tender smile caressed her shadowed features. "You have promised to make no complaint, no matter what I demanded of you," she reminded him in a throaty voice that caused excited tremors to scale his spine. "I want you to compensate for all the good nights of loving we have missed these past months . . . for all the times my stubborn pride has kept me from dashing into your arms. I want you to erase the endless nights I was forced to sleep beside Haden, hating him and loving you with every part of my being."

Sinking down beside him, Shianne reached out to thread her fingers through his hair. She inhaled the enticing scent of the man who had become her world. "I can forgive you for using me to get to Haden and to elicit aid from the Owl Prophet. Forgiving you was easy, my love." She bent, her lips whispering over his sensuous mouth. "But forgetting you will take forever. I don't think I could ever outlive this love I feel for you. It has grown so strong and compelling that it has taken command of my heart and soul."

Her gentle touch and quiet words melted bone and muscle. Wade became one of the weightless feathers in the mattress. He had expected the most hideous form of torture known to man—a foretaste of heaven before being thrust into the jaws of hell. Instead he was granted more than a glimpse of paradise. Lord, he didn't deserve her love, but Shianne had graciously offered him a second chance. He wasn't going to botch it up, not this time, not for all the treasure that lay buried in the cavern in Texas.

"Chad knew how I felt about you the first day I met

him," Shianne explained as her adventurous hands tracked across his shoulders. "He purposely set out to make you jealous, even though I feared nothing could affect a man who was so cynical of everlasting love."

Wade laughed softly. His fingers stroked the wild raven locks that fell across his chest. "I think my brother's pleasure from needling me was twofold. He was thoroughly enjoying the excuse of spending so much time with you, and I resented every minute of it." His expression grew solemn. His eyes turned a darker shade of green. "Shae, I thought I could walk out of your life, and it would be best for both of us; but I want to be around to watch you blossom and grow more lovely with each passing day. I want to see every change you undergo. Even if I managed to walk away, I don't think I could ever stop loving you. It has become as natural as breathing. You are every step I take, a part of me time has not been able to erase."

"I pray you will never stop loving me," she breathed against his cheek. "I can't go back to those days when I stood alone. You have become my reason for living, Wade. I would endure most anything just to have you love me as much as I love you."

Wade's heart swelled until it very nearly burst. God, how he adored this dark-eyed nymph. She was like a kaleidoscope of emotions, ever-changing, in constant motion. She affected him with her many moods, touching off a chain reaction of sensations that never seemed to cease before one feeling blended to create another.

Shianne stretched out beside him, her shapely form molding itself to his muscular contours. "Love me, Wade," she commanded. "It is the only retribution I seek. Love me for all the empty yesterdays, for the nights I longed to hold you and never let you go. . . ."

Like a rousing lion, Wade crouched beside her. His

muscles bulged and then relaxed as he hovered only inches away. Wade peered down into that exquisite face that had haunted his dreams, and he sighed appreciatively. He had seen many women whom he had considered pretty and others he deemed comely, but Shianne was absolutely exquisite, every well-sculptured inch of her. She was the kind of woman a man could be content to gaze upon for hours on end, absorbing her dazzling beauty.

Reverently, he trailed his index finger over her creamy cheek, mesmerized by her flawless features. His eyes worshipped her, while his hands caressed. He was satisfied just to map the landscape of silky flesh, to give and take the pleasure of touching her.

It seemed inconceivable that she loved him. He had done very little to earn the respect and devotion of this free-spirited nymph. Did she hold him in the same regard she held that bronzed-skinned bodyguard who followed after her like an obedient puppy? God, how envious he had been of the mystical oracle of the Kiowas and Comanches. Wade wanted to be Shianne's champion, the invincible knight who galloped through her childhood dreams.

He would give Shianne every reason to respect him, Wade vowed to himself as his loving caresses wandered over her pliant flesh. "I'm going to love you, Shae, like I've never loved another woman. You are not like the rest of them. I know there will be other men who will covet what I have come to treasure most, but you will have no reason to turn away, for I intend to love you with that precious emotion I have offered no one else." His lips joined hers while his sensitive caresses weaved a spell of magic upon her skin. "Let me show you what I have been saving for the one woman who is bold enough to earn my devotion and gentle enough to create lasting love, even when I was skeptical of its existence."

Shianne trembled beneath a kiss potent enough to melt the moon and leave it dripping on the stars. Wade had kissed her many times but never quite like this. He had touched her before but never with such patient tenderness. He treated her as if she were made of fragile crystal. His hands drifted ever so lightly over the peaks of her breasts before swirling across her stomach. His palms splayed across her thighs and then retraced the rousing path, leaving a million fires burning in the wake of his loving touch.

A moan of pleasure rippled through the silence. The tantalizing wave that engulfed her was not a violent tremor but rather a quiet quake that began to crumble the foundation of each and every emotion. His touch was like the tide rolling onto a sandy shore, erasing all that had come before. Over and over again, his skillful hands glided across her flesh, eliciting one ardent response after another. His lovemaking was creating a unique feeling of pleasure, the tenderest, most satisfying brand of rapture.

Shianne's womanly body roused by degrees. It was as if she were ascending a staircase. Each new level brought yet another dimension of ecstasy. She didn't want him to stop. She reveled in the erotic sensations he was offering. Yet, the burning ache grew so intense that Shianne became impatient to appease the gnawing craving that granted no peace. Passion bordered on the edge of insanity. It instilled a fierce need that his intimate fondling could not satiate. She wanted to feel his hair-matted flesh upon hers, to feel his heart beating in accelerated rhythm with hers. She wanted to be a living, breathing part of him—one heart, one soul existing in rapture's paradise.

"Wade?" she begged breathlessly, drawing him nearer.

He lifted himself above her, his body taut with unfulfilled desire. The dark fire in her eyes lured him closer. He could see the expression of his own emotions, a need so fierce and consuming that nothing could satisfy it except the purest form of passionate love. His body moved upon hers, glorying in the sensations of possessing and being possessed.

Wade would dare to love only once in his life. He was thankful that Shianne had surrendered to no other man. The thought of this gorgeous vixen lying in someone else's arms sliced his soul. He knew it was selfish for him not to allow her to know other men as he had known other women, but he couldn't bear to think of his precious angel being touched by another human's hands. Shianne belonged to him. He had been the first, and he prayed he would be the last.

His pensive contemplations diverged when Shianne arched toward him, whispering her need and her love. Wade's mind ceased to function when ineffable sensations swamped and buffeted him. His body was moving on its own accord, seeking ultimate depths of intimacy. The words he had offered no other woman tumbled from his tongue, quivering with genuine emotion. It seemed so right, so natural to offer his confession to this raven-haired temptress. She was his love, his life, the answer to an elusive dream.

When a heart-stopping tremor shook him, Wade groaned in sweet agony. His body instinctively surged toward hers, clinging to that blissful moment that held time suspended. Emotions poured through every part of his being, followed by soul-quaking aftershocks that destroyed composure.

"It's like flying into the sun," Wade breathed in awe.

Shianne giggled giddishly as she looped her arms around his neck. "And even with your eyes closed, could you see the splinters of white-hot light slashing

461

holes in the darkness?"

Wade drew back, his eyes wide with wonder. "Did you see them too?" he rasped, his voice heavy with the aftereffects of passion.

She gave her head a small nod and then lifted a delicate brow. "I thought you sorely resented the description of such intimacy. Is this the same man who crept into my boudoir one night so long ago, insisting that passion for passion's sake needed no labels or comparisons?"

Wade grinned sheepishly. "I've broadened my horizons since I blurted out that narrow-minded remark." Suddenly, Wade rolled away to stare at the moonlit sky that was framed by the open window. "Shae, are you certain you love me?" he couldn't help but ask. "You were so naive, so innocent of men. How can you know what love *is* when you have not been around enough to know what love is *not?* How long will it be before you begin to wonder how it would feel to experience another man's lovemaking? I don't want another man to touch you. The thought drives me crazy. How am I to . . ."

Shianne leaned over him, pressing her index finger to his lips to shush him. "You are making an issue of an event that will never come to pass," she softly assured him. "Why go in search of something better when I have already found the best?" Her lashes fluttered against her cheek. Slowly, she brought her eyes back to his. "I fear we will always argue because we are both strong-willed and determined to have our own way, but the love I feel for you will bring me back to your arms, even when anger sends me away."

Easing down beside him, Shianne cupped her hand beneath his chin, holding his unblinking gaze. "I have longed for a man who possessed Jedediah Winston's gentle ways and generous heart. I also wished for

462

someone with Maman-ti's wild nobility and aura of primitive maleness, someone who commanded my respect without requesting it. I would have sought for a man with my father's sense of humor and positive outlook on life. When I was a child he could always make me smile, even when I didn't feel like it."

A melancholy expression settled on her features. "I wanted a love like the one my father experienced, though it was all too short. My father has lived on the previous memories of my mother because what they had was special. He instilled in me that craving to find perfection in the man I chose to spend my life with."

Wade wished she hadn't landed on that particular subject. He had procrastinated telling Shianne about her father. It wouldn't make it easier, knowing how she felt about her natural mother, loving the memory of a woman she barely knew.

The look on Wade's face brought a curious frown to Shianne's brow. "What's the matter?"

His emotions were guarded by a carefully blank stare. "What could possibly be the matter?" he questioned her question, ". . . except that I have several arousing thoughts on my mind, ones that have nothing to do with conversation."

Shianne hesitated for all of a half-second. Although she had the feeling Wade was keeping something from her, she could not resist his devil-may-care charm. His come-hither glance led her into his arms.

"What is it you have on your mind, cowboy?" she purred in such a provocative voice that goose bumps formed on his skin, and it was not from a sudden chill. Indeed there was enough heat radiating around their room to rival a Dutch oven.

"I feel like loving you again . . ." Wade growled seductively. "And again . . ." His leg slid between hers, pressing intimately against her thighs. "And again . . ."

His chest brushed against the taut pink buds of her breasts, permitting her to feel the rapid beat of his heart.

His mouth opened on hers, savoring the taste of a kiss that sent trickling drops of sensations spilling through every nerve and muscle. Wade closed his eyes and sighed as pleasure flooded over him, the pleasure of loving and being loved. It was a unique feeling, and he never wanted it to go away. Admitting to loving Shianne was the most difficult task he had ever faced, but loving her with every beat of his heart was the easiest thing he had ever done.

How empty his life had been without her, he realized as his hands migrated across the smooth curve of her hip. She had become the eternal flame that burned within him, the fire that raging passion could not extinguish. Each moment of ecstasy with this Texas temptress was like that very first night he had crept into her room. It was always new and exciting, like exploring another chamber in that mysterious underground cavern. Each step took him deeper into that dark realm of sensual pleasure, bringing each of his senses to new heights of awareness.

God, how he loved touching her, bringing her desires to a fervent pitch. How he craved the taste of kisses that melted like a gentle rain upon his lips. Wade sighed in the pleasure of it all, delirious with the rapture of their union.

Later, he would explain about her father, Wade procrastinated. But for now he would love this lovely goddess the way she deserved to be loved—tenderly, deliberately . . . until dawn. . . .

Chapter 23

Chad glanced up to see the two riders approaching from the southeast. It had been three days since Wade had taken Shianne in tow and disappeared over the rolling hills. Even at a distance, Chad could detect the smile that affected every feature on his brother's face. It was obvious Shianne and Wade had come to some sort of understanding. Chad had the depressing feeling the fascination he held for this sultry beauty would have to be tucked in the shadowed corner of his heart.

His gaze strayed to Juan who had been rehearsing the sermon he had intended to deliver to Wade upon his return. "I think you have been practicing your soliloquy for naught," he commented. "My big brother looks as content as a babe in arms."

Juan's smile broadened into a pleased grin. *"Si,* from the look of things, I think the señora has removed the burr that laid beneath the *gringo's* saddle."

When Wade approached, his speculative gaze swung back and forth between the two gloating men. "Well, what are you two looking so smug about?" he demanded.

Juan and Chad were momentarily sidetracked when Shianne rode up beside Wade. The form-fitting gown

465

Wade had stewed and fussed about in Wichita caused the reaction he had anticipated. Both men were drooling over the shapely nymph whose endearing assets were more noticeable than they had been since she joined the trail drive. Wade had been assured of Shianne's love, time and time again for the past few days, but it still frustrated him to see his brother and his friend fantasizing about how Shianne would look if she were wearing not a stitch.

His eyes drifted over his shoulder to see the herd leisurely grazing on the meadow that stood knee high in grass and wild flowers. "It is still another eighty miles to Abilene," he reminded them gruffly. "Do you intend to let these longhorns lollygag all day, or were you planning to herd them up the trail?"

Chad unfastened his gaze from Shianne's voluptuous figure, knowing full well what had caused the unpleasant edge on Wade's voice. "You're the drover, big brother," he insisted. "Juan and I were only trying to hold the herd together until you finally returned." His blue eyes twinkled in wicked amusement as they circled back to the enticing display of bosom revealed by Shianne's gown. "Had we known it would take the better part of three days to purchase the lady's wardrobe, we would have struck out without you." His gaze swung to Wade who had long ago ceased to smile. "That *was* the only reason you were detained, wasn't it? Shianne's clothes? Or was it, perhaps, her lack of them?"

Chad knew he was risking life and limb by provoking Wade's temper, and he knew Wade well enough to know how far to push and the exact moment to retreat before his older brother reached his high threshold of patience. Wade was simmering, Chad diagnosed. It was time to make a hasty exit before Wade exploded. With a taunting chuckle, Chad reined his horse around and thundered off to give orders to the swing riders.

Judging by the hint of smoke that was drifting from the collar of Wade's cream-colored shirt, Juan decided to make himself scarce. Riding a wide circle, he trotted around the grazing herd to inform the vaqueros that they would follow the path marked by the mounds of dirt which Joseph McCoy had left to direct trail herds enroute between Wichita and Abilene.

"That ornery brat," Wade muttered as he watched Chad bring the longhorns into an orderly procession. "Mother spared the rod and spoiled that boy rotten. I'd like to put a clamp on that tongue of his."

Shianne giggled at the acrid expression that puckered Wade's face. "Teasing you has become the source of Chad's amusement. The more dramatically you react to his jibes, the more he needles you." Shianne shook her head disappointedly. "What has happened to that good-natured cowboy I met in San Antonio, the one who could smile through the most difficult situations?"

"He married the most bewitching rose in Texas, and the entire male population seems eager to tend the garden," Wade muttered sourly. "I'm plagued by the insane urge to take a rake after every man who comes within ten feet of you." When Shianne scoffed at his threat, Wade pinned her to the saddle with his narrowed gaze. "How would you react if women were drooling all over me, pursuing thoughts that would have a priest blushing in his robes?"

Shianne contemplated the possibility for a moment. It didn't take long to recall the night at the Casino Club when women were speculating how this handsome mass of brawn and muscle would look in the altogether. She had not appreciated all the attention Wade had received from his female admirers, but neither had she slapped any faces for staring so boldly.

467

The sound of approaching horses brought quick death to their debate. Shianne glanced sideways to see a mob of armed farmers thundering toward them. The men were dressed in hunting shirts, homespun pantaloons and coonskin caps. They looked more threatening than the band of Osage Indians who had approached the previous week, demanding a few beeves in exchange for grazing rights.

The Kansas posse, hellbent on preventing tick-infested longhorns from crossing their land, came like an infantry answering the command to charge. Wade had every intention of using diplomacy with the Jayhawkers, but the men had not come to debate the issue. They came to voice their grievances and make an example of this cattle drover. Only too late Wade realized there was no talking to this angry mob of farmers. When he rode out to meet them, they immediately surrounded him, mocking his southern drawl and jeering at him for taking the opposing side during the war.

Shianne stared in disbelief when the Jayhawkers flung their lariats around Wade and yanked him from his horse. As they dragged Wade away they attempted to set a fire beneath the peaceful herd. Rifles cracked the silence, causing the longhorns to scatter in seven different directions. The vaqueros could not come to Wade's aid, not when four thousand head of cattle were threatening to trample over them.

Spurred by fear, Shianne gouged Delgado, sending him off in the direction that part of the posse had taken Wade. She grasped her steed's neck, swinging herself to the opposite side of Delgado's saddle—the way Maman-ti had taught her to ride when faced with a barrage of bullets.

*   *   *

468

Wade strained against the confining ropes and kicked at the men who were hustling him toward the tree they had selected for their lynching. It took every bit of self-control he possessed not to provoke them further, even though he itched to spit in their faces. If he didn't do some fast talking, and quickly, he would find his neck stretched out like a giraffe's.

"Any last words, Johnny Reb?" Jacob Sanders snorted as he and his men hauled Wade back onto his horse and set the noose on their victim's shoulders.

Wade stared the red-haired lynchman straight in the eye. "You may kill me, but it will accomplish nothing," he told Jacob solemnly. "There is no crime in driving Texas cattle across Kansas to reach the railroad."

"We consider it a crime," Jacob growled and then tightened the noose. "We got wind that you and your diseased longhorns were on your way, and we don't want the likes of you and your beeves tromping across our pastures."

"These cattle were inspected at the Texas border," Wade insisted. "It is a common practice aimed to prevent diseased herds from crossing boundary lines. We will be happy to compensate for any damage by offering you a few head if you will . . ."

Wade was interrupted by Jacob's derisive laugh. "Hell, we don't want your filthy cattle, and we don't want rebels like you trespassing on our property. A lynching is a sure-fire way to discourage other drovers from trailing across our part of Kansas."

In the distance, Haden Reems sat licking his lips in anticipation. He had slipped from Indian Territory, clinging to the cover of underbrush, traveling by night. Determined to dispose of Wade, he approached a Kansas community and forewarned them of the herd

469

led by Wade Burdett. It had taken very little to incite a riot. The Jayhawkers were already up in arms. When he assured the farmers that Burdett's herd was crawling with ticks, the men grabbed their rifles and tore off in search of the approaching longhorns.

Haden watched in fiendish satisfaction as the irate mob led Wade under a sturdy tree and prepared him to meet his maker. If he couldn't recover his herd, Haden vowed to wipe that bastard off the face of the earth. It was a fitting end for that trouble-maker, Haden thought vindictively.

Shianne could not believe her eyes when she thundered over the hill to see Wade's hands tied behind his back, a rope around his neck and a dozen rifles aimed at various parts of his body. Clutching the saddle horn, Shianne pushed back into an upright position on Delgado's back. Gulping down the lump of fear in her throat, she charged toward the mob, praying they would not stoop to gunning down a woman.

A dozen pair of eyes shifted to the black stallion and his mistress. Growling at the interruption, Jacob Sanders reined his horse away from his captive to confront the intruder.

"Turn yourself around and ride out of here, girl," he ordered gruffly. "This isn't the place for a woman. We've got a job to do, and we are anxious to be done with it. . . ." A gasp escaped Jacob's lips when Shianne pointed her revolver at his chest with her left hand and aimed her rifle at his head with the other. He had made the drastic mistake of judging the lady to be some starry-eyed farmer's daughter who had foolishly gotten herself mixed up with these renegades who were transporting cattle into Kansas. "Now, hold on, girl!" he croaked, frog-eyed.

"No, *you* hold on," Shianne hissed venomously. Her gaze darted to the men who had twisted in the saddle to see what Jacob was squawking about. "You may hang my husband, but I promise you, mister, you won't be riding back home with the rest of your friends. There will be two funerals on the plains of Kansas."

The look in Shianne's dark eyes assured Jacob that he had blundered onto a woman who voiced no idle threat. He could imagine the size of holes this fiery beauty was contemplating blowing in his homespun clothes. Left with no choice, Jacob signaled his friends to cut Wade loose.

"Take your man and see that he heads back in the direction he came," Jacob ordered gruffly. "You aren't welcome in Kansas. We don't want a bunch of rebels hauling contaminated cattle into our land to infect our herds."

As Wade moved away from the glaring farmers, the crack of a distant rifle split the air. Wade sucked in his breath when a searing pain sliced across his shoulder. His concerned gaze flew to Shianne who had been distracted just long enough to find herself in a wrestling match with Jacob Sanders. Digging his spurs into Galahad's flanks, Wade charged toward Shianne. Using his good arm, Wade leaned out to unhorse Jacob and leave him in a tangled heap on the ground.

Shianne swiveled her head around as she urged Delgado into his swiftest pace. The angry mob had regrouped to come thundering after them. Her heart tore loose in her chest and wedged between her ribs as she and Wade galloped back toward the herd. She had made too many split second decisions the past few minutes, and her numbed brain refused to function. Blindly, she followed Wade's lead, hoping he had some notion as to how they were going to rescue themselves from the scrape they were in.

471

Although Chad and the vaqueros had managed to control the cattle, the herd was milling uneasily. Another round of rifle fire set them into panic. Wade hurriedly surveyed the herd and then glanced back at the approaching mob that had opened fire in hopes of stampeding the herd and turning them south.

Gesturing for Shianne to follow his lead, Wade slapped Galahad on the rump, demanding that the horse circle the herd at his fastest gait. Before Wade could signal the trail hands to converge and confront the irate farmers, scores of rifles were exploding around them, making it impossible to control the wild-eyed cattle. Wade watched helplessly as the herd circled and split.

His gaze flew to Chad who still maintained the swing position on the east side of the herd. He dragged his hat from his head, gesturing toward the east.

"What are we going to do?" Shianne questioned, her eyes glued to the approaching mob.

"We'll let the Jayhawkers come through the middle of us," Wade informed her as he leaned out to snatch the rifle from her hand. Spinning about, he fell in beside the oncoming column of longhorns. "Help me send these wild animals west and let them run!"

Shianne clutched her pistol and urged Delgado into a gallop. Riding in Wade's wake, she discouraged the thundering cattle from scattering in several directions. Chad and Juan followed suit. The right flank of longhorns charged over the hill, spurred northeast-ward by the exploding pistols of the vaqueros.

The Jayhawkers found themselves confronting four thousand stampeding longhorns. For several anxious minutes they could do nothing but attempt to hold their seats and roll with the flow of beef on the hoof. The mob split to give chase to both herds, their purpose defeated. Suddenly they found themselves driving the

Texas cattle deeper into Kansas territory.

Although the Texans had outmaneuvered the angry mob, they still had a stampede on their hands. Shianne's overworked heart was bouncing off her ribs as she tried to guide the unruly longhorns northwest. The ground was rushing past her at such an incredible speed that she feared Delgado would step into a prairie dog hole and fling her beneath the charging longhorns.

Shianne prayed nonstop for more than thirty minutes, wondering how many trail hands would be trampled by the time the cattle tired of their dead run and slowed on their own accord. Her worried gaze kept leaping to Wade, even while she popped the bull whip to discourage any longhorns from colliding with her steed.

Wade had come to life, his eyes keen, his body flowing with adrenalin. While in full gallop, he twisted in the saddle to note that the farmers had finally given up the chase. Although Wade could not see the other half of the herd that Chad had driven east, he could detect the billowing dust cloud in the distance. He directed Shianne's attention toward the right, silently commanding her to veer toward the other half of the herd.

As Wade raced alongside the lead cattle, Shianne swallowed what was left of her breath. Wade was flirting with disaster! He brushed against the longhorns, forcing them to swerve right. Shianne gasped in alarm when a deadly horn collided with his right leg, but it didn't slow Wade down, even when blood surfaced to stain his chaps. He kept pushing the herd, bellowing at them, demanding that they turn in the direction he wanted them to go.

After stampeding for six miles the cattle converged into a single herd. Wade pointed toward the valley to the northeast. Although the vale was thick with blackjack oaks, it provided a blockade at the far end. The cattle were forced to circle when they were bottled up in the neck of the dale that boasted steep walls of rock and scattered oaks.

Once the longhorns were content to catch their breath and drink from the creek, Shianne bounded from her steed. When she reached Wade, she groaned in dismay. His shirt sleeve was stained with blood to match the red splotches on his breeches.

"Reckless daredevil," she scolded gruffly.

"Me?" Wade snorted just as gruffly. Grimacing, he swung from the saddle to put weight on his injured leg. "Who the hell was it who came charging over the hill to *single-handedly* rescue me from a lynching? Dammit, woman, you could have gotten yourself killed!"

"Then we could have gone together," Shianne snapped back at him. "You threw yourself in harm's way so many times while you were guiding those stampeding longhorns that I swore you were suicidal!"

"What did you expect me to do?" he grumbled. "Hide behind the trees and allow the herd to scatter to kingdom come?"

"Well, you didn't have to ride in amongst them!" Shianne flared. "No one expected you to take control of the herd *single-handedly!*"

Forcing Wade to sprawl on the ground, Shianne tugged on the hem of his breeches, revealing the jagged wound just below his knee. "Oh, Wade, for heaven sake. The horn gored a hole all the way to the bone!"

His good shoulder lifted in a careless shrug. "You're the resident doctor. Patch me up," he requested.

Shianne yanked his shirt from his chest to inspect the flesh wound caused by an unknown assailant. Muttering, she bounded to her feet, but not before she flashed Wade a disgruntled frown. "I wish I would have married a man with a little common sense. The one I

474

wed obviously wasn't born with any. He sees himself as some immortal centaur who can accomplish phenomenal feats!"

After Shianne had stomped off to gather her medical supplies, Chad strode up to survey his brother's rash of injuries. "I thought everything was coming up roses after you and Shianne trotted off to rendezvous in Wichita." His gaze followed Shianne as she stormed toward the wagon.

Wade investigated the tender flesh on his leg and then glanced absently at his brother. "It's obvious you don't know your new sister as well as you think. If you did, you would realize she is quick to temper." He sank back on his elbow and stared his brother squarely in the eye. "I love her, Chad, but she is not the shy, retiring type who declines from speaking her mind. When that spitfire becomes angry, everyone knows it."

A rueful smile touched Chad's lips. Wade's confession had not gone unnoticed. It was Wade's subtle way of requesting that Chad back away, even though he cared deeply for that saucy firebrand. "You would never have been satisfied with Shianne if you could have walked all over her," Chad said quietly. "That is what drew both of us to her in the first place."

Wade stared at his brother for a long, silent moment. "You know if it were any other woman, I would have backed off and allowed you to win her affection," he murmured, absently rubbing the wound on his shoulder.

Chad jammed his hands into the pockets of his breeches. His head dropped, his gaze focused on the toes of his boots. "If it had been any other woman we wouldn't have found ourselves in competition," he remarked. "If I didn't know how much she cared about you, I might have pressured her far more than I did." Chad heaved a defeated sigh and lifted his eyes to study

Wade's face. "I won't say I can stop wanting her every time I look at her, but I will respect your right to her."

Both men fell silent when Shianne barreled toward them, toting her medical supplies. With no attempt at gentleness or compassion, Shianne slopped whiskey on Wade's shoulder and then dumped a good portion into the wound on his leg.

"Ouch . . . damn!" he yelped. "That hurts worse than being bushwhacked and gored by a longhorn!"

"That's the price one pays when one is a daredevil," Shianne sniffed caustically. Pressing her hands to his chest, Shianne shoved him off balance. "Lay back and quit squirming. It will take a while to stitch you back together."

Predicting that Wade was in for a rough time, Chad hastened to the chuck wagon to retrieve another bottle of whiskey. When he returned, he offered Wade a drink. Smiling in gratitude, Wade grasped the bottle and downed a gulp.

With steady hands Shianne cleansed the wounds and applied more whiskey. Reasonably certain any lingering germs were swimming in liquor, Shianne stitched Wade back together and bandaged both wounds. Satisfied with her handiwork, she rose to her feet and gave him strict orders to stay off his leg.

Wade grumbled at the command and defiantly rolled to his knees. He had every intention of moving the herd before the swarm of irate farmers came to finish what they had begun. The trail herders had been fortunate once. Wade doubted if they could outfox the angry mob again.

In the process of unfolding himself from the ground Wade herd the click of a revolver. To his amazement he glanced up to find himself staring down the barrel of a Colt .45. Shianne lifted a booted foot, pressed it to Wade's good shoulder, and sent him back to the ground.

"I said to give the wound a rest." She stuffed the pistol in Chad's hand and stared pointedly at him. "If your brother tries to get up again, blow off his other leg," she commanded, her eyes dancing with deviltry. "That should keep him off his feet."

Wade rolled his eyes in disgust. There was a mutiny in progress. Shianne had but to make a request, and Chad became her devoted slave. "This is one helluva note," he muttered, propping himself into a sitting position.

Chad chuckled in amusement. "I see what you mean. The lady is full of fire, and I wouldn't think to disobey her for fear of getting burned."

"I ought to let her take command of this trail drive," Wade grumbled spitefully. "Then she would realize there are some things a woman is incapable of handling."

"Oh?" Chad arched a taunting brow. "I wouldn't have thought to put anything past that feisty little hoyden," he smirked.

Wade flung his brother a silencing frown. "You've got stars in your eyes, little brother. She is resourceful, I'll admit, but she is not without limitations. If I let her stand in my stead, she would come crawling back, begging me to climb into the saddle and relieve her of her duties."

"Would you like to wager Shianne can't manage the chore?" Chad challenged, his blue eyes dancing with amusement.

Wade scowled to himself. "You and Juan seem to think that minx can do anything, even become the drover of a trail drive."

Chad tucked the revolver in his belt and sank down beside his sulking brother. Lifting an arm, he gestured to the left. "She is already passing orders among the men. We shall see if she can put four thousand head of longhorns back on the trail."

Wade looked on as Shianne persuaded the congregation of weary cowboys to take their positions and guide the herd from the vale. He also found himself dumped in the back of the supply wagon, along with the rest of the paraphernalia.

Staring at the dust cloud that rose beneath the wagon wheels, Wade asked himself why it slashed a gash in his male pride to learn that Shianne had filled his boots with such experienced ease. He knew Shianne had managed the vast Texas ranch during her father's absence. He knew how adept she was at lassoing cattle and riding all over a horse like her Indian cousins. Indeed, there was very little Shianne couldn't do and do well, especially when she set her mind to it.

Dammit, there were times when Wade wanted to be her champion, to be the object of her admiration. Not once had he saved that distressing damsel from disaster. Not even when Haden had tried to lead Shianne up the incline of the arroyo could Wade boast about being responsible for her rescue. It was more the result of a lame horse and Haden's haste to escape. How could he ever win Shianne's respect if he was being carted in the back of a wagon like excess baggage? That thought alone was enough to turn his mood black as pitch.

Wade glared at the bay stallion that had been tied to the wagon. "Galahad, ole boy, you don't know how lucky you are," he grumbled at his horse. "When a man finds a woman he can't live without, and he makes the fool mistake of saying so, he's got more trouble than he did when he found himself battling the attraction. Women! They are hell on a man's emotions."

478

Twisting around, Wade peered at Shianne and Chad who were poised on the hill in front of the herd. That was where Wade should have been, certainly not draped in the back of a wagon! Huffily, Wade flounced on his blanket, seeking a position that didn't bruise his wounded pride, but there was none. No matter which way he turned a pair of dark eyes were staring at him, tormenting him. If not for Shianne, he would have patched up his leg and arm and taken his place at point, gritting out his pain. Damnation, he should have known better than to fall in love with a nurse. Every time he sustained a scratch she would keep him bedfast for a week.

Wade was a leader, not a follower. He was accustomed to being in command, and he had very little trouble persuading other men to follow him. It just came naturally. When there was a job to be done, Wade calculated his actions and plunged ahead. It got his goat to realize Shianne would never blindly follow him. The circumstances of her past had forced her to become a leader and she had adapted amazingly well.

What kind of marriage would this be if both of them were determined to take charge, and they wound up pulling in opposite directions? Wade punched his fist into his pallet. How was this going to work with two headstrong, dominating individuals who almost had *too* much in common to be compatible?

Granted, he loved Shae with all his heart, but was he man enough to love a woman who was as capable and resourceful as he was? Shianne had survived (and quite nicely) in a man's domain. Was that vixen ever out of her element? It was for damned sure Wade would have to step out of *his* if he ever hoped to discover the answer to that question.

*　　　*　　　*

By the time Shianne and Chad decided to bed the cattle down for the night, Wade had worked himself into a full-fledged snit. He accepted the fact that he loved Shianne and that she loved him, but things were not quite right between them. When they were in each other's arms, all was right with the world, but when Shianne was filling his boots and the cattle drive was progressing without a hitch, Wade found himself resenting the very qualities that impressed him in the beginning—her determined will, her perseverance, her competent ability to assume command.

Weary but content, Shianne trotted her horse back to the wagon and slid from the saddle. A bemused frown knitted her brow when she noted the glum expression that was plastered on Wade's bronzed features.

"Are you feeling worse?" Concerned, she hopped up beside Wade to inspect his wounds, only to have her hands slapped away. Her lashes fluttered up, her bewildered gaze focused on Wade's chiseled features. "What is wrong with you?"

"Nothing," Wade snapped grouchily.

Shianne sank back to study Wade for a pensive moment. "Have I done something to annoy you?"

"What could you have possibly done wrong?" Wade snorted sarcastically. "You confined me to the wagon to mend. You took control of the herd, scouted the trail ahead of us and convinced a bunch of tired vaqueros to push another six miles before bedding down for the night. How could I possibly find complaint with that?"

Shianne was beginning to see reflections of another time not so long ago when she felt as useless as a worn-out boot. A knowing smile crept to her lips. Wade's male pride had been wounded, just as she had felt the sting of insult when he waltzed into her hacienda to assume her responsibilities.

Carefully, Shianne rolled up his breeches' leg and unwrapped the bandage. The wound was not bleeding as heavily since Wade had allowed his leg the chance to rest. "Your wound seems to be mending nicely." She tossed him a quick glance before concentrating on his leg. "I wish I could say the same for your injured pride."

Wade jerked back as if she had stabbed him. "What the hell is that supposed to mean?" he snapped sharply.

"Oh, I think you know exactly what I mean," Shianne said with a casual shrug. "I took your place at the head of the herd, and you are incensed that this cattle parade didn't break down without you at the front, waving your baton."

She reached over to retrieve the salve, intending to pack the wound, but Wade snatched the poultice away to see to the chore himself.

"I don't need you or anyone else hovering over me like a mother hen," he growled crabbily. "Since you are so damned capable, why don't you trot back to your sidekick so the both of you can poke fun at the cripple. You don't need a husband, honey. You need a lackey to fetch and heel for you while you are ramrodding this cattle operation with a competency that rivals the best of men."

Wade couldn't have hurt her anymore if he had kicked her in the midsection, and he realized that when he finally pulled in the reins on his runaway tongue. Never had he seen such a wounded expression on her exquisite features.

Fighting for hard-won composure Shianne eased off the back of the wagon. Her lips trembled as she glanced up to meet the scowl that claimed his face. "I resented you when you took control of my ranch, and it burned my pride even more when you handled the situation with such ease and capability. I felt betrayed when the vaqueros accepted you, no questions asked." Shianne inhaled a deep breath, fighting like hell to keep tears from clouding her vision and giving evidence that his harsh remarks had penetrated deeper than any knife. "It should be a compliment to your expertise that others who have watched your every move have learned to step in to take your place when you have been injured in the line of duty. A competent instructor should not see the deed as a personal insult but rather as an extension of his own handiwork."

Shianne licked her bone-dry lips and forced herself not to look away until she had finished saying what she wanted to say. "As you once told me, Wade, there is no such thing as a knight on his white charger or a helpless damsel in distress. I have accepted the fact that a man has to be as tough as leather to survive in this lawless land. You have your rough edges and your undeniable strengths. Does it make me less of a woman because I have learned to adapt and rely on ingenuity? Would you prefer me to be a whining, simpering female who complained about the accommodations and lack of civility on the wide open range? Would you have been happier if I would have fallen to pieces when that mob of farmers decided to lynch you? Or perhaps you would be better satisfied with a clinging vine draped so tightly around your neck that you couldn't move without the risk of being strangled. Perhaps you long for a weeper who would come crying to you when a howling thunderstorm approached. Did you have your heart set on a squeamish female who couldn't aim a pistol and use it if she must to save the man she loved from imposing doom?" She drew herself up to a proud stature. "I'm sorry I cannot be any of those things that makes a man feel more needed than he already is, things that bolster a man's pride. I will not pretend to be what I'm not. If I were helpless, I wouldn't be alive today."

Her misty gaze swung to Delgado. Shianne reached out to grasp the trailing reins and then sent the sober-faced cowboy another glance. "I took your place today because I wanted to give you time to recuperate. I cursed your daring when you were guiding the stampeding herd, even while I was admiring your poise and determination in the face of serious difficulty. I wanted to protect you because I care so deeply." She heaved a heavy sigh and clasped her hand on the pommel of the saddle. "I suppose I was being selfish when I chided you for your daring recklessness. I feared you would fall beneath the trampling hooves." Her gaze drifted back to Wade who was propped in the back of the wagon, staring at the toes of his boots as if something demanded his undivided attention. "And quite frankly, I wasn't sure I wanted to live without you—loving you the way I do—loving you because of the man you are, not because of the material things you might be able to give me or because I seek security and protection. I care for you, and I need you to make me feel whole and alive, to give my life meaning."

When Shianne popped her foot into the stirrup and galloped toward the creek, Wade expelled the breath he had been holding since he contracted foot-in-mouth disease a few minutes earlier. He felt as tall as a wagon spoke, and he had turned so many circles he couldn't determine which way was up. He had certainly exposed his stupid side when he blurted out that snide remark. After spending the afternoon taking doses of the same medicine he had stuffed down Shianne's throat, his disposition had turned sour enough to spoil a bucket of curds.

Shianne had tolerated his interference in her life a helluva lot more gracefully than he had accepted hers. But dammit, how did a man accept the fact that his wife was every bit as cunning and efficient as he was? Hell's bells, he didn't want a choking vine or a weeper who used his shirt for her crying towel. He preferred this sultry nymph who had grown up like a wild flower.

Now, the question was: Was he man enough to praise Shianne's strong will and determination, or was he going to continue resenting her like some arrogant ass who considered a woman to be a second-rate citizen? True, Wade was not accustomed to having a woman standing in his limelight while he was shoved into the shadows. True, Shianne was receiving all sorts of glowing accolades because she was capable of functioning in a man's world. And true, his pride had been wrinkled like an accordion.

Wade put the question up again for a second consideration. Did he possess enough self-confidence to accept Shianne for what she was, or was his monumental pride going to stand as an insurmountable obstacle between them? Wade deliberated for a long, soul-searching moment. He had to decide if he was big enough to cope with his vanity when confronted with a young woman of Shianne's rare abilities. He would have to learn to share the limelight and listen to other men sing praises to his resourceful wife. He would have to consider her feelings and learn to compromise—something he had refused to do the last few months.

When Chad and Juan rode up to the wagon, gloating and grinning like two weasels who had helped themselves to a chicken house, Wade dug his hand into his pocket to toss his brother a gold piece.

"I suppose you came by for this," he grumbled.

Chad nodded affirmatively and then tucked away the coin. "She was everything I thought she would be," he bragged.

"I envy you, *hombre*," Juan admitted without hesitation. "A man could be blessed with no greater treasure than to lay claim to a woman who would risk her life for him, and who would stand in his stead after he nearly got himself killed twice in the same day."

"No, I suppose a man would be a fool not to count his blessings," Wade mumbled more to himself than to his companions.

"*Sí*, he would be very foolish indeed," Juan concurred. "But I have always maintained that it would take more than the average man to handle a woman like the señora." There was admiration in his eyes when he bent his gaze to Wade. "I think she has found the right man for her."

The quiet compliment brought Wade off the end of the wagon. He glanced around to locate a tree limb that would serve as a cane. Spotting a sturdy branch, Wade limped over to retrieve it.

Juan frowned disapprovingly. "The señora will not be happy to see you putting pressure on your leg until it mends properly."

Hobbling around, Wade peered up at the Mexican. A wry smile bordered his lips. "I will heal much quicker with tender loving care. Tell the rest of the men to steer clear of the creek, will you?"

Although both men nodded agreeably, Chad's expression held a hint of envy. "You and your lady won't be disturbed," he promised.

"I'm counting on that," he murmured.

Wade turned himself and his thoughts toward the secluded creek. This time he took care not to run headlong into any skunks that might be lurking in the underbrush. He had already behaved like an ass. Wade had no inclination to approach Shianne, wearing the offensive cologne of one of those furry little creatures with white stripes painted down the middle of their backs.

Haden scowled under his breath when he realized his

attempt to dispose of Wade had met with defeat. Shianne had come riding in to throw a wrench in the lynching before Jacob Sanders could leave Wade dangling from a tree branch. Fearing his careful scheme was about to be foiled, Haden had jerked his rifle from its case on the saddle and took aim at Wade's back, but he had only winged Burdett. The cunning cowboy had not only managed to escape, but he had outfoxed the rioting farmers and stampeded the longhorns around them.

Frowning pensively, Haden considered his next retaliation. There had to be a way to repay the Burdetts for all the trouble they had caused him. And Juan . . . Haden cursed aloud when he remembered how his hired gunman had turned traitor. By damned, he was going to dispose of them all, Haden vowed to himself. He could not return to his own ranch until he was certain none of his adversaries were around to point an accusing finger at him.

A sinister smile crossed his features when an idea hatched in his mind. Taking up the reins, Haden aimed himself toward his destination. It was time he employed one of Burdett's conniving tricks, he decided. This time the whole lot of them would be caught in their own trap.

Chapter 24

Shianne sighed as she sank down to cleanse the dirt and grime from her face. After glancing around to ensure none of the men had wandered down to the rivulet, Shianne peeled off her gown and waded into the water. Since Wade had been behaving like a possessive mother bear the past few weeks, she knew he would make certain no one intruded on her privacy.

When she eased into the water, her spirits sank to the creek bed. She should be deliriously happy, she chided herself. Wade loved her, but Shianne was plagued with the uneasy feeling that he didn't love her enough to accept her for the woman she was. Perhaps the truth of the matter was that a man and woman could not survive on love alone. She and Wade had only recently declared their affection for each other, and already there were sour grapes in the fruit bowl of love. What would it take to ensure a peaceful coexistence between them, she wondered.

She was a misfit, and she would be the first to admit to that. Woman though she was, she could shoot as well as any man. Maman-ti had taught her to master the knife, and he had also instructed her to ride like the unexcelled warriors of the plains. She had been forced to assume all her father's responsibilities because necessity dictated it. While others fell back to allow someone else to take the lead, Shianne assumed command of her situations. Dammit, Wade knew what she was and how she reacted to difficult problems. She didn't freeze up; she came uncoiled. Why couldn't Wade accept her the way she was without trying to change her? Would they ever be compatible unless they were in bed? Was that all there was to this love of theirs?

Shianne glided her arms through the water, sending ripples fanning out in all directions. A pensive frown knitted her brow. Would Wade find less fault with her if she were a helpless female who leaned heavily upon him for protection? She admired *his* strengths. Why couldn't he at least tolerate hers?

It suddenly occurred to her that Wade had yet to overcome his licentious philosophy. He wanted to enjoy all the pleasures of marriage without the annoying inconveniences. He wanted her love and passion, but he was not particularly interested in her opinions or her assistance.

Shianne laughed bitterly when she realized that Wade had suddenly become the one who was living in the outdated dream of daring knights and fairyland castles. Well, this wasn't Camelot; this was Kansas. If they were to survive in this rugged land where each new dawn brought another string of catastrophes, they must unite. She and Wade could not continue crossways of each other and expect to hold their marriage together.

There had to be a compromise, Shianne reminded herself. She would try to restrain her dominant traits, but Wade would have to meet her halfway. He could not go on thinking her aim and ambition in life was to put dents in his pride. Dammit, she had only done what needed doing. Why couldn't that wooden-headed man see that? Because his brain was carved from knotty pine and it had petrified with time, she answered bitterly.

The rustling in the bushes dragged Shianne from her contemplations. She sank deeper into the water and glanced up to see Wade hobbling toward her on his improvised cane. Her first impulse was to scold him for being on his feet, but Shianne bit back the words, lest she sound more overbearing than he already deemed her to be.

Wade struck a gallant pose and lifted his cane as if he had drawn his mighty sword. "Fair damsel, are there any dragons hereabout I might slay for thee to bolster my knightly pride? Or point me in the direction of some evil prince that I might bring him to his knees." With a flair for the melodramatic Wade bowed before her. "M'lady, grant me at least one challenging crusade. I wish to prove myself to be a noble knight, worthy of your royal love."

All the bitter thoughts that were spinning through her mind dissolved when Wade flashed her that charismatic smile of his. For the life of her she couldn't remember why she was annoyed with him. Shianne burst into merry giggles when Wade began fencing the underbrush with his crooked sword. He was limping to and fro, slashing the scales off the imaginary dragon and stabbing holes in the armor of a make-believe foe who closely resembled cottonwood seedlings.

Wade pirouetted on his good leg, presenting Shianne with another exaggerated bow. This time, with a flair for the ridiculous, he drew himself up to full stature and laid his woody sword to his chest, formally saluting the naked queen who was bathing in the stream.

"The deed is done, m'lady." He gestured toward the wounded army that lay strewn about him. With the crooked point of his sword, he indicated the fallen dragon. "Your kingdom is free of the evil warriors and beasts that might think to harm you," he declared.

"Do you have any idea how silly you look?" she questioned between snickers.

Wade leaned on his sword-cane and graced her with an apologetic smile. "Surely I cannot look any more ridiculous than I feel," he told her quietly. His eyes dropped to study the tuft of grass beneath his feet. "Shae, I'm sorry. Instead of resenting your abilities I should have been complimenting them . . . like the rest of the men who have been applauding your daring feats."

His shoulders slumped, and his gaze drifted across the stream to focus on Shianne's bewitching face. "I suppose I have always wanted to impress you, to appear your invincible champion." Bitter laughter bubbled from his chest. "But it isn't easy when the woman a man longs to impress possesses more saving graces than *he* does. A man's arrogance and stubbornness often make him behave like an idiot." His green eyes bored into her, shimmering with genuine emotion. "Just because I have been acting like a fool, don't hesitate to be every bit the woman you are. You are not obligated to spare my overinflated pride." Wade let out his breath in a rush. "Dammit, Shae, I don't want to lose you. I know I would not be content with any other woman. No one can compare to you. I should know. I have spent several months trying to convince myself you were like all the others, and it didn't work worth a damn."

His words brought sentimental tears to her eyes. It took a great deal of courage for a man like Wade to make such a confession. He was a proud, determined man who was uncomfortable unless he was in full command. He called no one master, and the thought of equally sharing responsibilities with a woman was

490

obviously something that would take some adjustment; but he was trying to make amends, and Shianne was not about to lose the man she loved because of a silly power struggle.

"Come, my handsome prince. Your valiant deeds prove you worthy of knighthood. Let us waste no time in performing the ceremony," Shianne insisted.

Grinning, Wade limped into the water, clothes and all. Shianne grasped his cane-sword and touched it to each broad shoulder, careful not to aggravate his wound.

"I dub thee my most cherished knight. Your heroic deeds, above and beyond the call of duty, grant you any privilege that meets your whim."

A rakish leer spread across his tanned face. He devoured the sea of bare flesh that lay exposed to his gaze. Wade slid his arm around her waist and pulled her full length against him. "So much for the pomp and circumstance, princess. Let's get down to the good stuff."

"Good stuff?" Shianne raised a perfectly arched brow. She was obviously caught in a time warp. While she was still drifting in a world of gallant knights and fair damsels, Wade had flown back to present day Kansas.

"This is the good stuff," Wade informed her. His voice was husky with desire. "I never did give a damn about medals and honors. I'd trade them all for a dozen kisses just like this one. . . ."

When Wade settled down to the serious business of demonstrating what satisfied him most, Shianne melted all over him. Her lips parted to accept his questing tongue. Her body roused to the feel of his hard length pressing suggestively against hers. His experienced caresses descended to her hips, pressing her closer, making her wish he had taken the time to rip off his clothes before he waded into the water.

"Oh, Wade, I didn't mean to unman you or insult you this afternoon. I only wanted to help, to give you time to mend," she said breathlessly.

"I was the one who took offense when there was none intended," he insisted. "Now, enough talk. Where were we? . . ."

"Here . . ." Shianne prompted, bringing his head back to hers.

Her arms slid beneath the hem of his shirt to run her fingertips over his muscled flesh. Her head tilted, granting him free access to the swanlike column of her neck . . . and any other inch of flesh he felt inclined to kiss or caress.

Wade's body shuddered uncontrollably. His moist breath whispered across the rapid pulsations of her throat and skimmed her shoulder. His hands slid along her ribs to fold around each full mound; his fingers kneading her satiny skin aroused her with each gentle touch.

"I love you, Shae," he rasped as his mouth came back to hers. "Please don't stop loving me, even when I find myself battling my stubborn male pride."

She leaned back to gaze into those entrancing green eyes that were flecked with gold. Reverently, she trailed her finger over the smile lines that carved attractive creases in his face. "You are too much man to ever feel threatened by a woman," she softly assured him. "If the truth be known, perhaps it was I who was trying a little too hard to impress *you*. I wanted to be your eyes when you finally allowed yourself to sleep. I wanted to be your supporting arm when difficult odds caused you to stumble. I want my love for you to give you strength, *never* diminish it."

Wade stared at the young beauty who seemed wise beyond her years. She had gained insight from reacting like a man when she was thrust into a man's world, but he had never attempted to think like a woman and didn't have the foggiest notion how to go about it.

Shianne was teaching him things he had no inclination to learn . . . until now. It was difficult to admit that he had been a womanizer and every bit the rogue. He had never given his women much consideration. They had been necessary creatures, each one providing temporary satisfaction. But not this dark-eyed nymph. She had always demanded more than a smile and a moment. Shianne had become an integral part of his thoughts. Because he cared so deeply for her he had become aware of her feelings and her needs.

After dropping a kiss to her upturned lips, Wade nuzzled his forehead against hers. "Come along, princess. I think you have treaded water long enough. I have something more stimulating in mind for you."

His seductive tone provoked Shianne to raise an interested brow. "Oh, what could a wounded man possibly have on his mind besides recuperation?" she questioned in mock innocence.

A rakish grin tugged the corners of his mouth upward. "Don't play coy with me, minx. I may have a gash in my arm and leg, but you know me well enough to realize it has little effect on other parts of my anatomy."

When they reached the creek bank, Wade wasted no time in doffing his wet clothes. His thoughts were on the raven-haired beauty who kept his emotions in constant turmoil. It seemed there was no such thing as a peaceful existence after Shianne took hold of a man's life. Their relationship would never be a complacent affair. Boredom would never set in. Shianne was too high-spirited, and neither of them would outgrow *all* their stubbornness. When this minx reacted, she did so with all her heart. Wade finally understood that she, like he, never did anything halfway. It simply was not part of their emotional constitution.

The moment she flew into his arms, showering him with ardent kisses, Wade derailed from his train of thought. It felt so good to hold her, to feel her body respond to him and him alone. He wanted to pleasure her in all the glorious ways she pleased him.

When her hands began to weave their potent magic, Wade moaned in sweet torment. He knew where this dark-haired angel would take him and they could not depart soon enough. His craving for Shianne was a constant thing, a need that fed on passion and created even more intense desires.

Shianne combed her fingers through his midnight hair and then trailed her hand along the corded tendons in his neck. Her worshipping gaze followed in the wake of her wandering caresses as they glided over the slope of his shoulder to measure the wide expanse of his chest. She adored touching him. He was a mass of sinewed strength—a powerful, imposing creature, half man, half beast. He was a cunning, calculating male who had learned to survive by his wits.

It was inconceivable that Wade could even think she could compare to him. He was like a lithe, unconquerable lion who could uncoil and pounce, devastating his victim. He was half wild, majestic in the way he moved and seemingly invincible. Even when he sustained an injury, it might slow him down, but it never distracted him from his purpose. Wade was like an unstoppable force, driven by incredible inner strength.

No, this pantherlike creature had nothing to fear from her, Shianne mused as her hand splayed across the thick matting of hair on his chest. She could not compare to him. She had saved him from a lynching, and they had galloped away, but her mind went blank at the sight of unruly cattle ahead of them and an angry mob behind them. Yet Wade, dazed and wounded, had rescued them all from impending doom. It was that tireless strength, that perseverant drive that fascinated her as much as his magnificent body and his uncanny ability to melt her into a liquid pool of desire. He was all man, every muscled inch of him. Shianne loved him, hopelessly, completely.

As her caresses made another tauntingly delicious descent across his flesh, Wade was reduced to fire and smoke. He gasped for breath, overcome by the dark, engulfing cloud of passion. The last remnants of stubborn pride fell away, and Wade surrendered to rapture.

He *loved*. Each obstacle he faced seemed inconsequential in the face of that intangible emotion he had come to know as love. When he gazed into Shianne's expressive eyes, he saw the gateway to a sensual world they had only begun to explore. It was there beyond the smoke clouds and leaping flames.

Hand in hand, they glided beyond reality's horizon. They soared like an eagle winging across a boundless sky, spiraling and diving, suspended in flight by that mystical draft of wind—love in its purest, most magnificent form.

Shianne could make him feel every bit a man when she surrendered her heart and soul to him. The next time one of his men boasted about Shianne's rare talents, Wade would smile quietly to himself and nod in agreement. For only *he* knew just how remarkable she truly was, and *that* made all the difference.

The following ten days proved to be the least difficult of the three month cattle drive from San Antonio to

Abilene, Kansas. The Texans met with no more irate farmers, only a seasonal thunderstorm that dumped buckets of rain and kept the cattle bogged down in mud. While the herd was left to graze on the prairie west of town, Wade, Shianne and Chad rode into Abilene to make the arrangements for selling and shipping the cattle.

Shianne stared curiously at the cow town that had sprung up on the east side of Mud Creek. There were a dozen log cabins, roofed with dirt and several log-house businesses. The Bratton hotel, which modestly boasted six rooms, set beside the stable and blacksmith shop. East of the hotel was the saloon owned by Josiah Jones. Beyond the saloon was Frontier Store, a one room building that stocked groceries and dry goods, and served as a post office.

Her disbelieving gaze swept to the west side of Mud Creek to survey Tim Hersey's log cabin and two-story stage station. To the northeast lay the shipping yard built to accommodate Texas cattle. Shianne wasn't certain what she expected from the railway town that set at the end of a long, grueling trail, but Abilene provided little more than a place to feed one's hunger pangs and ease one's need to sleep in a customary bed.

Wade gestured toward the second hotel near the train station. "I think you'll find Drover's Cottage more to your liking, madam," he enthused. "We have invested in the fifteen thousand dollar hotel, and your father has been here the past few months, overseeing its construction."

Shianne assessed the imposing structure and sighed appreciatively. "Drover's Cottage does look more accommodating than the other hotel," she agreed. "I only hope I can obtain a bath and more appropriate clothes before encountering my father."

Chad made a critical sweep of Shianne's daring

gown. Although she looked a little worse for wear, he had no complaints about her appearance. "Don't you think your father will recognize his only daughter?" he chuckled. "Believe me, lovely lady, even if I were not to see you for a decade, I would have no trouble placing the face *or* the body attached to it."

Shianne blushed at Chad's bold remark and then cast Wade a discreet glance. She was relieved to note that Wade had not taken offense. He was still smiling, just as he had been for more than a week.

What a glorious ten days it had been, Shianne thought. Wade had returned to his easygoing ways, making her love him all the more. He no longer felt his manhood threatened, and he had been so playful and attentive that she often wondered if she had awakened in someone else's dream.

"A . . . Shae . . . there is . . . a," Wade himhawed, realizing he had neglected to speak to Shianne about her father. He had procrastinated until the very last moment, and now he was left to blurt out the truth.

Joseph McCoy rushed out of his office to greet the Burdetts, and Wade's announcement was immediately forgotten. "We have been anxiously waiting for you," Joseph burst out as he reached up to shake hands with Wade. "How many head did you bring up the trail?"

"Four thousand," Wade informed him and then made the quick introductions.

After a hasty round of how do you dos, Joseph assessed the shapely bundle who sat atop her coal black stallion. He was surprised to learn Blake's daughter had made the rugged journey. There had been very few women to undertake the task, and most of them arrived looking much more bedraggled than this fetching beauty.

"We have rooms waiting for you at the Cottage," Joseph told Shianne and then turned his attention to

Wade and Chad. "While the lady is freshening up from her journey, you two can join me in the office, and we will get the paper work out of the way."

While Wade was being led away by the enthusiastic cattle buyer, his head swiveled around to cast Shianne a parting glance. He had intended to tell her about her new mother, but Joseph's interruption caused another delay. He could only hope he arrived in the room before Shianne crossed paths with her father. If he didn't, Blake could break the news to her himself, Wade decided. After all, he had set the stage and explained the circumstances. Blake could take it from there.

After tying Delgado to the hitching post, Shianne bounded up the steps of the three-story frame hotel. A large livery stable set across the street, but Shianne decided to make herself presentable before she found a stall for her steed.

As she ambled inside she glanced sideways to survey the billiard room, bar and restaurant. Turning her attention to the waiting clerk Shianne requested a room and a bath. With her saddle bag draped over her shoulder, she aimed herself toward the steps, only to find her father descending them.

"Papa?" Shianne's face lit up like a lantern. She had hoped to bathe and change before greeting her father, but now that she had met him face to face, she didn't care how she looked, only that she was looking at him in the flesh for the first time in ages!

Blake left the woman at his side to greet his trail-worn daughter with a zealous hug. "My lord, girl, what are you doing here? And look at you, you're all grown up!"

"Time has a way of doing that to people," Shianne chortled, content in the circle of her father's stout arms.

"I assume by that greeting that I have been forgiven,"

Blake breathed in relief. "It's been a rough few years, honey, and I've lived with the guilt of not returning to you." He aimed Shianne toward the older woman who was patiently waiting on the landing. "But now that we are all together I want you to meet my wife. Isn't she lovely, Shianne? She has filled up the empty region around my heart."

If Blake hadn't been propping her up, Shianne swore she would have fallen flat on her face. The news hit her like a hard slap on the cheek. All the resentment she had battled when there had been no word from her father rose like cream on fresh milk. The memory of the love between her father and mother shattered, to be replaced by a heart-aching sense of hurt and betrayal.

Shianne jerked her arm from her father's grasp and glared at the petite woman who was smiling down at her. All sorts of bitter thoughts whipped through Shianne's mind. Who was this woman? How had she managed to latch on to Blake, a man who had survived on a precious memory? Had this aging harlot schemed to catch Blake, preying on his loneliness and his trials during the war?

Of course, she had, Shianne's mind screamed. This woman had bewitched Blake, intending to drain him of his wealth, planning to keep him from his only daughter forever. If Shianne had not made the journey, she probably never would have seen her father again. His scheming wife would have seen to that!

Well, if Blake and his immaculately dressed wife thought they could win her over with a hug and a gracious smile, they thought wrong! Shianne was nursing her resentment, and she was in no mood to be diplomatic, not after the hell she had endured the past few years—all because this conniving woman had stolen her father from the daughter who had needed him so desperately.

Snapping brown eyes riveted over Micara's comely features. Attractive though she was, Shianne viewed the auburn-haired woman as nothing more than a spellcasting witch. "You wouldn't let him come home, would you?" she hissed. "What had you intended to do, keep him here in Abilene the rest of his days, refusing to allow him to return to his own child, one who needed him far more than you did?" Her gaze raked Micara whose face instantly whitewashed when pelleted by Shianne's abrasive tone. "Surely you could have laid your hands on some Yankee who could afford your expensive tastes instead of . . ."

"Shianne!" Blake looked as if he had been hit by a fast-moving train. "What the devil is the matter with you? That is no way to talk to . . ."

"Oh?" Shianne scoffed, cutting her father off in midsentence. "How should one talk to this adventuress whose intent it is to bleed you of your money. One is not required to treat a scheming consort with an ounce of respect!"

Blake did something he had never done in his life. He raised his hand and slapped Shianne across the cheek. Shianne stared at him in disbelief, certain this cunning female had turned her own father against her. Tears sprang to her eyes, and she raced up the steps two at a time to seek out her room.

"Shianne, come back here!" Blake bellowed. Helplessly, Blake peered at Micara who was clutching the banister to keep from wilting. "Don't be upset. Shianne didn't mean the hateful things she said."

Micara choked on a sob. "I think perhaps she did, Blake," she murmured brokenly. "And she had every right to say them." Her misty gaze fell to Blake. "I kept you from your own flesh and blood. Your daughter needed you, and I selfishly clung to you when my world collapsed around me."

Blake glanced about him, indecision etching his brow. He didn't know whether to break down Shianne's door and throttle her for her disrespectful outburst or gather Micara in his arms and comfort her. To turn to one woman seemed to indicate that he was rejecting the other. In frustration, Blake stood there, mulling over the conversation, bit by bit. It suddenly occurred to him that Shianne appeared shocked to learn that he had married, and there could only be one reason for that, he reckoned.

A dark frown claimed his weathered features. Muttering under his breath, Blake wheeled around and stalked down the steps. His swift strides took him down the street to McCoy's office. Blake cursed Wade every step of the way. By the time he reached the log office, he was mad as hell.

Hearing the click of boot heels on the planked floor, Wade glanced up from the contract he was preparing to sign and offered the intruder a greeting smile. "Hello, Blake. . . ."

Blake shot McCoy a foreboding look—the way a hunter might glance at a rabbit on his way to fell a grizzly bear. When he turned his furious glare on Wade, sparks flew from his eyes. Blake greeted Wade with a doubled fist that sent stars circling around the younger man's head. The force of the blow caused the chair in which Wade was sitting to rear on its hind legs before it tumbled backward, unseating its occupant.

Rubbing his stinging jaw, Wade lifted himself onto one elbow to stare bewilderedly at the fuming man who was towering over him. Wade had the feeling that somewhere in that simple greeting, he had said something very wrong. "What the hell was that for?" he questioned out the unbruised side of his mouth.

"You didn't tell her, did you?" Blake spouted, his chest heaving in such frustrated breaths that he very nearly popped the buttons off his shirt. "Damnation, man. What do you think I sent you to Texas to do? And what is my daughter doing here in the first place? How dare you expose her to such a hazardous trip!" Blake's voice grew louder until he was yelling in Wade's battered face.

Cautiously, Wade dragged his feet beneath him and stood up to tower over his enraged father-in-law. "The moment was never right to explain," Wade ground out the answer to the first question and then glared at Blake while he spat out the second response. "And I didn't have a choice. Haden Reems kidnapped Shianne and the entire herd of longhorns. Chad and I were buried alive in the cave when Haden trekked across Texas with Shianne in tow!"

Blake swore under his breath and spared a glance at the two men who were nervously shifting from one foot to another. "You never got around to tell her I married your mother when you've had the better part of six months to do it? That's the flimsiest excuse I have ever heard!"

"I had my hands full," Wade defended tersely. "In case you didn't know, your daughter is a firebrand, and if that were not enough, it took a score of man hours to round up mavericks and tame them enough to put them on the trail north. I wasn't sitting around twiddling my thumbs, for God's sake!"

"Well, you couldn't prove it by me," Blake snorted sarcastically. "I thought you had nerves of steel." He raked the taller man with scornful mockery. "Little did I know you would fall to pieces when confronted by a mere wisp of a woman and a few *cimarrones* in the brush country. That will teach me to send a *boy* to do a man's job." Blake suddenly realized that Chad was standing beside him, and it dawned on him that the younger Burdett had set out for parts unknown. "What

502

the hell are you doing here?" he questioned abruptly.

Chad grinned and scratched his disheveled head of hair. "I came to watch Wade explain his way out of this mess," he snickered.

"You're a lot of help," Wade grunted, his tone belying his words. His annoyed gaze swung back to Blake. "I assume you and Shianne had words over your marriage."

"Words?" Blake hooted. "Shianne went at Micara with claws bared. She called her names I didn't think the girl even knew! She left your mother feeling an inch tall and put me in a tailspin. And I have you to blame for it." He expelled an irritated breath and glared holes in Wade's faded shirt. "If I had known you neglected to tell my daughter about the marriage I would have broken it to her gently instead of blurting it out like an idiotic fool. There I was, boasting about Micara to assure Shianne that my wife meant the world to me and that I was a happy, contented man. When all the while, Shianne was taking it as a personal insult. The whole idea of you breaking the news to Shianne was to allow her time to adjust. Now I've got one helluva mess!"

Blake threw up his hands in a gesture of frustration. "Micara is probably in our room crying buckets of tears, feeling she has caused conflict between me and my daughter, and Shianne is in her room demolishing the furniture, pretending I am every stick of wood she beats against the walls! Hell, I've already fought two wars, I didn't know I was going to find myself in the middle of another one when my wife and daughter chanced to meet!"

Grumbling under his breath, Wade veered around Blake's stocky frame and propelled himself toward the hotel.

"What are you going to do?" Blake called after him.

"I'm going to have a private conversation with my

wife," he threw over his shoulder and then stopped stock-still in his tracks, realizing he had just blurted out information that had reached Blake's ears for the first time. Tensely, Wade awaited the inevitable burst of surprise that erupted from Blake's lips.

"Your wife?" Blake staggered and braced his hand on the edge of the desk.

Wade did not wait to be scolded a second time in less than five minutes. The best tactic of defense was a strong offense, he reminded himself. "Yes, my wife," he repeated, his voice sharp, his gaze sharper. "That was what you hoped would happen when I laid eyes on that little hellcat you allowed to grow up like a windblown wild flower. You had several reasons for sending me to San Antonio while you and Mother headed north, didn't you, Blake?" Wade wagged a finger in Blake's guilty face. "You sent me to bear the news and explain the happenings of the past few years, but you also had in mind for me to fall hopelessly in love with Shianne, marry her and protect her from Reems. Well, you got your wish. I fell in love with her and I married her. So don't act so damned surprised that your scheme met with success."

Wade drew himself up like a soldier preparing to approach the battlefield. "Now, if you will excuse me, I'm going to go see if there is any way to convince that *mere wisp of a woman* from going on the warpath." He took one long stride toward the door and then wheeled back around to fling Blake an accusing glare. "And that's another thing. You neglected to tell me she was part wild Indian and that I would have to fight the medicine man of the Kiowas and Comanches to have her!"

As Wade stalked down the street, Blake lifted incredulous eyes to Chad's wry smile. "What the blazes is he raving about?"

504

Sympathetically, Chad patted him on the back. "After you finish calming Mother and smoothing over the initial clash between her new daughter and/or daughter-in-law, we'll sit down to supper and have a nice long chat."

Blake massaged his belly. He already had a severe case of indigestion. He wasn't sure he could stomach the details of the last few months over a meal. "I only hope the Cottage is serving chicken soup. Anything else will probably give me heartburn when I hear the rendition of the events that led you up the trail to Abilene."

Chad shrugged nonchalantly. "Other than the kidnapping, hailstorms, treacherous river crossings, stampedes and a near lynching, it was a quiet trip."

Blake gulped down his apprehension. He had the uneasy feeling Shianne had endured a most miserable time, only to be delivered a blow that her father had married and did not have enough nerve to face her himself.

His gaze lifted to the three-story hotel, wishing he could have been in two places at once. Micara needed him desperately after the war, and Shianne had needed a father. Blake had made the choice, and Shianne had paid for his sacrifice. If Shianne never spoke to him again he probably deserved the silent treatment, Blake thought dismally. It might take Wade the rest of the afternoon to calm Shianne down. Keeping that in mind, Blake strode back to the hotel, certain he was in for a long wait.

Chapter 25

Shianne climbed out of the tub and hurriedly dried herself. She had insisted on a cold bath after her tête-a-tête with her father and that *hussy* he had made his wife, but even cool water hadn't fazed her blazing temper. Shianne felt raw inside, and her pride was smarting.

When Wade had explained that her father had remained in Louisiana after the war to aid the Burdetts, she had understood Blake's need to offer compassion, and she had forgiven him for his absence at the ranch. But this! Shianne was so frustrated she wanted to tear out her hair. This betrayal of her mother's memory was unforgivable! How could Blake have succumbed to that . . . that strumpet?

No doubt, the woman had been booted out of the bawdy house because of her age. Desperate, she had tied herself into the trappings of a gently bred lady and had gone husband hunting. Blake was probably so smitten that he never bothered to ask how the wench had spent the days and *nights* of her past.

It all made sense to her now. Blake had not returned to Texas because his new wife would not permit it, and he was probably suffering from his guilt. At least he *should* have been after leaving his teenage daughter in Carlos and Ramona's care. Not that the Santos's had not loved her like a mother and father. Not that she and Carlos had not been capable of holding the K Bar together, but dammit, Blake had neglected his daughter to chase after that cruel, scheming woman!

The sharp rap at the door jarred Shianne from her troubled contemplations. "Go away!" she commanded harshly.

"It's me . . . Wade," he called from the other side of the door.

Shianne didn't care who it was at the moment. She was in no mood to converse with anyone until she had regained control of her temper.

"Shae, open the door." Wade's voice had a threatening ring to it, but Shianne did not respond.

Shoving his boot heel against the portal, Wade broke the lock and forcefully gained entrance. As the door crashed against the wall, Shianne wiggled into her clean gown. Her disapproving glare lanced off the sagging door and pelleted over Wade.

"I want to be alone just now," she ground out, attempting to refrain from venting her anger on Wade.

"No, you need to apologize for your tantrum *just now,*" Wade insisted.

So Wade knew about the scene with her father and his new bride, did he? And he was taking her father's side. Shianne felt betrayed all over again. "Me? Apologize?" Shianne scoffed at the absurdity. "I'm not the one who was dillydallying all over Kansas and Illinois while there was a ranch to run in Texas! I wasn't the one who turned my back on my own flesh and blood to go waltzing off with that scheming hussy!"

Wade closed the door as best he could, considering it was dangling from its hinges. Deliberately, he strode over to Shianne. "I think you are being a bit hard on

507

both of them. After all, you don't even know the woman. You have no right to pass judgment on her until the two of you have become better acquainted."

"I don't ever want to see her again," Shianne muttered resentfully. "And as for my father . . ." She wasn't certain how she felt. All the joy and excitement of seeing Blake again had been dashed by the news that she had a stepmother. That was the last thing she wanted!

Wade reached out to curl his finger beneath her chin, forcing her to meet his unblinking gaze. "I never thought you to be the kind of woman who would begrudge someone else's happiness."

"I am all for an abundance of joy, but not at *my* expense," Shianne grumbled resentfully.

"Your father is very much in love, and you have made a difficult situation unbearable," Wade scolded her.

Shianne presented her back and glared at the bare wall. "How would you feel if your mother showed up on the arm of some ne'er-do-well who had taken advantage of her loneliness and latched onto her wealth, only to grant himself security?"

A wry smile slanted across Wade's lips. "I would probably be hopping up and down with indignation. But my mother didn't marry a worthless drifter, and your father didn't marry some loose woman who was latching on to him for companionship and security. The lady happens to be in love with your father, and she has her own fortune to sustain her through her declining years."

Pivoting, Shianne flung Wade a skeptical glance. "How can you be so certain? Have you demanded a financial statement from your new mother-in-law?" she queried, her voice dripping with sarcasm.

Wade grasped Shianne's arm and led her to the bed,

gesturing for her to sit down. "When I came to Texas, I explained that Blake had put me in charge of the roundup and requested that I become your guardian. It is true that he was harboring feelings of guilt because he had not returned home. He wanted me to inform you of the marriage and allow you time to adjust to the thought of stepping aside to make room for another woman in the hacienda." He raked his fingers through his hair and then let his arm drop loosely at his side. "I thought you had enough to cope with and I kept procrastinating. You resented my interference in your life, and I was hesitant to spring the news on you. Then things started happening so fast, and I was too preoccupied to tell you about your father's marriage."

Wade folded his tall frame onto the edge of the bed and stared straight into Shianne's wounded eyes. "You see, it was only natural that I assume responsibility for you and that your father grant me power of attorney in his absence. I'm your step-brother, Shae. Blake's wife is my mother."

Stunned, Shianne gaped at him. The spiteful thoughts that had raced through her mind the past hour scattered in a thousand directions. Shianne couldn't find her tongue to speak because she had swallowed it.

"Your mother?" she finally chirped.

Wade nodded affirmatively. "I have told you of the tragedies my family encountered in the last months of the war. I tried to explain about the strong bond that had grown between your father and my mother. It was as if destiny brought them together. They found in each other something that had long been missing from their lives. It began as a friendship and appears to have blossomed into something very potent. They both needed someone." Wade heaved a heavy sigh. "I know it is hard for you to accept, knowing you presumed your father to be satisfied to live out the rest of his days on a memory of the past. In the beginning, Chad resented Blake's intrusion in our mother's life. He looked up to our father, patterning himself after the man who died serving the cause of the South. Now Chad realizes Micara and Blake care deeply for each other. He has accepted the fact that our parents' feelings for each other died long before my father lost his life."

"But why didn't Papa write and tell me where he was and what was going on in his life?" Shianne questioned bemusedly. "I would have understood. To betray my mother's memory was one thing, but to leave me wondering if he were dead or alive was quite another. I'm beginning to wonder if I really know my father at all!"

Wade grasped Shianne by both arms, giving her a firm shake. "Stop blaming Blake for something he couldn't control. He handled the situation the way he thought best, whether it was right or wrong in your eyes. How would you have accepted the news in a letter, one that would have taken months to reach you, if at all? Communication lines were virtually non-existent in the South during that time. We were under military rule and feelings between Yankees and rebels were barely tolerable. The North clamped down on the broken South, ensuring there would be no more rebellion. The mere act of posting a letter during those critical times was enough to provoke an investigation.

"You cannot begin to imagine the devastation, the turmoil. Texas was virtually untouched by the ravages of war, but the deep South lay in charred embers. Even if Blake could have sneaked a letter through the federal troops what could he have said? *My dearest daughter, I'm married to a lovely woman who needs me much more than you do at the moment.* And what would you have thought of him, not knowing the hell he was enduring, the total hopelessness of the situation?"

His tone grew softer, his emerald gaze holding her captive. "No, Shae, there are some things I don't think a man could tell his daughter in a letter. It would have made matters worse. Blake left you hanging in limbo, certain the truth would only hurt you more, and he also believed that his absence would keep you from succumbing to Haden. He feared your bitterness toward him might cause you to turn to Haden, if only for spite. Blake felt as if he was setting on a keg of dynamite. He didn't want you to wed Haden Reems, and he didn't want you to suffer any more than you already had. The war had far-reaching repercussions. During those critical times it was often difficult to know how to proceed. Life was a complex attempt at survival. It will take a great deal of time to put this country and its people back together after it has been ripped in two. You heard the way the Jayhawkers taunted me. They haven't forgotten. No one will, not for a long, long time to come."

Gathering Shianne's reluctant body into his arms, Wade rested his chin on top of her head. "You know how I feel about you, how difficult it is to think of ever leaving you. Is it inconceivable that your father could feel the same way about my mother?" Wade expelled a breath. "They both deserve a little happiness after the hell they have lived through. My mother lived with a man who had become a stranger, and your father lived on a memory. They filled an emptiness in each other's lives. Don't begrudge what they have together. It is very precious to both of them."

Shianne was ashamed of herself for spouting such insulting remarks to her father and Wade's mother, but the situation had taken her completely by surprise, and she had allowed her bitterness and hurt to grasp control of her tongue. She had found a special love. How could she resent her father's affection for Micara? He was her father, but he was also a man. Shianne realized that she had no right to sit in judgment of her father's feelings and obligations. Blake had known she was in capable hands, and he had stayed in Louisiana to help the Burdetts pick up the shattered pieces of their lives.

The faintest hint of a smile found the corner of her mouth. Shianne drew her feet beneath her and twisted around, exposing her shapely derriere to Wade's startled gaze. "Well, go ahead. Kick me," she invited. "I deserve it after all the hateful remarks I made about your mother."

A rakish grin claimed his bronzed features. That was the same request he had made to Shianne when they were in Wichita. "I don't have any inclination to issue a swift kick to your lovely backside, madam." His smile stretched into a wolfish leer. "I have another form of punishment in mind to compensate for the slanderous remarks you made about my dear, sweet mother."

Shianne returned his mischievous smile. "Don't keep me in suspense, dear brother. What is it you have on your mind?"

Wade looped his arms around her, yanking her onto his lap. "Nothing *brotherly,* on that you can depend."

"I will always depend on that," she murmured with an intimate smile. "Facing your mother after my disrespectful outburst is going to be punishment enough."

"I spoke to her before I came to our room," Wade said quietly. "She thought you had every right to be upset. You see, she feels guilty for keeping Blake from you. But Mother holds no grudge. She only wishes that the two of you become friends. As a matter of fact, the rest of the family is waiting in the restaurant to enjoy a peace treaty meal."

Reluctantly, Shianne slid from Wade's lap. "I know I will feel much better after we get this over with, but I do not anticipate facing your mother *or* my father again."

Wade gave her a loving squeeze. "Forgiveness will be forthcoming from both sides," he assured her softly. "You can eat your words, and Blake and Micara can swallow the guilt of leaving you to fend for yourself in Texas."

Nodding mutely, Shianne allowed Wade to escort her down the steps and into the dining hall. It was as he promised. Micara graciously accepted Shianne's apology and begged forgiveness for keeping Blake from his obligations as a father. Then, to Shianne's surprise, Blake apologized for taking a punch at Wade.

Shianne's wide-eyed gaze swung to Wade, noting the welt she had overlooked earlier. "You didn't say anything about Papa hitting you. Why did he do that?" she questioned bemusedly. "*I* was the one who threw the tantrum."

Wade grinned across the table at Blake. "I have the feeling I was his scapegoat."

Blake smiled sheepishly and shrugged. "I was so frustrated I felt like hitting someone. Wade's jaw just happened to collide with my fist."

"You still pack a wallop," Wade admitted, touching his tender cheek. "Even for an old man."

"I don't feel a day over thirty," Blake boasted, drawing himself up in his chair. His gaze slid to Shianne and then settled firmly on Wade. "I am still waiting to hear about this hasty marriage to my daughter. Although I did have hopes that such a union would come to pass, I most certainly expected to be there to give the bride away. Heaven knows I have been around to do little else these past few years!"

The guilt that seeped into Blake's voice did not lessen

Wade's uneasiness. He doubted that any explanation he gave would satisfy Blake who was bursting with pride for his lovely daughter. The man had been apologizing all over the place since they entered the restaurant, praising Shianne's abilities to assume control of the ranch and carry on in his long absence. How could he tell Blake that he had scooped Shianne off her wobbly legs and married her while she was up to her eyebrows in whiskey? That was not the sort of thing a father wanted to hear!

The discreet glances passing back and forth between Wade and Shianne drew Blake's wary frown. "Is there something I should know?" Blake demanded impatiently.

Shianne reached over to fold her hand over Wade's. "Yes, Papa," she murmured, the feelings from her heart shone in her eyes. "I fell in love with Wade the first time I saw him." It was no lie she gave. She was only twisting the truth a smidgen. "Indeed, I could not take my eyes off of him."

Wade returned her wry smile before sparing Blake a quick glance. "I found the woman I wanted, and I saw no reason to waste six months, waiting for you to return to Texas. Besides, Haden was pressuring me to announce *his* engagement to Shianne. That, I could not tolerate."

The mention of Haden Reems brought a pensive silence. It was Wade who broke the tension with his announcement. "I intend to set out after that scoundrel while you take the stagecoach to Wichita."

Blake gave his head a negative shake. "We are traveling to Texas together. We'll send the vaqueros home with the remuda of horses while we *all* employ the stage line. Our families have been split apart long enough. Haden cannot fight all of us, nor will he dare to show his face in San Antonio again. Let him live like

514

a hunted animal who is wary of his own shadow. A man who is accused of attempted murder, cattle stealing and kidnapping cannot dispose of all of those who would testify against him." Blake smiled confidently. "There is safety in numbers. I think Haden knows he has been beaten."

Wade wasn't so certain. He had the uneasy feeling that Haden would find a way to seek revenge. Haden's brand of evil never went away. It only faded into the background . . . temporarily.

One glance at Chad assured Wade that his brother had no intention of allowing Haden to roam the country without paying penance, but for the sake of peace, Wade kept his opinion to himself. He and Chad *appeared* to be satisfied with Blake's decision for the entire family to return to Texas by stagecoach, but neither of them would rest until Haden was punished for his wickedness. One day Haden would hang for his criminal offenses, Wade vowed to himself.

When the men adjourned to McCoy's office to complete the preparations for driving the cattle to the stock pens in Abilene, Shianne found herself staring into Micara's apprehensive features. Shianne cursed herself for her hateful remarks. If Shianne had not been in such a snit, she would have realized this gently bred lady was no aging harlot looking for security.

As they ambled back to their rooms, Micara paused to offer Shianne a heart-felt smile. "I don't know if I will ever overcome this sense of guilt, Shianne. I feel as if I have deprived you of years with your father."

"There is no need for you to . . ." Shianne began, only to be cut off by Micara's insistence.

"There is a *great* need, my dear," Micara told her earnestly. "I could say that what happened between your father and me was the product of disastrous times, times when we needed someone to lean on, to

515

depend on." She inhaled a deep breath and looked
Shianne straight in the eye. "But it was more than that.
We had suffered many trials together and our
friendship blossomed into an even stronger devotion.
There was much to be done to put our lives back in
order, and it took a good deal of time, just as the
restoration of the South will take decades.

"I suggested that Blake return to Texas, even though
I thought I would die if he left me, but I knew you
needed him as much as I did. He assured me that you
were in capable hands, and I allowed myself to believe
it because I could not bear to see him go. Nor was I
prepared to travel with him. I was still torn between my
love for Blake and my conflicting feelings for my first
husband. I did not wish to betray or cheapen his
memory, but I was so afraid of losing Blake after I had
lost most everything else."

Micara breathed a tremulous sigh and shed a few
tears. "I feared you would resent me as Chad resented
your father in the beginning. After all that had
happened I wasn't certain I could cope with a
stepdaughter who detested the sight of me and who
begrudged my intrusion in her life."

Shianne thoughtfully chewed on her bottom lip.
Would she have made life miserable for Micara?
Shianne would have preferred to think she was a bigger
person than that, but after the tantrum she had thrown
that afternoon, she wondered if she would have
gracefully accepted another woman in Blake's life.
Only now, knowing how dearly she loved Wade, could
Shianne understand her father's fierce need to stay by
Micara's side. No, she could not have comprehended
that compelling attachment until she had experienced
it herself, Shianne realized.

A smile, embroidered with genuine emotion, traced
Shianne's lips as she peered in Micara's misty blue eyes.

"I bear no ill feelings for you or my father," she assured Micara. "Although I may never know all the tortures of hell you endured because of the destruction of war, I understand what it is like to love someone with all my heart and soul. If my father had returned, I may never have met Wade." Shianne squeezed Micara's hand and held her level gaze. "The past does not seem as important as the present and future. You could not bear to endure a day without my father, and I cannot imagine life without Wade."

Micara was touched by Shianne's confession. Her apprehension fell away. It seemed at last she could get on with her life without wondering if Shianne would accept her as part of her family, but Micara was still plagued with a hint of uneasiness. She had seen the way Chad stared at this sultry beauty when he thought no one was looking. Micara had the feeling both of her sons were helplessly drawn to Shianne. Although Micara had not dared to interrogate either of her sons, she had the feeling Chad was harboring a secret affection, one that might cause conflict with his older brother.

"Shianne, I must ask something of you, something I hesitate to ask Chad." Micara took a deep breath and plunged on before she lost her nerve. "Are you aware of the affection my younger son feels for you?"

Shianne gaped at Micara. Her perceptiveness startled Shianne. Nothing had been said about Chad's attempt to make Wade jealous. Yet Micara had somehow sensed the strain of Chad's emotions.

Micara smiled demurely. "I can see that it surprises you that I noticed the way Chad stares at you. A mother can detect subtle signs in her sons. I know how Wade feels about you by the way he responds to you. I have never seen him so warm and attentive toward a woman, but I can also see what Chad is trying to hide.

Forgive me for asking, but are you torn between my sons?"

"I care for Chad," Shianne admitted. "But Chad knows where my loyalty lies. Somewhere there is a woman waiting for Chad to walk into her life, just as Wade walked into mine and filled up my world."

"Then this is something Chad will have to work out by himself," Micara said with a pensive nod. "I will not expect him to stay long in Texas, knowing how he feels about you. I suspect he will come to me with some excuse as to why he should strike out on his own. You and Wade must not attempt to convince him to stay. Until Chad comes to terms with his emotions, he will not be satisfied in Texas."

"You will let him go, not knowing where he is or what difficulties he faces in the untamed wilderness?" Shianne questioned bewilderedly.

Micara curled her hand around Shianne's arm, aiming her down the hall. "I have to, my dear, because it is best for Chad. Begging him to stay would only cause him misery. One day, when he has accepted his role as your brother-in-law *and* your stepbrother, he can look upon you without wanting what he cannot have. Chad is not as bitter as he once was, but he still has a long road to hoe before he becomes a man who is truly at peace with himself, a man who has accepted the tragedies of the past and will allow them to die a quiet death."

"If ever I begrudged your entrance into my father's life, I feel no bitterness now," Shianne said sincerely. "You are a remarkable woman."

"Thank you, Shianne." Her eyes twinkled in amusement. "And so are you. If not, my two sons would not be so taken with you. It seems that you defy everything they had come to expect from women. I could not be more pleased with Wade's choice, even if

518

he didn't wait until Blake returned to give you away. As in your case *and* mine, precious time was wasting. . . ."

Shianne returned Micara's sly smile, wondering if love at fifty could be as splendid as it was at twenty-one. Judging by the sparkle in Micara's eyes, Shianne concluded that it was, and she chastised herself for resenting Blake and Micara for even a minute. They both deserved the same brand of happiness that made Shianne's heart swell each time she gazed into Wade's craggy features.

Satisfied that she and Micara would become friends and confidants, Shianne returned to her room to await Wade. The empty hacienda near San Antonio would be bursting with joy and laughter once again. Shianne could hardly wait to arrive in Texas. It would be a wonderful new beginning!

Haden Reems stepped into the rustic office that had once been headquarters for the Texas Rangers during the Civil War. The outpost at Fleetwood, just below the Red River in Texas, was now the location of the state police whose duty it was to patrol the border, control the Indian offensives and inspect herds that passed through that region of the country. Although the transplanted Yankees did little more than collect their pay and swindle cattle from trail drovers, they were exactly what Haden needed to settle his feud with the Burdetts and the Kimballs.

After sneaking through the northeastern section of Indian Territory, Haden wired for money to be sent to him at Fleetwood from the bank in San Antonio. He was certain it would cost him several coins to pad the pockets of these carpetbag badge toters known as the Texas state police, but he was willing to make the sacrifice. With his money belt strapped around his waist, Haden approached Commander Benjamin Reynolds to present his case and request assistance.

"What can we do for you, Mr. Reems?" the elderly commander questioned.

"I find myself in dire straits," Haden began. "My cattle herd was stolen in Indian Territory by a gang of rustlers led by a rebel named Wade Burdett. I tried in vain to stop him, but he herded my longhorns to Abilene and sold them, pocketing the entire profit. Burdett is ruthless and calculating. If I confront him alone I would expect to pay with my life."

Commander Reynolds frowned. "Did you know of Burdett before your encounter in Indian Territory?"

Haden nodded affirmatively. "Burdett and his family had been conspiring against me for more than six months. He has persuaded his brother to falsely accuse me of attempted murder. He has married the woman who was my fiancée and convinced her to lie to incriminate me. He even went so far as to leave a message with a lawyer in San Antonio, naming me as the prime suspect should *he* meet with disaster," Haden explained. "My hands were virtually tied! If I attempted to right the injustices, Burdett would have *me* look the culprit. His ultimate purpose is to frame me for crimes I did not commit and then assume command of my ranch.

"My ex-fiancée even followed me on the trail to Kansas, begging forgiveness for marrying the wrong man. When Burdett caught up with her, he accused *me* of kidnapping her! He was furious with her for betraying him. I even saw Burdett lay the whip to her back for defying him."

Reynolds was beginning to detest this vengeful rebel, sight unseen. He was not particularly pleased with the duty he had been given after the war, and he was always eager to put a belligerent Southern sympathizer in his

520

proper place. Although Reynolds had not stooped to stealing cattle from the herds that filed through the area, he had often turned his back when some of his men harassed drovers and forced them to sacrifice several beeves in exchange for a permit to drive longhorns across the border. Perhaps his sense of justice had been warped after the war, but he would not allow a man like Wade Burdett to walk away unscathed!

"My men and I will see what we can do to right the wrong, but first we have to locate Burdett. That might take some doing, Mr. Reems. There are miles of border between Indian Territory and Texas," Reynolds reminded him.

"Within the week, Burdett and his family of liars and thieves should be arriving by stagecoach in Preston, by way of the Shawnee Trail. Do not be surprised if Burdett twists everything I have told you and proclaims that *I* am the one who has committed hideous crimes. His brother was tortured by the Comanches, and Wade encouraged him to testify that it was *I* who carved him up with a knife. No doubt Wade will also accuse me of starting the rockslide that buried him and his brother inside a cavern near San Antonio."

Haden threw up his hands as if he were utterly exasperated. "I swear the man has an uncanny knack of falsely accusing me of anything that might win him the deed to my vast holdings near San Antonio. He despises me because I was a Yankee sympathizer during the war. Since Burdett lost his plantation in Louisiana he intends to make a new life for himself on *my* ranch." A look of helpless frustration swallowed Haden's bony features, milking the commander's sympathy. "How does a man go about fighting someone who is so embittered by war that he will do *anything* to get what he wants?"

521

"I will personally see to the matter," Reynolds promised faithfully. "We will bring this man in for questioning and attempt to retrieve your money from the cattle drive."

Haden unstrapped his money belt and laid it before the commander. "I intend to prove to you that what I say is true." He gestured toward the roll of cash that lined the belt. "I am a wealthy man. If I do not receive my profits from the cattle drive I will still be able to keep my ranch functioning. Indeed, I would gladly put up the money you confiscate from Burdett as a reward for apprehending the dastardly criminal, but what I want most of all is satisfaction and the restoration of my good name, one Burdett has been dragging through the mud. He has my friends and neighbors questioning my integrity. If Burdett is not brought to justice, it will take months, even years to reestablish my reputation with the citizens of San Antonio. Rumors can be damaging." Haden laughed bitterly. "I should know. Burdett has twisted the truth until no one knows for certain what is right or wrong. Beware the man. He and his family will have *you* questioning *me*."

His eyes focused intently on Reynolds, determined to use Wade's own tactic against him. "If I should meet my demise, I promise you Wade Burdett will somehow be responsible. No jury could withstand the pack of lies given by him and his family. He deserves no better than a hasty hanging. Should I die for attempting to bring this scoundrel to justice, my tormented soul will not rest until Burdett is roasting in hell!"

Haden peeled off several bills and laid them in Reynolds's hand. "This is to incur any expenses during your journey to Preston. The rest of your reward will be paid when you bring the Burdetts to the post at Fleetwood. If I did not fear that I would be murdered by that unscrupulous band of outlaws, I would ac-

522

company you. But, knowing them, I would not live to plead my case in a court of justice, much less defend myself during an inquisition in your office."

When Haden strode out the door to return to his room at the hotel, Reynolds slumped back in his seat. He would have to prepare himself to confront the wily fox Haden Reems had described. Reynolds had met his share of scalawags during his hitch in the Union army. No doubt he was about to lay eyes on another. Texas was crawling with homeless rebels who would slither on their bellies to make a new start, and they didn't care who they crushed in their crusade to reestablish rebel pride.

"Damn war," Reynolds muttered under his breath. It would take a century to reunite the country. There were too many ill feelings between Yankees and rebels. Even *he* was having difficulty forgetting the atrocities he had seen.

One thing was certain. He would see that Wade Burdett became an example to all other rebels who thought to cheat an honest man out of his home and his livelihood. Haden Reems would receive full compensation for what had happened. Reynolds would not fall prey to a pack of lies aimed to turn the tables on Haden Reems.

Chapter 26

A muddled frown etched Shianne's brow as she peered out the stagecoach window to see the regiment of state police congregating about them. Her gaze swung back to Wade who shrugged at the question in her eyes.

"Wade Burdett, I wish a word with you," Commander Reynolds announced stiffly.

Wade unfolded himself from the cramped coach and stepped to the ground. Reynolds surveyed the tall, muscularly built man who stood before him. The natural smile that curved Wade's lips caused Reynolds to frown curiously. This man did not fit the image Reynolds had conjured up in his mind. This was the conniving desperado Haden had described? The commander recalled that Haden had warned him to beware of the deceptive serpent. Burdett's outward appearance gave the impression that he was a personable individual . . . until he was crossed. Bearing that in mind, Reynolds resolved not to trust Burdett any farther than he could throw him.

"You and the members of your family are under arrest for the theft of a cattle herd recently sold in Abilene, Kansas."

"What?" Wade couldn't believe what he was hearing.

Neither could Blake Kimball. He bolted from the coach to set the matter straight. "Now wait just a damned minute," he growled as he stalked toward the commander. "Haden Reems stole our herd and kidnapped my daughter. If anyone needs to be put under arrest it's that rotten excuse for a man!"

Reynolds smiled haughtily. "That is exactly what Mr. Reems predicted you would say when confronted with the accusations." Gesturing to the coach, he silently requested Wade and Blake to resume their places in preparation for a detour in their journey. "You will have your opportunity to speak in your defense when we reach headquarters."

Scowling, Wade wedged into the narrow niche beside Shianne and cast Juan Mendez a somber glance. "What do you suppose the bastard has up his sleeve this time?"

Juan flexed his mending hand, his eyes glowing with vengeance. "More trouble, *hombre,*" he muttered acrimoniously. "If I know Haden, he has found a way to make all of us pay betraying him."

"He may not live to accuse anyone of wrongdoing," Chad growled vindictively.

"There is a strong possibility of that," Shianne hissed venomously. "I have every right to slit his throat after what he did to me."

"You can go for his throat *after* I carve my name on his chest," Juan muttered sourly. "He owes me for maiming my hand and slashing my belly with his blade."

"And he owes me for using me as his whipping post," Chad grumbled. "The rest of you will have to wait your turn. I was the first to fall prey to his malicious ways."

Wade held up his hand to silence the vindictive threats that were buzzing around the coach. "God knows we each have just cause to cut Haden into bite-sized pieces, but if we march into Fleetwood, spouting our hatred for Haden, we will be signing our own death warrants. That is exactly what Haden expects us to do."

"What is it you suggest, big brother?" Chad smirked caustically. "The last time you devised a scheme to bring Haden to his knees we found ourselves buried beneath tons of dirt and boulders. I think one of us should kill him and be done with it."

"Chad!" Micara gasped. "You cannot just walk into a man's room and gun him down!"

Chad loosened the buttons of his shirt to expose the crisscross scars on his chest. "When a man does this to a total stranger without asking any questions, he deserves to die a violent death."

The color seeped from Micara's features when she spied the scars that left white streaks across her son's midsection. "Oh my God," she breathed raggedly.

Blake's tanned features wore a harsh glare. "Why that miserable bastard," he swore.

"If we march into the state police headquarters, thirsting for Haden's blood, we will find ourselves herded into jail before we can proclaim our innocence and Haden's guilt," Wade cut in, his expression solemn.

"What chance do we have with the state police?" Shianne sniffed disgustedly. "I would bet my right arm Haden bought them off. The whole lot of them are as crooked as he is!"

Voicing that thought brought another strained silence. Each passenger in the stagecoach was mentally speculating on the outcome of this so-called trial to establish justice.

Shianne was not at all certain the diplomatic approach would serve any purpose. Chad had been hungering for revenge for more than a year. Juan itched to slice Haden to bits. Blake was wishing he had found a way to destroy Haden years ago, and Wade was wondering how such a pleasant day could have turned so sour.

Wade's thoughtful green eyes swung to each passenger, speculating on which one of them, himself included, would resort to drastic measures. He knew how each one felt about Haden and with just cause. He was harboring his own hatred, which was playing havoc with his common sense. Wade knew it would be futile to dispose of Haden until the matter was resolved, but God, he was just as vindictive as the rest of his family. Haden had escaped unscathed once too often. If Haden won this round, there would be no punishing him, nor could anyone stop him from continuing his tyranny.

Frustrated, Wade pulled the brim of his hat down over his forehead and leaned back to close his eyes and ponder. Shianne nudged him with her elbow, annoyed that he could even think of catching a catnap when they were on their way to the gallows.

"I had hoped you would take this matter more seriously," she scolded. "How can you sleep when you could be swinging from a rope by this time tomorrow?"

Wade's long lashes fluttered up, and he flung his fretting wife an infuriating smile. "I was merely trying to think this through," he defended. "But it is damned difficult with all this racket."

Wearing a pouting frown, Shianne crossed her arms beneath her breasts and sat stiffly beside him. "Well, you better dream up an ingenious scheme . . . and quickly," she insisted. "Because if you cannot, there are those among us who might decide to fight fire with fire."

By the time the coach stopped at the stage station for

527

the night, nerves were frayed and tempers were boiling. The fact that guards were posted outside each door did nothing to improve dispositions. Shianne paced the room like a caged predator, wishing she could wrap her fingers around Haden's neck and choke the life out of him.

"Shae, come to bed," Wade ordered. "Wearing a hole in the floor is not going to solve our problems."

"At least it's a release for my frustrated energy," she grumbled grouchily. "Did you ever stop to think how I am going to live if the state police tote you off to prison or if Haden convinces them to string you up by your neck?"

Wade cast his shirt aside and strode over to gather Shianne in his arms. "Surely Commander Reynolds will recognize the truth after each of us has testified to Haden's treachery. How could he believe one man while four others are pointing accusing fingers at Haden?"

"Haden would have never gone to the state police if he didn't think he could battle us and win," Shianne blurted out and then wiggled free when Wade's wandering caresses began to flood over her hips. "Stop that. How can you think of sleep, or anything else for that matter, when we are up to our necks in trouble?"

A rakish grin tugged at the corner of his mouth. "How can I not think of making love to you when this is the first time in weeks that we have been allowed privacy. In every other stage station we were crammed into sleeping quarters with the rest of the family. I can only behave myself for so long. . . ."

Shianne tossed him a withering glance, but when Wade took her captive with his longing gaze, she melted into mush. How could she resist spending the night in his loving arms, knowing Haden might find a way to tear Wade from her forever? If passion would ease these disturbing premonitions that had ridden in her shadow throughout the course of the afternoon, Shianne decided it was well worth it.

She came back to his arms without an ounce of reserve, waiting for his loving touch to erase her torment and paint the world with rainbows. "Oh, Wade, if anything should . . ."

His fingertip moved across her lips. "Hush, love. Right now there are only the two of us," he murmured, staring into her dark eyes. "I want to forget everything that has any resemblance to reality. Kiss me, and don't stop kissing me until my mind is clouded with the dense fog of passion."

Shianne responded to his request. As her lips found his, her lashes fluttered down to blot out the world. For a time there would be nothing but the manly aroma that invaded her nostrils, the feel of his protective arms molding her body to the hardness of his, the taste of kisses that were laced with love.

Each of his caresses worshipped her skin and smoothed the wrinkles from her nerves. She clung to him, afraid to let go, afraid tomorrow would bring disaster, and their love would become a bittersweet memory. She detested Haden even more for putting her through this misery. If he managed to destroy Wade, she would not allow Haden to live long enough to enjoy his satisfaction, she promised herself. There was no law to speak of in Texas, and she would not think twice about taking matters into her own hands. Haden did not deserve to live.

That was the last sane thought to traverse Shianne's mind. Wade erased her vindictive musings with his tender caress as he came to her, murmuring his love. Shianne surrendered to the erotic sensations he always evoked from her. This bold, powerful breed of man could send her to the heights and depths of ecstasy, and she never wanted to leave that mystical domain.

"Shae, promise me you won't do anything foolish," Wade whispered in the aftermath of love. "No matter what happens I want your promise. . . ."

Shianne couldn't make that vow, not after the one she had made to herself. They were in direct contrast. "You ask too much of me," she murmured, refusing to meet his steady gaze.

His hand curled beneath her chin, bringing her eyes back to his. "I am the one accused of theft," he reminded her. "Let me deal with Haden as I see fit."

"And if diplomacy doesn't work, what then?" she demanded softly.

Wade gave his raven head a slow shake. "I haven't quite thought it out yet," he admitted.

"Blast it, there are times when I wish you weren't so deliberate," Shianne grumbled resentfully.

"Then perhaps you should have married my brother," Wade snapped more harshly than he intended. "The two of you could have left a path of destruction behind you, disposing of everyone who tested your tempers."

Shianne didn't want to fight with Wade, not when time was so precious. Her hand glided across his stony features, mellowing his severe expression. "I would be satisfied with no other man. Don't you know that? It is only that I am frustrated and afraid that I might lose what I cherish most. If wishing would make it so, Haden would disappear into thin air, never to be seen or heard from again. I don't want to lose you, Wade. I love you."

A wry smile slid across his lips, making the gold flecks in his eyes sparkle in the lantern light. "Prove it. . . ."

Shianne returned his challenging grin as she pressed him to his back. "Beyond a shadow of a doubt?" she

530

questioned, her hands working their sweet magic.

"Mmmmm . . . yes," he breathed, his body rousing to her loving touch.

And she did.

Although the previous night had chased away Shianne's fears, her apprehension returned in full force when the coach rolled up to the headquarters in Fleetwood. The small settlement contained an outfitting store for cattle drovers, a hotel, a saloon and several buildings used by the state police. The barracks provided little in the way of luxury, but at least everyone was allowed the privacy of a room. All too soon Shianne realized she would have preferred to live without that privacy. Each family member was left in his separate chamber, complete with a posted guard. One by one, they were summoned to Commander Reynolds's office to be interrogated about their relationship with Haden Reems.

All the while the bastard sat in his chair, smiling self-righteously. Haden was so sure of himself that Shianne fought the urge to claw that gloating smirk off his face. After she explained what had occurred, Haden was granted the opportunity to present his rendition of each incident. Shianne sat there in disbelief, wondering how the man could twist the truth into such an incredible knot of lies and make it sound so convincing. By the time she was ushered back to her room, she was so frustrated she felt like screaming at the top of her lungs.

The day dragged on at a snail's pace, and Shianne was beside herself, wondering how the others had fared when they confronted Haden and Commander Reynolds. When the clanging of a distant bell jostled her from her pensive musings, Shianne came to her feet and opened the door to her room. To her amazement she watched the guard abandon his post to answer the call of emergency.

This was her opportunity to seek out Haden and force him to admit to the truth. Easing open the door to ensure the guard had not returned, Shianne surveyed the dark hall. The commander had positioned the other members of the family in different wings of the barracks, allowing them no opportunity to exchange or rehearse the information they offered during the investigation. Since there was no one in the hall, Shianne crept from her room, wondering how many other family members were contemplating the same tactic that was buzzing through her mind. No doubt she would find Haden in his hotel room with a long string of visitors waiting to get their hands on him.

Darting through the shadows, Shianne made her way to the small hotel. Without bothering to knock, she burst inside the room to face Haden who had already expected all sorts of company that evening. He waited, sitting leisurely on his bed, his pistol laying within easy reach.

"Ah, my dear Shianne. How nice of you to happen by to ease my loneliness. I'm sure Commander Reynolds will be interested to learn that you came to beg forgiveness for the vicious lies you spouted in his office today. Have you come to share my bed, hoping I will take you back when your treacherous husband is hanged for his crimes?"

Shianne stared incredulously at Haden. The man was utterly mad! He had concocted so many lies that he had begun to believe them. His twisted mind left him living in a world of pretense and fabrication. He honestly thought he had been put upon by the Burdetts and the Kimballs.

"You are insane," Shianne hissed at him.

Haden chuckled carelessly. "Nothing you say affects me now, Shianne. Don't you realize that? I listened to each and every one of you falsely accuse me of malicious crimes, none of which I committed." He sighed heavily. "I know you have deep affection for me, but I'm afraid it is too late for us. I cannot forgive you for what you tried to do to me. When the state police hang your husband, I will not be there to console you."

His demented gaze flooded over her appetizing figure, one that had long been a tormenting obsession for him. "I will consider keeping you as my whore, but nothing more. I must consider my pride and my reputation in the community." There was a hint of madness in his smile as he swung his spindly legs over the edge of the bed and stood up. "Perhaps if you offer me a foretaste of your charms, I could be persuaded to change my mind. . . ."

Change his mind? Haden didn't have one left! Shianne stared long and hard at the revolver that lay on the bed. Then her eyes shifted to the dagger he carried in his belt. How she itched to turn both his weapons on him for even suggesting she would allow his repulsive touch!

Haden would never live through the night, Shianne told herself. Someone was going to put him out of his misery, no matter what the consequences. He had become so poisoned by his own treachery that it had transformed him into a raving lunatic. Haden could not distinguish between fantasy and reality. Now he was even more dangerous than before. Commander Reynolds would believe anything Haden told him because Haden seemed so sure of himself, so confident of his innocence.

As Haden skulked toward her with a leer stamped on his features, Shianne retreated. In frustration, Shianne fled out the door. Something had to be done and quickly. She could almost see the noose settling about Wade's neck, just as it had the day the Kansas mob attempted to hang him. Panic overcame her. To hell with diplomacy, her mind screamed. Commander Reynolds would never recognize the truth while Haden was there to parry with lies!

While Shianne was debating about how to handle the situation, Wade had sneaked from his room to confront Haden. He doubted he would be the first or last visitor to file toward the hotel. Indeed, the scattering of guards would allow every friend and family member to pay Haden a call.

Wade had come to the same conclusion that tormented Shianne when he laid eyes on Haden. The man was demented. Haden calmly assured Wade that as soon as he was hanged for thieving, Shianne would be in her ex-fiancé's arms.

Haden wouldn't last the night, Wade predicted. One or the other of them would yield to the temptation of returning to dispose of the madman who had wrought grief with every step he took.

Scowling, Wade returned to his room to pace the floor. How could he control the rest of his family when he was stricken by the same urge to snatch up Haden's pistol and blow him off the face of the earth? The man had put each and every one of them through hell the past year . . . except for Micara, he reminded himself. Since his mother was the least likely suspect, she would probably be the first to contemplate the crime. Even Micara had been taken to Reynolds's office to undergo questioning, and she had never met Haden Reems! Knowing Micara, she would probably decide it was her place to see the matter done to spare the rest of her family the torment.

Or Blake . . . Wade frowned at the thought. He knew Blake was upset about this entire ordeal. He held himself personally responsible for not putting a stop to Reems's skulduggery years ago. Then there was Juan—the outlaw-turned-good. Juan was very capable of reverting to his old ways in this instance. He had killed for Haden in the past, and he might be thinking it was time to dispose of the man who had instigated most of the crimes committed in Bexar County.

Of course, one could not overlook Chad, Wade dismally reminded himself. Chad had been itching to walk in and gun Haden down since the beginning. It would take very little to provoke Chad to follow through with his instinctive retaliation.

In frustration, Wade stared at the closed door, debating whether to go or stay. If he tarried much longer, the guard might return to check on him. If he stayed, someone else might attempt to dispose of Haden. What repercussions would follow? Lord, he knew how impulsive his own wife was. If she dared to . . . Wade refused to allow himself to complete the thought. He well remembered how Shianne had come riding over the hill to save him when he had been accosted by irate Jayhawkers, showing no concern for her own welfare. When Wade had asked for her promise not to do something rash, she had refused to give it. Lord, he would much prefer to be swinging from a tree than to watch Commander Reynolds lead Shianne away for committing a crime for the sake of love. . . .

Benjamin Reynolds scowled in irritation and glanced about the demolished saloon. A rowdy group of trail herders had thundered into town to turn the place upside down. It had taken every available man to break up the brawl provoked by one of the mischievous Calico Queens who had pitted one man against the other.

Once order was restored and the accidental fire had been extinguished, Commander Reynolds ordered his men back to their posts to stand watch over the Kimballs and Burdetts. After hearing the testimonies and the counterdefense presented by Haden Reems, Benjamin had made his decision. He was anxious to see justice served and settle the feud that had given him one hellacious headache.

It was three o'clock in the morning when he assembled the members of the family from each wing of the barracks. Benjamin did not need to sleep on his deliberations. He had decided what was to be done and the sooner the better.

Clasping his hands behind him, Benjamin paced the hall. "I have given the matter careful consideration. After hearing the accusations presented by you and by Haden Reems, I have reached my decision about who is telling the truth and who is lying."

Shianne clung tensely to Wade's arm, awaiting Reynolds's decision. To her dismay, he paused from his pacing and gestured for the entire group to follow in his wake.

"We will adjourn to Mr. Reems's room at the hotel. When I pass sentence, I intend for everyone concerned to be present."

In silence, the congregation proceeded down the street and filed down the hall that led to Haden's room. Strange, muffled noises came from behind the door. Frowning bemusedly, Commander Reynolds rapped on the portal, only to hear another round of odd sounds. When he attemped to draw open the door, something on the inside seemed to be restricting it from swinging back toward him in the usual manner.

Bracing his feet, Reynolds clasped both hands around the door knob and forcefully yanked it toward him.

A muffled groan reached his ears, intermingling with the crash of a chair against the planked floor. Peering around the edge of the partially opened door, Reynolds gasped at the scene that lay before him. "Good God!"

His angry gaze swung to each somber face. "Which one of you is responsible for this?" he demanded gruffly.

No one uttered a word. If a pin had dropped on the floor, it would have sounded like an anvil crashing on the planks.

Muttering, Reynolds pulled the door completely open. There hung Haden, his neck stretched past its limits, swinging from a rope that was attached to the ceiling beam. Haden's hands had been tied behind him, and his red bandana had been stuffed in his mouth. Another rope had been strung around the leg of the chair on which Haden had been standing and, in turn, tied to the door knob. When the commander yanked open the door, the chair was dragged out from under Haden, and he was left dangling in midair.

Reynolds glanced around him, speculating on which one of these men had sneaked from his room during the ruckus at the saloon and ventured to the hotel to dispose of Haden. After hearing the testimony of each person, Reynolds wasn't certain he would put it past any of them: Wade, Chad, Juan or Blake. He immediately ruled out either woman, certain a female would not have possessed the strength to manipulate Reems into what had been a fatal position on the chair.

"Help me cut him down," Reynolds growled at his men.

After Haden's body had been carried away, each person in the room stared curiously at the others, wondering who had dared to put action to the thoughts that had been flitting across his mind throughout the evening. Never had Reynolds seen a room filled with so many deadpan expressions.

"Is no one going to confess to this clever scheme?" he snorted impatiently. "Or do each of you intend to defend the other?"

Still there was nothing but silence. When Wade broke into a lopsided smile, Reynolds frowned. "What is it you find so amusing? A man has been killed, and I am confronted with a roomful of suspects, each one brimming with motives."

He gestured an accusing finger at Chad. "This one claims to have been slashed and whipped by Haden Reems."

Reynolds indicated the Mexican who was as sober as a judge. "And this one swears he lost the use of his gun hand, not to mention having his belly split with Haden's blade."

The commander focused narrowed eyes on Wade. "Here we have another prime suspect who was supposedly stripped from his clothes, staked to the ground and robbed before he was buried alive. Haden was certain that if he met his demise, you would somehow be responsible."

His gaze swung to Blake. "And Mr. Kimball openly admitted to me that he could kick himself for not dragging Haden Reems to the sheriff's office years ago."

Benjamin breathed a frustrated sigh. "I would go so far as to accuse the young lady if I thought she had the strength to deliver Haden to his own lynching."

"Haven't you overlooked one of us?" Wade questioned, wearing a sly smile.

"Who? Your mother?" Reynolds scoffed at the absurdity. *"Her* testimony convinced me that Haden Reems was a raving lunatic. You tried to dissuade me

538

from bringing Micara into my office for interrogation because she had never met the man," he reminded Wade. "When Haden accused her of lying and insisted that they had met in San Antonio, I knew something was amiss. Haden had an iron-clad defense for every incriminating incident. He was too calm and self-assured." Reynolds gave his head a negative shake. "No, I don't think I have overlooked anyone who might have been responsible for Haden's death. I agree that he deserved no better after all the crimes he committed against each of you, and the irony of it is that I would have suggested the punishment he received."

"I was not referring to my mother," Wade informed the commander, relieved that, if nothing else, Reynolds had seen through the vicious lies to pluck out the truth. "I was referring to *you,* sir."

The color ebbed from Benjamin Reynolds's features. "Me?"

Wade nodded affirmatively, indicating the rope that was dangling from the door knob. "You are the one who yanked open the door and pulled the chair out from under Reems. It seems you are the one who delivered his punishment. Does it matter so much in this instance who took the condemned man to the gallows?"

Benjamin glanced at the congregation, finding not a repentant face in the crowd. And for good reason, he mused. He thought about it for a moment and then expelled the breath he had been holding since Wade accused him of causing Haden's demise. "No, in this case, I suppose it doesn't," he admitted. "The man was utterly mad. I'm most thankful I realized it before another innocent victim fell prey to the lunatic's scheming. I'm not certain how I am going to effectively report this incident to my superiors, but I am asking no more questions. Indeed, I don't think I want to know who was responsible for setting me up as the gaoler in this lynching."

Reynolds strode toward the door and then paused to glance back at each pensive face. "You are free to go. I regret that I did not see through Reems's lies in the beginning. I could have spared us all this unfortunate incident."

When the commander strode away, Shianne discreetly reached over to retrieve the object that lay on the ledge of the open window. Tucking it in her hand, she fell into step behind Wade.

"Have you any speculations as to which one of us ensured that Haden paid his due?" Wade questioned as they ambled back to the barracks.

Shianne nodded soberly and unfolded her hand to reveal the object she had taken from the window ledge. A slow smile worked its way across Wade's features as he stared at the shred of evidence, but he did not utter a word.

"How do you suppose he knew we . . ." Shianne's voice trailed off. She knew the answer to the question the moment she put it to tongue.

The faint call of an owl intermingled with the sounds of the darkness. Shianne clutched the feather in her hand and raised her beseeching gaze to Wade. "Let me go to him . . ." she softly requested.

"We'll go together," Wade insisted.

After they had borrowed mounts from Commander Reynolds, Wade and Shianne rode into the plush valley of the Red River. The moment the Owl Prophet stepped from the swaying shadows Shianne slid from her horse and dashed into Maman-ti's open arms.

"I had a dream," he murmured against the top of her head. "It led me from my village by Medicine Creek to this great river. I saw you flee from the barracks to the

540

hotel, and I crouched beneath the window when you visited the white man, Reems." Maman-ti's dark eyes lifted to study Wade's somber expression. "When your husband made his second visit to the madman's room I came in through the window."

Shianne's eyes flew to Wade and then circled back to the Owl Prophet.

"When the evil white man tried to put a bullet through me, Wade Burdett wrestled him to the floor," Maman-ti explained.

"It was the first time the two of us had worked together instead of pulling in opposite directions," Wade murmured, casting the Indian a quiet smile.

"I would have lifted his scalp," Maman-ti declared. "But Wade did not wish to bring the wrath of Texas down on the Comanches and Kiowas. He wanted to let Reems suffer in torment, knowing the end would come, and he could do nothing to stop it." The faintest hint of a smile touched the Owl Prophet's lips as he glanced at Wade. "Wade Burdett thought it best to let Commander Reynolds become the executioner. It is best that only the three of us know what truly happened to Haden Reems. It does not matter who sent the evil white man from this world, only that he received his just reward. Many have suffered because of him, and justice was a long time in coming."

Maman-ti bent to press a parting kiss to Shianne's forehead. "The deed is done. The wicked white man brought this on himself." Curling an arm around Shianne's waist, Maman-ti turned to address the man he had finally come to call friend. "You and your family will live in peace with the Comanche and Kiowa."

As Maman-ti extended his hand, Wade grasped it tightly, staring into the Owl Prophet's dark eyes. "The next time you and your braves venture into Texas there will be a herd of mustangs waiting for you. They will be a gift from my family to yours, Maman-ti. It is a gesture of thanks for helping me keep that which I treasure most." Wade's loving gaze fell to Shianne's shadowed face. "The state police have no more reasons to harass your people. No one will ever know that the Owl Prophet, great medicine man of the Comanche and Kiowa, was my accomplice. It will remain our secret."

A wry smile pursed Maman-ti's lips as he lifted Shianne onto her mount. His dark eyes settled on the muscular cowboy who sat proudly in the saddle. "You are a good man, Wade Burdett . . . for a pale face." His admiring gaze slid to the attractive beauty who had often come into his dreams. "It is as it should be . . . even if I am reluctant to admit it."

"Until the spring," Wade murmured, a knowing smile bordering his lips. "Until then, I will take good care of Shae, the best. . . ."

Shianne peered over at Wade as they rode back toward Fleetwood. The looming black cloud that Haden had kept over them had dissipated, and Maman-ti had finally come to call Wade friend. Her eyes swung south. Now, at long last, they could make a new beginning, she mused with a contented sigh.

Her gaze drifted to the silhouette of the man who rode silently beside her. Shianne felt her heart warm with pride. Wade had seen to it that none of his family would take the blame for what happened to Haden. Commander Reynolds could accuse none of them of disposing of Reems when he was the one who was the direct cause of the lynching.

As always, Wade calculated his actions and then proceeded. He had considered the repercussions the Owl Prophet might have faced if he were suspected of being in the area near Fleetwood. Wade had also felt the responsibility of dealing with Haden for his entire family. If one of the others had laid a hand on Haden, they could have been accused and convicted, even if Haden were a raving lunatic, but Wade had seen to it that none of those he loved would suffer another atrocity because of Haden Reems.

Shianne reached out to grasp his hand, giving it an affectionate squeeze.

Wade arched a heavy brow and smiled into her moonlit features. "What was that for?" he questioned.

"Because you are you, and I love you," she murmured.

Overextending himself, Wade stretched between the two horses to plant a passionate kiss on her lips. "Does that mean I'm forgiven for not allowing you and my brother to take care of Haden your own ways?"

Shianne studied his craggy features for a long, pensive moment. "You aren't going to tell the others what really happened, are you?"

Wade gave his ebony head a negative shake. "No, it's better this way. Now each of them will look upon the other with quiet admiration. It is one of those secrets that is better left untold. Juan will admire Chad for seeing the matter done while Chad is thinking the same thing about me and Juan and Blake. *Not* knowing will bring us closer." A wary frown plowed his brow when he noticed the mischief dancing in Shianne's eyes. "You won't betray my secret, will you, Shae?"

"I won't if you buy my silence," she baited.

A grin replaced his dubious frown. "And just what will it cost me to keep the secret, minx?"

"I think you know the answer to that, my dear husband," Shianne purred seductively.

He most certainly did and he saw to the matter just as soon as he and Shianne were closeted in his room at the barracks. Wade vowed Shianne would have no

543

recollection of the meeting beside the Red River or the conversation they indulged in on the way back to Fleetwood. And she didn't. Her memory was clouded with the image of a man with twinkling green eyes and a rakish smile, a man who filled up her world and her thoughts when he took her in his arms and accompanied her on the most intimate of journeys into ecstasy. . . .

Chapter 27

A faint smile tugged at Blake's mouth as he gazed down at Shianne. His eyes shifted to the sprawling valley that lay before him. The past few months had been hectic, but the vaqueros had successfully excavated the dirt and rock to reopen the entrance to the cave. All the precious keepsakes, minus one chair that had been destroyed during Chad and Wade's escape from their would-be sepulcher, had been retrieved and transported to the K Bar. Haden's property had been sold at public auction, and Wade had purchased the hacienda and ranch land for a reasonable price. The Lazy R had been renamed the Circle B, and Shianne and Wade had remodeled the hacienda, giving it a warm, cozy atmosphere.

All was well in Texas, except for the fact that Chad had announced his intentions to set out for parts unknown, just as he had planned to do the previous year. Blake was disappointed to see Chad go, but he knew there was a strange restlessness within the younger Burdett, something that urged him to wander.

As Chad and Wade rode away from the K Bar, Blake draped his arm around Shianne's shoulder and stared thoughtfully at the Burdetts' departing backs. "I hope

Chad finds what he is looking for," Blake mused aloud. "I think the only reason he stayed this long was to pacify Micara." His gaze strayed over his shoulder, following the path the teary-eyed Micara had taken after bidding her youngest son adieu.

Shianne nodded mutely, her gaze fixed on Wade's broad back and the striking picture he presented in the early afternoon light. It seemed inconceivable that four months had elapsed since they had returned to Texas. Those had been the most satisfying months of her life. The love she and Wade shared had blossomed, even when Shianne was certain he had already filled up every corner of her heart. Together they had chased away the dark, foreboding shadows that had surrounded Haden's ranch during his reign of terror. Now the halls of the Spanish-styled mansion rang with laughter.

The only dark spot in their bright world was Chad's departure. Shianne knew it would come, just as Micara had prophesied. Micara had held her composure amazingly well until Wade accompanied Chad down the path that led west toward Fort Bliss and points beyond. Courageously, Micara had pasted on a smile and watched her restless son ride away; but at what great cost to her self-control, Shianne thought to herself. Micara knew she had to let Chad go, but it nearly killed her to see him leave, knowing it might be years before he returned. The moment Chad and Wade were out of earshot, Micara burst into tears and hurried into the hacienda.

Shianne also lamented Chad's leaving. Chad, Wade and Juan had been inseparable these past months, working tirelessly to make the Circle B every bit the ranch the K Bar was. Although Juan stayed on as foreman, Chad felt the urge to explore the West, to find that which was missing in his life—that inner peace Shianne and Wade shared. Personally, she thought Chad was heading off in the wrong direction if he was searching for a woman to give his life meaning. Women in the West were few and far between. Shianne thought it wiser to head east but she had kept her opinions to herself.

Blake's fierce bear hug startled Shianne from her silent reverie. She glanced at her father, wondering why he suddenly felt the urge to squeeze her in two.

"Did I ever tell you how proud I am of you?" Blake murmured affectionately. "You rode out the unsettling years of the war like a trooper. If I had not known what a strong, competent young woman you would turn out to be, I would never have been able to remain in Louisiana with Micara."

Shianne returned her father's fond squeeze. "And if you hadn't sent Wade in your stead, I would never have known what love was and why Louisiana held such lure for you."

Blake chuckled at the dreamy expression on his daughter's flawless features. "We were both very fortunate. Strange, isn't it? Our long separation turned out to be a blessing in disguise." Heaving a sigh, Blake released Shianne and turned to stare at the door of the hacienda. "Well, I suppose I better find a way to cheer up Micara. She's going to miss Chad terribly."

"Why don't you show her your impression of a monkey?" Shianne suggested with a mischievous smile. "It used to cheer me up when I was feeling low."

Blake skewed up his face and hunkered over like an ape lumbering on its hind legs. "You think this will bring her a smile?"

"Without a doubt," Shianne enthused, confirming her words by grinning at the ridiculous look on Blake's face.

Dropping his gorilla impersonation momentarily,

Blake turned back to Shianne. "I almost forgot. Wade wanted you to meet him by the spring after he bid his private farewell to Chad."

Shianne frowned bemusedly. "Why?"

"Dunno," Blake mumbled before clambering through the door like a clumsy ape.

Shianne ambled across the veranda and then strode to the barn to fetch Delgado. She was curious about the rendezvous at Speaking Springs. It must be to check on the corral of mustangs he had rounded up in preparation for Maman-ti's return, she decided. Wade had built the pens, and Chad had spent hours taming the skittish colts. It had been the perfect distraction during Chad's long sojourn at the K Bar.

Swinging onto the black stallion's back, Shianne aimed herself north, certain she was about to spend the better part of the afternoon gentling the more contrary steeds in the remuda. But the day wouldn't be a total loss, she mused with a sly smile. When Wade was underfoot, and they were granted privacy, there would be a few minutes for more pleasurable diversions. She would see to it!

A pensive silence stretched between Wade and Chad. Wade stood up in the stirrups and then sank back in his saddle after giving his backside a rest. "I guess this is good-by, little brother," he breathed. "Do you have the slightest notion where you're going?"

Chad shrugged noncommittally. "Maybe to New Mexico or Colorado. Wherever the wind blows me, I suppose."

Wade's green eyes focused intently on Chad. "You know there will always be a place for you here," he said quietly.

"Not until I . . ." Chad's voice trailed off. These past

months with Wade had smoothed off some of his rough edges. Chad wasn't as blunt and outspoken as he had once been, but he still had the habit of speaking his mind. "Hell, you know why I have to go and when I'll be back. Damn, what a gentleman I've turned out to be." He laughed mirthlessly. "A year ago, who would have thought *I* would have done the noble thing by leaving." His blue eyes swung back to Wade. "Who knows, maye one day I'll even turn out to be as gallant as you are, big brother. You have known all along what I wanted, but you didn't run me off."

"Chad, I . . ."

Chad held up his hand to forestall Wade. "Don't make this any more difficult than it already is. I can't have the woman I want when she belongs to my brother, the one I admire and respect for a hell of a lot of reasons." His gaze fastened poignantly on Wade who had suddenly found an incredible fascination with the pommel of his saddle. "And I guess I never got around to thanking you for disposing of Haden in your own clever way."

Wade raised his gaze to meet Chad's wry smile. "Don't be so sure I was the one who took care of Haden. Here all this time I thought it was you who plotted his demise."

"I would have shot him through his hard heart before it would have occurred to me to employ a more practical method of disposing of him," Chad snorted. "You knew that and that was why you handled the situation the way you did."

"You're giving me a helluva lot more credit than I deserve," Wade grunted, determined not to commit himself. He had vowed to keep the secret, and he fully intended to let it remain a mystery.

"No," Chad argued, a fond smile bordering his lips. "You deserve a lot of credit, and when I can be the man you have become I'll be back." His grin faded as he nudged his steed toward the West. "Take good care of that feisty little misfit, big brother. I don't think there is another one like her anywhere."

Wade's shoulders slumped. His gaze followed Chad as he thundered across the open range. "I hope time and distance provide you with what you're looking for," he mused aloud. "But, knowing why you can't stay leaves me to wonder how long it will take you to forget her."

Dammit, why did he and Chad have to be so magnetically drawn to one woman? What a cruel twist of fate.

Grumbling, Wade reined Galahad toward Speaking Springs. He had promised to pay close attention to the steeds that would soon belong to Maman-ti. As a distraction, Chad had thrown himself into working with the mustangs. The method had not proved one hundred percent successful, but it had preoccupied Chad when he found himself wanting what he couldn't have.

Shianne's bewitching image materialized out of nowhere, leaving Wade to wonder if he and his brother were being visited simultaneously by the same alluring specter. A wry smile bordered his lips. It had been his intention to break the last of the mustangs to halter this afternoon, but suddenly he was anticipating more from the day than manhandling contrary horses.

Chewing on that delicious thought, Wade urged Galahad into a gallop. He was determined to arrive at Speaking Springs before Shianne. What he had in mind was a surprise for his lovely wife, something that would keep both of them from brooding over Chad's leaving.

* * *

A startled gasp burst from Shianne's lips when her absent gaze landed on the creek bank. She had to pinch herself to ensure she wasn't seeing a mirage, the exact same one she had stumbled on ten months earlier.

There, wearing nothing but a seductive grin, lay Wade. The bright April sun was burning down upon his naked flesh, making it glow golden-brown in the afternoon light. His hair, as black as a raven's wing, lay recklessly across his forehead. His hands were folded beneath his head and his legs were casually crossed at the ankles. He reminded Shianne of the ominous knights of old, the invincible warrior who was carved of brawn and rippling muscle.

Shianne's all-consuming gaze flooded over his powerful, well-sculptured physique, not overlooking even the smallest detail. Breaking into a mischievous smile, she nudged Delgado closer to get a bird's eye view of the naked knight who was basking in the sun.

"Pardon me, sir." When Wade pried open one eye and elevated a dark brow, Shianne raked him again, her ebony eyes twinkling with amusement. "Isn't this where I came in?"

A deep skirl of laughter echoed in his chest. "Mmmm . . . I do believe it is," he concurred. The resonance of his voice rolled toward her, provoking a fleet of tingles to cruise down her spine. "Last time we met like this, you tore off like a house afire." Wade propped himself on an elbow, drinking in the sight of the shapely beauty who sat atop her prancing black stallion. "Why don't you step down and join me, madam. This lovely afternoon was created for lounging in the sun."

Shianne glanced about, frowning warily. "Aren't you afraid someone might happen upon us? After all, it is broad daylight."

Wade cocked his head to stare at the pen of

mustangs. "Who the devil is going to see us? There are no other creatures around except the horses, and contrary to what you might have heard, horses do not carry tales."

A provocative smile blossomed on her heart-shaped lips. "Well, in that case . . ."

Shianne reached up to tug the pins from her mane of raven hair, allowing it to tumble to her waist. Her tapered fingers moved to the buttons of her blouse while Wade watched on with rakish anticipation. When she had shrugged off the first layer, she drew the chemise over her head. After hooking both garments over the pommel of the saddle, she swung to the ground. As Shianne pivoted around, she noted the flames of desire flickering in Wade's eyes, assuring her that their minds were running on the same titillating track.

When her black merino skirt cascaded down into a pool at her ankles, Wade's devouring gaze ascended to sketch her perfect figure. "God, you're lovely," he breathed appreciatively.

"I'm not as beautiful as you are," Shianne insisted as she tossed her boots aside and sashayed toward him.

"A man does not take kindly to being labeled beautiful," he scolded, his tone too soft and throaty with desire to sound abrasive.

Shianne dropped down beside him on the plush carpet of grass that lined the creek bank. "Then perhaps *magnificent* would make a more appropriate description," she amended. Bending over him, Shianne spread featherlight caresses across the wide expanse of his shoulders. "Or maybe *awesome.*" Her fingertips roamed down the thick hair that covered his chest. "Or perhaps . . ."

Wade caught her teasing hand, pulling her down on top of him. "Hush up, woman. I did not summon you

552

here to increase my vocabulary."

One perfectly arched brow lifted questioningly. "Oh? Then what was your motive for calling me to Speaking Springs? To fiddle with the horses you have penned up?"

His fingers tunneled through her hair, bringing her head to his. "Do I look like a man who has an obsession for mustangs?" he queried huskily.

"Yes," Shianne declared, her dark eyes dancing with deviltry. "You have spent more time with those blasted horses than you have with me these past few weeks. I was beginning to think the only way to gain your attention was to sprout a mane and tail."

Wade halted his amorous advances when his lips were only a few breathless inches from Shianne's mouth. "Have you been feeling neglected, princess?" he inquired. His intent gaze memorized her exquisite features.

"Terribly," she murmured. Her eyes were on the sensuous curve of his lips. She was hungry for the taste of him.

"Then we will immediately remedy that. It has never been my intention to deprive you of anything. . . ."

The moment his mouth slanted across hers, Shianne *was* deprived—of oxygen. Wade's devouring kiss stripped the breath from her lungs. Yet, she wasn't objecting; she was responding, wildly, helplessly. Her body arched to fit itself against his hard muscled planes, aching to appease the craving that only those delirious moments of ecstasy brought on by their lovemaking could satisfy. But, like a never-ending spring, the emotions bubbled forth each time they kissed and touched.

"Wade, I love you," Shianne whispered when he finally granted her a breath of air.

His quiet laughter tickled her senses. His thick lashes

fluttered up to reveal those shining emerald-green eyes that could entrance her and draw her into their mysterious depths. "You're only saying that because you want to have your way with me. I've met women like you before. You want to use my body for your pleasure, and then you will fling me aside when I have served my purpose."

Shianne could not resist his playful banter. It was as it had always been with Wade. He could loft her spirits and send them spiraling. "I beg to differ, sir," she purred. Her leg slid between his, causing him to flinch at her intimate touch. "Granted, you do have something I crave, but when I finish with you, I'll still have use for your services . . . as many times as you can rise to the occasion. . . ."

That sounded like a most intriguing challenge. Wade hooked his arm around her waist. With one lithe move he pressed Shianne to the grass. Propping himself on one forearm, he peered down into her bewitching face. The alluring sight of her left Wade estimating how long it would take Chad to forget what he was missing. Wade swore if *he* had been the one to go, he would never be back. It would take forever to forget the way Shianne made him feel when she gave herself up to the ardent passion that exploded between them, the way her eyes glistened when she smiled, the way she moved with seductive grace, the soft resonance of her voice and the velvety texture of her skin. . . . Those were the things he would never forget, at least not in this lifetime.

Everything about this spirited nymph aroused him. Each time he left her, he found himself anxious to return to her waiting arms. Shianne was a living, breathing part of him, and with each passing day Wade found himself even more in love than he had been the day before. At times it seemed incredible that a man could come to care so much for a woman. Before Shianne came along, Wade never thought it possible to grow more in love. But Lord, how wrong he had been!

Reverently, Wade reached down to cup her chin in his hand. He tilted her face, studying her as if she were a cherished portrait. Bending close, he brushed butterfly kisses across her moist lips and then withdrew to stare into the fathomless depths of her eyes.

"Each time I look at you, touch you, I ask myself what I could have done to deserve your love. Whatever it was, I'd gladly do it over and over again if it will ensure that you will be mine until the end of time. You are the one woman I never expected to find. Now that I have, I don't ever want to lose you. I think I could endure anything but that. I love you, Shae. You have taught me the meaning of forever. . . ."

A warm tide of emotion surged over Shianne. This man who smiled so easily, who loved so tenderly, had filled up the essence of her being with a flame. It was like a slow burning memory that was ever present in her mind. It was there, waiting to set fire to passion. Yet, it was so much more. Her love for him gave her unconquerable strength and allowed her to display incredible gentleness. Knowing she had earned Wade's love made everything seem possible.

Lovingly, she combed her fingers through his crisp, wavy hair and then drew his full lips to hers. "Do you suppose, in all the world, there are other husbands and wives who have discovered the same kind of love we share?" she questioned him.

His lips parted in a wry smile as they grazed her mouth. His muscled body molded into her feminine curves, kindling the eternal fire. "Some of them, perhaps," he speculated. "But I must confess I haven't given it much thought, princess." He moved, his sinewed body half covering hers. "I pity those who have never learned what love is or how deep the emotion runs. Lord, if they only knew what they were missing. . . ."

Shianne looped her arms over his shoulders, reveling in the tantalizing sensations that spilled through her. "Wade, I . . ."

"I didn't come here to chat," he murmured against the swanlike column of her throat. "I came in search of rainbows."

"Then you shall have a pocketful of them," she promised huskily.

Wade's rich laughter whispered in the spring breeze. "This particular suit of clothing I'm presently wearing is void of pockets," he teased as his caresses flowed over a sea of bare flesh, loving the feel of her satiny skin beneath his hands.

Shianne twisted away to hover over him, her eyes shimmering with black magic. "But I like you best in this particular suit of clothing," she teased him back.

Wade's patience had become legendary—in most situations. This, however, was not one of them. The last few minutes had been hard on his blood pressure. He had not the slightest inclination to indulge in further conversation.

The playful smile evaporated from his craggy features. "If you don't quit talking and kiss me, I'm afraid I'll be forced to take a cold dip in yonder creek," he growled, gesturing his head toward the lazy flowing stream.

"Is this what you want, my impatient husband?" she murmured as she came to him, her breasts brushing wantonly against his laboring chest.

"It's a start," he breathed against her lips. "But I might as well warn you, a kiss will hardly be enough to satisfy the monstrous craving you have instilled in me."

"I was hoping you would say something like that,"

she giggled beneath what was meant to be a most passionate kiss.

"Will you be serious for just one minute, woman?" Wade grumbled. "I'd like to make love to you if you can stop laughing!"

She did and he did, but that *one minute* stretched out to encompass eternity. When Shianne touched him in that tender, unique way of hers, passion fed the flame. The fire began to burn and grow until it engulfed him. As they set out in search of rainbows the world took on the pastel hues of every color that had ever been sprinkled through the universe. Wade reached out to gather the translucent beams in the palm of his hand, marveling at their radiance, feeling their mystical warmth. This dark-eyed nymph had spun a kaliedoscope of emotions about him, and she had given each splendorous feeling its own distinct color. For him, she had created a glorious, precious spectrum of enduring love.

FIERY ROMANCE
From Zebra Books

AUTUMN'S FURY (1763, $3.95)
by Emma Merritt
Lone Wolf had known many women, but none had captured his heart the way Catherine had . . . with her he felt a hunger he hadn't experienced with any of the maidens of his own tribe. He would make Catherine his captive, his slave of love — until she would willingly surrender to the magic of AUTUMN'S FURY.

PASSION'S PARADISE (1618, $3.75)
by Sonya T. Pelton
When she is kidnapped by the cruel, captivating Captain Ty, fair-haired Angel Sherwood fears not for her life, but for her honor! Yet she can't help but be warmed by his manly touch, and secretly longs for PASSION'S PARADISE.

LOVE'S ELUSIVE FLAME (1836, $3.75)
by Phoebe Conn
Golden-haired Flame was determined to find the man of her dreams even if it took forever, but she didn't have long to wait once she met the handsome rogue Joaquin. He made her respond to his ardent kisses and caresses . . . but if he wanted her completely, she would have to be his only woman — she wouldn't settle for anything less. Joaquin had always taken women as he wanted . . . but none of them was Flame. Only one night of wanton ecstasy just wasn't enough — once he was touched by LOVE'S ELUSIVE FLAME.

SAVAGE SPLENDOR (1855, $3.95)
by Constance O'Banyon
By day Mara questioned her decision to remain in her husband's world. But by night, when Tajarez crushed her in his strong, muscular arms, taking her to the peaks of rapture, she knew she could never live without him.

SATIN SURRENDER (1861, $3.95)
by Carol Finch
Dante Folwer found innocent Erica Bennett in his bed in the most fashionable whorehouse in New Orleans. Expecting a woman of experience, Dante instead stole the innocence of the most magnificent creature he'd ever seen. He would forever make her succumb to . . . SATIN SURRENDER.

Available wherever paperbacks are sold, or order direct from the Publisher. Send cover price plus 50¢ per copy for mailing and handling to Zebra Books, Dept. 2158, 475 Park Avenue South, New York, N.Y. 10016. Residents of New York, New Jersey and Pennsylvania must include sales tax. DO NOT SEND CASH.